BEAUTIFUL SIN SERIES BOOK 3

Beautiful Chaos

JENNILYNN WYER

II

CONTENTS

COPYRIGHT	1
SYNOPSIS	4
DEDICATION	6
DEAR READER	7
RECAP	9
CHAPTER 1	17
CHAPTER 2	26
CHAPTER 3	32
CHAPTER 4	42
CHAPTER 5	48
CHAPTER 6	56
CHAPTER 7	62
CHAPTER 8	75
CHAPTER 9	82
CHAPTER 10	94
CHAPTER 11	101
CHAPTER 12	106
CHAPTER 13	113

CHAPTER 14	125
CHAPTER 15	134
CHAPTER 16	146
CHAPTER 17	155
CHAPTER 18	161
CHAPTER 19	169
CHAPTER 20	174
CHAPTER 21	183
CHAPTER 22	192
CHAPTER 23	198
CHAPTER 24	206
CHAPTER 25	214
CHAPTER 26	222
CHAPTER 27	230
CHAPTER 28	236
CHAPTER 29	245
CHAPTER 30	252
CHAPTER 31	260
CHAPTER 32	271
CHAPTER 33	282
CHAPTER 34	287
CHAPTER 35	297
CHAPTER 36	308
CHAPTER 37	317
CHAPTER 38	320
CHAPTER 39	328

CHAPTER 40	333
CHAPTER 41	343
CHAPTER 42	355
EPILOGUE	374
Also by the Author	382
Letter to Readers	385
About the Author	388

COPYRIGHT

Beautiful Chaos (Beautiful Sin Series Book 3) © 2024 Jennilynn Wyer

This book is a work of fiction. Names, characters, businesses, places, events, brands, media, and incidents are either the products of the author's imagination or are used fictitiously. The author acknowledges the trademarked status and trademark owners of various products referenced in this work of fiction, which have been used without permission. The publication/use of these trademarks is not authorized, associated with, or sponsored by the trademark owners. Any resemblance to actual events or persons, living or dead, is entirely coincidental.

All Rights Reserved, including the right to reproduce this book or portions thereof in any form whatsoever. No part of this book may be reproduced in any form or by any electronic or mechanical means, including information storage and retrieval systems, without the written permission from the author, except for the use of brief quotations in a book review.

GENERATIVE AI TRAINING BY ANY PLATFORM OR ENTITY OF THIS BOOK OR THE CONTENTS THEREIN IS PROHIBITED. Work in any manner for purposes of training artificial intelligence technologies to generate text, including without limitation, technologies that are capable of generating works in the same style, trope, or genre as the Work, is STRICTLY PROHIBITED.

Cover Design: Angela Haddon

Photographer: Wander Aguiar

Model: Vinicious

Copy Editor: Ellie Folden @ My Brother's Editor

Formatting By: Jennilynn Wyer

Reader's Note: Intended for mature audiences due to sexual and mature content. Beautiful Sinners is dark reverse harem that contains scenes that may be triggering for sensitive readers (scenes depicting torture, violence/abuse/blood, foul language and f-bombs, praise kink, bondage, and MF/MFM/MFMM scenes).

Connect with the Author

Website: https://www.jennilynnwyer.com
Linktree: https://linktr.ee/jennilynnwyer
Email: jennilynnwyerauthor@gmail.com
Facebook: https://www.facebook.com/JennilynnWyerAuthor
Twitter: https://www.twitter.com/JennilynnWyer
Instagram: https://www.instagram.com/jennilynnwyer
TikTok: https://www.tiktok.com/@jennilynnwyer
Goodreads: https://www.goodreads.com/author/show/20502667.Jennilynn_Wyer

Bookbub: https://www.bookbub.com/authors/jennilynn-wyer

Books2Read: https://books2read.com/ap/nAAgBb/Jennilynn-Wyer

Amazon Author Page: https://www.amazon.com/author/jennilynnwyer

Newsletter: https://forms.gle/vYX64JHJVBX7iQvy8

SUBSCRIBE TO MY NEWSLETTER at https://forms.gle/vYX64JHJVBX7iQvy8 for news on upcoming releases, cover reveals, sneak peeks, author giveaways, and other fun stuff!

JOIN THE J-CREW: A JENNILYNN WYER ROMANCE READER GROUP

Join link https://www.facebook.com/groups/jennilynnsjcrewreadergroup

SYNOPSIS

Beautiful Chaos is the highly anticipated conclusion of the Beautiful Sin Series.

Blurb contains spoilers from books 1 and 2.

***

Constantine, Hendrix, Tristan, and Aleksander. Four dangerous men who will do anything to protect me.

Constantine Ferreira, Tristan Amato, and Hendrix Knight. My three childhood best friends who grew into ruthless, powerful men. Constantine is my sanctuary. Tristan is my strength. Hendrix is my freedom. And then there's Aleksander Stepanoff. Let's just say, things are very complicated when it comes to my former enemy.

These four men see the scars that mark my body as perfection and my darkness as beautiful chaos. A chaos that I will unleash upon the Society and the people who took everything from me.

I've been used by everyone in my life. As a weapon, a pawn, and a bargaining chip. No more. I am Aoife Fitzpatrick. Daughter of James and Caroline Fitzpatrick and heir to the Council. I am also Syn Carmichael. The girl with the battle scars who rose from the ashes like a phoenix reborn. The heartbeat of two strong women beats inside my chest. *As does revenge.*

With the support of the three men I love and the enemy I have come to trust, I'm going to take back my father's legacy and punish those who betrayed my family...

...and hopefully, somewhere along the road to vengeance, I'll find my own happy-ever-after.

For readers who like dark romance and why choose with:
- four smoking hot, possessive MMCs
- a strong and fierce FMC
- forced proximity
- opposites attract
- secret society
- found family
- twists and turns that will leave you gasping (literally)
- a much deserved HEA

"Obsessed. I am completely obsessed with this series." – Rebecca, Goodreads

Beautiful Chaos is a full-length why choose romance with dark themes and possessive MMCs. It is book three and the conclusion in the Beautiful Sin series. Recommended for mature readers. Please check Reader's Note in the front matter of the book for potential TWs.

Beautiful Sin Series
#1 Beautiful Sin
#2 Beautiful Sinners
#3 Beautiful Chaos

DEDICATION

To my readers who love when I take a walk on the dark side.

DEAR READER

How are we here? How is it the end? I'm not ready! I love these characters so much, and I don't want to say goodbye.

Thank you so much for picking up my book baby, Beautiful Chaos. It's the third book and the conclusion to the Beautiful Sin series, a dark reverse harem/why choose romance. Thank you for coming on this journey with me, Syn, Constantine, Hendrix, Tristan, and Aleksander. I hope you enjoy their much-deserved HEA.

We're in the honeymoon stage of the story, which means more sex (compared to books 1 and 2). Again, I have no clue how to perceive 'chili peppers,' as readers' perspectives are very subjective. One reader may rate a book 5 scorching hot chilis, while another sees it as a 1.5. In *Beautiful Chaos*, I wanted to focus more on the individual relationships between Syn and her guys, as well as their group dynamic, so expect date nights. We're also at the point where Syn gets her revenge, so be aware of those trigger warnings.

Also, Andie, Keane, Jax, Liam, and Rafael return in *Beautiful Chaos*. If you're curious about the characters from *Savage Princess*, *Savage Kings*, or *Savage Kingdom*, you can find those books on Amazon, Kindle Unlimited, or grab the audiobooks (audiobooks are available wide at most retailers, including your local public library).

Oh, and a little name game for you. Aoife is pronounced ee-fa; Fénix is pronounced phoenix; Niamh is pronounced neev, and Caoimhe is pronounced kee-va. I throw in some new Irish Gaelic phrases for you, too, but I'll let you translate those using Google. It's more fun that way ;-)

Okay. Are you ready for the end? I'm not, but here we go!

Don't forget to look for those Easter eggs and references I love to put in every one of my books. I sprinkled a few from Fallen Brook in here.

Shoot! Almost forgot about those triggers. The Beautiful Sin Series contain scenes depicting torture, gun violence/abuse/blood, foul language and f-bombs, praise kink, bondage, biting, and sexually explicit MF/MFM/MFMM scenes.

Love and happy reading,

JENNILYNN WYER
ROMANCE AUTHOR

RECAP

In case you forgot those cliffhangers from Beautiful Sinners...

The most god awful noise I've ever heard assaults my ears and brings me out of a deep sleep. Cocky Bastard crows again, and it's like listening to a thousand cats dying. Worse than fingernails down a chalkboard.

"What the fuck is that?" Hendrix startles awake, and I'm lucky he doesn't knee me in the balls.

"Rooster," Con groggily replies.

"Fucking hell," Hendrix grouses and pulls a pillow over his head. "Firefly, shut your bastard up."

Out of all the animals she could have chosen, leave it to Aoife to have a pet rooster and name it Cocky Bastard.

I roll over to wake her, only to discover she's not there. "Aoife?" I call out.

When she doesn't respond, Con sits up and drapes his

legs over the side of the bed. "What time is it?"

I dig my palms into my eye sockets to wipe away the sleep and look over at the small digital clock on my nightstand. "Four."

Con stands and stretches. "Want some coffee?"

Getting up as well, I reply, "Coffee would be good."

Hendrix makes a grunted noise of discontent. "I'm going back to sleep. Make sure Aoife wakes me up before she leaves, so I can walk her to class."

I toss Con a pair of basketball shorts after I slip on some gray sweatpants.

"I was going to do that."

"I called dibs. Now fuck off."

"Fuck you."

Not the best comeback, but whatever.

Piano music starts playing from somewhere in the house.

"Do you hear that?"

Hendrix lifts up onto his elbows before collapsing back down. "It's someone's phone."

I stumble out into the hallway just as the music cuts off and starts up again.

"Sounds like it's coming from Aoife's room," Con says.

Why would anyone be calling her at four in the morning?

"Red," I say when we enter her room, only to find it empty. The phone stops ringing and begins again, but it's not coming from in here; it's coming from down the hall. "Hendrix, you jackass, it was your phone!" I yell.

He shouts something back, but I don't hear him through the sudden rush of white noise that fills my head when I see what's on the bed. A gust of air brushes my arm when Con edges up next to me.

"The fuck?"

Aligned in a straight row on top of the bedcovers are five photographs that look like they were taken at the Knight Foundation benefit in London last year. And each one has a dark red letter written on it in jagged slashes of what looks like blood.

L-I-A-R-S

Darlington's familiar streets, bathed in the ethereal glow of the moon, take on an entirely new character in the early hours of the morning. The solitude is both eerie and peaceful, a stark contrast to the bustling life that envelops the town and its campus during the day. There's an undeniable darkness lurking beneath its charming façade, where every shadow holds its own secret—something I refused to see when I first moved here.

The rubber soles of my tennis shoes pad silently on the black asphalt as I round the corner into the alleyway. I watch my shadow elongate and shrink, then elongate again, as I pass under the dingy, yellowish light that shines down from the top of the building. The cooler night air helps dampen the stench of rotting garbage overflowing out of the trash receptacles, but the sour smell is pervasive and inescapable.

Approaching the back service exit of the Bierkeller, I trail my fingers over the coarse brick until I feel the circular indentation of a bullet hole.

Funny how you always end up right back where you started.

"I'm glad you called."

Aleksander steps out into the open, his face a harsh mask of trenchant angles created by the light of the waxing moon. The severeness of his face is softened somewhat by the slight cupid bow shape of his mouth and the light pewter of his eyes.

"Cut the bullshit, Aleksander. How long have you known?"

He runs a hand through his short hair, mussing it up. "Not long. A year, perhaps."

His words from the bar make much more sense now. *"Oh, they're still very much alive. I wouldn't want to spoil your fun."*

"How long have *they* known?"

Aleksander's broad shoulders hunch as he breathes in deeply through his nose. "Malin is Francesco's fixer and right-hand man—"

He wasn't before. I would've remembered him.

"—so, I can only assume that Tristan has known all along."

Pain lances my chest, its blade sharp and hot. I remember Constantine's reaction in the shower when I told him about the constellation man. I point-blank asked him today about it. He fucking knew who I was talking about, yet he said nothing.

Betrayal sinks its fangs into me, delivering the bitter

poison of their deceit straight to my heart. As my thoughts swirl in a maelstrom of doubt and anguish, I question every moment, every memory, every touch between us.

Meeting Aleksander's penetrating stare, I let the pain I feel erupt, molten and scalding.

"That's his name? Malin?"

I can barely say it out loud, the visceral pain so intense, I almost double over from the severity of it.

"Yes."

"There was another man. He had a scar on his face."

I hear my mother's screams echoing around the alley, and my vision obscures with the crimson tincture of vengeance.

Aleksander's brows knit with a confusticated downturn. "Another man?"

Without warning, I rush Aleksander and slam him against the wall of the building. By the time it takes him to recover, I have my knife out, the point of the blade cutting into the tender flesh of his neck.

"Do *not* lie to me."

He barely reacts when I press deeper, just a breath's-width away from where his pulse thrums rapidly. The gray of his irises blot black when his pupils dilate, but it's not fear I see. It's something else entirely.

"Don't," I warn, a tremor lacing my voice when he raises his hand to my face. His calloused fingertips are insistent, like a burning brand on my cheek, and yet there's a reverence in his touch.

"Let me help you," he implores. "Let me give you your revenge."

My gaze bores into him, the knife in my hand steady. One more inch, and I'll sever a major artery.

"I don't want your fucking help. Everything you've done has been to benefit yourself."

Aleksander has been playing me from the beginning. I'm little more than a mouse to his cat.

"Everything I've done," he retorts, his tone carrying an ache of unspoken regret, "has been for you."

Disgusted that he would lay the blame for what he's done on me, I hiss, "Don't you dare use me as the excuse to justify the bloodshed and destruction you've caused. We barely know each other. I am nothing to you!"

His mouth twists in pain as he whispers hoarsely, "You are not nothing, Aoife. You're my wife."

LET'S DIVE RIGHT IN, SHALL WE?

ARE YOU READY FOR THE END?

CHAPTER 1

"Do not be afraid; our fate cannot be taken from us; it is a gift." —Dante Alighieri, *Dante's Inferno*

A slow, steady rain starts to fall and pelts the window, creating tiny rivulets that drip down the glass like teardrops. My fingertip follows the haphazard patterns they create as they trickle down the outside of the pane. Chaos theory helps explain why their paths look random and chaotic, when in fact, they're not. Like everything in life, there are inherent repetitions, patterns, and feedback loops. Everything is interconnected in some way.

Wrapping my arms around myself, I try to chase away the sudden chill, but the cold that has embedded its icy fingers in me goes bone deep. As deep as the betrayal I'm drowning in.

The men I trusted lied to me. Alana lied to me. And my mother... God, I hate her for what she did. I was her daughter. She was supposed to love and protect me. Instead, I was nothing more than a business transaction. She sold me off just like Francesco sold Alana.

I glance down at the floor where the signed contract with my mother's elegantly distinctive signature rests at my feet in a crumpled ball, then lift my gaze to find Aleksander in the reflection of the glass, warily watching me from across the room.

"I may have been promised to you, but I *am not* your wife."

I never consented. I never said, "I do." I was nine fucking years old when the contract was signed between my mother and Nikolai Stepanoff.

In the eyes of the Society, it won't matter. The legalities of things mean little to an organization that thrives on doing whatever the hell it wants with no repercussions.

Was this the betrayal my father spoke about that night?

When Aleksander doesn't say anything, I cross the living room and take a seat on the coffee table in front of him. I shouldn't feel an iota of sympathy for this man. He may not have had control over the things that happened when he was younger, but he's an adult now. Everything he's done, he did so by choice. Yet, I can't help but feel sorry for him. In a way, Aleksander and I are very similar.

"Let me take a look."

Bright crimson blots the white terrycloth he's holding to his neck.

"I'm good. Just a scratch."

Just a scratch, my ass. I shove his hand out of the way. The blood hasn't clotted yet and slowly weeps from the wound.

"Where's your first aid kit?"

"I'll get it," he says and tries to stand, but I none-too-gently push him back down.

"I'll do it. Just point me the way."

He motions with a tilt of his blond head in the direction of the kitchen. "There's one in the cabinet underneath the sink."

On my way to the kitchen, I study the layout of the place. Nice, modern décor. Clean. There are maybe two bedrooms down the hallway that leads from the living room. The kitchen is small and utilitarian. Hendrix would hate it.

I miss them.

For fuck's sake, stop thinking about them.

Opening the bottom cabinet under the sink, I immediately spot the first aid kit… along with a small revolver duct-taped to the inside of the cabinet door. My fingers itch with temptation when I lightly touch the hilt.

It would be so easy.

Ignoring it, I hastily grab the small plastic box and go back to the living room.

"I hope you're up to date with your tetanus booster."

"I am."

His eyes briefly fall to my right hand when I kneel in front of him and something akin to relief flashes over his face. He knew damn well the gun was there when he told me where the first aid kit was. He was testing me.

"If I was going to kill you, I'd have done it in the alley.

No cameras. I don't play games, Aleksander, so don't play them with me."

The side of his mouth curves in a bemused half smile. "Noted."

I roughly jerk his chin up so I can clean and dress the wound. "Speaking of games, you're an asshole for leaving those photographs in my journal for me to find."

Ripping open an alcohol wipe, I clean away the crusted blood and inspect where I sliced into his neck with my knife.

His vocal cords vibrate under my fingers when he replies, "You would have never believed me without proof."

I don't disagree because he's right.

After dabbing antibiotic ointment over the area, I use two butterfly strips to keep the cut closed so it heals properly, then choose a large, waterproof adhesive pad instead of gauze and gently smooth out the edges to make sure it stays secure.

"You'll live," I tell him when I'm done.

He covers my hand with his and softly says, "Thank you, Aoife."

Aoife was the girl I used to be. The woman I am now is someone entirely different. In order for me to begin taking back my life, I have to make a choice. Be the naïve girl whose life wasn't her own or become a strong woman who will never let anyone control her again.

"It's Syn," I reply intentionally. I pack everything back into the first aid kit and move over to sit on the couch across from him. "And you can thank me by telling me where to find the man with constellation tattoos."

I refuse to say his name out loud. The next time I utter it will be the last thing he hears before I kill him.

Considering me, Aleksander props his elbow on the arm of the chair and touches his thumb to each finger, pinky to index and back again.

"Tristan hasn't told you anything, has he?"

My heart painfully slams against my chest. No matter how much they've hurt me, I can't just shut off my feelings or make myself stop loving them by flipping an invisible off switch.

"If there's something you want to say, spit it out."

He leans forward, and by the seriousness on his face, I know I'm not going to like what's about to come out of his mouth.

"Tristan came by looking for you last night. He also wanted to know where our father was."

Our father?

Whatever I was going to say abruptly dies on the tip of my tongue. And then I get angry. Fuck him. My tolerance for manipulative bullshit is at capacity.

Unable to listen to one more person lie to me, I'm off the couch and walking toward the elevator.

"Syn, don't leave."

"I won't let you use me for your stupid vendetta against Tristan."

"Don't go," he implores, sounding almost panicked.

Incensed, I stab at the down button.

Aleksander bounds out of the chair and makes the mistake of grabbing me. Twisting out of his hold, I spin around to his back and kick out his knee. The hard wood judders under my feet when he hits the floor.

"You don't ever fucking touch me without my permission."

He twists his body around and looks up at me. I'm taken aback by the visceral sadness that clouds his storm-gray eyes. Aleksander is twice my size, but right now, he looks so much like the shy boy I remember from the gala ten years ago.

Bending his legs to his chest, he cups the back of his neck with both hands and drops his face to his knees.

"I'm sorry. I just... please, don't leave."

I glare down at him. "Give me one good reason I should stay."

I said something similar to Tristan not too long ago.

His deep, gruff voice is muffled and barely coherent when he replies, "Because I have no one else."

Damn him for saying that. I know that pit of loneliness all too well. I'd been submerged in it for the last ten years. The guys mentioned that Nikolai died several years ago. I don't know what happened to his mother, Nina. And Aleksei... *fuck*.

I hadn't felt any remorse for what I did to Aleksei until this very moment. I took Aleksander's brother from him. *But Aleksei isn't his only brother.*

Before I can convince myself that this is a really bad idea, I lower to the floor and sit cross-legged, facing him.

"You said '*our father*.'"

Uncomfortable silence descends and smothers the air around us.

Just when I'm about to say *screw this* and plow over him to get to the elevator and leave, he says, "I found out the night of the gala when I asked you to dance." He chuckles quietly, but it's hollow and devoid of any humor. "Helena Amato has a big fucking mouth when she's drunk and high."

Warily, I scoot a little closer. "Tell me."

This is the last chance I'm giving him to be honest

and real. A chance he doesn't deserve, but one my guilty conscience wants to offer him.

"Tristan was with me when Helena spilled the secret."

My heart breaks for the second time tonight. I search my memories, trying to wrap my head around it. Tristan never said anything, but I knew something was wrong when I couldn't find him after their fight.

The antagonistic relationship between Tristan and the twins makes more sense, but it also doesn't. They're not responsible for what their parents did, so why do they hate each other so much? And Alana—she's his half sister. She didn't do anything to him.

Aleksander pulls me from my thoughts when he says, "When I confronted Mom about it, she broke down. I'd never seen my mother cry before, not even when Dad beat her. She blurted out that Francesco had raped her. She swore me to secrecy." His biceps bulge as he grips the back of his neck harder. "I never even told Aleksei."

Compassion pushes my anger away, and my hand unconsciously wraps around his forearm in a gesture of comfort. What he said hits me hard because of what happened to my mother.

My rage flash-freezes to a bitter, icy cold when I think about how scared Nina must have been. Did my parents know that happened to her? Did they do nothing, just like Papa did nothing after Gabriel almost killed Constantine? I know damn well the Society wouldn't have lifted a finger to help her or to punish Francesco for what he did.

Aleksander's chest expands with a single, ragged breath. "She said it happened when Dad was away that summer. He'd been in Russia on business. She discovered she was pregnant right before he returned. Mom said he never suspected anything."

Nikolai Stepanoff must have been the most clueless man on the planet. Surely, he would've looked at the ultrasounds or gone to one of Nina's appointments and had questions about the date of conception.

"If Nina made you promise not to tell anyone, then how did Helena find out?" I gently query.

A snarled curse leaps from his lips. "Somehow, Francesco knew Aleksei and I were his. Admitted it to my face. Called me a dirty little bastard. Said I was nothing but the unwanted result of a bad fuck."

I still have questions, but I don't push for more.

Taking a chance, I cup the sides of his stubbled face and force him to look at me.

"From what I remember of Nina, she was kind and always nice to me. I'm so sorry. For her and for you. But it's not Tristan's fault. You can't blame him for what his father did. He hates Francesco."

Aleksander's cruel fingers claw into my wrists with an iron grip. "You're so fucking blind when it comes to him. He's the reason your parents are dead."

"No, he's not," I snap.

Outraged by what he said, I struggle against his punishing grasp, trying to break free.

He lifts my scarred arm between us. "He's the reason for *this*. Why do you think your father hid you in Ireland? James made a deal with Francesco. You were supposed to belong to Tristan. Your mother found out and made sure that would never happen. Francesco retaliated. If Tristan couldn't have you, no one else would."

"Shut up!"

With a strength born from rage, I use his hold on me to yank him closer. Wrapping my legs around his torso, I push forward and pin him forcefully to the floor, but he uses the momentum of his large body to flip us over and trap me underneath him.

"Get the fuck off me!"

Aleksander's weight presses down, trying to subdue my efforts to escape. "I promised you revenge. I can give you Francesco and Malin."

His words reverberate enticingly, quieting my struggles, their allure too much to resist.

"How?"

"Because I know where they are."

Our intense stare-off is interrupted by a loud chime. Aleksander slowly lifts off me and takes his phone out from his side pocket. Whatever it is has his brows drawing down.

I sit up when he turns his phone, allowing me to see the live video feed playing on the screen.

"You have a visitor."

CHAPTER 2

"Aoife!"
"Check downstairs."
Running footsteps pound the floor.
I'm reluctantly yanked from my sleepy stupor when Tristan and Con's loud-ass racket out in the hallway has me dragging my weary butt out of bed.
 "Can you both shut the hell up?" I grumble, half-awake and irritated.
Cocky Bastard picks that moment to crow. I hate that damn rooster. There has to be a way to muzzle it, so it doesn't crow all fucking night long. Our neighbors will probably show up on our doorstep with pitchforks and torches if he keeps going. I'll join them. My fried chicken with biscuits and gravy is delicious.
Like a half-dead zombie, I shuffle slowly out of the room. Since I'm up, may as well bake Syn some apple-cinnamon muffins. They're her second favorite behind pancakes.

Con yells from the foyer, "How the hell did she leave without the alarm going off?"

The frantic way he says it has my eyebrows shooting up questioningly at Tristan when he rushes out of Syn's room.

"Fuck. *Fuck!*" Tristan spears his hands harshly through his hair, then leans over the balcony railing. "I showed her the goddamn code!"

Confused, I ask, "Did Syn leave already? I told you to wake me up so I could walk her to class."

Tristan unceremoniously shoves me in the direction of my room. "Put on some clothes. We need to find her."

Find her?

I grab his arm before he can take off down the stairs. "What's going on?" Tristan's expression is grave, but it's the look of guilt that crosses his face that kicks me in the gut and has me worried. "Where's Syn?"

If she pulled another disappearing act like yesterday, I'm going to spank her beautiful ass, then chain her to the bed for a week. My dick gets excited about all the possibilities that entails. Last night was incredible. I love how open she is to exploring her boundaries, and I can't wait to continue testing them.

Tristan growls in frustration. "I fucked up."

What in the hell does that mean? "Fucked up how?"

Con is practically panting when he reaches the top of the stairs. "We need to tell him."

"Tell me what?" I ask, pinging them with a furrowed brow. If I ask one more question that no one answers, things are going to get violent.

Tristan makes a sweeping gesture at my groin. "I can't talk to you with your dick on display."

Seriously?

Giving him the middle finger, I walk swiftly into his bedroom and snatch some clothes from his dresser, then hurriedly get dressed. When I come back out, he and Con are arguing in hushed, angry whispers. I catch snippets of words like Aleksander and Malin, and a sense of foreboding runs through me as my heart races faster than my mind can process what it all means.

With my patience rapidly waning, I harshly snap out, "My dick is covered. Talk."

"Tell him, or I will," Con says.

I find it a little disconcerting when Tristan backs up a few steps, creating distance between us. His mouth opens and closes in mute stammers before finally surrendering to silence.

Officially at my limit for further prevarication, I threaten, "If one of you doesn't start talking, I'm going to throw you over the fucking balcony."

"Malin was sent to kill Aoife and her parents. He's the one who hurt her."

Tristan speaks in a rush, his words muddled, and I can barely make out what he says.

"What?"

"Malin. It was Malin who attacked Aoife."

Every molecule of oxygen gets sucked right out of my lungs in a painful torrent. Malin did those horrific things to her? Refusing to believe it, I shake my head in denial. Malin couldn't even scratch his own ass without Francesco's permission.

Dear god, no.

I spear Tristan with a murderous glare, and he wisely takes a few more steps away from me.

"Your father was behind what happened to her?"

Tristan's simple 'yes' has the power to bring me to my

knees, but it's the perfidy I feel emanating off him that spikes my rage. I can read my best friend like a fucking book, and right now, he looks guilty as hell. Has he known this entire time?

I shift my gaze between Con and Tristan, searching their faces for answers. When Tristan averts his eyes and won't look at me, I cut Con an accusatory glower that demands the truth before I lose my shit.

"The man with the constellation tattoo on the right side of his neck. She said that to me at Cillian's. She wrote it in her journal. That's how I found out. I told Tristan."

He told Tristan, but not me. They both knew and decided to keep me in the dark. *Jesus fucking Christ.*

I read her journal inside and out the night Con told us who Syn really was. The answers to what happened to her were right there, and I didn't connect the dots. Fucking Francesco Amato and his lapdog. They took my sunshine from me. They hurt her in the most gruesome way and left her to die.

My thoughts funnel to that dark place I would escape to whenever Dad would beat me, or… *Don't go there. Syn needs you. You can't lose her again. You won't survive it.*

"Where is she?" I roar, advancing on Tristan because he has the unfortunate luck of being within reach.

Con's body becomes an impenetrable barricade when he lunges forward and gets in front of me, shoving me back.

"I don't know!" Tristan bellows. "I don't know how she got the pictures. I think Aleksander—"

"What pictures?" I shout over him.

"On her bed," Con replies and lets me go.

"Shit, Hen, wait," Tristan calls after me, but I'm past

the point of caring what their deceiving asses have to say.

As soon as I see the LIARS written in what looks like blood on photographs of us with Malin, my whole world detonates as understanding sinks in. We promised her we would help her find who murdered her parents, and she thinks we betrayed her. I slide a finger through the dark, sticky liquid, smearing the A. *God, baby, I didn't fucking know.*

"I was going to tell you," Tristan says from behind me, and something inside me snaps.

She's gone because of them. She left us, and it's their fault.

"You motherfucker!" The words erupt out of me as I explode and ram into him, our combined masses crashing to the floor in a sprawling heap.

Bearing all my weight on his chest, I rain down blow after blow on his face, desperate to inflict as much pain as possible. Wanting to tear him apart, I'm able to get in four solid hits before Con intervenes and grabs me by the shoulders.

"Calm down."

Wrong thing to say.

Con is stronger and a better fighter, but the punches I hurl at Tristan are fueled by heartbreak and desperation. Becoming an outlet for my rage, he takes the brunt of my onslaught without fighting back.

"Hen, stop!" Con shouts in my ear.

I can't.

My body goes weightless as it flies through the air and hits the wall. I sag to the floor and watch as Con helps lift Tristan to a sitting position. Blood drips from his face and smears across his cheek when he wipes at his busted lip with the back of his hand.

"I'll fix this. I'll get her back."

I hate him so much right now, and it takes every ounce of strength I have not to hit him again.

"I think you've both done enough. I'll find her and bring her back."

I push to stand, threading bloodied fingers through my hair as I think. Where would she go? The only other people she knows here are Evan, Raquelle, and Shelby from the bar, and I doubt she'd fly back to Texas.

"Can we track her through her phone?"

Con extinguishes that small sliver of hope when he replies, "She left it on her nightstand."

Smart girl.

Tristan hesitates for a moment before slowly getting to his feet. "I think I know where she went."

CHAPTER 3

SYN

When the elevator door opens, my stupid heart goes wild when I'm met with the menacing silhouette of Hendrix standing a few feet away. Bathed in the soft white light from the wall sconces, he's six-feet-three-inches of gorgeously inked, blue-eyed lethality with sexy, sleep-mussed hair.

Love and hurt meld and comingle. My first impulse is to run to him, needing to feel his arms around me and hear him tell me that everything is going to be okay. Instead, I tear my gaze away from his alluring visage and look past him toward the entrance.

He peers over his shoulder, then back at me. "I came alone."

Part of me is relieved while the other part is greatly disappointed.

"You shouldn't have come at all," I immediately rejoin. "What do you want, Hendrix?"

Feet planted shoulder-width apart, he casually settles his hands at his sides, but the banked tension rolling off him is smothering.

"I want you to come home."

Goddamn this man. I'm emotionally drained and not mentally strong enough right now to protect my heart from him, because God help me, all I see when I look at him is my childhood best friend and the man I love, not the lying bastard he really is.

Gathering every last minutia of willpower I can muster, I reply, "No. Please leave."

"No."

I hate how much I love the smartass smirk that twitches his lips, so I smooth a hand across my forehead to hide my reaction and sigh.

"I can't do this with you right now. I need you to go."

There's no hint of playfulness when he practically snarls, "You'd rather stay here with that twatfuck than come home where you belong?"

"Aleksander isn't the one who lied to me!"

It's a mountain I'm willing to die on. I don't trust them anymore. I don't trust Alana. I don't trust anyone. Too many ugly revelations have been thrown at me over the last few days, and I'm suffocating. I need space and room to process.

I stand my ground when Hendrix suddenly advances.

"I didn't lie. I didn't fucking know!"

Laughter spills out unbidden at his audacity. He can try to convince me of a lot of things but not that; however, a sliver of doubt starts to creep in.

Not able to fight my emotions when he's so close I could reach out and touch him, I raise tear-glossed, beggar's eyes. "Tell me the photographs were doctored. That you, Tristan, and Constantine weren't standing right next to the man who forced me to watch my parents die in front of me, then smiled as he tortured me for hours. Tell me none of it is real."

His intoxicating cedar and citrus scent wraps around me when his large body guides me backward until my spine flattens against the wall. I can't prevent the moan I make when his hand settles around my throat, lightly squeezing. He knows my weaknesses and is masterfully using them against me.

With his sensuous lips at my ear, he growls in that slight British accent, "I. Didn't. Know."

"Liar," I hiss.

"We'll see who's lying." His thumb tilts my chin, and he takes my lips, his kiss possessive and demanding.

As soon as his tongue strokes the inside of my mouth, the walls of my resistance crumble like a sandcastle at high tide. Whatever anger I was tenuously holding onto changes into a wildfire of need.

My body does what my embattled heart is afraid to do. Fisting his shirt, I pull him closer, moaning louder when his hot palm covers my breast through my shirt. I can't deny the desperation I feel at his touch. Hendrix, Tristan, and Constantine are my obsession—my everything. Which is why it hurts so damn much when I press my hands to his chest and push him away.

"All that kiss proves is that you're just another person who takes something from me without my permission."

It's an idiotic thing to say because I kissed him back. Hendrix is aware of it, too, and I know I'm in trouble when his eyes glint cerulean fire.

"Is that so?" he silkily asks. I don't stop him when he slides a hand down the front of my shorts to find me soaking and needy. "Who's the liar now?" he taunts, rubbing circles on my clit that have an explosion of desire racing through me.

I berate myself for allowing this to happen at the same time I open my legs wider, craving the release he's promising. Pleasure pulses and swirls as he cleverly and deliberately edges me toward climax.

His smoldering gaze holds mine with challenge as he slips a finger inside my wet heat. "Come home with me."

I shake my head, wanting to say no, but all that comes out is a long moan when his skillful fingers drive me to a quick orgasm that leaves me delirious and wanting more.

"*Come home with me*," he repeats, and punishes my G-spot until I come hard a second time.

Holy shit. My legs buckle, and I'd plummet to the floor if he wasn't holding me up.

He leans his forehead against mine—his breaths nothing more than panted puffs of air over my flushed face—and paints my cum over my parted lips before tenderly kissing me.

"You promised you'd never leave me again. Please, Aoife."

It's the heartbreak I hear that shatters me completely and has me close to giving in.

Snick.

"Get away from her." Aleksander's quiet baritone is laced with threatening command.

Hendrix tenses beneath my hands. There's a violent shift in the color of his eyes from aquamarine to molten, electric blue.

"Hendrix, no."

My nails score into his arms, digging in to prevent him from turning around and attacking Aleksander.

"Now," Aleksander says.

Hendrix's hands fall away from my face. "If you think I'm leaving here without her, you might as well shoot me."

"Gladly."

It's all juvenile, masculine posturing and testosterone-fueled bullshit. Why do guys act like that?

In a desperate attempt to avoid any confrontation between them, I duck under Hendrix's arm and position myself on his other side, but he pivots around and pulls me protectively to him, anchoring me with a muscled arm wrapped around my waist.

Aleksander's gray gaze flickers a warning at Hendrix before shifting to me. His posture gradually relaxes, and he lowers his weapon.

"Are you okay?"

"Fuck you," Hendrix hurls at the same time I reply, "I'm okay. I'll be up in a minute."

"The fuck you will," Hendrix barks.

His arm painfully constricts across my midriff, the belly chain cutting deep into my skin like a branding iron of ownership.

Speaking to Hendrix, Aleksander says, "She knows everything. Every dirty little secret you've kept from her. You can't control her anymore. She gets to decide what happens next."

My eyes flare with surprise. The power to choose is something a man often takes away from a woman. Just like Hendrix knows my weaknesses, so does Aleksander. He doesn't see me as lesser; he sees me as his equal, able to make my own choices and choose my own path.

Something Andie said hits home. *"If it's important to you, then they'll support you, regardless of whether they agree with you or not. That's what loving someone entails."*

"Whatever she knows is the twisted version you've told her," Hendrix replies.

"Can I have a minute?" I say to Aleksander.

Without argument, he turns and leaves. Hendrix and I watch in silence as he disappears into a dark alcove to the left of the elevator. So that's where the stairs are. I was wondering how he got down here without using the elevator.

With how firmly Hendrix is holding me, it proves difficult to turn in his arms. When I'm finally able to look up at him, I take his beautiful face and bend his gaze to meet mine, needing to see his eyes. The truth always shows in the eyes. The way someone looks away or the slight dilation of the pupils. Watching someone's eyes is as good as hooking them up to a lie detector—unless you're Constantine and have the ability to cloak your expression in a wall of bored apathy.

"Aoife, please—"

"Did you know who killed my parents?"

There's no hesitation. "No. And Con said he only figured it out when you told him about the man with the constellation tattoos."

"Did you know that my mother made a deal with Nikolai? Did you know about the marriage contract?"

His hands dive into my hair, cupping the back of my head. "That contract is bullshit. You were never Aleksander's. You're ours, Aoife."

Before, being claimed like that gave me a thrill of excitement. It made me feel loved and desired. Now, however, it just makes me sad.

"I'm not a thing you buy, Hendrix. No one *owns* me."

I've been used by everyone in my life. As a weapon, a

pawn, a bargaining chip. No more. I may not be able to choose my fate in this life, but I'm damn well going to choose my destiny.

Hendrix's face slackens in panic when I pull away.

"Aoife... Syn. *Please*, baby. Please. Don't."

My soul cries out for him with each step I take.

"I love you, Hendrix. I've loved you since the day we met, and you pulled my pigtails. But I'm not going back with you."

I'm going after Francesco and Malin. I'm going to kill all of them.

And God help anyone who gets in my way.

Aleksander is sitting on the couch, drink in hand, when I step out of the elevator. His body language appears relaxed, but his posture is stiff, and his eyes follow me warily.

"I didn't think you'd come back."

The curtains that frame the large picture window are pulled back, giving a spectacular view of the lightening horizon as the sun starts its journey into morning. Walking over, I press my fingertips to the glass. Tiny circles of condensation create a pattern much like the arrangement of stars tattooed on the side of Malin's neck. As soon as I lift my fingers, they disappear.

"I used to search the night sky for him."

The leather of the couch squeaks as Aleksander shifts, hooking an arm over the back, drink dangling from his fingers.

"Once I found out what Francesco did—God, I hate him." Aleksander tips the rest of his drink back in one swallow, sets it on the coffee table, and rises to his feet. "Everything I've done was to avenge you. It was never about Tristan."

An eyebrow arches with a hefty amount of cynicism. "The Knight Estate," I remind him.

With a boyish chagrin, he says, "Okay. Maybe a little about Tristan."

Tristan and Aleksander have been fighting a war with one another when they should have been fighting together. They need each other. Not as enemies but as brothers. Aleksander has Alana, too. He needs the kind of love she'd be able to give him. A love that could help heal some of his broken pieces. It did for me.

I turn and prop my butt on the windowsill, hands curved over the ledge. "You've had plenty of opportunities to kill Francesco and... *him*. Why haven't you?"

"I wanted him to suffer. Take everything he covets until there's nothing left."

I contemplate that and him for a long time. "I'm starving. Got anything to eat?"

He frowns at my abrupt change of subject, but I don't wait for him to answer and start walking toward the kitchen.

Wanting a grilled cheese sandwich, I raid his fridge for sharp cheddar and butter. Seeing the package of swiss cheese, I grab that, too.

Aleksander comes around the counter and takes the items from me. "Aren't you going to ask where Francesco and Malin are?"

Every time I hear his name spoken aloud, my

stomach lurches.

"Pans?"

Looking a bit dazed, he points to the pull-out drawer below the double ovens. I grab one of the flat non-stick griddles and put it down on the front burner. Spying the bread box, I choose the loaf of pre-sliced white bread, even though the French baguette looks good.

Taking four slices out, I look over at him. "I know where they are. Butter knife?"

He pulls one out of a drawer and hands it to me. "How? I didn't tell you."

I turn on the burner and coat the pan with butter, then let the bread toast on one side while I slice the cheddar.

"You didn't have to. They're at the Society compound."

The gala is this weekend. I put two-and-two together and came up with four. It wasn't hard. It's what I would've done. Aleksander wants to humiliate Francesco. What better way than in front of the most important members of the Society who will be attending the annual gathering.

His mouth falls open, then he bursts into unexpected laughter. "You're scary… wife."

Pulling the metal spatula hanging from a hook of cooking utensils, I smack him with it. "You have no idea. And I'm not your fucking wife."

I once made a promise that my enemies would regret ever bringing Aoife Fitzpatrick back. However, they're about to find out what Syn Carmichael is capable of.

"Do you know how to pick a lock?" I ask him, opening cabinets one after the other in search of where he keeps the plates.

"I'm rusty, but yeah. Why?"

Finally finding where his dishware is stored, I take a plate out, then decide to get another so I can share my grilled cheese with him.

"I need to get into my apartment."

I tense when I feel Aleksander come up behind me. Looming and large and slightly intimidating.

"You're more than welcome to stay here. I'd like the company."

Plates in hand, I turn around and almost knock into him. The guy is just so... big. And *right there*.

I squash the guilt I feel over Aleksei. I can't let Aleksander use it to get me to do what he wants.

"First, that's not a good idea for many obvious reasons. Second, I need clean clothes."

I left a lot of my things at my apartment, thinking my stay at the guys' house was temporary. I also need a dress for the gala. I'd ask Raquelle, but I don't think she'd like getting it back with blood stains on it, which means I need to procure something soon since I plan to go to New York tomorrow after my last class... without him.

A heady thrill courses through me when I think about what awaits me at the Society compound. Can you feel it, Malin? Can you feel death coming for you?

CHAPTER 4

TRISTAN

"*The days when the sun and the moon can be seen together in the bright blue sky are my favorite. I equate the moon to be a woman and the sun a man. The man gives chase, and every so often, the woman will let him catch her.*"

I smile as I read the entry Aoife made in her journal. She didn't date any of the pages, so I don't know when she wrote it. It's one of her more beautiful thoughts stuck between pages filled with her nightmares.

"Anything?" Con asks, dropping down beside me on the couch. I pass him the journal but keep the pressed flower I gave to her and check my phone.

It doesn't matter that I keep checking it every ten seconds. Each time I turn the screen on, I expect to see a message from Hen saying that he found her and is bringing her back.

"Nothing."

Con bends forward and sets her journal on the coffee table, then buries his face in his hands.

"*Fuck.*" He slams back into the couch and stares up at the ceiling. "We should've told her."

I check my phone again because I'm clearly an optimistic idiot. "We were protecting her."

Aoife repressed her memories for a reason. The shit with Aleksei in the garden forced them back before she was ready. Who knows what additional psychological trauma we would have caused if we told her now. She was already dealing with too damn much, and now Aleksander had to make things worse with those fucking photographs. And how the hell did he find out about Malin? Con and I didn't know until a few days ago.

"Do you think Aleksander told her about—"

"I'm certain of it."

He's going to use every weapon in his arsenal to turn her against us. Half-truths, manipulation, whatever it takes to wreak vengeance on Francesco and punish me.

"Hen was pissed," Con says.

Yeah, he was. A pissed-off Hendrix is not someone I want to deal with. He tends to go off the rails when he's upset, which means we'll need to keep a close eye on him.

The phone Andie gave Aoife rings, and I answer it immediately.

"Aoife?"

A spark of hope ignites only to die execution style when it's not her voice on the other end.

"Hello? Synthia?"

Con's posture piques in interest. *Dierdre*, I silently mouth to him.

Putting the phone to my ear, I pace to the other side of the living room. "Hey, sis."

I'd think the phone call disconnected if it weren't for

the fact that I can hear her breathing.

"Tristan? Where's Synthia?"

Since seeing her standing on the other side of the elevator doors at Falcon Tower, my sister has been acting like she wants nothing to do with me. Then again, I've been avoiding her as well. Apparently, time apart *does not* make the heart grow fonder; it seems that decade has only made us more distant.

Evading her question, I ask, "How's Ireland?"

"She said she hadn't told you." She sounds surprised.

Ten years' worth of resentment passes over the connection when I reply, "*You* should've told me—about everything. What the fuck, Dierdre?"

Carrying the phone with me, I step out onto the back patio into the dusky pinkish-yellow hue of early morning. It's barely half past six, and the sun is about to make its arrival. Cocky Bastard is sitting on the roosting perch that extends out from the front of the henhouse, or whatever the fuck it's called. His tiny, beaked head tilts curiously when he sees me, and I glare murder at the demon bird, daring it to crow again. I swear the fucking thing smirks at me.

There's a hint of melancholy when Dierdre says, "You were twelve, Tristan. There's nothing you could've done to protect me from Gabriel. You know damn well what our father would've done to me if I refused. Mom didn't give a shit about me. She wouldn't have stood up to him. I did what I had to do. I won't apologize for it."

My hand tightens around the phone. "And what about Aoife?"

I can mostly understand why Dierdre faked her death, but hiding Aoife from us? Never.

"I *did* what I *had* to *do*," Dierdre enunciates slowly, but her voice is strained.

Something doesn't add up, and I make sure to call my sister on it. "If you were protecting her, why send her here to Darlington?"

Aoife made the same accusation, so I'm only repeating what she said.

I hear Dierdre's sudden intake of breath.

"Dierdre, answer me."

"It's what James wanted," she answers quickly before adding, "That's all I can say. You need to talk to Cillian."

Guilt clings to her tone like sandburs, and I pray for patience.

"I don't want to talk to fucking Cillian. I'm asking you."

An eternity of silence passes before she speaks again.

"I've got to go. Could you tell Synthia to call me later, please?"

"Don't you dare hang up!" I shout into the phone, but she's already gone. "Goddamn it!"

Cocky Bastard flaps his wings in annoyance at my outburst and crows his disapproval.

Pocketing the phone, I open the back door, pry the lid off the sealed container that contains the flock raiser crumbles I had delivered, and scoop a large handful of feed. Dew sticks to the grass and wets my bare feet as I walk over to the coop.

"I've never had a pet and have no fucking clue what I'm doing, so you're going to have to bear with me, okay?" I say to the rooster as I scatter feed out onto the ground.

He looks at the food, then at me, before hopping down from his perch. Instead of eating, he puffs out his plumage and struts back and forth with an arrogant swagger.

"You really are a cocky bastard. We'll need to get you some hens to lord over," I tell him, amused, and head back inside.

Con comes into the kitchen just as I grab a mug from the cabinet.

"That was quick."

I set the Keurig going and wash my hands. "She hung up on me. I know things aren't good between us, but she acts like she can't stand me. And then there's the stuff she said to me when we were in Texas."

Con pours himself a bowl of cereal and starts eating it dry. "What did she say?"

"She doesn't belong with you."

"Just some offhanded remark about me and Aoife." When the Keurig shuts off, I grab my coffee and sit down on one of the barstools. "Do you think James's offshore accounts still exist?"

Con shrugs a shoulder as he eats. "Won't know until I do some digging."

The guys and I have more money than we know what to do with and can take care of Aoife, but the Fitzpatrick fortune belongs to her. If James placed Aoife's guardianship into Cillian's care, he may have also done the same with his money. I hope not. And if he did, Cillian better not have touched a penny of it.

Con rinses his bowl and puts it in the dishwasher, then leans forward over the counter island, hands clasped together.

"She's going to kill him," he comments about Malin.

"I fucking hope so."

But Aleksander shouldn't be the one with her when she does. Con, Hen, and I also want our pound of flesh from that murdering motherfucker.

"She's not going to let you hurt Aleksander," Con says next.

I scowl at him. My half brother is a very smart man. He's been maneuvering the chess pieces of this game I didn't know we'd been playing for a while, carefully and strategically positioning us exactly where he wants us.

My head twists around when the front door closes. Con hasn't figured out yet what Aoife did to the security system, but nothing works. Not the notifications or the cameras or the alarm. It's how she was able to leave in the middle of the night without us hearing.

Con and I rush out of the kitchen just as Hendrix comes around the corner, looking worse for wear and angry as hell.

He takes one look at our optimistic expressions and shakes his head.

"I'm sorry. I tried. Fuck!" he shouts and punches a fist through the drywall, leaving a large circular hole next to the framed watercolor of a French rural town. Like a man defeated, he presses his back to the wall and slides down until his ass hits the floor. "I begged her to come home, but she wouldn't. What do we do now?"

With a determined resolve that lights a fire within me, I go to my haunches in front of him.

"Hey. Look at me." I wait until his bloodshot eyes meet mine. "What we're going to do is get our fucking girl back."

CHAPTER 5

SYN

"Stop hovering," Aleksander says as he fidgets with the two lock picks.

I'm supposed to be keeping an eye out for nosy neighbors, but what he's doing is more interesting.

Practically draping myself over his back so I can see, I reply, "I'm curious."

He turns his head. "You're distracting me."

With an annoyed huff, I give him room to continue working. It takes less than a minute before there's a click, and the door to my apartment opens.

"You're teaching me how to do that," I tell him and step over the threshold.

It's been almost two weeks since I've been gone, and the place desperately needs airing out.

"Cute," Aleksander says when he enters.

Pulling the latches, I open the living room window and breathe in the fresh air that rushes in.

"It's tiny, but I like it," I absentmindedly comment

because my attentions are elsewhere.

Things are not where I left them. I don't have much, so it's easy to notice that the throw pillows that sat on my floral couch are missing, and the glass I left out on the kitchen counter isn't there.

"You have a cat?"

Perplexed about why he would ask that, I reply, "No. A rooster."

I experience a pang of guilt because I left Cocky B by himself in a new home that would seem strange and unfamiliar to him. But I know the guys will take care of him until I figure out what I want to do.

"You have a rooster in the apartment?"

"Of course not," I reply.

Aleksander walks over to my couch, pointing out the stuffing bulging out from tears in the cushions. Constantine said he found the guy from the alley snooping around. The same guy he finally admitted he killed. Did he kill him inside my apartment?

"I got the sofa secondhand at a garage sale. It came like that," I badly lie and quickly walk away before he can call me on my blatant fib.

As soon as I step foot in my bedroom, I can smell it. The metallic stench of death. It's faint and barely noticeable for someone who isn't intimately acquainted with it, but it's there. *Constantine, what in the hell did you do?* I'm going to have to bleach the entire place, then buy a bunch of plug-in air fresheners before I'll be able to sleep in my room. Guess I'll be crashing at Aleksander's tonight after all.

Flinging open my closet door, I yank clothes off their hangers. My suitcase is at the guys' house along with everything else. Keys, clothes, backpack. I really didn't give much thought about them when I snuck out. I left my phone on purpose, knowing they could track my location with it.

"Your bedroom smells like dead fish."

Aleksander's unexpected intrusion makes me jump. Pirouetting on my toes, I implore, "Don't ask."

"Syn, what the fuck is going—"

Before I fall down the rabbit hole with him about why there's an old blood smell in my bedroom, I unceremoniously thrust the bundle of clothes I'm holding at him.

"You've got yourself a roommate for the next few days. Hold those for a sec. I'll get a trash bag to put them in."

Pulling open the top dresser drawer, I frown when I see the state of my undergarments. *Are you fucking kidding me?* My perfectly rolled underwear is a mess of haphazard colors, and the expensive black lace thong I bought online before I moved to Darlington isn't there. It was delicate and sexy, and I purchased it on a whim, hoping that one day I'd meet a man worth wearing it for. *Or three men.*

Not wanting to wear anything that a stranger may have touched, I slam the drawer closed and search for my spare pair of sandals.

"I'll need to go clothes shopping after class today," I inform him, spotting my cheap pink watch I wear for work.

I grab it and put it on. I've got two hours before Comparative Literature. Enough time to drop by Danby to see if I can catch Raquelle before my first class.

Aleksander follows me into the kitchen where I keep a box of tall kitchen garbage bags in the tiny three shelf pantry to the right of the fridge.

"Give me a list of what you want and your sizes, and I can have a personal shopper get the things you need."

I keep forgetting how wealthy he is. Tristan told me that Aleksander took over when Nikolai died. Something to do with private equity, but I'm not entirely sure. I should ask.

"Thank you, but I'd rather do it myself."

Andie gave me enough cash to tide me over until I can get to the bank—which means I'll have to go back to the house eventually. I can't get money out of my checking account without my debit card, and it would take a few days for one to come in the mail if I logged into my online banking and requested a replacement. And then there's my driver's license and student ID.

I really didn't think things through, did I? Then again, once I saw the photographs, anger and heartache were driving my impulses. Fight or flight, and I chose flight.

Aleksander's face pinches with displeasure when I motion for him to dump the clothes into the plastic bag.

"Don't you own a suitcase or a duffel bag?"

"Don't be snotty. This is fine."

He gives me a droll look. "Not wanting you to carry your stuff around in a trash bag is not me being snotty."

Pulling the drawstrings closed, I tie them in a bow instead of a knot. Easier to get open.

"What?" I ask him when he just stares at me.

"We need to talk about the gala."

Suddenly twitchy, I open the refrigerator to find only bottles of water. I had planned to go to the grocery store the morning after my Friday night shift at the Bierkeller.

"We can discuss the gala later. Right now, I want to

get the hell out of here."

Because I'm not a dorm resident and don't have my student ID, I have to wait outside the front doors of Danby until someone walks out. Luckily, I don't have to wait long.

"Thanks," I say to the guy who holds the door open for me.

As soon as I stroll inside, Evan looks up from behind the reception desk and smiles.

"Hey," he cheerily greets when I reach him and folds the corner of the page he was reading to keep his place. The book is a recent science fiction release I've seen posts about on bookstagram.

"Hey back."

Evan mentioned that he worked the reception desk from four to eight on Wednesdays and Thursdays. Knowing who he is now and who his father is makes me wonder why he said he was here at Darlington on financial aid. Cillian doesn't seem to be hurting for money. His house was the size of a small country. None of my business, I decide.

"You look pretty this morning. Love the shirt," he comments.

I'm wearing one of my rooster tees and decided to go full farm girl by Dutch-braiding my hair into pigtails.

I lift the small white paper bag containing still-warm pastries and offer it to him. "I brought yummies. Stopped by the donut place across the street from the Bierkeller on my way."

He eagerly snatches the bag out of my hand, opens it, and inhales deeply with a pleased hum. "You are a hungry man's food angel."

I smile at the silly compliment.

Scanning the immediate area, I ask, "Has Raquelle come down?"

"Haven't seen her yet."

He tears the paper bag down the middle and uses it as a makeshift placemat, then takes one of the napkins and picks up a *pain au chocolat*.

"Don't make me eat alone," he muffles as he chews.

I already ate two, but what the hell. Choosing one, I squeeze the flaky pastry until filling oozes out, then lick up the chocolaty goodness.

Sensing Evan watching me eat, my stupid face flushes with embarrassment.

"I have weird eating habits."

A grin teases his lips. "I didn't say anything."

A stampede of people come off the elevator, and the space fills with their happy faces and excited chatter. That was me a week ago. The recluse farm girl from Dilliwyll with hopes and dreams and a worldview skewed by rose-tinted glasses and deep-seated repressed memories—and I hate how that innocent, expectant part of me no longer exists. Will I ever be that girl again? Do I want to be?

"Where's the guy who's been following Raquelle?" I ask, not seeing him anywhere.

Evan finishes off the food and balls up the paper bag to throw away. "Outside."

Huh. I didn't notice him. Evan must have spoken to him about being less obvious.

"He's not needed anymore."

He executes a flawless free throw shot into the large trash receptacle.

"You sure? Dad will want to know why."

My fingernails tap out piano keys on the black lacquered top of the reception desk as I think about how I want to approach the sticky subject that is Aleksander Stepanoff. Best course of action is to jump right in. A *rip-the-Band-Aid-off* kind of thing. Then I decide against it.

"Tell Cillian thanks, but Aleksander isn't going to be a problem, and there really isn't a reason for someone to continue following her around all over the place."

I smile brightly until my cheeks hurt, begging Evan with my eyes not to ask any more questions. I've already used my one free lie for the day with Aleksander when we were in my apartment.

Evan opens his mouth to say something, but all that comes out is a long, drawn out, "*Okaaay*."

I point at the electronic tablet on the swivel stand. "I don't have my ID on me. Is it alright if I go up without signing in?"

Skepticism rolls off him when his hazel eyes narrow behind his glasses, and I suppress the urge to pull away when he covers my hand under his. I'm still not used to other people who aren't Alana or the guys touching me. I've gotten better at not retreating when Raquelle gives me one of her happy hugs.

"You know you can come to me for anything."

His concern makes me squirm.

"I appreciate that."

"I'm serious, Syn. I want you to come to me if you need anything." After a beat, he adds, "We're family."

The only family I have left is Tristan, Constantine, Hendrix, and Alana. Four people who said they loved

me, hurt me in the worst imaginable way.
   And how fucking sad is that?

CHAPTER 6

S Y N

The auditorium where my Comparative Literature class is held is a good ten-minute speedwalk across campus. When I see Daniel, one of the TAs, start to close the double doors, my fast walk becomes a full jog.

"Am I late?" I ask, breathless and slightly flustered.

After a short visit with Raquelle, I found myself in the butterfly garden Constantine took me to for our picnic. Lost in thought, I hadn't noticed that was where my feet were taking me until I got there.

"Just in time," Daniel says, holding the door open for me to pass through.

Professor Gilchrist's heels *click-clack* as she walks across the stage to the podium and attaches a wireless mic to her blouse.

"Good morning, everyone."

Professor Gilchrist has a policy that if you can't arrive on time, well, tough shit. If she sees you coming in after the doors close, she'll kick your ass right back out.

She and the professor who does my biology lab must be related.

"Sorry," I whisper to the girl whose legs I bump as I step over the bag she left in the middle of the aisle.

Hoping to be inconspicuous, I silently slide into the first unoccupied seat I find near the back… and freeze midway down when I lock gazes with heartbreakingly broody dark eyes. And damn my traitorous heart for the explosion of pure happiness I feel.

With my pulse thundering loudly in my ears, I take my seat and try my best to ignore the gorgeous, tattooed badass right next to me.

It's an asinine, futile effort. Especially when he smells so freaking good.

After a full minute of failing to pretend Constantine isn't there, I give up.

"What are you doing here?"

A girl in front of us turns her head, giving him an interested perusal that instantly brings out my jealous streak. I kick the back of her chair and glare a warning for her to mind her own business. I may be mad at him, but he's still *my fucking boyfriend*.

"Fuck. Off," I hiss at her, and she whips back around in her seat.

Constantine leans closer, his enticing body heat and the pleasant scent of his sandalwood soap accosting me in the best way possible.

"I miss you."

Air clogs my lungs as my throat constricts with emotion. It's been only hours, but I miss him, too.

It takes an immense effort of will not to leave my seat, crawl into his lap, and bury deep into him. Feel his arms around me. His lips pressed to my skin. Hear his gravelly, broken voice.

Choosing to keep my mouth shut, I stare straight ahead, feigning interest in what Professor Gilchrist is saying but not hearing a word of it.

Constantine throws his arm across the back of my seat and manspreads his long legs. Tingles race up my thighs where our knees touch, at the same time goose bumps pop, one by one, along my neck when his fingers begin playing with one of my braids.

When those fingers start drawing over the exposed skin of my neck, I give up on listening to the professor and hyperfocus on what he's doing. A heart. Letters that spell out *I LOVE U*. Some other shape I can't decipher. He brushes each one away with a feather-stroke of his thumb before tracing something new.

The next hour is excruciating as I sit there like a statue made of cold, hard granite while Constantine sets my body on fire with his casual, *intentional*, caresses. By the time class ends, my back and neck muscles are sore from how rigid I'd kept my posture, even though my insides are liquefied. I'm literally panting and more turned on than I've ever been in my life, which is a horrible predicament to be in with an auditorium full of people.

I remain in my seat while everyone shuffles out of the auditorium. As soon as we have complete privacy, I turn toward him, arms crossed over my chest. The therapist Alana had me see used to tell me people cross their arms when they feel defensive or anxious or need a way to self-soothe. Check, check, and check.

"You should have told me."

His too-handsome face goes somber. "We were."

I uncross my arms and pin him with annoyed eyes,

irritated that he doesn't get it.

"No we, Constantine. *You. You* should have told me as soon as you figured out who the man with the constellation tattoo was."

I'm not prepared for him to fire back at me. "What kind of cruel assholes would we have been to dump that on you when you were already dealing with so fucking much? Jesus, Aoife. I get why you're mad, but put yourself in our position."

Constantine has never been angry with me before, and his reasoning takes the wind right out of the sails of my ire. I slump back in the auditorium chair, not willing to concede he's right but also not wanting to remind him that he's wrong. The gray area between the two is muddied and thick like quicksand.

Yes, the last few days have been nothing but neverending chaos. But I'm the one Malin stabbed. I'm the one who was forced to watch the horrific things he and the other man did to my parents. He set me on *fucking fire* and left me with permanent burns and ugly scars that will remind me every day for the rest of my life of what *he* did to me. I'm damaged because of him—physically, mentally, emotionally—and that kind of trauma won't ever go away no matter how many therapy sessions I go to or surgeries I have.

They promised that they would help me find who was responsible. They knew who it was when I point-blank asked for their help, and that's what I'm having trouble getting past. A lie of omission, even if it's done with good intentions, is still a lie, and I'm so goddamn tired of everyone lying to me.

His phone chimes, and he doesn't appear to be happy when he looks at whatever message comes in.

Abruptly standing, he bends to kiss me on the top of the head. "I need to go, but don't think for a second this conversation is over."

"Anything wrong?" I ask because I don't like the tight frown lines that have etched themselves into his forehead.

"Hen is freaking out. He can't find Tristan's meds."

Worry crashes into me. If Tristan needs his meds, it means his migraine is bad. Stubborn man refuses to take them until he's almost incapacitated.

Aleksander put Tristan's medication in my backpack when he returned it to me.

"They're in the front pocket of my bag. I left it on the floor next to the bed."

"About that." Constantine picks my pack up off the floor and hands it to me. "I thought you'd need it."

I'd swoon at the thoughtfulness if I wasn't so concerned about Tristan.

Quickly unzipping the front outer pocket, I take out the small orange bottle and give it to Constantine. Our eyes meet and hold, both of us saying so much without saying anything at all.

"Love you, sweet girl."

My eyes flutter close when his hand strokes my cheek, then he leaves without another word.

Why does it feel like he's taking my heart with him?

One forever second… two…

I last three whole seconds after he disappears through the double doors before I'm up and chasing after him. Not seeing him in the hallway, I dash outside and catch a glimpse of his dark head of hair before he turns down the walkway that leads to one of the student parking lots.

"Constantine! Wait!"

CHAPTER 7

Constantine unlocks the front door and pushes it open. A peculiar stillness greets me, as if the house itself is sad, but I'm sure that's more psychosomatic on my part and a projection of my own feelings.

Constantine notices me hesitate at the threshold and patiently waits me out.

"This is still your home."

Home was always Dilliwyll with Alana, but home is also *them*.

Taking a deep breath, I walk inside and immediately feel trepidation coursing through my veins in a slow, persistent ache. The foyer is draped in shadows, the morning light still shyly avoiding this side of the house. The stained-glass windows aren't painting the walls with their usual kaleidoscope of colors like they do when the late afternoon sunlight shines through them.

Beneath my feet, the distressed wood floorboards groan in reluctant acknowledgment, echoing the hesitancy that clings to me like an invisible shroud. Slipping my sandals off at the door, the spanner rug that runs the expanse of the foyer absorbs the sound of my cautious footsteps. I look up when I sense eyes on me.

Hendrix looms at the top of the stairs, his mouth set in a pissed-off, grim line as he scowls down at me.

"Fucking love how you'll come home when Con asks you to but not when I do."

Climbing the steps until I'm in front of him, I throw as much attitude at him as his stupid accusation deserves.

"He didn't ask. Tristan's meds were in my backpack."

Those jealous, possessive blue eyes narrow, but eventually he gets out of my way so I can get past him.

"Is he in his room?"

"Had to carry him up. It's bad this time."

I remember the first night I was here. How Tristan slurred his words and could barely move when one of his bad migraines hit. He was so out of it, my first assumption was that he was stoned out of his mind.

"I'll do what I can," I assure Hendrix, sliding my hand down his arm. A simple brush of comforting touch that I think we both need right now.

"Here," Constantine says. He hands me the bottle of pills from his pocket.

"Could you get me a bowl of ice water, a washcloth, and a glass of water with a straw so he can take his meds?"

"I'll get them," Hendrix replies, looks away, runs a hand through his hair. "Just do your voodoo shit and make him okay."

His faltering movements give away how much he's worried. The three of them love one another, their bonds of brotherhood soul deep. *Sometimes the best families are the ones you create, not the ones you're born into.*

"I'll take good care of him," I reply, turning the knob and slipping inside Tristan's room. I leave the door cracked open for Hendrix and Constantine to come in without disturbing him.

The blackout curtains are drawn tight, making it almost impossible to see even an inch in front of me, and the lingering scent of sex has memories from last night instantly filling my vision. How can so much happen in such a short amount of time?

Carefully navigating the room, I slide the strap of my backpack from my shoulder and set it down next to the nightstand. Tristan emits a pained moan, the sound pitiful and gut-wrenching.

I move to the other side of the bed and slowly position myself beside him as gingerly as I can.

"Aoife?" he slurs. His entire face pinches in agony at the sound of his own voice.

"I'm here."

I grab one of the pillows and place it in my lap, then gently help him roll over to his back so that he's lying between the wide vee of my legs. Tenderly, I run my fingers over his temples and through his soft, dark mahogany hair.

"Try to relax," I whisper and begin targeting the pressure points on his face and around his ears.

His breathing evens out after a minute, but there are strained grooves wrinkling his stubbled face.

I glance up when Hendrix and Constantine come in carrying the things I asked for. The room returns to total darkness when Constantine quickly shuts the door so light from the hallway doesn't filter in.

"Where do you want this?" Hendrix's voice hushes out, and I can only assume he's referring to the bowl.

"On the nightstand. Soak the washcloth and wring it out, please."

With careful effort, Constantine helps me prop up Tristan so he can take his medication. He's nothing but dead weight, and it takes both of us to get him to swallow his pill.

"I'm… sorry. Love you… so much. Don't… hate me," he mumbles.

"I could never hate you, Boston," I softly reply.

"Here," Hendrix says.

Droplets of icy water splash on my forearm. I take the washcloth, fold it lengthwise, and press the cold compress to Tristan's forehead.

I don't know if it's five minutes or thirty before I'm sure Tristan is fast asleep. Kissing the tips of my fingers, I press them to his lips. He doesn't even twitch.

"Only sweet dreams," I tell him and carefully ease out of the bed.

As soon as we get out into the hallway, Hendrix starts down the stairs. "I'm going to get the pizza dough started."

My stomach perks up at the thought of homemade pizza. I check my plastic watch and see that I have another hour and a half before my next class.

I want to sink into the comfort of Constantine's warm hand when he possessively splays it along my lower lumbar… which is why I don't. Falling into old habits would be too easy, and the road to earning my trust back is long.

My emotions are a jumbled mess and all over the

freaking place when it comes to them. The hurt is still there, barely masking the love that is rooted deep. However, until I'm able to face the devil who destroyed me, I can't move forward. With them. With my life. With anything. I'm stuck in a perpetual loop of hate and revenge, and I'm terrified of the woman I'll have to become to do what I know needs to be done.

Something I remember reading comes to mind. A quote from Octavia Butler: *"In order to rise from its own ashes, a phoenix first must burn."*

"You sticking around?" he asks.

I look up at the man who used to say so much without saying anything at all. His voice is getting stronger the more he uses it.

My smile is unsure when I reply, "Pizza sounds nice."

Hendrix is already measuring out flour by the time Constantine and I enter the kitchen. I love how this room always smells of something delicious. Right now, the air is fragranced with a hint of yeast.

"Can I help?"

I expect Hendrix to say no, so I'm shocked when he says, "There are bags of fresh oregano, parsley, and rosemary in the fridge that you can fine-chop. Grab the jar of sauce while you're at it."

I'm about to make a quip that he would lower his culinary standards and use store-bought pizza sauce when I see the unlabeled mason jar sitting on the top shelf next to the packets of herbs. Of course Hendrix made sauce from scratch.

He places a cutting board and knife out for me when I unload everything onto the counter island. As I wash the parsley, my eyes wander to the backyard and the chicken coop.

"Has Cocky B been fed?"

Hendrix roughly folds and rolls the dough with his hands. "That bloody rooster is a terror. He needs a damn muzzle. Wouldn't shut the fuck up."

I wipe my hands dry using the kitchen towel Hendrix has thrown over his shoulder.

"Be right back." Scooping some feed from the container by the back door, I head outside. "Hey, big man," I say as I open the side gate and walk into the enclosure.

I'll ask Constantine if he can buy more fencing to extend the chicken run so Cocky B has more space to roam. He won't be able to free range the backyard without supervision because of the possibility of feral or stray cats or other predators. The coop and run will also need to be cleaned once a week and fresh bedding laid down. Deep cleans are only done twice a year.

Cocky B pecks circles around my feet as I scatter the feed on the ground.

"We'll need to get you a few girlfriends to keep you company."

Penny, Henny, and Jenny were his favorite hens back home—which reminds me that I need to talk to Alana about what to do about the farm. She can't expect Mike to care for the animals indefinitely.

Crouching down, I stroke along the ridge of Cocky B's comb, then down the feathers of his neck. "You be good and don't give Hendrix any reason to cook you for dinner."

He bobs and cocks his head and gives me what I call rooster attitude when he crows loudly.

It's official. All the men in my life are stubborn and difficult.

Going back inside, I'm a little exasperated when I find that Hendrix is already chopping the herbs.

"I was going to do that." I hip-bump him out of the way, so I can wash my hands.

He hip-bumps me back. "I'm doing it now."

"Kitchen diva," I retort and jump out of his way to avoid the ass slap I see coming.

Constantine sits on the other side of the island, his face set in a stone of concentration as he clacks away on his laptop.

"Studying?"

His focus briefly flicks from the screen to my face. "Hunting."

The way he says it sends predatory shivers down my spine. The really good kind.

Because I'm nosy, I come around the counter. His laptop screen is filled with computer code I don't have the first clue in knowing how to decipher. Basic commands I understand, but this is something else entirely.

Intrigued, I scoot in close. He shifts on the barstool and pulls me down to sit on his thigh. Slipping his left arm around my waist, his fingers delve under the bottom hem of my shirt to play with the links of the belly chain, and my stomach tightens with flutters of arousal.

"Hunting for what?" I croak when goose bumps explode over every inch of my body.

"The Society dissolved what was left of your family's estate—"

I hadn't given a second thought to my childhood home or what happened to it. The only things I have left of my parents would be in that house.

"—but there has to be hidden accounts somewhere. Money James or Caroline hid in private or offshore accounts. Your inheritance."

Inheritance because my parents are dead.

But so am I.

Aoife Fitzpatrick doesn't exist anymore. To the world, she's been dead for over ten years, what was left of her body buried alongside the ashes of her father and mother in the Fitzpatrick family crypt in Cork, Ireland. Something I found out over breakfast when I asked Aleksander about it.

Constantine slides a sapphire blue credit card across the slick granite. "It has no spending limit."

I blink at it. I know what type of credit card this is.

"I can't take your money." I slide it back to him, only to have him reverse its direction until it's right in front of me again.

"*Our* money," he emphasizes.

There's a metallic clank when Hendrix slams down the knife. "Take the fucking card. Why do you have to be so bloody difficult about every fucking thing?"

Our willful gazes clash.

"Because I don't like charity."

It's a petty excuse and one born out of stubbornness. I'm used to working hard to get what I want. I may not have much, but the things I do have are things I earned.

Hendrix rolls his beautiful blue eyes. "Charity, my ass. For a smart woman, you really are stupid."

"And you're a… a…"

I can't think of a good comeback when he's smirking at me with that sexy half-tip grin that melts my insides and makes me think *very* dirty thoughts.

"Fine." I snatch the card off the counter and stuff it

into my back pocket, then temper my irritation with a sincere, "Thank you."

I'll be paying them back every cent I spend.

When the timer on the oven goes off, Hendrix removes the plastic wrap from the bowl and takes out the round, puffy ball of dough. I watch, completely entranced, as he deftly hand-stretches and tosses it like a pro.

Hendrix notices my obvious interest. "Want to give it a try?"

I'm off Constantine's lap in an instant. "What do I do?"

Hendrix gestures at the bag of flour. "Since you already washed your hands, rub some of that on them. Don't want the dough to stick."

Once my hands are coated, he comes behind me and lowers his arms over my head, effectively caging me in.

"You'll want to keep your hands palms-down and only use your knuckles. Let gravity do the work for you."

He demonstrates the technique then transitions the dough over the backs of my hands for me to try.

When the dough droops more on one side, I can't suppress my giggle. "It looks like one of those melting clocks from that Salvador Dalí painting."

A jolt of pure electricity sizzles through me when Hendrix lightly bites the tendon at the base of my neck.

"Keep moving it around in a circular motion."

Tremors race up my arms when his hands caress their way to my breasts, and my back arches, pushing my aroused nipples into his palms.

"It's kind of hard to do that when you're feeling me up," I rasp.

He double-downs by pinching my nipples through my T-shirt. This man knows exactly how to play my body, and I know if I don't stop where this is quickly heading, Hendrix will be fucking me bent over the counter island. As much as I want that *and* him, mind-blowing sex and earth-shattering orgasms aren't going to fix what's broken between us.

I lay the dough flat on the parchment paper he spread out over a pizza pan and duck under his arms to escape temptation.

"Do you know what happened to the house?" I ask, brushing off the flour handprints Hendrix left on my shirt.

Constantine and Hendrix share a heavy look, which has me thinking worst-case scenario.

"Just tell me," I press.

Constantine closes his laptop. "It's gone, sweet girl."

A whoosh of pent-up breath I didn't know I'd been holding in expels from my lungs. "How?"

"We were told lightning hit it."

Lightning? That can only mean...

Fire.

Francesco burned my fucking house down? He decimated my life and for what? Because he wanted my father's position on the Council? Because my mother didn't want me to marry Tristan?

My fingertips sink into my left arm where my scorched skin prickles.

A strange odor, both acrid and sweet, assaults my nose, but I'm not able to process it over the searing pain of the knife being shoved into my side. The pain comes again and again, each time hurting a little less until there's no pain at all.

A whoosh whispers in my ear as a bright light erupts behind my closed eyelids. Heat scorches all around me, tiny licks of fire dancing across my body like magical forest sprites.

I wonder if I'll become a phoenix once the fire burns me to ash, like the one in the story Papa reads to me at bedtime. I'd like that. I'd like to be able to spread my wings and fly.

I feel like I'm flying now. Higher and higher toward a bright light. It's beautiful. Peaceful. I am the phoenix.

"Aoife."

Startled out of the horrific memory, my head snaps up when I hear Constantine say my name.

"What?"

There's a hard tug on my hand, and I can't hide my horror when my gaze falls from his face to the prep knife I'm clutching dangerously close to his throat. My veins turn to ice as reality slams into brutal focus. *Oh my fucking god.*

Hendrix gently pries the blade from the death grip I have on it and puts it back in the butcher's block, then takes my face in his hands and guides my vision so that I see only him.

"Focus on me, baby, and breathe."

I can't. There's no air.

A guttural whimper tears from my throat as the realization of what I had almost done suffocates me.

My mortified gaze fixes on Constantine, begging him to forgive me.

"I would never..." My voice cracks on a gasp. "I'm so sorry," I stammer.

"I'm okay. You didn't hurt me."

"Stop saying that!" I shout. "Stop telling me everything is okay!"

Why am I losing time again? It shouldn't be happening now that I remember everything.

The room shrinks around me as I begin to spiral into that hidden, dark place inside me where I bury things I don't want to confront.

I'm not here.

I'm not here.

I am no one.

No! I won't let myself be that girl. I won't hide from the monsters ever again.

"Let me go, Hendrix."

His grip tightens, ironclad and unrelenting. "Not until—"

"Let me go!"

As soon as he does, I bolt out of the house. The early morning cirrus clouds have burned away to reveal a gorgeous crystalline blue, cloudless sky that I wish I was in a better headspace to enjoy.

I fist my hands into tight balls because they haven't stopped shaking. I held a knife to Constantine's throat. My sweet, dark angel who has suffered so much. What in the hell is wrong with me? It's an easy question to answer. I'm just... broken.

I hate this. I hate feeling like this. I need the pain to stop. I need to be free from my nightmares. And the only way to destroy the demons that have held me prisoner for the last ten years...

...is to kill them.

I tip my face up to the heavens and feel the sun's golden filaments dance across my eyelids as a cool, caressing breeze plays with wisps of my hair.

Papa, I need you. Please give me the strength to do what must be done.

Of course, he doesn't answer back. There is no divine intervention that will guide me along the right path because there is no right path. The only road laid out before me is one paved in blood.

Opening my eyes, I look behind me, expecting to see Constantine or Hendrix and am disappointed when I don't. Hypocritical of me to feel because they're doing what I asked.

What's that saying? *If you love someone, set them free. If they come back, they're yours.*

But who will that person be?

I guess I'm about to find out.

CHAPTER 8

CONSTANTINE

I block Hendrix when he tries to chase after Aoife.

"Don't," I warn him even though every fiber of my being is screaming at me to go get her and bring her back.

With agitated hands, Hendrix yanks at his hair and whirls around to pace the kitchen, worry and fear spilling out of him.

"What the fuck was that? She flipped again. Why is she not getting better?"

I graze my thumb over where the knife pressed to my neck. My beautifully broken girl.

"What did you expect would happen? She's been through too goddamn much, and we're only making things worse. She doesn't trust us. We need to prove to her that she can."

Aoife has had too much forced on her all at once. She needs time to process and to heal. She needs us to be there for her. To be her strength and give her a soft place to land when she falls. All we've done is fuck things up. Kept things from her, believing it was for her own good. Pushed and pushed. If we lose her, it'll be our own fucking fault.

Hendrix angrily advances on me, but I don't flinch.

"And whose fucking fault is that? You and T kept it from me, too, but I'm being lumped in with the blame. You should have told me."

He shoves me back and raises his fist. I won't fight him if this is what he needs because letting him beat the shit out of me would be absolutely justified. Tristan and I messed up, good intentions be damned.

Hendrix vibrates with chaotic violence, needing an outlet to channel it.

"Do it," I tell him when he hesitates.

He lowers his arm. "Fuck you." With a growl of frustration, he slumps back against the pantry door and cinches his eyes tightly closed as if he's in pain. "I can't breathe without her."

I cuff the back of his neck until he has no other choice but to look at me.

"Neither can I. But can't you see that's part of the problem? By some miracle, we got our angel back, but we keep trying to compel her to be the girl we remember and not the woman she is now. We can't hide her away. We can't protect her from her demons. She needs to know that no matter what, we're right there beside her, fighting them with her."

My voice cracks at the end, and I detest the reminder that I won't ever be able to talk normally. I can speak for longer periods without it hurting. I know it's getting better, but that raspy crackle will be there every day to remind me that my father wishes I was never born.

Filling a glass with water, I pop it into the microwave.

Hendrix moves from the pantry door and takes over making the chamomile and honey tea that's my go-to whenever my throat bothers me.

"I hate you right now," he says, ripping open the Tazo foil pack and taking out the tea bag.

He doesn't hate me. He's mad, and that's okay. We'll get through this like we always do. Together.

Hendrix is quick to anger, but that anger is also quick to diffuse, so I leave him alone to grouse around the kitchen.

Flipping my laptop back open, I check on the progress of the code I've been running in the background. Hendrix not-so-gently slams the mug of hot tea next to me, sloshing its contents.

"Motherfucking fuck," he curses and rips off a sheet of paper towel to clean up the mess.

After kicking the trash can a few times, he leans over the counter island and buries his face in his hands.

"Find anything?" he mumbles, sounding a little calmer.

"Maybe." I blow on the steam rising from the mug before taking a sip.

Millions of dollars found their way into one of Francesco's private accounts around the time we were told Aoife and her parents were dead. I need to find out where the money came from. It could be something innocuous, or it could be something else entirely.

Quiet descends as I jump into the rabbit hole of mysterious monetary funds. I don't notice that almost two hours have passed until Hendrix takes out a pan of homemade biscuits from the oven.

I check the time on the bottom right of my screen. Shit. I missed my class. Maybe I should drop out like

Tristan and Hen did, but I honestly like my courses.

Cocky Bastard belts out a crow just as there's a knock on the front door. I really need to get our security system back online.

Hendrix drops the pan on top of the stove, and the hopeful expression he wears is the same one I feel.

"She came back."

God, I hope so.

I'm hot on his heels when he rushes out of the kitchen.

Unfortunately, the person standing on the other side of the door is the last person I'd expect to ever darken our front porch.

"She really has a pet rooster? I thought she was making it up."

Aleksander's bemusement pisses me off. Why would Aoife share anything personal with him?

"Oh, hell no," Hendrix says and tries to slam the door shut, but Aleksander sticks his Timberland boot in the way.

"I need to speak with Tristan."

"He doesn't want to speak with you," Hendrix retorts and plows his way into Aleksander's personal space. "And you've got a death wish showing up here after what you did."

Aleksander meets Hendrix's rage with a casual brush-off. "Could say the same to you, Knight, seeing as you showed up this morning, uninvited and most definitely unwelcome. How many times did Syn ask you to leave?"

Knowing exactly where to bury the knife to cause the most damage, Hendrix says, "Heard Aleksei is fertilizing the petunias."

A flicker of unbridled emotion appears before Aleksander schools his features and forces a smug grin. "Same could be said about Eva. Have you spoken to Patrick yet?"

I swiftly step between them before they try to kill each other.

Arms crossed and my cold stare blank, I block the doorway. "Tristan is busy. What do you want?"

Aleksander's eyebrows shoot up, and I despise how much he looks like Tristan when he does that.

"You can talk?"

I refuse to dignify that stupid-ass question with a response.

"You have five seconds to say what you need to say before I step out of the way and let Hendrix have his fun."

Unfazed, Aleksander peers over my shoulder. "I'd like to speak with Tristan, so why don't you go fetch him."

Unbelievable asshole.

When my throat starts to burn, I cover my cough with my fist. "I'm not a fucking dog. If Tristan wants to talk to you, he knows where to find you."

Tristan is in no condition right now to deal with Aleksander's bullshit.

The letters spelling out ANGEL and DEVIL inked on Aleksander's knuckles contort and stretch when he pushes up the sleeves of his black Henley.

"I came as a courtesy to discuss the gala and am only here because regardless of what you or my half brother thinks, I care about Syn and—"

"Like hell you do!" Hendrix explodes, nearly knocking me over when he launches for Aleksander's throat.

I struggle to hold him at bay and wonder why I'm

putting forth the effort. I should just step out of the way and let Hen tear him apart.

Cocky Bastard must have heard the outburst because he starts making a repetitive *pee-caw* sound.

Footsteps slowly plod down the stairs behind me, and I feel Hendrix bristle at my back.

"Let him in," Tristan says, his words running together.

"T, we can handle this twat," Hendrix tells him just as I resignedly move out of the way.

Aleksander enters the house and takes a cursory look around. The entire time we've been at Darlington, he's never been inside.

"Quaint... and pretentious," he remarks, his gaze eventually landing on Tristan. "You look like shit."

"Thanks." Tristan eases down to sit on the bottom step.

He shouldn't even be up. His migraine is still raging, evidenced by his pained expression and squinted eyes.

Aleksander is observant and perceptive, so it doesn't surprise me when he asks, "Are you drunk?"

Tristan's denial is swift. "No. And what you're trying to do won't work."

A master of calculated provocations, Aleksander sports an arrogant half-grin. "What do you think I'm trying to do?"

Lowering his head between his bent knees, Tristan pulls in several long gulps of air before saying, "Punish me for what Francesco did. Take Aoife from us."

"It's called karma. I also find it very hypocritical. Reap what you sow, brother."

The foyer crackles with unspoken animosity, each barb thrown adding more gasoline to the fire that has sustained their rivalry for over a decade.

"That's it, motherfucker. Kindly let the door hit you on the ass as you leave."

Hendrix shoves Aleksander, and I'm forced to intervene once again.

"Touch me again, and it'll be a month before you have full use of your hand," Aleksander bites out.

"Touch him, and it'll be the last thing you fucking do," I threaten.

I'm trying so damn hard to remain calm for Aoife's sake. When we were in Texas, she made me promise not to hurt him—and as long as I draw breath, I will never break a promise to her—but I'm two seconds away from choking him out.

Smirking like a jackass, Aleksander pulls out his phone. His grin drops.

"To be continued," he says before answering it.

"Get out of my way, Con!"

"Shut up." I have to muzzle Hendrix's loud mouth so I can hear what's being said.

I don't catch much, but it's the "Syn, I can hear you breathing," that gets my full attention.

Something's not right. Call it a gut feeling. *Sweet girl, what trouble are you getting yourself into now?*

I'm on him as soon as he ends the call. "Aleksander, where's Syn?"

CHAPTER 9

SYN

"You can pull over here," I tell the taxi driver.

The man's beady eyes find me in the rearview mirror. "You sure, lady?"

I never offered my name, and he never asked it, but I know his from the identification bolted in the middle of the dash. Edgar Dutchman.

Other than to direct Edgar where to go, the two-hour car ride has been done in thankful silence.

"Yes," I reply.

The blurred scenery outside my window takes shape as the cab slows and jerks to a stop in the gravel on the shoulder of the road. We're in the middle of nowhere, surrounded by nothing but thick forests of trees on either side, but I know exactly where we are.

Edgar snubs out his cigarette in the overflowing ashtray and twists around in his seat to peer back at me. The deep creases in his craggy face give testament to the long, hard life he's lived. Yellow, nicotine-stained fingertips tap against the edge of the opening in the clear partition that separates the front from the back. The car reeks of the stale stench of cigarettes that his three green tree-shaped air fresheners hanging from the rearview can't mask. Even with his window rolled down, the acrimonious odor fills the small space and clings to my skin, clothes, and hair like sticky soot.

"Need me to wait?"

"No."

The fare tallies to hundreds of dollars. I hand over a roll of cash, giving him most of what I have left from the money Andie gave me.

Edgar balks at the exorbitant amount as he flips through the bills, then quickly secures the cash in a lockbox he pulls out from underneath his seat.

"Appreciate the lift." I grab the duffel from the floorboard that I stole from Aleksander's room and open the back passenger door to get out.

"Take care, Red," the man says.

Hearing Tristan's nickname for me pierces my heart like a serrated dagger.

I love you, Boston. Please understand.

Standing along the shoulder, I watch as Edgar pulls away and wait until the cab crests over the hill before I disappear into the thick autumnal foliage of deciduous trees.

Finding a thicket of underbrush that hides me from the road, I set down the heavy bag and unzip it. My nose wrinkles in disgust when I smell the cloying tobacco clinging to me. I take a cursory look around before I strip down to my undergarments. Rifling through the duffel's contents, I take out the clean set of clothes I packed. Black tank top and black yoga leggings. Once I secure the laces of my old pair of tennis shoes, I pull the elastic band from my wrist and tie back my hair, then grab the Glock I also stole from Aleksander and set off at a leisurely jog.

The woods aren't difficult to navigate in the light of day. It wouldn't matter if the sun was out or not. The layout of the property is as clear as a map inside my brain. Where the hidden cameras used to be located. The perimeter wall. The secret underground tunnel. Papa taught me well.

My soft footfalls crunch the leaf litter underfoot, startling a squirrel perched high in a branch above. He gives a chittering screech of warning to the forest animals that there's a predator nearby.

It takes me eight minutes to jog the mile from the road to the private drive that leads to the gatehouse and main entrance of the Society compound. I'm not here for subtlety. I'm here to make a fucking statement.

As soon as I break the tree line and step out onto the smooth, black tarmac, adrenaline spikes like a drug through my bloodstream. My senses hyperfocus, cataloging everything. Sights. Smells. Sounds. There's an immediate tension in the air as I approach the gates.

Two guards move about inside the gatehouse, and I know exactly when the security cameras detect me because both their heads snap in my direction with precise synchronicity. The taller, lankier man walks out, mocking amusement in his eyes and a slimy grin on his face. His right hand is propped on his gun holster, his posture relaxed. I'm a woman. He doesn't see me as a threat.

"You lost, gorgeous?" he asks, checking me out with a lecherous roam of the eyes.

But then his gaze drops to my scarred arm, and his smile fades away, replaced with revulsion.

I stop in front of him. "I'm exactly where I need to be."

Without warning, I crush his windpipe with a precise strike to the throat. His body falls like a limp ragdoll to the ground, his hands gripping his throat as he tries to choke in desperately needed oxygen. He'll be dead in two minutes.

"The fuck?" I hear the other man's stunned shout from inside the gatehouse before his voice is muted by the echoing gunshot that punches the air.

Brain matter splatters the glass windows like an abstract painting when I put a bullet through his skull. I step over his lifeless, crumpled body at the door and hit the control that opens the tall iron gates. The gears grind and whine as they slowly swing open.

I regard the man on the floor. I feel… nothing. No remorse. No sympathy. No regret. He worked for the Society. Killed for them. A choice he made, and not one that was forced upon him like the servants who are compelled to cater to their every whim. This guy is just as guilty as the men who sit at the Council table, and I'm the fucking Reaper come to collect.

"You won't be needing this," I tell him as I unclip his sidepiece and slide it under the elastic waistband of my leggings at my back.

As I ascend the narrow private drive, the foreboding stone mansion stands like a brooding sentinel overlooking the land below. The Society compound is a decaying monument to opulence and power, a corrupt symbol of its legacy. The mansion's limestone façade is weathered and worn and bears the scars of over a century's abuse from nature's elements. Ivy clings to its outer walls, a green tapestry that weaves tales of how long the structure has existed on this hill like a decrepit king sitting on his throne. Windows, dark and lifeless, stare out with vacant eyes, revealing nothing of the malevolence that's concealed within.

With every step that brings me closer to my nightmare, the ominous shadows cast by the looming trees seem to reach out, their long spectral fingers pointed at the house, damning it as if they know what's about to happen.

With me sitting snuggled on his lap, Papa twirls his thick finger around a curl of my blonde hair and loops it behind my ear. The wood fire warms my bare toes and draws a sleepy yawn from my lips. Drowsy and content, I rest my head in the crook of his shoulder, breathing in the comforting notes of the vanilla in his aftershave as he tells me the story of Boudicca, a Celtic queen. Upon her husband's death, she rebelled against the Romans who had seized her kingdom, raped her daughters, and publicly whipped her as a message not to defy them.

"And when the Romans took everything Boudicca loved, the queen vowed, 'Win the battle or perish, that is what I, a woman, will do.'" Taking my chin, he tips my face up and pecks a soft kiss to the button of my nose. "You are my fierce little queen, Aoife. Even when all seems lost, never stop fighting."

There's a static crackle of shouted masculine voices coming from all directions as armed guards race out into the open, their guns drawn and locked on me. Buzzing fills my ears as I give myself over to the darkness and set the monster free.

Kill them all.

One by one, men crash to the ground as my finger

squeezes the trigger again and again and again, leaving a gory trail of blood and destruction in my wake. I pay no attention to the screams of panic or cries for help that echo around me as bullets discharge without hesitation under my unforgiving hand of retribution.

And then, all is blessedly quiet.

I stand amid the massacre I just created and look up at the sky. Clouds have rolled in, obscuring the sun, and a chill wind rushes past me as thunder resonates overhead, announcing the quick approach of an early afternoon stormfront. A bolt of lightning forks a jagged path from cloud to cloud, ripping the air apart with its power. It's as if I conjured nature's fury, and it's feeding off the chaos churning inside me.

I move with purpose up the front portico marble steps, an invisible force guiding me like a beacon. Just as I get to the massive double doors, one side opens, and another guard appears in the doorway, his gun held to the head of an elderly man. I recognize him.

Most of the servants who work for the Society don't do so to earn an honest living. They are forced into servitude to pay off a debt. It's either that or death, and once you've agreed, there is no way out.

Using the old man as a human shield, the guard shouts, "Drop your weapon!"

Fucking coward. I shoot him right between the eyes before he has a chance to blink.

The old man covers his ears with wrinkled, trembling hands and stands motionless as the guard timbers backward like a felled tree.

Out of ammunition, I switch out the Glock for the pistol I took.

"How many more in the house?"

"T... two, I think. I'm not sure," he whispers hoarsely.

I took down eight. With the gala happening this weekend, the place should have been teaming with them. Then again, Aleksander never told me what he had planned. For all I know, I might have just killed his own men.

"Helena Amato?"

He swallows thickly. "Mistress Amato is to remain in the Rose Room. Master Stepanoff's orders. Master Amato is being detained elsewhere."

I feel a sick sort of morbid giddiness. "Where?"

He points a shaky finger down at the floor, but I understand what he's referring to. I had already deduced that's where Aleksander had imprisoned him and Malin.

Stepping inside, I do a quick reconnaissance of the foyer. The grand chandelier suspends from the domed ceiling and illuminates the dust motes that dance around it. Rain begins to beat against the stained-glass windows that follow the curvature of the Pantheon-like dome stretching high above my head. The interior of the house is exactly the same as I remember. Ornate antiques. Beautiful gold-leaf framed oil paintings. Antique silk wall coverings. Its beauty belies the malevolent secrets that lie hidden within its oppressive walls.

Another flash of lightning precedes a roll of thunder that rumbles menacingly outside, its compressive sound waves hitting the glass windows and making them rattle.

Never taking my awareness off my surroundings, I tenderly cup the man's frail arm and give it a squeeze of reassurance. "I'm not going to hurt you, Mister Jones."

His confused face rises when I address him by name. Pale-blue eyes that have seen so much in his lifetime bore into me with kindled recognition.

"Dear God, it can't be," he hushes out, shock turning his complexion white.

"I need you to do me a favor. Leave and never return. You no longer owe a debt to the Society."

He inclines his gray head and worries his hands, wringing them together. "But my son... and granddaughter... she just turned nine..."

The terror I hear in his voice enrages me. Threats toward family members were one of the many 'incentives' the Society used to ensure compliance. Papa could have changed things, made things better, helped these people. But he didn't, did he?

I was conditioned from birth to view our world wearing blinders to the evil happening around me. That what we did was normal. That youthful naivety is long gone, and for the first time, I'm ashamed of my father and the complacency he perpetuated.

"They're free, just as you are free. Now, go."

I hope he heeds my words and does what I ask.

Ever vigilant, I make my way to the secret door that leads to the catacombs underneath the foundation of the house. With muted stealth, I navigate the labyrinth of hallways—past the ballroom and the kitchens and the other rooms that we were never allowed inside. I don't encounter anyone else, which is odd. In fact, the house is silent as a tomb. Instead of putting me at ease, the lack of people has me on edge. *Aleksander, what have you been up to?*

Goose flesh scatters chills over my skin when I'm standing in front of an imposing black door. As a child,

I had an image in my mind of what the gates of hell looked like, and every time I stood in front of this doorway, I was certain this was it. Because that's how it felt to my young mind every time I walked through this doorway—like I was walking straight into hell.

"'*Lasciate ogne speranza, voi ch'intrate*. Abandon all hope, ye who enter here.'"

I murmur the passage from Dante's *Inferno* as I press my palm flat to the thick, solid wood. My pulse is throbbing so fast, I can physically feel it through my hand. The devil is on the other side of this door, and once I open it, everything changes. I won't come back out the same person I was when I entered.

Taking a deep breath, I rotate my shoulders clockwise to release some of the tension coiled tightly inside my chest and eye the security panel mounted on the wall. The damn thing mocks me. I can't get in without a passcode.

Taking a chance, I enter the code Papa made me memorize and am very surprised when it still works.

"Oh, Francesco, you stupid, stupid man."

The door moans on its hinges when I push on it and expose the limestone steps that lead underground. With every step I descend, my lungs fill with the musty whispers that tinge the air like a sinister promise. One step. Two. Three. I continue on until the stairs open into a cavernous, dimly lit room.

Familiar red velvet tapestries hang from the ceiling like opaque waterfalls of blood. Gold trinkets and fine sculptures sit atop six-foot Doric columns made of black obsidian that are evenly spaced in a circle in the middle of the room. The last time I was down here was for Constantine's initiation ceremony on his twelfth birthday. It was the same night Papa stole me away to Ireland and made me leave the three boys who were my everything.

My tennis shoes scuffle across the cold stone floor until I'm in front of the four ornately carved seats that belong to the founding Council families. With reverence, I trail my fingertips along the back of my father's chair, the Fitzpatrick heraldic crest carved into the ebony wood of the seat back. I follow the upturned curve of the lion's tail to its paw as it fights the dragon beneath it.

A glint of sanguine catches my eye and draws my attention to the jeweled onyx box. Like a siren's song, I'm drawn to it and the promise of what I know I'll find nestled inside. Opening the lid, I take out the ruby-encrusted medieval dagger and turn it this way and that. It feels heavy in my hand, its weight carrying the burden of every soul it has taken.

Grasping the dagger by its hilt, a slow smile blooms on my lips as I cross to the other side of the room. The beating muscle in my chest strikes against my breastbone like mallets hitting a bass drum. I slip like a wraith through the darkness down the passage that leads to the catacombs.

"Hello again."

ShitShitShit!

I stop in my tracks when the barrel of a gun pushes against the back of my head. However, I have a gun *and* a knife. The odds are in my favor.

"Please don't," the man says when he notices my hands tighten around my weapons. "Aleksander would have my head if I laid a finger on yours, and I very much like my head exactly where it is."

Brows knitted together in a perplexed frown, I slowly turn around.

"Mrs. Stepanoff. Nice to see you again."

The man who was with Aleksander when he trapped me and Alana in the restroom at the bar in Texas smiles at me.

"Wish I could say the same," I reply, but he cuts me off with a finger held to his lips.

Did he seriously just shush me?

He taps the earpiece in his left ear, then says, "Aleks, you're never going to guess who I'm looking at right now… Uh-huh… No. Your wife."

"I *am not* his fucking wife," I whisper-hiss.

His smile broadens as he looks me over.

"A little blood-splattered but seems fine to me… How the hell would I know…? They're all dead… Well, she's your wife, asshole…"

Oh, for fuck's sake. "I am not his—"

The infuriating ass shushes me again. And why am I standing here, putting up with this? He held a gun on my mother. The least he deserves is a punch to the face.

"Hold on," he says.

He dislodges the earpiece and offers it to me. It's one of those Bluetooth ones that connects to your phone or watch. He shouldn't be able to get cell reception down here.

When I don't take it, he gives a humor-filled shake of the head and slips it into the hollow of my ear. I want to smack his hand away, but I'd probably slice it off with the dagger by mistake. Would serve him right.

"Syn, I can hear you breathing," Aleksander says in my ear.

I keep my mouth closed and glare at the other man

in front of me. He's blond like Aleksander, not as tall or muscled, and his eyes are green, not gray.

Aleksander sighs heavily over the earpiece. "You are a very exasperating woman. I'll see you in an hour. And it's not Pyotr's fault. He's only doing what I asked him to."

Who the fuck is Peter?

That's the last thought I have before my body goes limp and everything goes black.

CHAPTER 10

SYN

My awareness kicks in slowly, like I'm walking through a thick blanket of fog into dim sunlight. Loud, angry shouts bombard my fuzzy, cotton-filled brain. The cacophonic noise does little to chase away the elephants stampeding through my head.

I touch the throbbing pulse at my temple where the headache has taken up residence. What the hell did Pyotr do to me? Damn you, Aleksander.

With languid eye blinks, things around me start to come into focus—

—including the broody, dark-eyed man sitting in the corner of the room.

At first, I think I'm imagining him. A dream similar to the first time I woke up in Tristan's bed to see Constantine sitting in the chair, the glow from his phone creating odd shadows on his handsome face. And like that time, a small gasp escapes when I find that pseudo-onyx gaze looking right at me.

Constantine doesn't say a word, just watches me with that unemotive stare I loathe because I can't tell what he's thinking or feeling.

Wishing the bed I'm lying on would swallow me whole, I gingerly sit up and gather the courage to say something, *anything*, that will help ease the guilt I feel at the thin, red line on Constantine's throat that is as conspicuous as a glaring neon sign.

"Did I hurt you? Are you okay?" I lightly tap my fingertips to the column of my neck before letting my hand fall to my lap when Constantine's face remains impassive.

The arguing that brought me out of unconsciousness rages on outside the bedroom door. Tristan's unmistakable Bostonian lilt, Hendrix's angry British undertone, and… Aleksander's deep timbre.

They're all here? This is *not* good.

I hold back the nausea that hits me when I fling my legs over the side of the bed and stand up. Next time I see Pyotr, I'm going to kick his ass. Aleksander's, too. He promised me revenge, then had his man stop me when I was so close to getting it. Malin and Francesco were *right fucking there*.

"I'm not okay."

My eyes dart to Constantine when he speaks. His admission piles on more guilt to the mountain I'm already buried under because I know he's not referring to me blipping out earlier at the house.

With lethal grace, he unfolds himself from the chair and slowly approaches me. My heart rate flitters like the wing beats of a hummingbird, then triple times when he drops to his knees in front of me.

Those wonderful, inked hands slide up my thighs

to my hips, then circle around me in an embrace. My fingers dive into his thick, soft hair when he presses his cheek to my abdomen.

"You are not alone in this," he says, the rasp of his voice raw against my skin.

How can this man of few words know exactly what to say?

Instead of lambasting me for what I did, Constantine holds me and tells me that I'm not alone. Tristan and Hendrix are here with Aleksander, their enemy. The fact that they are holds such immense significance.

I'm at a crossroads. I either let anger guide me along a solitary path, or I follow my broken compass back to them. And the truth is, I need them. We are stronger together, and I really don't want to do this alone.

Slipping my hand from his hair to his rough-stubbled cheek, I say, "*Você é meu coração,* Constantine Matias Valentim Ferreira."

At the use of his full name, he gives me a silly grin that melts my freaking heart.

Something I used to do as a child was to look up the meaning of names. Most of the time, parents pick whatever because they like the sound of it, not knowing its derivative or significance. Aoife is Gaelic for beauty and radiance. I'd find it ironic given the scars I carry, but the guys tell me I'm beautiful every day—that my scars are part of what makes me beautiful.

Constantine's middle names, Matias and Valentim, mean gift of God and strong, respectively, but it's his first name that carries the truth of who he really is. Steadfast and constant. My safe place and comfort.

"I'm still angry."

Constantine presses a kiss to my navel. "I know."

They're going to have to do some serious groveling to mend the hurt they caused. But that's the thing about love. You fight hard but love harder, and damn if I don't love them to the core of my soul.

"*Really* angry," I stress.

He bumps my shirt up with his nose and kisses along the belly chain.

"I *know*."

I try not to smile, but he makes it impossible.

I wait for him to rise to his full height before stepping into his big body and circling my arms around his tapered waist.

I take a minute to breathe him in and get my bearings. I think we're in the Lilac suite based on the various lavender colors of the room. I never liked this room. Too much purple.

"I love you, pretty boy," I tell him.

"Love you more, pretty girl." He kisses the crown of my head. "It's not your fault, Aoife. What happened at the house. So don't you fucking dare carry that around. You didn't hurt me."

A fat crocodile tear slips free unbidden. "I'm not any better."

And I'm terrified that I'll be like this for the rest of my life. Losing time and not in control of my anger. Letting the monster inside take over. It's a helpless feeling, not being in control of your own body and actions, regardless of if that monster serves a purpose.

Constantine hugs me harder. "You *are* better, sweetheart. That doesn't mean you won't have setbacks. Can you promise us something?"

I don't miss his use of *us* and not *me*.

"When this is over, will you consider talking to

someone?"

I take a deep breath and exhale it out. He means seeing a therapist. It's something Alana had me do, and in hindsight, something I should still be doing.

"Okay," I quietly answer just as more shouting ensues outside the room.

I don't want to let him go, but I know I need to stop whatever is happening out in the hallway.

"How did you know I was here?" I ask, hand on the doorknob.

"Aleksander came by the house."

That's unexpected. Aleksander is still breathing, so things must have stayed civil. I hope. The yelling says otherwise.

With a solid yank, I open the door... and stumble right into Hendrix. Denim-blue eyes blaze down at me.

Out of my three guys, Hendrix is the most volatile but it's only because his heart is the easiest to damage. It's why he tries to barricade himself behind a fortress of assholery. Despite his deplorable behavior, I think it's why I was so drawn to him when I refused to remember. The girl I was before knew who he really was deep down where it counted.

"Hen—"

Hendrix's hands are suddenly on me, and air whooshes out when my backside collides with the wall.

"Shut. Up." He takes my throat in one hand and steals every thought from my head with an aggressive, demanding kiss that I wholly and enthusiastically reciprocate.

I once thought that Hendrix kissed me like he had something to prove and was willing to destroy me to do it. And he does. Every single time.

As suddenly as the kiss started, it stops when he pulls away. His hand at my throat squeezes just enough to restrict my ability to draw breath.

"I'm fucking livid with you right now," he says at my lips, dipping his tongue inside before letting go.

I refuse to apologize for why I came and for what I did once I was here. There are only so many *'sorrys'* I'm willing to give, and this is not one of those times.

My eyes land on Tristan. He's standing beside Aleksander. I see it now. The resemblance. Even though they couldn't be more different physically, they have the same full mouth and shape of the eyes.

"You're going to let him treat her like that?" Aleksander says.

"Heard you've done worse to Serena," Hendrix fires back.

Just the mention of her name stokes those embers of rage. I don't care who Serena sleeps with, but I don't need the reminder of all the times Hendrix fucked her. No woman wants to have her man's past relationships thrown in her face. Serena is also a catty bitch.

"Can we not right now?" I implore.

Like I'm tethered to him, I'm pulled forward by an invisible force until only a breadth's-width separates me from Tristan. Going up on tiptoe, I search his whiskey eyes for any sign of the migraine and am relieved to see that his pupils are normal.

His eyelids fall shut when I softly caress his cheek. "I think it's time we sat down and talked."

He takes my face in his hands and brushes the barest of kisses across my lips. "I think that's a good idea." Dark brown brows dip into a vee. Held at arm's length, he inspects me with a critical once-over. "Is that blood?"

I peer down at myself. I'm wearing all black and don't see anything.

"If it is, it isn't mine," I reply.

I spin around and punch Aleksander in the face.

"The fuck, Syn!" he bellows, cupping the side of his jaw.

No one jumps in to intervene—surprise, surprise—so I hit him again because he deserves it.

"I am not your goddamn wife. You do not get to make decisions for me, and you absolutely will not sic your man on me again like you have a right to decide what's best for me. You made me a promise, and you're damn well going to keep it." Not through with my tirade, I point an enraged finger at Tristan, Hendrix, and Constantine. "Andie said something that really hit home. She said that if it's important to me, then you'll support me, regardless of whether you agree with me or not. She said that's what loving someone entails." I pound a fist to my chest where my heart beats a song of revenge. "I need you to love me enough to let me do what I came here to do. What I fucking *need* to do. And stop smirking, or I'll punch you next," I tell Hendrix, who appears way too happy that I hit Aleksander.

With a sexy pop of dimples, he sends me a challenging grin. "You know I like it rough, Trouble."

My body responds to him like it always does when he's being an ass, and arousal sneaks its way underneath the irritation.

Tristan grabs my wrist and pries open my closed fist, then threads his fingers with mine.

"We'd burn the world down for you, Red."

Ironically, that's exactly what I intend to do.

After I kill Malin.

CHAPTER 11

SYN

The silence booms loudly in my ears as I stand on the precipice of confronting the man who took everything from me and left me scarred. My chest feels heavy with the weight of a reckoning long overdue; my footfalls deliberate, each one echoing the burning hatred that fuels my every move. The blackness of the catacombs seeps deeply into my soul, feeding the darkness within me. Every fiber of my being screams for retribution the closer I get to *him*.

But this time, I'm not alone.

"I hate this fucking place." Hendrix's voice echoes between the stone walls.

I hadn't considered how they would feel coming down here. Their perspectives are tarnished by the initiation ceremonies they were forced to endure on their twelfth birthdays. I was here for Tristan's and Constantine's, the memories still fresh like a macabre photograph. How witnessing them kill an innocent man didn't bother me as much as seeing the sybaritic delight on the faces of the Society members who were watching.

My reply is as morose as my thoughts. "Me, too."

Always knowing exactly what I need, Constantine takes my hand, giving me his strength.

Hendrix presses close to my back, his warmth chasing away the chill that has been building. "You don't have to do this."

"Yes, I do."

I detest how my voice wavers when I say it.

Being down here a second time feels different. I'm no longer riding a wave of bloodlust. I'm back to being that confused, angry, and scared little girl who witnessed something so horrific, she made herself forget. I am also a woman transformed into a weapon, ready to reclaim the shreds of my life Malin ripped apart. It's a confusing maelstrom of emotions that I don't know how to deal with.

Ever my protector, Tristan says, "If it's too much or you change your mind, we'll do it."

They would kill Malin for me, no hesitation whatsoever. It makes me love them so much more knowing that. Fucked up, but the truth.

I steel my spine and fortify my resolve. "I won't change my mind," I assure him.

Hendrix swipes my hair to the side and kisses my neck. "You are fucking titanium, baby girl."

I find solace in his praise, soak it up like sand in a desert after the first drops of rain.

Aleksander's gray eyes score into me. He has been quietly observing, almost as if he's fascinated by the dynamics between the guys and me. Were he and Aleksei close? Identical twins are said to have an intense bond because they share DNA and were born from the same fertilized egg. Does he feel like half of himself is missing now? I know I did when Papa hid me away in Ireland. The longing for Tristan, Constantine, and Hendrix was worse than any pain I had ever felt. Worse than what Malin did to me. Even when I didn't remember, I always felt like I had lost something vital. I hope one day that Aleksander and Tristan see what's right in front of them.

With my hand clasped securely in Constantine's, I make my way down the corridor that leads to what Papa called the dungeon. We don't run into Pyotr. Aleksander was smart to tell him to stay out of sight.

"Francesco is in there with him," Aleksander says, and I go ramrod rigid, stopping in my tracks.

My heart jack hammers against my ribcage so hard, it physically hurts. Both of them. In the same cell. Together.

Aleksander moves in front of me, but I don't see him through the flash fire of fury burning behind my cornflower-blue eyes.

"I have plans for him. I need him alive."

Tristan lunges forward and slams Aleksander to the wall. "You can shove those plans right up your ass, or is what you said about giving it all up for her just the same old bullshit and lies?"

"You always miss the bigger picture, *brother*. What better revenge than to make an example of him in front of everyone?"

What he says penetrates through the haze of rage. That's actually a good idea. The highest-ranking members of the Society will be here tomorrow for the gala. The ultimate endgame.

"Okay," I acquiesce.

Tristan's head snaps around, his eyes hard as flint. "Be fucking sure, Aoife."

With a nod from me, Tristan backs away from Aleksander and pulls me into a rough embrace. My fingernails dig into the cotton fabric of his shirt, clinging to him and never wanting to let go.

"I'm afraid I won't come back."

I'm terrified that the darkness will take over, and I'll be lost again.

"We love you. Every part of you. Dark and light. Aoife and Syn."

Hendrix and Constantine join our huddle, bundling me in the middle of them. I'm surrounded by their love, stronger because of it.

"We won't let you, firefly. Where you go, we go. Our hearts will find yours."

Hearing my promise given back to me erases any doubt about what I'm going to do.

"You ready?" Aleksander says, his fingers poised over the security panel that will unlock the door that will lead me into hell.

Yes.

No.

Something heavy and cold slips into my hand, and when I look down, I see my red-handled pocketknife snug in my grip. *Hendrix.*

"Go play, baby girl."

I find him over my shoulder and mouth the words, *I love you.* He mouths back, *I know.*

With his gun drawn, Aleksander pushes on the door, metal sliding over stone like the tines of a fork being scraped across a ceramic plate. I block out the shouts that follow when Tristan and Aleksander rush into the room, followed by Hendrix and Constantine.

"Don't look, baby. Close your eyes and don't look. It'll be okay."

Papa's dead stare blindly watches as blood oozes out of the hole in his head.

Mama's lies turn into cries of pain and pleas of mercy to spare me as the man with the scar rapes her.

I'm not here.

I'm not here.

I'm not here.

I step inside.

My mind has been consumed with dark fantasies and gruesome plans, envisioning the moment when I would finally confront my living nightmare. Every waking hour has been spent obsessing over this day of reckoning, relishing in the thought of making Malin suffer for every ounce of pain he inflicted upon me and my parents. With twisted satisfaction, I planned to prolong his death, extending his agony until he begged for mercy, and I finally ended his life. I imagined the thousands of ways I could torture him. But morbid thoughts and vengeful wishes pale with the raw, chilling reality that stares back at me.

"What the fuck is going on? Who the hell are you?" the voice of the devil says.

A smile slowly creeps across my face when I find Malin in the corner of the dank room.

"I am no one."

CHAPTER 12

TRISTAN

"Hey, Dad. Look who came by to visit," Aleksander announces.

Francesco appears a little worse for wear. His eyes are rimmed with the purple smudges of fatigue. His usually clean-shaven face now sports a salt-and-pepper short beard. And his hair is no longer immaculately coiffed to perfection. Unwashed chunks are sticking up at stiff angles, and the gray of age that he hates to acknowledge and tries to hide with regular salon appointments to have it dyed is more pronounced. It makes me childishly happy to see him so unkempt.

"Get your fucking gun off me, you filthy little bastard."

Defiant and condescending, even with a gun aimed at his head.

"Saying stuff like that might hurt my feelings," Aleksander *tsks*. "If I gave a damn."

I don't miss the relief or the hope that kindles in my

father's eyes when he sees me, thinking that I'm there to rescue him from Aleksander.

"Tristan."

I ignore him, preferring to watch my girl. This is her moment. Her revenge. Mine will come soon enough.

"Mister Amato," Malin says desperately, his gaze pinging between Con and Hen as they corner him.

Like a frightened rabbit that knows there's no escape, Malin slinks back farther against the wall.

Aoife just stands there and stares at him with cold calculation. A predator stalking its prey. It's eerie and fascinating and sends chills down my spine, especially when Hendrix begins to whistle the melody for "Fake Your Death" by My Chemical Romance.

"What the fuck is going on? Who the hell are you?"

A deadly smile slowly spreads across her face. "I am no one."

Pain lances my fucking heart. How many times had I uttered those exact four words while my father took a whip to my back?

"Tristan, tell Aleksander to let me go! I am the head of the Council! I order you to obey!" Dad uselessly demands.

I unwillingly tear my gaze from Aoife. Typical of him to only think about himself. Malin has served my father like an obedient dog for years, and my father couldn't care less. He'd happily sacrifice him to save his own ass.

"Did you think I wouldn't find out?"

His mouth frowns in consternation, the symbolism of my question lost on him. It was what he said to me right before he snuffed out his cigar on my hand.

I cinch his cheeks in a crushing grip, forcing him to look directly at Aoife.

Pressing in close, I take immense satisfaction when I tell him, "You thought you could take her from me, but my girl is fucking strong. She survived. Your lies can't protect you anymore."

Through a clenched jaw, he snarls, "I don't know what you're talking about. I haven't done anything to Hendrix's whore."

Aleksander punches Francesco in the side of the head with the butt of his gun. "Call her a whore again, and I'll end you right here."

"She's Aoife Fitzpatrick, you son of a bitch."

All the air rushes from his lungs in a deluge of realization. "*What?*" he wheezes, unable to look away from her.

Does he see it? The angel of death that has come for him.

A tremor shudders through his body, and his skin turns to ice under my fingers. "No. It can't be."

Aoife slides the flat part of her knife down her tongue as though she's relishing a taste of Malin's blood.

"Want to know who I really am?" Aoife sweetly asks, tracing the burned skin on her left arm with the tip of her blade. "Guess you could say I am the phoenix."

"Crazy cunt." Malin spits at her, but the blob of mucus lands with a sad *plop* at his feet.

Hendrix stops whistling. "What did you just say?"

In swift retaliation, Constantine kicks out Malin's knee and drops the fucker to kneel in front of her. There's an audible *crack* when he hits the unforgiving stone floor. Malin cries out, and I want to roll my damn eyes. Such a pussy.

"Tristan, I'm your father! Obey!"

Aleksander bursts out laughing. "Is he serious?" he

asks me.

Disgust for the man who sired me spews out. "He stabbed her. Set her on fire. Left her for dead *on your orders*. She was ten fucking years old. Think of all that hate that has been building. The things she's going to do to you."

People react to fear in different ways. A few literally piss their pants. Others plead for mercy or try to hide. And then there is my father, who decides to say some really dumb shit.

"Caroline betrayed me. Your legacy was being threatened. I did it for you."

The sheer audacity of his bald-faced lie is astonishing.

"You're delusional if you think I'd even believe that for a second. Nothing you have ever done has been for me. I have the whip marks on my back that prove it."

I don't care for the way Aleksander looks at me, a curious tilt to his head. I don't want or need his pity.

"I made you strong!" Francesco bellows. "Amatos are kings!"

"I never wanted the fucking throne!"

I just wanted Aoife and Con and Hen and Dierdre. A family. Love. A semblance of happiness. To be normal.

Done listening to him, I say to Aleksander, "You said alive, not unharmed."

"Sounds about right," Aleksander replies.

I slam my father's head against the dolomitic brick. "She's going to kill you." My fist to his gut doubles him over. "And I'm going to love... every. Fucking. Second."

I punctuate each word as I hit him. It's not enough for what he's done, but it feels damn good.

I had planned to tell Dad that Dierdre was alive, just

like Aoife was alive. Rub his failures in his face.

I don't.

Dierdre is dead as far as my parents and the Society are concerned. She deserves to live the normal life I never got a chance to experience. If being Alana and raising chickens on a farm makes her happy, I want that for her.

"He's out cold," Aleksander says, lifting Francesco's listless head and letting it drop.

Crimson froth dribbles from his mouth and down his chin. One eye is already swollen shut, and a large bruise puffs his right cheek.

"Where's my mother?"

Aleksander slides his gun under the waistband of his trousers. "Helena is upstairs. East wing. Fourth door to the right. Pyotr's watching her. I'll let him know you're coming."

I settle back against the wall to enjoy the show. "I'm not in any hurry."

Aoife hacks off bits of Malin's clothes, piece by piece, like squares of a quilt, until he's completely naked.

"In case you forgot my name, it's Aoife Fitzpatrick, but you can call me Syn."

I can see the exact second Malin's tiny brain puts things together. The disbelief that she's alive and standing in front of him. How his eyes snap to my father, afraid of the punishment he'll receive for his epic failure because he didn't wait around that night to make sure she was dead—and the relief that shows when he sees that Francesco is unconscious.

"Where's your friend, the one with the scar? The one who raped my mother?"

Teeth bared, he snarls a feral growl, hurling a string

of curse words at her that meld into each other and come out as nonsensical gibberish.

He uselessly fights against Con and Hen's hold until he exhausts all his energy.

"He's dead, you bitch! I killed him! She was supposed to be my reward. Mine to fuck."

Aoife's entire body shakes, her fury palpable. I want to go to her. Hold her. Protect her from the hurtful venom spewing out of his mouth.

"Guess it's just you and me then. You should know…" She pins his head to the side at a severe angle with her forearm. "…that I'm going to enjoy this very, very much."

Malin's screams are a symphony of terror, piercing the air and filling it with hopeless agony as Aoife's sharp blade begins to meticulously slice away at the constellation tattoo etched into his neck. Blood flows like a scarlet river from the large, jaggedly hewn wound, its metallic scent perfuming the room.

She decorates his flesh from chest to thigh with thin lines from her knife. The gut-wrenching wails emanating from him as she works bring a sick satisfaction to my ears, like a sweet concerto of violins played on twisted strings.

It doesn't take long before the spineless bastard starts to beg.

"Please! I'll do anything! Please, stop!"

It's pathetic listening to his whimpers for mercy. Did he stop when Aoife begged him? Did he hesitate or have second thoughts when he stabbed her? Burned her? It's taking every ounce of restraint not to intervene and kill him myself.

Aoife spits in his face. "Not even God can save you

from me," she says and proceeds to cut out his tongue. Fuck, she's beautiful.

CHAPTER 13

SYN

"Sweet girl."

I look up at Constantine from where I'm sitting on the floor in the middle of the gore and carnage I created. Pieces of Malin are scattered around me like a jigsaw puzzle I'm taking apart.

He's been dead for a while, but I keep cutting and cutting. I can't stop.

I thought killing the man who destroyed me would bring me peace. All it has done is made me... numb. I will never get closure. Malin will never be truly dead. All I have to do is look in the mirror, at my scars and burns, and he'll be right fucking there, looking back at me.

"Let's get you cleaned up," Constantine softly says.

I know I look like a horror movie. Blood paints my body, my hair, my clothes. I'm covered in Malin.

"In a minute."

I go back to disemboweling the corpse. A funny thought pops into my head as I rip out his internal organs. I think I want to be a surgeon when I go to medical school.

"Aoife—"

"In a minute."

Hendrix sits down on the floor behind me, fitting me between his legs. He drops his chin to my shoulder, his hands on my thighs, and presses a tender kiss to the shell of my ear. If anyone can understand my chaos, it's him.

"Do you remember that song that was playing the first time we danced?" he asks.

A smile tips the corners of my mouth at the memory. Another gala. I was eight, gangly and awkward, and had such a huge crush on him. I stepped on his toes twice because I was so nervous.

"'The First Time Ever I Saw Your Face.' The string quartet did a really good instrumental."

Hendrix nibbles my neck. "You looked so pretty in your pink dress. Your hair was down in those big, soft waves with strings of tiny pearls woven in the strands. I thought you were a tiny fairy princess."

I pause what I'm doing and turn my head. Hendrix has the bluest eyes, ocean eyes, turbulent and captivating.

"You remember that?"

"I remember everything about you, firefly."

I peck a kiss to his lips and go back to what I was doing, quietly humming the song Hendrix and I waltzed to.

"Where's Tristan?" I ask when I become aware of his absence. Aleksander is gone as well. Francesco, too.

"Helena," Constantine replies.

I don't know what Tristan plans to do with his

mother, but she isn't my concern. He can let her go or have her die with the rest of them. Doesn't matter to me, but I'm leaning more toward the latter. She never once intervened when Francesco beat Tristan. She didn't protect Alana when she was sold like a whore to Gabriel. Helena deserves whatever is coming to her.

"I want a shower."

The muscles in my legs protest when I unfold them and stand up. Hendrix rises with me.

Running my blood-soaked hands over my face and through my hair, I survey the mess that used to be Malin scattered all over the floor. I shouldn't have killed him so quickly. I should have kept him alive, only so I could enjoy dousing him in gasoline and lighting the match.

Fuck you, Malin.

I startle when Constantine tenderly lifts me in his arms, then go stiff as a board, not wanting to smear blood all over him.

"I'm a little gross."

"You're beautiful," he replies, not caring that Malin's filth is getting on his clothes.

I don't argue. I'm exhausted. Not physically, but mentally. I need to shut down for a few hours. Forget about Malin. Feel something other than numb.

"Hold tight, baby."

I wrap every part of myself around him and lay my cheek on his shoulder as Constantine carries me who knows where.

Breathing him in to help dispel the smell of death that clings to me like sticky tree sap, I close my eyes, only to see my parents. Their details are fuzzy, like I'm looking at them through frosted glass. It's been so long since I've seen them. I've noticed that they've become a little blurrier in my mind. I fear the day I won't be able to conjure them at all, only the essence of what my ten-year-old self remembers of them. But right now, they're smiling. Happy. I take a mental snapshot and store the image away.

"I don't have any pictures of them."

There's nothing left of my parents. The guys said Francesco destroyed my childhood home. My existence is the only proof that James and Caroline Fitzpatrick were real.

Hendrix smooths a hand down my hair as we walk. "We can check the archives. I'm sure we'll be able to find something."

I don't want pictures of them that will remind me of the Society. I want the family photographs that used to line our fireplace mantle and sit on my dresser. Images of Papa holding me in his arms, an ear-to-ear grin on his face as we look at each other. I want the photograph of me and Mama laughing because we were caked in mud after spending all day out in the garden planting iris bulbs. I want the picture of us on the beach, holding hands, our backs to the camera as we walked along the shore with the setting sun blazing red and orange on the horizon.

My eyes blink open at the sound of a door closing and latching. We're in one of the upstairs bedrooms, the one my governess would stay in. Beatrice was her name. Sweet woman. Soft-spoken. Loved to read me poetry at bedtime. I wonder what happened to her.

Constantine takes me to the adjoining en suite and sits me down on top of the black and gold marble vanity. With an inordinate amount of care, he carefully undresses me as Hendrix turns on the shower.

"How hot do you want it?" Hendrix asks, stripping out of his clothes.

Fascinated by his tattoos and his dick piercings, it takes a second before my brain registers what he said.

I want every trace of Malin scrubbed off me with the hottest water imaginable.

"Scalding." Moving my belly chain out of the way, I lift my hips so Constantine can pull my leggings off.

Hendrix reaches into the shower, touching the spray, then flicks water at me.

"I'd say it's close to spewing out lava."

A small snort escapes at his lame joke. "Hotter," I reply.

He takes his heavy cock in one hand and strokes it with sensuous glides of his fist. "Hot enough now?"

Another joke. I'm not used to this playful side of him, but I know he's doing it for my benefit.

Pulling my bottom lip between my teeth, I nod. Hendrix Knight pleasuring himself is unequivocally hot.

"Tell us what you need," Constantine says.

My head falls back on a sigh when his mouth touches the scarred skin along my left hipbone. He places open-mouthed kisses down my stomach to my pubis, nuzzling his nose in the soft, curly hairs of my mound. With a delicate nudge of his fingertips, my thighs fall open for his exploration, desire thrumming through my blood as he teases me with soft licks to my clit.

I once made the comparison that Constantine made love to me like I'm precious, while Hendrix fucked me like I'm unbreakable. I love both equally because they complete each half of me and make me whole. I need that right now—for them to fill the hollow emptiness that killing Malin chiseled out of me.

"I need you," I answer, lifting my head and meeting Hendrix's cobalt scrutiny.

I need them to make me feel... something... anything other than this god awful nothingness that has taken root.

Never taking my eyes off Hendrix, I say, "I need it to hurt."

All the playfulness from before erases from his gorgeous face. He knows exactly what I mean, and I know he'll be the one to give it to me.

Pain is the only thing that lets me know I'm alive. I'm conditioned to it. Crave it like Hendrix does. Existed in it in one form or another for most of my life. It's a perverted, deviant, unhealthy thing to want. I don't care.

"Fuck, you're perfect."

At his praise, a blush heats my cheeks, and warm tingles spread through me like a waterfall of glitter.

"And adorable."

Pursing my lips, I give Hendrix a chastising glower. My arms and face are covered in blood, I'm naked, legs spread with Constantine's face practically buried in my pussy, and Hendrix thinks I'm adorable.

Once Constantine sheds his clothes, I'm lifted again and placed inside the shower. Hot steam fills the small stall in a dense fog, the sauna-like heat soothing my sore muscles. I stand idle and stare off into space as Hendrix moves to my back. He passes Constantine a bottle of shampoo.

"Lean back."

My spine conforms to the hard planes of Hendrix's chest. His erection nestles in the crack of my ass, prompting a flurry of illicit thoughts that have my nipples hardening and arousal pooling between my legs. I go almost catatonic when he begins washing my hair, and a low moan trickles out when he digs his fingers into my scalp and massages the sudsy cherry blossom foam into my hair. Constantine lathers my skin, his hands running down the curvature of my neck, shoulders, and arms.

"I love your hair." Hendrix eases my head forward and rinses the shampoo out. He lifts the heavy mass and combs his fingers through the wet tresses.

I watch the red-tinted water swirl at my feet and disappear down the drain.

"It feels so anticlimactic."

"What does?" Constantine asks, going to his knees and raising my right foot. He places it on his thigh and rubs soap between my toes.

"Malin."

It feels too abrupt, the buildup too huge for things to end so quickly. I don't have a sense of relief that it's over. It's like something is missing, but I can't figure out what it is.

Hendrix cups my breasts, his lips at my cheek. "You are goddamn amazing. So fucking strong, baby girl. You awe the hell out of me."

Well, shit. Tears I hadn't yet shed now run tracks down my face and get carried away by the water raining down from the showerhead. Tears show weakness, but dammit, I am weak when it comes to them. I love them. Heart, mind, body, and soul. It's the kind of love born from childhood friendships and shared trauma. A love that weaves its web into the fabric of your being, its threads hardening and solidifying into unbreakable bonds as each day passes. It's a love that transcends everything.

Quoting Maya Angelou, I say to them in Gaelic, "*Ar fud an domhain, níl aon chroí dom cosúil le do chroí. Ar fud an domhain, níl aon ghrá duit cosúil le mo ghrá.*"

Hendrix twists my face to the side and covers my mouth with his, his tongue like velvet when he kisses me. I push my ass back into his hard cock, not being subtle at all.

Gripping my throat in the way that I love, he says, "You going to be a good girl?"

My immediate, breathy "yes" morphs into a needy moan when Hendrix pinches my nipples.

"You going to let Con eat that sweet pussy, so we can fuck you?"

"*Yes.*"

Constantine wastes no time. Draping my leg over his shoulder, he drags the flat of his tongue through my folds, then scrapes his teeth over my clit. His pillow-soft lips seal around the tiny nub, sucking with long pulls of his tongue that cause a rush of desire to coil tightly in my belly.

I mold my hands over Hendrix's as he plays with my breasts, urging him to be rougher.

He nips a stinging bite below my ear. "Greedy."

I can't help wanting more of the wonderful things they do to me. Sex with the three of them has become an almost religious experience where I die and go to heaven every time they make me come.

I look down at my broody, fallen angel and am met with a primal intensity that burns within the depths of his inky eyes. I writhe and buck in Hendrix's arms as Constantine builds my orgasm, my moans beckoning him to dominate me. Take me. And he does. Constantine devours me like a man starved. Every muscle clenches taut in ecstasy when his skilled fingers slide inside me, pulsing in perfect synchronicity with the rhythm of his tongue. The darkness that had been plaguing my thoughts dissipates under the intensity of pleasure he builds so effortlessly. He presses his fingers to my inner walls when they begin to flutter, then sinks his teeth into my sensitive flesh—and I come hard, sobbing his name.

My quivering leg falls off his shoulder when he suddenly lurches up and pins me between him and Hendrix. Constantine's kiss is savage. Punishing. His calloused touch bruising. He's giving me what I asked for and not holding back. There is no gentle or tender in my sweet man.

My feet dangle on air when Constantine spins me around and slams me against the cold tile of the shower wall.

"Oh, fuck, yes!" I shout when he lines himself up and thrusts into me.

I scrabble to get purchase, using my thigh muscles to hold onto his waist as he pounds me into oblivion.

Hendrix watches us fuck like animals, his expression filled with lust and sadistic enjoyment when I quickly climax a second time.

Still intimately connected, Constantine flips our position. My back arches like a preening cat's when Hendrix skims his fingers down the dip of my spine. He stops on my lower lumbar, sweeping his thumb back and forth across my gluteal cleft.

"Be sure," his husky voice rasps.

His thumb moves lower, and I suck in an excited

breath when he rims my forbidden hole. Anal is something I never thought I'd be into, but it's another facet of my newfound sexuality that I want to explore with them because I know they will make it amazing.

"I want it to be you. I want you to be my first."

I may have given Constantine my virginity, but I'm still a virgin in a lot of ways, and it makes me happy that I can give Hendrix a piece of me that will belong only to him.

Hendrix breathes in a deep, pleased breath, pressing the pad of his thumb to the puckered skin. "Thank you for such a wonderful gift."

"I love you," I simply reply.

I let go of Constantine's shoulders and cup his face, liking how his coarse stubble abrades my palms. I'm not as tactile as Tristan, but I could spend eternity exploring their bodies. The valleys and swells of chiseled muscle. The unique details of their faces. Constantine and Hendrix's gorgeous body art. Tristan's scars.

"Both of you. So very much," I tell them.

And that's really all that matters. Not our arguments or our fights. Not the secrets or the enemies that surround us. I won't get lost in the darkness that wants to consume me because their love is my guiding light. They are my broken compass that really isn't broken at all, is it? It brought me back to them.

"When this is over, I want to come home."

Constantine's cock jerks inside of me in response, but it's his radiant smile that lights me up like freaking Christmas.

Hendrix kisses my shoulder blade. "You never left. You are our home," he replies, then, "Sorry, man. I need to lube."

What?

"Oh, god," I whimper when Hendrix slicks through my arousal around the base of my labia, touching Constantine in the process.

He drags his thumb over my perineum to the puckered skin at my back entrance, and a full-body shudder overtakes me.

"Need to stretch you out first, so you can take me," he says, breaching past the barrier. "Fuck, you're tight. I can't wait to feel you. Absolute paradise."

I try to stay still while he stretches me, but it feels too… much. Too damn good. Having Constantine inside me while Hendrix slowly fucks my ass with his fingers is indescribable. It's like nothing I've ever felt before. There's a sense of fullness mixed with a slice of pain, but also this incredible euphoria.

"There's this sensitive spot right here…"

I don't know what he does, but I'm suddenly catapulted into orgasm. "*Hendrix!*"

"Fuck, Aoife. Shit." Constantine grits his teeth as my pussy strangles his cock. "Shit, I'm going to—"

His hands squeeze my waist in a vise, and he pumps into me furiously, not able to hold back. Pulses of warmth fill me when he comes on a long, masculine moan.

"God damn, firefly. It's incredible how responsive you are. Fucking perfect." Hendrix removes his fingers and spreads my ass cheeks. "Try to relax."

I can't do anything at the moment because I haven't stopped coming. I'm paralyzed in a blissed-out trance that won't let me go.

A hiss hushes past my lips when Hendrix eases inside

me, one excruciating inch at a time. His metal barbells raze my oversensitive walls, touching places inside me that I never knew existed. My body tries to adjust to his size, but his dick feels enormous, more so because Constantine hasn't pulled out. Unbelievably, he gets hard again, and it feels like they'll split me in two. I have an inclination that I'll be walking funny for a few days after they're through with me.

"You were made for this. For us. I love you, Aoife," Hendrix says.

He makes one final push until he's seated fully inside me.

Holy shit. How can it hurt so much but also feel amazing?

I pant in anticipation, waiting for one of them to move.

I lift my eyes to Constantine.

I love you.

I kiss his lips, tasting my essence clinging to his plush mouth.

Love you more.

And then they fuck me together.

Brutally.

Carnally.

I was right.

This is most definitely heaven.

CHAPTER 14

Tristan

My feet feel like lead moving across the Persian runner that stretches down the long hallway. Nothing has changed in this godforsaken place. Every carefully selected piece in this house is showy, ostentatious bullshit, and most of it is ugly as hell. The framed paintings, the sculptures, the tacky gold-embossed silk wallpaper. It's all just a slickly crafted veneer of wealth to hide the evil that takes place under the mansion's foundation.

"Let's get this over with."

Con and Hen will take care of Aoife, but I want to get back to her as soon as possible.

"I didn't know."

I don't look at Aleksander. I hate that I showed any weakness in front of him. That he heard what I allowed our father to do to me. I let Francesco beat me like a fucking dog day after day, and I never once fought back.

I rub the burn on the back of my hand against my leg. I'm an adult, and I still let the man put his abusive mark on me. Aleksander will use that knowledge to twist me apart. It's what he does.

Approaching the room my mother is held in, I slow my gait when another man walks toward us. Tall, blond hair, green eyes, arrogant smirk curving his mouth. Aleksander lifts his chin in greeting.

"Is that Pyotr?" I ask.

"That's him."

"How is she do—" Pyotr starts to say.

I grab his collar, yank him to me, and punch his stupid face.

"Fuck!" he yells, teetering backward from the force of the blow.

I use my grip on his shirt to pull him back upright.

"You ever lay a hand on my woman again, I'll kill you."

He wiggles his jaw back and forth, eyes narrowed with rage. "*Your* woman? Don't you mean his wi—"

Wrong thing to say. I push the asshole up against the wall in a chokehold, getting in his face so he hears me loud and clear.

"*My. Fucking. Woman.*"

Pyotr's angry gaze flicks from me to his boss.

"We've got it from here, Pyotr. I'd suggest staying out of sight for now. Syn isn't too happy with you."

I shove away from him and take a few steps back because the need to hit him again is tremendous.

"Fine," Pyotr replies, glaring retribution my way, and walks off.

Aleksander sighs, brushing imaginary lint from the sleeve of his shirt. Along with tapping his fingers together, it's another OCD tic I've noticed he has.

"I've known Pytor since I was a kid. He's a good man.

Loyal. Someone you want on your side."

"I don't fucking care. He put his hands on Aoife."

He does that head tilt thing I loathe. "She said something to me the other night about not touching her without her permission."

When I round on him, he throws his hands up, palms facing outward in capitulation. "I would never hurt her. I swear on my life. Did… did something happen to her?"

I'm taken aback by his concern, like he actually cares, before I remember who I'm talking to.

"Other than being stabbed and burned alive and going through years of painful graft surgeries?"

He visibly flinches at the descriptions I enumerate.

"You know what I'm referring to," he quietly states, eyes downcast to the floor, his fingers playing piano keys against his pants leg.

My insides churn at the thought of Aoife being sexually assaulted. Then it hits me. His mother, Nina. What Francesco did to her.

God dammit.

Tempering my tone, I reply, "She hasn't said anything, and we would know if she had been…" I let the rest of that die on my tongue.

The fact that she was, until recently, a virgin or how she lost her virginity is none of his fucking business, just like our relationship and how we choose to love one another is none of his fucking business, or anyone else's.

I get how the four of us together may seem taboo to the outside world, but those people never lived the lives we were forced to live or had to endure the trauma and abuse inflicted upon us daily. And I will not apologize or cower under those people's antiquated perceptions of what they deem right or wrong. We love Aoife, and she loves us back. Anyone who doesn't like it can screw themselves.

He expels a loud exhale. "Good. Good. Okay." Gesturing at the door to our right, he asks, "You ready to go in?"

I'm ready to get this entire weekend over with.

"Yeah."

He takes out a key from his side pocket and unlocks the door. No security panels up here, but the outside lock is new. He must have installed it just for Helena. Aleksander always plans ahead.

Helena looks up when the door opens. I can't tell whether she's happy or relieved or upset at seeing me. She's had so much plastic surgery, her face is frozen and without emotion.

Shakily standing from the armchair she's sitting in next to the barred window, she smooths down her hair and does the same to the pleats of the skirt she's wearing.

"Tristan?"

I prop my shoulder to the doorjamb and shove my hands into my front pockets. When I look at the woman who birthed me, it's like looking at a stranger. Her appearance has changed so much over the years, if you stuck a picture of her from ten years ago next to one from now, you'd think you were looking at two different people.

"Helena."

Her throat bobs as she swallows. "What's going on? Where's your father?"

"Do you honestly care?"

Her mouth opens, but nothing comes out. I have

a hunch she was hoping Aleksander had killed him already.

"Am I to assume that you are behind this atrocious maltreatment?"

Aleksander makes an incredulous scoff. "Luxurious accommodations. Three meals a day. Such a fucking hardship."

I really, really abhor that I completely agree with him. Helena has a predilection for the dramatics. If the thread count on the sheets isn't over one thousand, it's akin to cruel and unusual punishment.

"And if I was?"

Mother shakes her head and sits down on the upholstered footboard bench at the end of the bed, hands clasped together, and legs demurely crossed at the ankles—an elegant portrait of fatalist acceptance.

"If I may make a request, could it be quick and painless?"

She's talking about her death like she's ordering a burger at a fast-food restaurant. It also says a lot about our family dynamic. How easily it is for one of us to consider killing the other.

I take a good, hard look at her. The only bad thing I can say about Helena is that she's a shit mother. She's one of those people in the world who should never have had children. However, she didn't lift a hand to Dierdre or me. She just stood and watched while our father did. Perhaps she thought that it was better us than her. Who the fuck knows.

Needing to see her reaction, if she's even capable of making one, I inform her, "Whatever happens to you is up to Aoife."

Her eyes widen in surprise, even if the rest of her face

doesn't move. "Aoife?"

"She's alive."

Clutching at the non-existent pearls at her throat, she stammers, "That's not possible."

It's as if I reached across the room and slapped her. The horror and the guilt. It confirms what I suspected. She fucking knew.

Gut-wrenching pain fills me. I was their child, but they have done nothing but hurt me since the day I was born. But they also hurt Aoife, the only truly good thing I ever had, and that's what ultimately decides her fate.

That foolish, tiny ember of hope that my mother would someday love me, dies a quick death.

Hatred blazes a hole through my heart, and I spew it all over her in three words that don't do the emotion justice.

"I hate you."

"Tristan, wait! Please!" she cries, but I'm done.

Her futile fists pound on the door after Aleksander slams it shut in her duplicitous face.

He turns the lock and pockets the key. "Want a drink?"

What the hell. I need a minute to calm down before I return to the catacombs.

"I wouldn't turn down a whiskey or an entire bottle of vodka."

Aleksander walks in the direction of the private elevator. We ride the cage down in silence, and once off, head to the servants' kitchen. The lights automatically turn on when we enter.

"If I remember correctly, they keep the good stuff in here," he says, opening and closing cabinets.

The good stuff isn't the expensive champagnes or the

heavy crystal decanters of one-thousand-dollar liquor. It's the stuff you get at the grocery store that tastes like good times and bad decisions.

"Glass?"

There are no stools at the counter island, so I hop up and dangle my legs over the lip. "Bottle," I reply, and he hands it over.

I twist the silver metal cap off and take several long pulls, then hand it back to him. Fire burns its way down my esophagus and settles warmly in my stomach.

"You know that piece of paper Caroline and Nikolai signed isn't legal."

He eyes me over the bottle as he drinks. Wiping the back of his wrist over his mouth, he sets the vodka down between us on the counter.

"It may not be legal, but it means something to me."

My bark of laughter rattles around the kitchen. "You don't even know her. Besides, you've been drooling after Serena's bitchy ass for years."

He leans a hip to the counter island and crosses his arms. "And how many women have you and Knight fucked? Pretty hypocritical if you ask me."

God, I want to throat punch him. "We thought she was dead."

"So did I," he thunders. "If I had even an inkling she was alive, I'd have moved heaven and hell to find her."

I hop down and shove him, hoping he takes the first shot, wanting any scrap of justification to end him once and for all.

"Why the fuck do you care? Seriously? You know damn well she loves us and wants to be with us. Not you. You're fighting a battle you will never win. You can lie and scheme and try to twist things around, but none of it will work. Aoife will never be yours."

I knock his shoulder with mine when I push by him because fuck him. Fuck this. Fuck Dad and Mom and this house and the Society.

After rounding the corner that leads to the black door, I jog down the stone stairs. I'm not prepared to find the holding room empty with no sign of Aoife, Hen, or Con. I'm also not prepared for the nightmarish gore that greets me. *Jesus fucking Christ.* God, baby. I back out of the room. I've seen some awful shit, but this? This is something else. It's as if pure rage took on a material form and unleashed the worst parts of hell.

The mansion is so vast, it takes me a good ten minutes to get to the west wing. To the rooms that the Fitzpatricks used to stay in. I know every nook and cranny of this part of the compound because the guys and I would sneak into Aoife's room after her governess fell asleep. We'd go up to the roof and hang out, look at the stars. Goof around until almost sunrise. They were some of the best times in my life.

"Hey," I say when Constantine slinks out into the hallway.

His hair is wet and slicked back—and he's buck naked. Aoife just went through a traumatic experience, and they dicked her like horny teenagers?

"What the hell, Con?"

My eyebrows hike up when he turns and holds a finger to his lips for me to be quiet.

"She just fell asleep. I need to find her some clothes."

"Find yourself some, too. Is she okay?" I ask, cracking open the bedroom door and peeking inside.

It's a dumb thing to ask because she's not okay. But she will be. We'll be there for her every step of the way.

We won't let her get lost in the darkness.

There's enough light for me to see that she and Hen aren't in the bed. When there's subtle movement on the other side of the room, I find two prone silhouettes lying on the floor below the large window. Hen is on his back, Aoife lying on top of him, her face hidden in his shoulder. His arms are wrapped around her, one hand on her ass, the other splayed over her upper back.

"Why are they sleeping on the—" I look over my shoulder, but Con isn't there.

Sliding my phone from my back pocket, I walk to the end of the hall. Scrolling to the number I had recently stored in my contacts, I put the phone to my ear and wait. One ring. Two. Three.

There's a click and "Hello?"

"Fancy a trip to Darlington?"

A hum of discontent, then, "Why?"

"Syn needs her mom. She needs you... Alana."

CHAPTER 15

SYN

"*Don't look, baby. Close your eyes and don't look. It'll be okay.*"

My eyes fly open as I gasp for air.

Why won't the nightmares stop? How many more times will I be forced to relive that night? It's fucking torment. I just want it to be over.

A hand soothingly caresses through my hair. "Shh, baby. Go back to sleep. You're safe," Constantine murmurs.

I unglue my face smushed into Hendrix's neck. No wonder it felt like I couldn't breathe.

The room is dark, so not yet morning. I have no clue how long I slept. Probably not long at all since Tristan isn't here with us. I'm lying half-on, half-off Hendrix. I ache everywhere, mostly due to the ungodly uncomfortable, hard floor. It's been years since I stopped waking up under the bed at home, and my body has become accustomed to sleeping on a soft mattress.

This sucks.

Hendrix grunts when I try to move off him.

"A little help, please," I whisper.

Constantine lifts Hendrix's arm so I can slide off his chest.

"Aoife?"

Of course, he wakes up.

I lean over and kiss his lips, then his stubbled cheek. "Need to pee."

I don't.

"M'kay." He rolls over to his side and falls back asleep.

Wish it was that easy for me.

When I attempt to climb over Constantine, he stops me with his hands on my hips, and I have no other choice but to straddle his chest. He hardens instantly underneath me, and I contemplate rising up and impaling myself on him. How easy it would be to get lost in the euphoria of sex to help erase the nightmares.

"Hungry? I can go make you something."

This amazing man is forever taking care of me.

I slant a hand over his heart to feel its steady beat. Heartbeats are the music of the soul, and his is wonderful. Constantine thinks his soul is damned by the things he was made to do, but I know the truth. There is no one more beautiful, inside and out, than my dark angel.

"I'm not hungry, but thank you," I reply.

The thought of food makes my stomach queasy. I don't know if I'll be able to keep down anything for a couple of days with images of what I did to Malin still fresh and present. The really scary thing? Realizing how much I'm okay with what I did. Scarier is knowing that I'm capable of more.

"I'm going to head to the roof. Get some fresh air."

"I'll come with you," he insists.

I press down on his chest when he starts to sit up. "Stay here with Hendrix. I don't want him to be alone."

He didn't take me leaving well, even if I was gone for only a short time. I shouldn't have walked out in the middle of the night, justified as it was at the time. Relationships are hard enough, but a relationship with three stubborn men? We definitely need to sit down and have a long discussion when we get home. No more putting it off. No more walking away when I feel the rug pulled out from under me. I need to learn to plant my feet and fight. Was it Tristan who said something like *we fight, we fuck, then we get the hell over it*? I can't remember, but the sentiment is right.

Constantine cradles the back of my head and pulls me down, kissing me softly. Slowly. Melting my insides in the best way.

"Don't be gone long."

"I won't. I promise."

"Found some clothes for you. They're on the chair."

God, this wonderful man.

When he lets me go, I place a wet kiss, full of tongue, to the tip of his hard cock before getting to my feet.

A growl rumbles deep in his chest. "*Aoife.*"

I lick the saltiness of his precum from my mouth and blow him a kiss. "To be continued."

He looks down at his erection standing at attention and blows out a harsh breath. "Going to have to take care of that."

"Think of me when you do."

"Fuck."

He rolls to his feet, smacks my bare ass, and

disappears into the bathroom.

I find the clothes he procured—a powder-blue sundress, dark-blue wrap tunic, and men's black socks. A weird ensemble, but whatever, because there's no way I'm trekking through the woods to retrieve my duffel. I wouldn't want to put on the clothes I took off earlier anyway. The dress and sweater are at least clean and don't smell like secondhand smoke.

Once dressed, I tiptoe to the door and sneak out into the hallway... and stub my toe when I trip over Tristan's long legs.

"What are you doing out here?"

I plant my hand on the wall to keep my balance when he grabs my foot. "Fuck, baby, I'm sorry," he says and kisses my sock-clad big toe.

He looks ragged, like a man beaten down by life and is only holding on by a thread.

I gather the hem of the dress as I go to my knees in front of him. I crawl into his lap, trying not to wince because my ass is sore as hell.

"I'm fine. Are you?"

His arms come around me, his whiskey eyes tired. "Better now. You look very pretty."

My hair is a bird's nest, and the sundress is too tight and too short. Luckily the tunic reaches to my knees and is warm.

"I look like a mess."

He fiddles with the cloth belt of the sweater. "There's not one thing about you that isn't beautiful, Red." He pulls the ends of the sash together and ties a bow. "I'm sorry I wasn't there."

"You saw Helena?"

He drops his forehead to my chest, his hot breath

fanning goose bumps down the bodice of the dress. "Yeah."

He doesn't expound further, and I don't push. I think we've been through enough for one day.

I wind my fingers through the soft, brown strands of his hair, scraping my fingernails over his scalp in the way I know he likes.

"Want to go to the roof?"

His hair tickles my sternum when he nods yes.

Going to my haunches, I take both his hands and guide him up with me. Worry dips his brow when he sees my discomfort.

Before he can ask, I preempt him. "Just a little sore back there from... you know."

"Back there?"

A fire-hot blush scorches my body from neck to ankles at his stunned expression, then morphs into a wildfire of embarrassment when a very sexy, very smug grin slowly creases his cheeks, popping those wonderful dimples.

"Change of subject." With his hand held in mine, I turn sharply and start walking.

"But I want to talk about it now."

"Nope."

His playful whine of protest brings out a silly grin I can't suppress.

There's an access panel to a flight of metal stairs that leads up to the roof in the back of the storage closet at the end of the hall. Constantine was the first to discover it, and we'd use it all the time when we were kids to sneak around. Kind of like a secret tunnel. The mansion is full of them.

When we get to the closet, I wave a pretend wand

in the air and say the magical incantation from *Harry Potter* that opens doors. "*Alo-ho-mora.*"

His eyes cartwheel at the reminder of all the times I made him pretend to be Harry. I was Hermione, of course. Constantine was Ron, and because Hendrix would always complain, he had to be Draco. What nine-year-old wasn't obsessed with those books back then?

"This brings back memories," Tristan says, moving a vacuum cleaner out of the way. He pulls the panel off and sets it at an angle against the side wall. "Let me go first to make sure it's still safe."

Bending to clear the low opening, blackness swallows him as he steps through. Seconds later, his hand pokes out, and I grab it.

"I can't see anything."

"Hold on."

He turns on the flashlight on his phone. Gossamer cobwebs hang at odd angles from the railing. Not touching that. I hate spiders.

The metal pops and creaks as we climb the spiral staircase that takes us to the roof. Like most doors in the compound, you can only unlock it by entering the code into the security panel next to it. Tristan punches in the same numbers I used to get to the catacombs.

A brisk wind blasts our faces and whips my hair into a frenzy as soon as we walk outside. Nothing other than nature exists as far as the eye can see.

"Can I borrow your phone?" I ask.

He hands it to me, and I flip the camera view to forward-facing, then smoosh in close to Tristan.

"Smile," I say, taking a selfie.

I enter Raquelle's number into a text.

Me: Proof of life. Will be absent from calc class.

Spending the weekend with the guys.

His phone vibrates almost immediately. It doesn't surprise me that she's still up. The girl never sleeps, only paints.

Unknown: Again? You just got back.

Me: I know.

Unknown: They must have some serious BDE.

Tristan reads the texts over my shoulder. "What's BDE?"

"Big dick energy."

He barks a laugh. "Damn straight. Wait. You told her about us?"

Us as in the four of us.

"Well, yeah. I trust her. I'm also not going to hide our relationship. She approves, by the way."

He kisses my temple. "Wouldn't matter if she did, but I'm glad she does for your sake. I know how much you appreciate her friendship. She seems like a really nice person."

Coming from him, with how much he distrusts people in general, means a whole hell of a lot.

"Me, too. Is it okay if I tell her where the key to the house is hidden, so she can feed Cocky Bastard?"

"Already taken care of." He chuckles. "Con has been trying to figure out what you did to the security system."

I'm not tech savvy like Constantine, so I cut a few wires with kitchen scissors. He'll figure it out as soon as he realizes it isn't a technical issue but a mechanical one.

"Thank you for taking care of Cocky B."

A new text comes in.

Unknown: Hello? Where did you go?

Me: Sorry. Talking to Tristan. BTW, I lost my phone. This is Tristan's.

That excuse is as good as any since I intentionally left my new phone at the house so the guys couldn't track me. I should have known they'd find me anyway.

Unknown: You and phones are mortal enemies.

Me: Tell me about it. If you need to contact me this weekend, text him. We'll be back on Sunday.

Unknown: Will do. Oh! Drake is definitely coming for homecoming. I can't wait for you to meet him.

I type out a reply but don't send it. "This okay with you?" I ask Tristan.

"Fine with me."

I hit send.

Me: I can't wait. We can do a cookout at the house.

Unknown: Would love that. I'm bringing my sketchpad.

"She loves the house and wants to paint it," I explain to Tristan.

Me: Off to bed. Exhausted.

She sends me a good night GIF, and I send her one in return.

I give Tristan back his phone. "Thanks."

"Homecoming week is a big thing. There's a formal dance, campus parties, the big football game against Harvard. Lots of drunken fun."

"We're doing all of it, right?"

I've never been to a party or have done anything that would be considered frivolous fun, and I want to experience that part of college life with the guys.

"Of course," he replies.

I take in the view surrounding us. Parts of the property glow under the various landscaping lights strategically placed around the mansion. This section of the roof is flat, not sloped, with filigree wrought-iron railing running along the side of the deck that meets the edge of the roofline. Walking over, I look down. There's no movement other than the rustling of the leaves in the trees and bushes. No guards patrol the grounds. It's as if time stands still three stories below us.

I connect the dots of dark stains that blot the driveway, the only evidence left of the destructive path I took to the house. No one will ask questions. There won't be an investigation. Falsehoods will be told to family members and loved ones about how they died. Money will exchange hands, NDAs signed, and if warranted, threats will be issued. That's the way of the Society.

Tristan twirls me in a three-sixty like a ballerina, then bands his arms around me from behind, pulling my back flush with his chest. I relax into him as we sway back and forth and enjoy the silence. Not even the song of a cricket can be heard over the brisk breeze.

"I forgot how peaceful it was up here," he says.

I marvel at the star-filled night sky. "I won't have to search for the constellation anymore."

"Con and I were going to tell you."

Unease prickles my thoughts, dampening the serenity I'd been feeling. I don't want to fight about it anymore.

"From now on, no more secrets." I crick my neck to peer up at him. "I won't come back next time."

It's an ultimatum. A line in the sand. I love them. I love them so fucking much. It would absolutely destroy me to lose them again. But I have to love myself, too. I don't want a life filled with deception and betrayal. I've lived twenty years controlled by both, and I won't do it anymore.

"No more secrets," he replies, the truth of his promise spoken with conviction.

Turning in his arms, I lift up on my toes, which puts me eye level with his wonderful mouth that I want to kiss.

"I would have been proud to be your wife."

I wish I could understand why Mama betrayed Papa and gave me to Aleksander. Francesco is a bastard of the worst kind, but Tristan is not and will never be anything like his father. Besides, she knew how I felt about Tristan. How close we were. He was one of my best friends.

I'm suddenly crushed against him. "I hope I get to spend the rest of my life loving you with everything I have in me."

A future of possibilities opens up as I stare into this magnificent man's eyes. I find myself wanting things I never thought were possible. Children. A house with a white picket fence and a dog in the backyard. Roots. Andie took over a mafia empire and built a life with her four men and Sarah. I want to build one with mine.

I caress his face, temple to cheek. "I want our daughter to have your dimples and your smile."

"Fuck, Aoife. Fuck. Dammit." He swipes at his eyes, emotion choking his words as his tears fall freely.

I've never seen Tristan cry before. He abhors showing weakness of any kind. But he shows his vulnerability to me because he truly loves me. He knows I will protect his heart with my last dying breath.

He grabs my face, and my lips eagerly part for his kiss. And damn, does he kiss me.

Breathless, I pant, "I'm wearing a dress."

He licks across the seam of my mouth, then dips inside to taste me again. "It's a very pretty dress."

I feather my mouth to his ear and whisper seductively, "I'm not wearing any underwear underneath this very pretty dress."

I don't care how sore I am. I want him.

His Bostonian accent comes out stronger when he queries, "You don't say?"

Biting my lip, I nod yes. He palms my ass, slowly inching up the skirt of the sundress with his fingers. Night air hits the backs of my legs, popping gooseflesh everywhere.

"Want to feel how wet I am for you?" I tease.

A rumble rises up in his chest as he hikes my dress higher, his fingers digging into the flesh of my buttocks.

We look over when the access door clangs open.

"You gotta be fucking kidding me," Tristan grumbles.

Cotton fabric flutters down my legs as my dress is put to rights just as Aleksander's blond head comes into view.

He stops short like a deer in headlights. "Sorry. I, uh… I wasn't expecting anyone else to be up here."

"Then fuck off," Tristan snaps.

I pinch his side. There is no give whatsoever. He's all lean muscle and zero body fat.

Tristan wraps his arms around my waist, and I snuggle in, using my body to hide his very obvious erection.

Trying to dispel the sudden awkwardness, I comment, "I didn't know anyone else ever came up here."

"That night before the gala when we were kids, I

saw you guys go into the closet and not come back out. That's how I found—" Aleksander thumbs over his shoulder in the direction of the access door.

I picture a sullen Aleksander, watching us, wishing he could be part of the fun but never asking to join because he felt unwelcome and unwanted by the guys. By his own brother.

That lonely, bullied girl I used to be in Dilliwyll understands all too well how it feels to be the outcast.

I wait for either of them to extend the first olive branch, the uncomfortable silence between them louder than a bullhorn. I have a feeling I'll be waiting until the end of time. Tristan and Aleksander are two of the most obstinate people I have ever known.

Giving up when all they do is stand there and pretend neither exists, I suggest, "How about we head inside and scrounge up something to eat?"

I'll probably vomit up anything I try to swallow, but I'll endure a nauseous stomach if it helps open a line of communication between them.

Tristan doesn't audibly sigh, but I feel his chest expand, then concave. "Hendrix will be pissed if he catches us cooking without him."

"Then we'll be extra quiet. I also want to discuss some stuff with both of you about the gala tomorrow."

My inclusion of 'both of you' is deliberate. I know full well trying to force a relationship between them could end in disaster, but if I'm anything, it's determined.

Aleksander grins. "I have a feeling it's going to be a bloody good time."

He has no idea.

CHAPTER 16

SYN

Coffee.

I smell wonderful, glorious coffee.

And the aroma of breakfast. Not so wonderful if the twist in my gut has anything to say about it, but I'm going to lick my plate clean because everything Hendrix makes is flipping delicious.

"Whoever brought me coffee is getting a blow job."

I crack an eye open to see Constantine with a mug in his hand.

"That's not fucking fair since I'm the one who made you the fucking coffee."

The sheet falls away as I sit up in bed. Tristan must have brought me up and undressed me. I passed the hell out sometime around four in the morning. We'd been in the parlor, talking. As he and Aleksander argued—shocking, I know—Tristan started running his hands through my hair, and that's all it took. Lights out.

When I see a pyramid of freshly baked chocolate chip

muffins, I decide I'm very hungry after all.

Holding out both arms, I make grabby hands at them. "Gimme. Coffee first."

"Kiss first," Constantine says, keeping the mug just out of reach. Evil man.

I pucker up in the best duck face I can muster, and he laughs as he bends over and sweetly kisses me good morning.

Okay, kisses are absolutely better than coffee.

Getting on my hands and knees, I crawl to the end of the bed where Hendrix is standing next to a rattan butler tray table.

"Can I help you?" he asks in that slight British inflection.

"Kiss."

"Where?"

"On the lips."

I squeak when he pushes me back and grabs my ankles, messing up the bed covers when he roughly hauls me to him, spreading my legs apart.

"You never specified which lips," he says and covers my pussy with his mouth.

I change my mind again. Morning orgasms are *so much* better than coffee.

Tristan strolls out of the bathroom, towel wrapped low around his waist and all that damp, sexy chest hair on display.

"Are you capable of keeping your hands, mouth, and dick off her for more than two hours?"

I'd say something if I had the capability of producing coherent words other than the loud moans I'm currently making as I come.

"Nope." Hendrix licks me very close to *that area back*

there, and a shudder overtakes me.

"She winced all fucking night long every time she moved."

The biggest smile spreads across Hendrix's face.

Pulling a T-shirt over his head, Tristan pushes Hendrix off me.

"Morning, Red," he says and lifts me by the back of the neck to kiss me.

Coffee, breakfast in bed, my gorgeous men, one fabulous orgasm, and two kisses. Pretty damn good start to the morning.

Once Constantine gets situated behind me, I recline back and take the plate of food Hendrix offers, going for the muffin first. The chocolatey goodness literally melts in my mouth.

"Dear god, this is the most incredible thing I've ever eaten—don't say it." I point a finger at Hendrix to stop the retort I see coming about his dick being the best thing I've ever eaten.

Helping me out because chocolate is smeared over my fingers, Constantine holds the coffee cup steady for me to take a sip.

Tristan zips up his trousers but leaves the top button undone. "It's time."

Hendrix drops down beside me on the bed and spears a forkful of eggs. "Time for what?" he asks with his mouth full.

"What we've been planning for years. Endgame."

Hendrix's fork stops midway to his mouth. "Today?"

"The gala."

"Even better. Going to enjoy watching Dad beg on his knees in front of everyone before I end him," Hendrix replies, continuing to eat.

I set the piece of bacon I'm nibbling back on the plate when my stomach does a queasy flip. I wish we had another choice, but if there are people who shouldn't be left walking the earth and breathing its air, it's their fathers. The only way to rid the Society of its evil roots is to destroy them, scorched earth style.

There is a sad truth, however, that Tristan and Aleksander pointed out to me. Figuratively speaking, we cut off one head of the hydra, another will form to take its place in the power vacuum we leave behind. And there's only one way to stop that from happening.

"Dad is still in the wind. I reached out to my contacts. No one has heard from him in a couple of weeks," Constantine states.

"He'll be here tonight. He's Council," Tristan says.

"Not if Aleksander is playing us. Dad has been pushing for the Stepanoffs to get a seat for a while. What if the gala is a setup?"

I have ten years to catch up on, and I'm stumped on the whole Aleksander-Gabriel thing. In the alley, Aleksander claimed that everything he'd done since he found out that Francesco ordered my supposed death was for me. But what if there's something else going on that I'm not seeing? My gut is telling me to trust Aleksander, but I've been wrong before. I've allowed people to lie to me my entire life. People I loved and trusted. Fool me once, shame on me. Fool me twice… let's just say it won't end well for that person.

Giving my plate of food to Hendrix, I slide out from between Constantine's legs and stretch the soreness from my aching muscles. I get three very appreciative male hums when I bend over at the waist to touch my toes.

"Your body is a fucking wonderland," Hendrix says.

With a blush from his compliment pinking my cheeks, I straighten up and raise my arms over my head in a volcano yoga pose.

"We need someone to watch our backs tonight."

Tristan sidles up next to me and imitates my yoga position. "Aleksander has more men coming. I also called in some men who are loyal to the Amatos. To me, not my father. They should arrive before noon."

I drop my arms and turn toward him. "We need people who are not Society."

Not able to help himself because I'm standing in front of him stark naked, Tristan brushes his thumbs over my nipples until they harden. Tendrils of desire twine their filaments deep inside me when he replaces his thumb strokes with his mouth.

Constantine's raspy voice drops low when he asks, "What did you have in mind?"

Right this second? Sex.

Gasping when Tristan's lips roam down my torso, I reply, "How would you feel about going into business with the mafia?"

The heavy wooden door groans when I push it open, setting off the motion-sensor lights as they click on one by one and cast a warm ambience with their soft glow.

Bathed in the deeper hues of aged wood, the Society's archive room is more like an opulent library, reminiscent of the one Papa took me to in England when we spent a week in London for my sixth birthday. Bookshelves twelve-tiers high line the walls, their dark mahogany scaffolding reaching toward a baroque ceiling. Every shelf is laden with leather-bound tomes, their spines embossed in faded gold leaf and their pages filled with the accumulated history of the Society.

On one side of the room behind a large executive desk hangs a distressed, antique political map of the world, a visible symbol of the Society's far-reaching influence and power.

Navigating the large space, I run my fingertips along a row of books, inhaling the earthy, musty odor of decaying lignin coming from the paper. I absolutely love the scent of books. Whenever I'd get a new paperback, I would fan the pages just to smell them.

A cloud of dust dances in the air when I select one of the books and slide it out from its home. The smooth leather cover yields to my touch with a slight resistance when I flip to the first page.

"Hope I'm not interrupting. Saw you come in."

Aleksander stands in the doorway, looking unsure, waiting for me to invite him in.

He looks different today. Dressed in jeans with rips at the knees and wearing a plain black T-shirt, he seems more approachable, almost boyish.

"Hendrix made the suggestion that I could possibly find some old photographs of my parents down here."

"Want some help?"

I snap the book closed and put it back. "Sure."

The stiff tension he was carrying in his shoulders visibly dissipates.

Never letting my guard down around him, I ask, "What brings you down here?"

The archives are located in the north part of the underground caverns. When I descended the stone stairs, curiosity had me going to the room where I killed Malin. It had been bleached and cleaned, with no trace left of the horrors that took place inside its small confines.

"Francesco," he replies.

Tristan had mentioned they put him in another holding cell. Was I tempted to seek him out? Very much so, which is why I forced myself to turn around and leave. I can't let my hatred for the man ruin our plans for tonight.

Aleksander leaves the door open when he enters. Something I appreciate because the room suddenly feels smaller with him in it. He's a pretty big guy, but it has more to do with his presence. Papa had the same effect when he walked into a room. Constantine does, too.

"I'm surprised they let you out of their sight for more than two seconds."

His obvious effort to be friendly by making a joke backfires, even if what he said is mostly true. The guys want to protect me, but they also know I need my space. It's a precarious balancing act between what *they* want and what *I* want.

I grab a pen from the desk, twist my hair around it, then push it through to secure it in a low bun. Pens are handy instruments, not for writing, but because they make great weapons.

"When we leave tomorrow, I'm going home with them."

Aleksander's head cocks slightly in contemplation. "Can I ask you a personal question?"

"Okay," I answer cautiously.

He strolls to the other side of the room where an ornate chess set captures his attention. He picks up one of the intricately carved pawns from the mosaic of dark and light squares that make up the chessboard. In many ways, chess is like war. The game itself is one of carefully planned strategy, where each move is an intellectual battle being waged between the two players.

"Do you think… if things were different…" He moves the pawn a square.

I go to the other side of the game table and push one of the white pawns to counter his move. "If things were different…" I repeat when he doesn't continue.

Moonlight-gray eyes lift to meet mine as he maneuvers another chess piece. "The gala when we were kids. When I asked you to dance, we were interrupted, and I never got your answer."

Because of the fight with Tristan. The night they found out they were brothers.

"It would have been yes," I reply, sliding another piece across the chessboard.

He moves his knight, and I counter it by positioning another pawn to the center of the board to restrict his options for attack.

"And if I asked you to dance tonight, would you say yes?"

He wants to dance with me?

I stare at him. Aleksander Stepanoff is one of those riddles wrapped inside a mystery that's been shoved into an enigma.

"I would say—"

"Any luck, baby girl?"

Hendrix's question seems innocent, but the lethal look in his eyes aimed solely at Aleksander is not.

"No."

I haven't had a chance to start going through anything with the revolving door of people popping in unexpectedly.

Hendrix walks over and studies the chessboard. "Whose turn is it?"

"Mine," I reply.

He sets up an attack on Aleksander's king by moving my bishop. "Check," he says and loops his arms loosely around me. "Ready to go clothes shopping?"

I perk up at the mention of clothes. I want out of this damn sundress.

"We're going clothes shopping?"

He nods and kisses the tip of my nose. "Our badass queen needs something scandalously sexy to wear to the gala."

I'm a girl. I may not be overtly feminine, but the idea of dress shopping gets me excited.

"Take the helicopter. It'll be quicker. I'll have it prepped and ready to go in thirty minutes," Aleksander offers.

"Where are we going that requires a helicopter?"

"Baby, all the best shopping is in New York City," Hendrix says with a grin.

CHAPTER 17

SYN

Oh, god.

I'm going to throw up.

Leaning over the bathroom vanity sink, I gulp in oxygen, not able to take my eyes off my reflection in the mirror. I must have been out of my ever-loving mind letting Hendrix choose my dress, but he was so excited and wanted to surprise me, and I didn't have the heart to say no.

I should have said no.

The shimmery gold chain-link material drapes off my right shoulder and molds to every curve of my silhouette. But it's the diagonal slash from shoulder to navel, the large slit up the left side of the skirt, and the fact that it's basically see-through that has me on the verge of hyperventilating. Every scar and burn marking my body is on public display, including the area on my shoulder that's still healing where the bullet grazed me. Not to mention the hickeys and bites and bruises.

I touch the pinkish, sandpapery skin on my left arm. I'm going to kill him.

"Ouch. Dammit."

I slip my hand down the front opening to adjust my belly chain when it gets caught on the chainmail, contemplating for the millionth time taking the dress off and switching it for the godawful sundress.

Hendrix said I needed to make a statement. I think I'm going to make a fucking big one.

Using the makeup Hendrix purchased, I touch up my eyeshadow, being careful so that the smoky eye effect I create doesn't make me look like a raccoon. I finish the look with a nude lipstick and a sweep of mascara.

Using the flat iron I insisted on having, I finish straightening my wavy locks and apply glossing serum to tame the frizz, then gather it into a sleek ponytail, using a gold band to secure it.

Taking a step back, I turn from side to side to view the final results, and my heart deflates. I'm wearing a very expensive, very gorgeous dress, my makeup and hair are on point, but all I can see are the repulsive parts. No amount of makeup or dress up will turn this ugly duckling into a beautiful swan. I'm pretty much a fucked-up mess in a ten-thousand-dollar prom dress.

Tristan scares the crap out of me when he barges into the bathroom. The man does not understand the concept of privacy or closed doors.

"I thought Hendrix was the diva who took for-fucking-ever to get ready—*fuuuck me*."

"What? What is it?" I spin in a circle, trying to look behind me.

It would be my luck if my fat ass ripped the dress down the back and exposed my butt to the world. The skirt has a panel that helps conceal my intimate area in the front, but not in the back. The thong I had no choice but to wear won't provide any coverage back there, so I'm screwed.

"Aoife."

"Where's the tear?"

"Aoife."

"Is it bad? I don't see anything."

"Aoife."

The deep huskiness in his voice finally registers and stops my frantic twirling.

"There's nothing wrong with the dress, baby."

I blow out a relieved breath. Oh, thank god.

"You take my goddamn breath away."

Oh.

My confidence swells at his praise.

Tristan takes one deliberate step forward, lust blazing in his brown eyes. "You are the sexiest, most beautiful woman I have ever laid eyes on."

Oh.

"I'm going to fuck you in that dress."

I press my hand flat to his chest when he advances the final three feet between us.

"I just spent two hours getting ready, Tristan Amato, and you will not mess up all my hard work."

He grips my neck, thumb under my chin, and I soften like putty under his indelicate touch.

"I like you messy," he says and nips my bottom lip.

Every molecule of my being lights up as he kisses me with deep, penetrating strokes of his tongue.

Screw the lip gloss. I can reapply it.

"Who can't keep his hands, mouth, and dick off her?"

With an exorbitant amount of reluctance, Tristan

pulls away, and I'm pirouetted so Hendrix can get a good look. I'm greeted with a second libidinous head-to-toe examination that sends preening gratification racing through me. I love how they look at me because they don't see my flaws. They just see *me*.

"God *damn*, firefly. I knew that dress was made for you. We are so fucking you in that dress."

"That's what I was trying to do," Tristan grumbles, teasing a finger under the front opening and along the swell of my breast.

"And the heels."

Dangling from Hendrix's fingers are a pair of strappy translucent stilettos that look like something a modern-day Cinderella would wear.

Constantine appears over Hendrix's shoulder, his pupils flaring with unconcealed admiration.

You are a goddess, he signs.

My throat goes Sahara dry. Not from what he said, but because Constantine in a tuxedo is sex personified. The cut of the jacket fits him perfectly and only amplifies his raw masculinity. He's not wearing a bowtie and has left his shirt collar open, allowing the gorgeous, colorful ink on his neck to peek through. He must've done something with his hair because the wavy locks are tamed into a faded side part.

"I, uh… *Jesus*," I breathe when my gaze cuts between him to Hendrix and Tristan. I have to reach back and grip the edge of the vanity to keep my knees from giving out.

In my earlier panic, I hadn't noticed that they were also in their tuxedos, sans jackets. I'm overwhelmed by them. Filled with so much love for them. The boys I adored grew up to be three stunningly gorgeous men, and I'm the insanely lucky girl they want to be with.

My heart rate zips into the stratosphere when Hendrix goes down on one knee, slipping the stilettos on my feet and securing the ribbons around my calves. As he rises to stand, he lifts my hand to his mouth, genteelly placing a kiss on my wrist.

"Perfect."

My smile is watery when I look into his blue, blue eyes. "Thank you."

"Not done yet, pretty girl."

He pulls me from the bathroom on unsteady legs. Jacked up five extra inches, I feel like a newborn giraffe on ice.

My heart rate does a triple beat when Constantine holds out a small robin's egg blue jewelry case.

"Am I being *Pretty Woman*-ed?"

"Are you being what?" Tristan asks, yanking down the sleeves of his tuxedo jacket after he puts it on.

"The movie. Never mind," I mutter when I get three blank looks.

Even I know that movie. Raquelle would be proud.

Constantine opens the case and shows me the delicate, tear-drop earrings nestled inside.

I touch the small diamonds reverently. "They're stunning. I love them."

My belly button piercing, and now my belly chain, are the only jewelry I wear. I would have hated anything showy and gauche, but the earrings they bought me are exquisite. Simple, yet elegant.

"May I?" Constantine asks.

I dip my chin and tilt my head to the side and breathe in the sandalwood of his cologne when he steps in close. With a brush of his left hand, he sweeps my ponytail over my shoulder. The graceful glide of his finger down my neck is like sensuous foreplay, as is the kiss he gifts me on the sensitive skin behind my ear. He secures one earring, then the other, on my lobes.

"Beautiful."

I liquefy on the spot. It's the first word he spoke to me as Syn. We were in my apartment. I remember feeling this prodigious connection to him and not understanding why. The energy between us was like lightning in a bottle; a living, pulsating thing, barely contained.

Someone's phone goes off.

"It's Aleksander. Patrick's limo just pulled up," Tristan says with a grave tone.

The lovely moment we'd been sharing dies a withering death at the reminder of what tonight's gala entails. There is no fairy tale being played out where I get to be the princess dancing in the arms of her princes. Tonight means one thing only.

I fortify my spine with iron and hold my head high.

I am Aoife motherfucking Fitzpatrick. Daughter of James and Caroline Fitzpatrick and heir to the Council. I am also Syn Carmichael. The girl with the battle scars who rose from the ashes like a phoenix reborn. The heartbeat of two strong women beats inside my chest.

As does revenge.

CHAPTER 18

S Y N

"No one knows, do they?" I ask, wanting off the elevator.

If this sudden bout of claustrophobia is what Andie experiences every time she's in one, I feel sorry for her. It's like having ants crawl over your skin.

Constantine weaves our fingers together at the same time Hendrix takes my other hand.

Tristan reposes against the wood railing attached to the lift's mirrored walls. "Not a clue."

"What about Patrick or Gabriel? Has Aleksander said anything to you?"

The members attending tonight's gala are apparently blissfully unaware of the transgressions that have recently transpired. The power plays that were made for control or that Aleksander successfully orchestrated a coup. But how Patrick and Gabriel fit into Aleksander's plans is a mystery.

"Nope," Tristan replies, not acting concerned in

the least. "Doesn't matter. I've given orders to shoot without question if Aleksander tries anything."

I pray it doesn't come to that, but I'll be the first one to slit Aleksander's throat if he does anything to hurt my guys.

"Dad's been blowing up my phone the past two days. I've been sending him straight to voicemail," Hendrix says.

"What did he say?" Tristan asks.

Hendrix shrugs a nonchalant shoulder. "Don't know. Don't care. Didn't listen to any of them."

Tristan gestures for Hendrix to give him his phone. "I'll listen to them."

"Fuck off."

Hoping to preempt an argument, I ask, "Do you think anyone will recognize me?"

Would anyone remember the little girl with the curly blonde pigtails and big blue eyes?

"Not a chance. Red, *we* didn't even recognize you."

It's a bit sad to contemplate that I'm basically a ghost in a world that I grew up in.

I wobble in the death traps I have strapped to my feet when the elevator slows and bumps to a stop. I can only conclude that a man came up with the design for high heels because no woman in her right mind would ever think these horribly uncomfortable things were a good or practical idea.

"Ready?"

We take a deep, collective breath at the same time.

Hendrix tucks my arm into his and escorts me out of the elevator as soon as the door slides open.

"Head up, baby girl."

At his reminder, I square my shoulders and lift my

chin.

The heels of my stilettos make an eerie *click-clack* echo as I walk that is discordant with the metallic clinking of my dress. There is no hiding our arrival with the noise my clothing is making.

I try my best to tamp down my nerves when a few curious eyes drift in our direction. I feel too exposed in this dress, and it sets my nerves off-kilter. My nails score into Hendrix's forearm before I force my fingers to relax.

These people's opinions do not matter.

Constantine's warm hand fits to my lower back, a comfort and support that helps me put one foot in front of the other.

The loud din of orchestral music and overlapping conversation carries out from the ballroom and fills the hallway. A few couples I do not remember or know loiter just outside the massive double oak doors, their heads close together as they gossip and sip Cristal.

Tristan makes an annoyed groan. "Mathis is here."

One of the men, stout with a paunch belly that strains the button of his tuxedo jacket, excuses himself from his three much younger female companions and approaches us.

"Tristan, it's so good to see you," he boldly announces, exuberantly shaking Tristan's hand. "Has Francesco not arrived yet? I was wanting to have a word with him."

Tristan pries his hand from the man's grip. "He'll be here soon."

"That's Mathis Laurent. Katalina's father," Hendrix quietly speaks in my ear.

Katalina. Not a name I wanted to hear tonight. If she's here, so is Serena. Awesome.

My arm slides free when Hendrix shakes Mathis's hand in greeting. Constantine is next before Mathis turns to me.

"And who is this gorgeous…" The rest of his sentence hangs in the air when his gaze drops to my scars.

I self-consciously try to cover the burns on my left arm, something Tristan corrects immediately. He possessively hooks his arm around my waist.

"My girlfriend. If you'll excuse us," he says, none too politely, and walks off with me in tow before Mathis can say anything else.

Hendrix chuckles. "He looks pissed. You just ruined his dream of a Laurent-Amato match made in hell."

I inwardly cringe. Katalina is refined, poised, ethereal, and everything I'm not. She embodies what a man like Tristan would want in a wife. A well-bred armpiece to complement his stature in the Society.

Tristan side-eyes Hendrix. "That was *never* going to happen," he elucidates.

"Can't wait to see how Katalina reacts. You know he's going to go tattle." Hendrix peeks over his shoulder. "Yep. There he goes."

Pyotr suddenly materializes in front of us. He presses a finger to his ear. "They're here—oh fuck," he says when I surge forward, but I don't get far because Tristan pulls me back, giving Pyotr enough time to slink away.

"As much as I want to see you kick his ass, now is not the time."

"I'll bring the box of popcorn for that," Hendrix jests.

I squint my vexation. "Why are you in such a chipper mood?"

He's been acting almost giddy with excitement since this morning.

His grin is devilish. "Tonight's going to be beautiful chaos, baby."

Just as we're about to enter the ballroom, we're interrupted by more people wanting to speak with Tristan and Hendrix.

"Come on," Constantine says, grabbing my hand, and I happily let him pull me away.

No one may recognize me, but fuck if they aren't rubber-necking. And for once, it's not because of how I look, based on the loud whispers I can obviously hear. My presence on the arms of three of the most powerful men in the Society has tongues wagging.

We enter a scene straight from a fairy tale, and I'm transported back to the first time my parents brought me to a Society gala. I'm as mesmerized now as I was then.

Massive chandeliers drip from the high ceiling like icicles made from champagne diamonds. The crystals refract the candlelight and cast a warm, golden ambience over the room. Strategically placed nine-foot framed mirrors give the illusion of endless space. A pop of color against the creams and golds are provided by exotic blood-red orchids that adorn the glass tables scattered around the fringes of the dance floor.

It all screams wealth, power, prestige… Society… and unease surrounds me amid the flagrant extravagance. I'm both dazzled and alienated by everything, and after ten years of being separated from the life I was born into, I can't help but feel like an intruder. I'm a lone dandelion weed that has sprouted in the middle of a meticulously manicured rose garden. Being back in this house, in this ballroom and around these people, makes me realize that I never truly belonged, regardless of whose daughter I was. I was always the outlier. And I think Papa planned it that way. He didn't want me to conform. He wanted me to rise.

Constantine intrudes my thoughts when he asks, "Dance with me?"

Grateful for the distraction, I reply, "I would love to."

He ushers me through the sea of people already on the dance floor, and I ignore the blatant stares. When he sweeps a hand around to my back, I circle my arms around his neck and mold myself to his front. In the heels, I'm almost at eye level with him.

"You don't want to waltz?"

I glance at the people dipping and twirling, doing the same thing as everyone else, and shake my head. "I want to dance our way. Everyone else can waltz."

Being careful not to mess up my hair, he slides his hand under my ponytail and holds me as we sway cheek-to-cheek.

As the small orchestra creates a musical backdrop for the spectacle, my gaze alights on the female pianist tucked unobtrusively in the corner in front of the grand piano. I watch how her hands flow across the keys while the music of the violins and cello rise in a soft crescendo. If this were any other gala, I'd ask Tristan and Hendrix to play me something, just so I could sit on the floor beside them and listen.

"It's the same but different," I ruminate.

His clean-shaven cheek feels like satin when he rubs it against mine, almost like a kiss. "Do you miss it?"

I ease back and get lost in his midnight eyes. "Not one bit. I only missed you, Tristan, and Hendrix."

My skin bristles, and the hairs on my arms raise when I sense new eyes on us. Like a divining rod,

I immediately pick out the bleach-blonde in the red, glittery gown. Serena is standing next to Katalina near the ten-foot ice sculpture of a ballerina. Katalina glances over every so often, but Serena flat-out glares.

Shit. It was inevitable we would cross paths tonight.

"Will there be any ghosts of past girlfriends attending the gala that I should be aware of?"

Tonight is stressful enough as it is. I don't need any more jealous bitches coming at me.

"You're my only girlfriend."

"Nice save."

"It's the truth."

"Really nice save."

I kiss him full on the mouth. Screw Serena and Katalina and anyone else who's watching.

"Mind if I cut in?"

Constantine's face hardens into a stony mask at Aleksander's intrusion. "I do."

I was wondering when he would pop up. I searched for him when we first walked in but didn't see him.

Several heads swivel with nosy interest. I cup Constantine's hand and press it to my heart. "It's okay."

Constantine steps aside, and my eyes playfully pitch upward when Aleksander decorously bows.

"You look beautiful, *pevchaya ptitsa*. May I have this dance?"

"You may."

I settle my left arm gently on top of his right, my hand curving along his shoulder. He takes my other hand in his, and I align my elbow almost parallel to the floor. His wide palm stretches across my mid back just under the shoulder blade.

"Waltz?" I ask.

I giggle hysterically, which is embarrassing, when he suddenly dips me low, my back arched under the support of his hand.

"Hell no. Waltzes are for pretentious assholes."

He pulls me up and spins me around.

"Playing the charming gentleman suits you better than pretending to be the scary Russian."

"You think I'm charming?"

Before I have a chance to answer, I'm suddenly whisked out of his arms… and straight into Hendrix's.

"Fuck off. She's mine."

The mania exuding off him is palpable. His cobalt eyes are wild. Mean. Something's off.

Trying not to trip on the hem of my dress, I try to keep up with his long strides as he hauls me off the dance floor.

"Hendrix, what is it?"

"I need you."

CHAPTER 19

HENDRIX

"Eva mentioned the Knight Foundation was..."

My patience wears thin as the pompous prick prattles on about the last thing I want to talk about. My irritation only gets worse when he won't shut the hell up about Eva. Playing the role of Hendrix Knight, the entitled playboy heir of the Knight fortune, is suffocating, and I thank god I'll only be forced to portray him for a little while longer.

I nod and make meaningless noises of interest at his banality, but my complete focus is on the gorgeous redhead in the center of the room. Aoife laughs at something Con says, and her beatific smile lights up her entire face. The dress I bought her is driving me crazy—how it clings to her gorgeous body like a second skin, accentuating every curve, or how the almost see-through material teases me with glimpses of creamy flesh that I'm eager to mark. It's enough to tempt the most devout priest into committing lustful sins and be happy to go to hell for them.

I cut off Chester Fielding mid-sentence, not able to stand there and listen to him a second longer.

"Excuse me, but someone just arrived who requires my immediate attention."

"Please tell your mother…"

I tune him out. I won't be telling Eva anything since she's dead.

I meet Tristan's pleading gaze as I leave him to fend for himself.

"Asshole," he mouths, and I just smile.

Tristan has always been better at the diplomacy shit and ass-kissing, so I don't feel bad one bit for leaving him amid the jackals who have descended. Tonight's gala is the same as all the others. Under the table deals are made, money and allegiances change hands, and butts are kissed for promises of future favors. Political, social, financial, or something else more sinister like murder for hire.

Zeroing in on Aoife, I stumble to a halt when someone blocks my path.

"Hendrix."

Bloody hell.

"Dad." I return the monosyllabic greeting, not surprised to see him since Aleksander had texted that his limo had arrived.

"Why haven't you returned my calls?"

No hello. No how are you. No swapping of pointless pleasantries. And no mention of Eva.

"I've been busy."

He checks for anyone listening. He hates it when I talk back, but he can't do anything about it because we're surrounded by witnesses.

"Busy?"

"Yes."

I'm tempted to shove him out of the way. Or take an hors d'oeuvres pick and shiv him with it. I'd also enjoy having a repeat of last night with what Aoife did to Malin. That was a fucking amazing sight.

"Too busy for your mother's funeral?"

Ah, there we go. Need to play the part of the grieving husband in front of his peers. I hold my tongue about knowing he 'tit-for-tatted' with Aleksander to kill her in exchange for his Council vote.

"I'm shocked you even had a service instead of burying her in the backyard next to the dog."

When I was six, I found a stray on our property, going through the garbage, eating anything it could find. Some mongrel mutt with mangy calico hair. It was malnourished to the point I could count its ribs. I hid the dog away in the stables and cared for it. Snuck food out to it every night for three weeks and brought it back from the brink of death. I never gave it a name, but I loved that fucking dog. Dad somehow found out and shot it in the head, then made me bury it.

"Watch it. You may be an adult, but I still own you."

A sick thrill rushes through me at the thought of what's going to happen tonight. Reap the sins you sowed, fucker.

With menace oozing out of every word, I reply, "You lost your control over me years ago, *Patrick*."

His punishing grasp latches on to my shoulder, clamping down hard. His hand has delivered more than enough pain over the years that I don't even flinch. To anyone looking, it would seem like a father greeting his son.

There's a swish of fabric to my right. A foreboding familiarity. Black-tipped fingernails curl around my father's biceps.

"There you are."

No. God, no. Not here. Not now.

Fear solidifies my blood to ice at the sound of her voice, a Pavlovian response, even after twelve goddamn years.

The stunningly savage face I want to forget but can't blurs into view. Heavily lined green cat's eyes, a waterfall of sleek raven hair, augmented breasts that are way too big for her petite body size, and those blood-red lips that curve with a vicious smile. She looks exactly the same as my nightmares remember.

"Hello, Hendrix."

Nausea rises when she purrs my name, her emerald gaze wandering my body with sick delight.

She's not supposed to be here. She is supposed to be in Singapore. I've kept tabs on her over the years. Made sure to never be in the same place she is. Why isn't she in Singapore?

"Hendrix, you remember Natasha. She came to help me during this dark period for our family," Dad says, intimately drifting his hand down to rest right above her ass.

No one here would blink an eye if he was already sleeping with another woman before the dirt settled on Eva's grave.

Natasha glues herself to his side, her touch also intimate, and I want to throw up.

Her husky giggle is as fake as her tits. "Of course he does."

I've tried to forget. Tried to erase the things she did

to me. She ruined me. Corrupted me. Turned me into *this*. A debased animal who derives gratification from inflicting pain. Natasha Zephyros is a monster of the worst kind.

"It's so good to see you again." She bites her plump bottom lip. "You've grown up. Very handsome. Just like your father," she coos, rubbing his lapel.

I hate you. I hate you.

"I am nothing like him," I snap. With as much disgust as I feel, I say none too quietly to the man I despise as much as I despise her, "You really are a stupid bastard if you're sticking your dick in that."

Judge Ravensport's wife gasps at my crude remark as she and her husband walk past.

Dad's face reddens to an ugly shade of purple. He angles forward and hisses, "You watch your fucking mouth. What I do is none of your concern."

"Hendrix, why don't we go get a drink and catch up —" Natasha starts to suggest, and I back out of reach when she tries to touch me.

Never again.

"Fuck you both."

"Hendrix!"

I can't do this. I can't. I can't.

I need air. I need to get out. I need my angel to take the pain away.

CHAPTER 20

SYN

Hendrix barrels through people, dragging me out of the ballroom and down the hallway that leads to the back of the house. My arm almost rips out of its socket when he abruptly turns and smacks open a door that reveals a small powder room.

"Please tell me what's going on. You're freaking me out."

He slams the door closed; his breaths ragged. I want to touch him, but something stops me. An innate warning to tread carefully.

"Hendrix," I try again.

His fists pummel the door, each strike hitting me like a physical blow.

"She shouldn't be here," I think he says.

Something is definitely very, very wrong.

Desperation sinks in because I don't know what transpired in the last twenty minutes while Constantine and I were dancing. Hendrix had been with

Tristan, or so I assumed, and the 'she' he's referring to can't be Serena. He wouldn't go off the rails like this because of her.

"Please talk to me. What happened?"

In a blur of motion, Hendrix swings around and grabs me. The air gets violently knocked out of me when my stomach connects with the edge of the porcelain sink.

"Hendrix, what are you doing?"

The metal links of the dress clink like chains rattling when he flips the back of the dress up. I hear the pull of a zipper, and arousal drips down my inner thigh, my body wanting what's about to happen, even though my mind is screaming at me to stop this. Lust and logic battle it out. Lust wins when he rips my thong off like tissue paper.

"Need you."

My eyes fly to our reflection in the small oval mirror at his jagged benediction. His pupils are eclipsed in a glaze of insanity, his expression cold and unforgiving. But I see it. The pain. So much fucking pain, it shreds whatever resistance I have left. The demons that have taken over are in control. The man about to fuck me is not Hendrix.

Tears gather and spill over. My forearms tremble with how hard I brace the pedestal vanity. Whatever he needs, I'll give him, even if all he wants is my body and not my love.

"I'm yours. Always."

I'm not prepared for the brutal way he enters me. No foreplay or gentleness. His cock ravages me with every severe thrust of his hips, his piercings tearing me apart while also hurtling me toward an orgasm I can't hold back. Snarled growls and the sound of flesh slapping against flesh fill the tiny bathroom.

As soon as I cry out, convulsing around him, my airway suddenly constricts when he grabs the front of my neck, choking me. It's impossible to breathe, but I don't fight it. I cover his hand with mine, urging him on. *He needs you. He needs this. Be his strength.*

A scream lodges in my throat when he sinks his teeth into my shoulder, drawing blood. He bites me again and again, his pleasure feeding off my pain. Spots dance around the periphery of my vision as my lungs beg for oxygen—and then unconsciousness creeps its way in, bringing the darkness with it.

Come back to me. I'm here. I'm your safe place. Your home.

"I love you," I gasp. "I love you."

With a muffled, feral yell, he climaxes, pounding his cum into me as I drift into oblivion.

Salty raindrops splash across my lips.

"I'm so sorry. I'm so sorry. Baby, please. Please, wake up. Aoife, wake up."

More raindrops fall.

Thunderstorm.

Tristan.

Mist clings to my lashes, blurring my vision. Even in my red haze of anger, Tristan is so devastatingly handsome, it hurts to look at him. Or perhaps I'm the one hurting because I've come to care for him.

"You're not leaving, Syn."

The rain beats down more heavily, plastering my hair to my head. Bright flashes of lightning pulsate the sky with white light which is soon followed by a long procession of thunder.

"Then give me a reason to stay!"

I barely have enough time to brace before he moves. Arms band around me, and my feet come off the ground.

"I'm your goddamn reason."

"Oh god. I'm sorry. I'm so fucking sorry. Don't leave me. Aoife, wake up."

Hendrix. Not Tristan.

Hendrix needs me.

With a jolt, life comes crashing back into existence. Breathing feels like inhaling acid, the burn sending me into fits of coughing.

"I'm so sorry. I'm so sorry," Hendrix keeps repeating as he frantically rocks me in his arms.

We're on the floor with me curled up on his lap, his desolate sobs the most heartbreaking song ever played.

I lift a weak hand to his devastated face.

"I'm okay," I promise.

He clutches me like he'll never let me go. "I hurt you. I'm sorry. I'm sorry."

I ease to a sitting position, and my shoulder screams in agony where he bit me. Blood oozes from the open wounds and trickles down my back. Tristan and Constantine are going to lose their shit when they see them because it's on the same shoulder I was hit by the bullet.

"You didn't hurt me. I'm titanium, remember?"

Not knowing if it's the right thing to do, I press my mouth to his and hold it there. I don't kiss him. I let the connection between us sink deep.

"I love you, Hendrix Knight."

A shudder racks his tall frame.

Hoping to soothe him, I softly hum as I wait for him to come out of whatever hell he's caught in. It's a hell I'm all too familiar with. That 'flip' when I become someone else. When I hurt people, or worse.

"She ruined me."

He just opened the metaphorical door. Time to walk through.

"Who?"

He plants his face in my neck, shaking his head.

When my therapist suggested I write down my dreams, she said, *"Let the pages be the holder of your pain and let the words you write carry your burden."*

I can do that for him. Be that for him.

I clasp his face and say with a certainty forged from a lifetime of love, "Whatever you tell me won't lessen what I feel for you. I survived death to come back to you. You are my fucking heart, Hendrix." Using the pads of my thumbs, I wipe away the tears that stream from his beautiful blue eyes. *"Gheobhaidh mo chroí do chroí."*

He forces in a stilted inhalation. Then another. "Natasha."

I kiss away the wetness coating his cheeks when he pauses. It takes a few tries before he can continue.

"Natasha Zephyros."

A face from long ago comes forward at the mention of Natasha's name. Exotic looks. Dark hair. The only reason why I remember her is because she gave me the creeps. The last time I recall seeing her was here. Another gala. I was seven, I think.

"She was an acquaintance of Eva's. Stayed at the house that summer."

"Which summer?" I ask.

His teary eyes lift, their despair punching a hole through my chest.

"The summer I disappeared."

My pulse begins to frantically hammer.

"Do you mean that summer you were vacationing in India?"

There was a period of about four weeks where we didn't see or hear from Hendrix. Papa said he was away on holiday in India with his parents.

His chuckle is lifeless. "I wasn't on vacation."

Something ugly slithers across my skin. "Hendrix—"

"Dad was in India with his whore. Eva was livid. I heard her tell Natasha."

"Where were you?" I need to know, even though I knew it was going to wreck me.

His arms painfully constrict around me. "She did things to me. Made me do things. I didn't want to. I tried to fight back. Tried to get out, but the chains were too tight, and I was too weak from whatever Eva kept drugging me with. She watched. Always watched. Said I deserved it. Said I looked too much like him. I didn't want to. I didn't want to," he rambles.

No. No. Oh, Jesus.

Things click into place. Why he hated Eva and was glad she was dead. Like me, Hendrix shows signs of PTSD. He sleeps on the floor, a form of protection. He has a need to be in control and control his environment, like in the kitchen and especially with sex. He lashes out at the slightest provocation.

Self-hatred singes my soul. I should have known something was wrong. Sensed it. Felt it. When Hendrix came back from what I thought was his trip, he was different. He didn't smile. He was quiet. He wouldn't let anyone touch him. I would ask him what was wrong, but he would shrug it off and tell me it was nothing. I should have *fucking known.*

I caress his cheek, his brow, his neck. "I know you didn't. I know. It wasn't your fault, sweetheart. I love you so much. So damn much."

"It was worse after you disappeared."

His shoulders shake as he cries, and all I can do is hold him. Love him. Promise him that everything will be okay. That I'll protect him and keep the demons away.

I won't fail him again.

There's a series of four light knocks on the bathroom door.

"Aoife?" Constantine says through the pressed wood.

Hendrix stiffens.

"Yeah. Hold on," I call back. "Hey. Look at me," I tell Hendrix. "I love you."

He nods.

"*I love you.*" I will continue to tell him that until the end of time.

He nods.

"Trust me to protect you."

He nods.

I seal my lips over his mouth and kiss him.

"I love you. Be right back. I promise."

He pulls his knees to his chest when I stand up. He looks so broken. So small in that moment.

"Hendrix?"

He tips his face up.

"She will never hurt you again," I vow.

He nods.

As soon as I step out into the hallway, Constantine

pulls me to the side.

"You're bleeding. Why the fuck are you bleeding?"

The damn dress cuts off my circulation when I bend over to untie the straps of the stilettos. I slip them off my feet and kick them out of the way.

"Stay here with Hendrix."

"Did he do that to you? Aoife!" Constantine barks when I lift my dress and take off at a jog.

It needs to end. All of it. Now. Fuck Aleksander's plans.

My bare feet slow when I run into Tristan at the end of the hallway.

"Where the fuck have you been? I've been looking for you and Hen—what are you doing?" he asks when I search through his pockets and pat him down looking for a weapon. "Is that blood?"

Will everyone stop asking me that?

"Yes. Is Natasha Zephyros here?"

The slight widening of his eyes is his tell. "He told you." A statement, not a question.

"Is she here?"

Hendrix was triggered. She has to be here.

I spot Aleksander walking our way, but Tristan bands an arm around me when I try to circumvent him.

"Aoife, don't."

I balk at his temerity. "Don't? Are you fucking kidding me right now? You know what she did!"

Aleksander uses his body to block us from view. "People are looking." He sees the blood and pins Tristan with a murderous scowl. "Let her go," he warns.

"Have you seen Natasha Zephyros?" I ask Aleksander.

It feels like a piece of me gets torn out every time I say her name. My simmering hatred of the man with the constellation tattoos was an obsession, but the explosion of hatred I feel for the bitch who hurt Hendrix is all-consuming.

Aleksander's eyebrow quirks at my brusque tone. "She's with Patrick at the bar."

"Give me your gun."

"I swear to Christ, Aoife," Tristan grumbles, then dejectedly sighs out, "Give her your gun."

Aleksander takes out his Glock, checks the safety, then places it in my outstretched hand.

"Thank you. Barricade the doors. No one leaves."

"What about the people arriving or—Gabriel hasn't shown up—*Shit!*"

With a single-minded focus, my vision tunnels on the raven-haired woman with her hands all over Patrick Knight. I know it's him because he looks exactly the same as he did ten years ago.

Did she touch Hendrix that way? Intimately, like she had a right. He was a boy. There's a special place in hell for pieces of shit like her.

Keeping the gun hidden at my side, I barrel through couples dancing to get to the other side of the room. I ignore the contemptuous protests and snooty remarks of the people I shove out of the way. The lyrical music being played matches the steady beat of my heart. The darkness in me whispers in my ear, urging me to set it free.

"Natasha Zephyros."

Her laughing face turns when I call her name.

"Yes?"

The front of her skull explodes a millisecond after I pull the trigger.

Then all hell breaks loose.

CHAPTER 21

SYN

"I can control my destiny, but not my fate." - **Paulo Coelho**

Confusion. Panic. Mayhem.

But not from the man under my gun.

Natasha's limp, lifeless body slides off the stool and hits the floor with a thud at his feet.

Patrick's cold voice cuts through the chaos. "You must be Synthia Carmichael."

I smile.

He studies me with clinical detachment, taking in my left arm, the blood, my disheveled appearance.

"You're not what I expected of the poor country hick my wife so generously gave a scholarship to attend Darlington Founders. And you certainly don't fit my son's usual type. Hendrix prefers to fuck weak, brainless blondes."

He wants a reaction. He won't get one.

Patrick unfolds a napkin square and casually wipes off the brain matter and blood spray from his face. Removing his jacket, he drapes it over the bar, undoes his gold-and-diamond cufflinks, and rolls up his sleeves midway to his elbows.

"I told Aleksander it wasn't a coincidence that you were at the house that weekend. All this effort just to get to me? I must admit, it's rather flattering."

Stupid, arrogant man. It's so like Patrick to think that he's the center of the universe. However, I know better than to underestimate him. Patrick may be pretentious and excessively narcissistic, but he is also dangerous.

The noise level rapidly diminishes to hushed, urgent whispers as the room falls silent.

Patrick darts a glance at someone over my shoulder and smirks. "You won't make it out of here alive."

He thinks he's safe. That whoever is behind me will save him.

"I disagree. By the way, thanks for killing Eva. It's the only thing you ever did right as a father."

Hendrix wraps his hand over mine, and together we pull the trigger.

The sound is deafening, drowned out only by the horrified gasps that echo around us. Patrick's head snaps backward, whiplashing with a jerk, his face locked in wide-eyed shock. Seemingly frozen in time, he sways slightly before toppling sideways in slow motion.

"You okay?"

Without my heels, Hendrix towers above me. I tilt my head to his face, and relief washes over me. He looks like my Hendrix again.

Urging my arm down, he applies pressure to my

forefinger and discharges the Glock three times into Natasha.

"I will be."

I'll make sure of it. Constantine wants me to go back into therapy. Maybe Hendrix will be open to joining me. We can heal together.

Hendrix kisses the crown of my head. "Let's get this party started."

I scan the sea of faces in front of me. Some confused. Some terrified. Some angry. Some I know. Some of them unfamiliar. Most of the people here are the upper echelon of the Society. They ruin lives for money they don't need. Manipulate their positions—as judges, politicians, civil servants, businessmen—for power they don't deserve. They look down on the world and its people with disdain, believing themselves to be superior.

A few men rush the ballroom doors only to be subdued by the guards Aleksander and Tristan put in place. However, it's the woman with the violet eyes who beckons me from the corner of the room and gives me the assurance I need. Andie came. She kept her promise to have my back. And next to her are Constantine, Liam, Jax, Keane, and Rafe.

Hendrix pinches his fingers and holds them to his lips, releasing a shrill whistle that grabs everyone's attention. "Chill the fuck out and sit your asses down!"

Serena makes the mistake of speaking up, a false bravado that she's untouchable giving her deluded self-importance.

"You think because you're fucking them that you'll be able to come in here and take over? Whatever they promised you are lies. This is the Society, bitch. My father is a senator."

The man in question tries to shut his daughter up. "Serena, hush."

She slaps his hand away, not done with her little speech. "You're nothing but a whore. You're nobody. Hideous gutter trash. Do you honestly think he cares about you?" she says of Hendrix.

With a snarky British tone, Hendrix says, "I'd think very carefully before you say another word."

She rants right over him. "Hendrix will never be yours. He'll fuck you until he breaks you, then toss your ass out when you're no longer fun to play with."

All eyes turn toward me, the girl who has spent the last decade hiding in the shadows. I hate attention. I hate it when people never see *me*, only my scars. But I can't hide anymore.

Hendrix huffs a derisory snort. "Please go kick her ass so she'll shut the hell up."

Gladly.

Murmurs cascade around the room like a wave as I walk with purpose to where Serena and her father are crowded together with Katalina and Mathis Laurent.

"Young lady, what is the meaning of this? Why are we being held against our will?" Senator Worthington demands to know.

"I'll tell you in a minute," I reply, and face off with Serena when she hisses, "Ugly bitch."

"Do you have anything else you'd like to say to me? Burn girl, perhaps?"

She jabs a ruby-red fingernail into my burned arm. "You—*Ahh!*"

Her scream reverberates through the room when I grab her wrist in an *ura gyaku* wrist lock, a type of

Kyusho Jitsu pressure point that tears the tendons of the hand, middle, and index fingers. With a sharp twist and bend, I brace my left leg and push her to the floor. I keep the pressure on because I want her to suffer for every malicious word she has ever spoken to me. It's petty and vindictive, but I don't really care.

The senator says nothing as his daughter wails in agony, her tears uncomfortably dripping between my bare toes. I almost tell her to lick them off.

A raucous commotion breaks out when Aleksander and Tristan drag a kicking and grunting Francesco into the room. His face is battered and swollen, his hands bound with zip ties, and there's what looks like a balled-up hand towel shoved into his mouth.

I release Serena, relishing her cries that I broke her hand. I hope I did.

"What do you want? Why are you doing this?" someone shouts.

The chandelier above creates a spotlight effect that shines down upon me. This is it. My moment. My revenge. My destiny, no matter how hard I want to run from it.

"My name is Aoife Fitzpatrick. Only daughter of James Fitzpatrick. And I've come to seek justice against the man who betrayed my father and stole what rightfully belongs to my family."

"Dear god," Mathis Laurent gasps as murmurs of my name circulate the room.

"Francesco Amato is responsible for the brutal murder of my parents. My father was shot in the head. My mother, Caroline, raped and tortured in front of me. Malin, Francesco's loyal puppet, stabbed me and left me for dead. He doused me in gasoline and torched the house, hoping the fire would eradicate any evidence."

Having to recount the events of that night almost breaks me, but I stand there and let them see my truth. The trauma that still visibly mars the left side of my body serves as undeniable proof of the horrors I endured.

"Francesco has held his position as head of the Council through betrayal and lies, and it is my right as the legitimate heir to remove him from power and take my father's place at the table alongside Tristan Amato, Hendrix Knight, Constantine Ferreira, and Aleksander Stepanoff." Fierce resolution crosses my face when I turn to Andie. "The Levine-Agosti syndicate will also have seats at the Council table."

"You can't do that!" Mathis blusters.

"You are welcome to leave the Society if you do not like the new leadership."

"Dad, no," Katalina says, grappling at his arm.

She recoils when he backhands her across the face. "You said you could get Tristan to marry you. You're useless to me now."

In a flash of fury, I grab one of the cocktail forks from a nearby table and plunge it into his eye.

"You will never raise a hand to your daughter again," I seethe through clenched teeth, then yank the fork out.

Mathis crashes to the ground and howls like he's dying. He's not. I made sure not to penetrate the optic nerve into the brain. He'll lose the eye, but he'll live.

"Would anyone else like to voice their opinion?" I ask.

Katalina cradles her cheek and blinks at me. No one says a word.

One of the guards approaches, and with a nod from me, he grabs Mathis's collar and drags him away.

"The Society has become a disease, infecting everything it touches," I announce as I walk over to Francesco. "No more."

Tristan and Aleksander force him to his knees in front of me. His one good eye begs for mercy, but I have none to give.

"Brought you something," Tristan says and places the jeweled ceremonial dagger in my hand.

A surge of righteous anger snakes its way through my heart, and I make a show of holding the knife up for everyone to see.

"This is for my father." With a flick of my wrist, I slash the sharp edge across Francesco's face, cutting a deep, diagonal gash from temple to chin. "This is for my mother." I mirror the cut on the opposite side of his face. Leaning over him, I whisper in his ear, "And this is for me." I shove the knife deep into his side, just like Malin did to me.

Francesco convulses as he falls forward and face-plants onto the floor. He's not dead, but he'll soon wish he was.

I can't unleash the damage I want to inflict upon him because it's not only me that Francesco has hurt. It's up to Tristan and Aleksander to decide their father's fate.

Suddenly, Tristan's strong grip pulls me in close, his lips crashing onto mine, kissing me in front of everyone. "You are fucking magnificent."

Constantine and Hendrix come to either side of us, Andie and her men at our backs. It's a calculated display of strength and unity, a warning to all who would dare oppose us.

I extend my hand toward Aleksander, hoping he will take it. Wanting him to be a part of this found family.

Our family. I'm relieved when he twines his fingers with mine.

"Members of the Society, prove your worth," Tristan decrees.

It's a challenge and a test. Pledge obedience or suffer the consequences.

One by one, each person in the room steps forward and uses the dagger to carve their mark into Francesco's flesh. And then, finally, it's Tristan and Aleksander's turn.

Hendrix was right. Such beautiful chaos.

The night lights up with a roaring whoosh.

"Hey, cuz. You did good in there," Andie says.

I rest my head on her shoulder when she loops an arm around me, and we watch the raging fire reduce the Society compound to ash. Karma at her best. The news will report on the devastating fire that ruined the gala. A fire sparked by faulty electrical wiring in the ballroom. How Francesco lost his life trying to save his wife, who had barricaded herself in their bedroom suite upstairs. How Patrick Knight was the first to succumb to the flames that quickly engulfed the ballroom. How everyone else in attendance will say they were lucky to get out.

It's Shakespearean in a way, how it ends. Kind of like Macbeth. *"We still have judgement here that we but teach bloody instructions, which being taught, return to plague th'inventor."* Like I said. Karma.

There is one small problem.

Gabriel Ferreira never showed up.

"Thank you for coming."

We're the only ones that stayed, us and the guys. I couldn't leave just yet. I had to see it burn.

"Anytime, babe," Andie replies.

The whir of helicopter blades cuts through the night air; the downwash it creates whips my ponytail around.

"Our ride is here."

They need to leave before the authorities arrive. Too many questions would be raised if anyone noticed members of the mafia loitering around.

Andie clasps my upper arms, her expression serious. "Do not feel guilty for what happened here. Guilt has no place in our world. We do what has to be done to protect our family and the ones we love."

I make the first move to hug her. "I'll call you tomorrow."

There are so few people I can trust, and I'm so damn grateful that she's one of them.

"What are your plans? Are you heading back to university?" she asks. "You're always welcome to come stay with us if you need a little downtime."

What downtime? Between classes and the changes we will be making at the Society, I probably won't have a spare second.

"Rain check?" I glimpse to my left. At my three men. "Right now, I just want to go home."

CHAPTER 22

TRISTAN

Hendrix taps the back of his headrest. "T, we're home."

Sitting in the back row of seats next to Aleksander, I'd been blankly staring out the window, consumed with a million turbulent thoughts, most of them not good.

"I've got her," Constantine says.

He turns the engine off and gets out. Seconds later, the back passenger door opens, and he unbuckles a sleeping Aoife. She doesn't rouse. Completely dead to the world. Maybe not the best analogy considering what went down tonight.

"You coming?" Hendrix asks.

Aleksander's legs are stretched out in the aisle between the third and second row of seats. Instead of getting out on his side of the car, Hen intentionally kicks Aleksander's foot as he follows Con and Aoife.

"You are so fucking juvenile, Knight."

Hen blows him a kiss.

The only good thing about the short car ride to the

house was that it was done in blessed silence.

"I'll be there in a minute. Can you get her out of that dress?"

I can only imagine how uncomfortable it would be to sleep in. We did a quick clean and patch-up job on her shoulder in the helicopter. Something Hen and I will be talking about in private. I don't know what transpired between him and Aoife—I can only guess it had something to do with Natasha since he apparently told her what happened—but he went too far. He loses control when he's triggered, but he can't use her to purge his demons like that.

Hendrix looks back, his smile wicked. "You know I can."

He leaves the car door open, allowing fresh air to come in and dispel some of the stench left by death that coats our clothes.

"I assume I'm not welcome inside," Aleksander says.

The blood vessels at my temples pulsate with a heavy throb, warning me of an oncoming headache.

"Where's Gabriel?"

Con's father was a no-show at the gala, and the only conclusion I can come to is that he was tipped off.

Aleksander bends his knees and turns in his seat. "I don't know."

"Where's Gabriel?" I ask again.

"I don't fucking know, Tristan!"

I grab his open collar and shove him back in his seat. Anger pours out of me like poison. "And I don't fucking believe you. If you're hiding him, if he comes after Aoife or Deirdre, what happened to Malin will be nothing compared to what I will do to you. Now kindly walk your ass back to the bell tower and stay away from

Aoife. She needs to heal, not have you twist her around with more head games."

He goes still. "If you want to keep that hand, I'd suggest you remove it."

"Make me."

I'm acting just as immature as Hendrix because I want him to react. Hit me. Give me any excuse to retaliate and let loose this rage that keeps building. I had been groomed for years to be the next head of the Council. A prince destined to be king of an empire. Everything I went through, everything Francesco did to me, was to prepare me for the role I was to inherit. But now... Now, I'm stuck in a life I don't want anymore. We all are. Hen wanted to walk away. Con never wanted it in the first place. Aoife wants a normal life, medical school, kids, a home.

I don't care what I have to do. I will crawl into the gutter to make sure every dream she's ever wished for comes true.

"I hope you're proud of yourself. You've ruined her life."

The things he set into motion pulled her back in, and if he cares about her the way he keeps professing he does, I hope he chokes on that guilt.

There's a momentary flicker of remorse. "Tristan, wait."

I don't. Leaving him in the back seat, I storm into the house and slam the front door shut behind me.

"You look pissed."

Dierdre stands up from where she's sitting at the bottom of the stairs and wipes her hands down the front of her jeans. Her hair is pulled back in a single braid, her plaid shirt tied in a knot at her waist. She looks vastly different from the person I saw at Falcon Tower.

"You got here quick," I reply and go into the kitchen. I need a drink.

"I was at Cillian's place in Boston when you called. I never went to Ireland. I wanted to stay close in case Syn needed me."

"Have you spoken to her?" I pull two beers from the fridge and set one down on the counter island.

She takes the bottle and untwists the cap but doesn't drink it. "I stayed out of the way when they came in. Didn't want to wake her. Tristan, what in God's name happened?"

I take a long pull, wishing I had chosen something stronger. "They're dead."

Saying it out loud makes it real. Our parents are dead. I killed them. What kind of monster does that make me?

Her head drops, and she deflates like the weight of the world has been suddenly lifted off her shoulders. One lone tear falls to the floor.

"It's over then."

"Not exactly." I take my beer and walk outside onto the back patio.

Cocky Bastard makes a small noise. If that thing crows and wakes up Aoife, I'm going to pluck all his damn feathers.

The deck chair groans when I drop into it and kick my feet up onto the railing. No stars out tonight because of the clouds. The storm line that moved over the Society compound must've made its way here. There's a wet, musty odor wafting up from the mulch of the plant beds that reminds me too much of the catacombs.

Dierdre bumps into my legs, knocking them off their perch, and glowers at me, a hand on her hip.

"What do you mean, not exactly?"

I finish the beer in two swallows and swipe the untouched one from her hand. "Did you feed Cocky today?"

"Yes. And stop deflecting."

I haven't missed this part of a sibling relationship. The nosy, overbearing older sister.

Draining the beer, I set the empty bottle on the ground. The quick infusion of alcohol has mellowed me enough to allow the self-pity to seep in.

"Why do you hate me so much?"

Flabbergasted, she rocks back on her heels. "Don't be ridiculous. I don't hate you."

I glance over at where the chicken coop now stands. "I planted a redvein over there. I would sit next to that fucking bush almost every night and talk to you. I missed you so much." I turn my gaze back to her. "But you act like you can't stand the sight of me."

A strained, uncomfortable silence stretches between us that I'm too weary to fight. I close my eyes and try to will away the headache.

"You look like him. Like Dad."

I'm so damn tired of people comparing me to that abusive, twisted bastard.

I crack my eyes open. "Jesus fucking Christ, Dierdre. I can't control genetics. You look like him, too, but I never hated you for it."

Her face pinches. "It's not just that you look like him. You became him."

I shoot up out of the chair, hurt fueling my anger. "I am *nothing* like Francesco, and fuck you for even saying that," I snap. "You left me, Dierdre. You could have taken me with you, but you left me," I shout, striking a fist to my chest as tears clog my throat, smothering me. "You left me with him, knowing what he would do to me. So fuck you."

When I try to walk away, she throws herself at me, arms crushing me in a desperate embrace. Can she feel the scars that cover my back?

"I know I did. I'm sorry. I didn't know what else to do. I couldn't take another day under his fist. I wasn't strong enough. He broke me, Tristan."

The hand Dad burned with his cigar curls into a tight ball as I pull away from her.

"He broke me every single fucking day."

Dierdre's tear-streaked face crumbles. "I'm sorry."

I'm suddenly more tired than I've ever felt in my life. "I'm going to bed."

CHAPTER 23

SYN

Screams fill my ears, and I smile as I look at the dead bodies lying at my feet. Blood drips from my fingers, and I use it to paint lines across my face. A warrior's mark.

"Syn, this isn't you! Wake up!" the blonde-haired girl with cornflower-blue eyes cries.

A dagger forms in my hand, and I use it to cut her throat. In order for Syn to live, Aoife must die.

"No!" With a gasp, I come awake and fight the arms holding me.

"Shit, Aoife. What—"

I leap out of bed and barely make it to the bathroom before my stomach unloads its contents.

"Jesus, baby," Tristan says, gathering my hair in one hand while rubbing circles on my back as I heave into the toilet until there's nothing left to come up.

The sink turns on, and Constantine places a wet washcloth on my forehead when I collapse back on my butt.

Three worried faces look down at me.

"I'm okay. Bad dream." I frown when I feel cold tile on my bare ass. I'm naked on the bathroom floor. Awesome. "Help me up?"

Constantine lifts me under the arms and sets me on my feet, and I have an unfortunate first look at myself in the mirror. Dear god. I touch the deep purple finger bruises that circle my neck. Strategically applied makeup should be able to hide them, but I'll wear one of the guys' dry-fit running tops with the collar to make sure.

I catch Hendrix's horrified expression in the reflection.

"I'm so fucking sorry," he says before backing out of the bathroom.

"Hendrix."

Tristan turns me to the side before I can go after him. "Let him go," he says, removing the gauze and medical tape on my shoulder. He probes the area with a delicate finger. "He can't keep marking you like this."

"I think that's up to me to decide," I reply.

"And I think you'd let him do whatever the fuck he wants just to make him happy. There have to be boundaries set that he cannot cross, Red. Trust me."

I don't need the reminder of all the women they fucked together.

"And you need to trust *me*."

Tristan and I share a lengthy stare. I won't budge on this. What I do with my body or let someone else do to me is no one's business. Not even his. Hendrix needs different things when it comes to sex. Things I'm completely into and want as well. Yes, last night was different because he lost control. He was in pain and needed me. I could've stopped him at any time, but I didn't because I know to the depths of my soul that I'm safe with him. I trust him implicitly. He just needs to learn to trust himself.

Constantine props a hip to the counter and crosses his arms over his chest. "I'm on T's side about this."

I groan out a frustrated sigh because I don't want to argue about this. And that's when it hits me. Not the putrid stench of vomit, but the sour smell of old blood. Francesco's blood.

"Can we discuss this later please?" I turn on the shower and don't wait for the water to heat up before I step inside. "What time is it?" I ask, scrubbing my skin raw with soap.

I only see Constantine's silhouette through the frosted shower glass as steam begins to billow.

"A little after five."

I rinse off and attack my hair with shampoo. "Are you going to class today?"

"Are you?"

"Well, yeah," I reply like it's obvious.

Constantine pokes his head inside the shower. "I don't want you going anywhere without one of us. My father is still out there, and until I know his whereabouts, it's not safe."

With a twist, I wring out my hair and turn off the shower.

"We're not doing the whole 'Syn needs a babysitter' thing again."

I need the normalcy of everyday life. Classes. Raquelle. College life. My guys. The Society has taken far too much from me, but those things it can't have. They're mine.

"Aoife."

"Nope." I take the towel he's holding and kiss him on the cheek. "And it's Syn. No more Aoife."

The dream I had carried some truth. I can't be two people anymore. Syn is the person who exists in this world. She's the one in college, has a social security number, a driver's license. Aoife is buried in Ireland next to her parents.

He follows me out of the bathroom and into my bedroom. "Gabriel is dangerous."

I sort through the clothes I hung in my closet and pick out a shirt and jeans. "So am I."

He doesn't refute that, but he does get in my way when I try to get dressed.

"Why do you have to be so fucking stubborn?"

"You love me stubborn," I reply and toss the clothes onto the bed so I can put my hands on him.

He's in nothing but those tight, sexy Calvins. And he's hard. Unable to resist, I close my lips over his nipple, playing the tiny nub with my tongue.

"Aoife," he growls, and the sound travels straight to my clit.

"Syn," I remind him.

With ribald intent, I kiss my way down his body until I'm on my knees. I starfish my fingers over his taut abs and slide my thumbs across the waistband of his boxers.

Constantine gently wraps my wet hair around his fist, his coal eyes blazing down at me. "You wreck me in the best way."

My thighs clench together at his husky voice.

Keeping our gazes locked, I lick a line from his pubis to his belly button. "And you love me in the best way."

I drag at the elastic of his boxer briefs, nipping a trail

of kisses that follow the exposed skin uncovered as I push the cotton material over his tight ass and down his legs.

Liquid heat pools at my center and a throbbing pulses between my thighs when his cock springs free, beads of translucent liquid pearling the tip. Constantine is magnificent to look at—all golden sun-kissed skin, dark hair, and beautiful body art—and I want to worship every inch of him.

His head falls back on a moan when I take him into my mouth. Hollowing my cheeks, I suck him with hard pulls, making sure to drag the flat of my tongue over his piercings in the way he likes. Constantine's hand tightens in my hair, but he doesn't dictate the rhythm or take over.

"Fuck, baby, you feel incredible."

I run my fingers through the soft curls of his pubic hair, up the full length of him, and along the underside vein to the base where I grip his girth with a reverent touch. I stroke him with slow glides of my hand and lightly scrape my teeth across the bulbous head. He feels like satin over steel, his salty musk exploding on my tongue, and I hum my pleasure.

"Touch yourself," he rasps, his breaths becoming choppy as I deep throat him until I gag.

The towel I wrapped around my torso parts when I slip my hand between my legs, sliding a finger through the wetness soaking my folds. My middle finger slips over the tiny bundle of nerves, rubbing rough circles that spiral me to the sharp edge of the sweet bliss of orgasm.

"So beautiful. So fucking beautiful," he says, taking over and fucking my mouth like a man possessed.

His cock thickens and swells. His moans turn into hedonistic grunts. And when he climaxes, I watch how rapture morphs his face with masculine beauty.

I remove my fingers from inside me and use my essence to write M-I-N-E along his Adonis belt.

I'm suddenly hoisted off the floor, and Constantine's mouth crushes mine, our tongues meeting on twin moans.

My legs go around his waist when my back meets the wall. His cock presses against my pussy, demanding entrance. His still very hard cock.

"How can you still—"

The rest of what I was going to say is cut off with a gasp when he enters me in one stroke, stretching me deliciously. The way we go at each other isn't pretty or gentle. It's fucking in its purest form. Feral. Soul-shattering. Paradise.

My nails claw into the taut muscles of his upper back, digging in as he thrusts into me, his tongue following the same frantic rhythm as he kisses me.

"Give it to me, Syn. Give me everything."

And I do. Because I can't deny him anything.

With his next punishing thrust, my inner walls clamp down, and I shatter. His sweat-slicked face buries in my neck, and he groans a gloriously masculine sound when he comes.

His weight bears down on me when he collapses forward, his hot breath panting at my ear.

"Love you, sweet girl," he says, kissing me.

I let my fingers dive into his hair, scraping the damp curls away from his face.

"Love you more. You, too," I tell Tristan, who has a shoulder leaned against the doorjamb.

No idea how long he's been standing there, but by the curvature of his grin, long enough.

"FYI, you may want to close the door next time."

I give him a perplexed look. There is absolutely no modesty between the four of us. If they could enforce a no-clothes rule in the house, they would.

"The walls are thin, and sound carries." His grin increases in wattage.

Again, I'm confused.

He tries to smother his laughter but doesn't do a good job of it. "Dierdre is downstairs."

Oh. Shit.

"She's supposed to be in Ireland. Why is she here?"

"I asked her to come," he replies.

I can't be mad because he did it for me.

My voice is but a squeak when I ask, "Did she hear?"

Twin dimples pop on his gorgeous face. He's enjoying this.

A blush of mortification scorches me from head to toe. "I'll be down in a minute."

"I'd suggest putting on some clothes first. Or not."

I flip him off, and he laughs. The sound of it hits me like a wrecking ball. There hasn't been much to laugh or smile about lately, so hearing it makes me stupidly happy.

Constantine pulls out and places me on rubbery legs that refuse to hold me upright. Tristan produces a cup of coffee from behind his back, and I almost fall on my ass when I leap across the room to retrieve it. Eagerly accepting my liquid addiction, I pepper kisses all over his face.

"Thank you."

"Hurry up. Hen's making breakfast." He smacks my

butt to get me moving.

Constantine secures an arm around me when I make a dash for the bathroom.

"Nope. Don't shower. I want you to smell like me for the rest of the day."

My sweet Constantine has been possessed by Hendrix.

I love it.

CHAPTER 24

SYN

I walk into the kitchen with Constantine, acting like my heart isn't beating a mile a minute. Not from the knowledge that the woman I consider a mother heard me having sex with my boyfriend, but because of the confrontation I know is coming. I could feel the ominous tension from upstairs.

The kitchen is rife with bad energy. Hendrix is at the stove, his back turned, ignoring the room as if Alana and Tristan aren't arguing in hushed, angry whispers three feet away from him.

"Good morning," I cheerily greet.

Alana is like a plank of wood when I hug her. I kiss her cheek anyway, happy to see her even though she's bristling like a pissed-off cat.

"Are you out of your goddamn mind?"

And here we go.

"Christ, Dierdre," Tristan admonishes his sister.

If she wants to fight about the guys and me again like

she did in the restroom at the bar, I'm going to shut that shit down quick.

I take a seat on a bar stool and grab Tristan's shirt, pulling him down to me. Tristan knows exactly what I'm doing and deepens the kiss as soon as our lips touch.

I hook my finger through the belt loop of his trousers to keep him close. "Can you be more specific?" I ask.

"Don't do that."

"Do what? Kiss my boyfriend?"

If she's going to be obtuse and difficult, so am I.

Not meeting my eyes, Hendrix slides a plate stacked with my favorite chocolate chip pancakes over to me and turns back around. I'll need to deal with that soon—his guilt over thinking he hurt me.

I pinch off a piece of the top pancake and pop it into my mouth. There really is nothing Hendrix makes that isn't the most delicious thing I've ever tasted.

"Act like a brat," Alana replies.

"The fuck?" Tristan shouts.

Hendrix turns off the gas burner and points the spatula at Alana. "You wanna fucking repeat that, you ungrateful bitch? You have no idea, *no fucking idea*, what she's been through to protect you."

I get off the stool and move in front of Hendrix before he does something that he'll regret later. Reaching back, I curve a hand around his hip, hoping my touch will instill some calm.

"I never mouthed off to you in our home, and you will not do so in theirs."

"Ours," Tristan interjects.

"I get that you're worried. But I'm twenty years old, not twelve. I decide what is right for me, and it doesn't matter whether you agree with my choices or not. I choose them. I choose this life. And what happened at the gala yesterday, I chose that, too."

"That's not what James wanted!"

Sick and tired of others—Alana and my parents included—trying to manipulate my life for their own purposes, I fire back, "I don't care what he wanted! He doesn't get to preordain my future any more than you do."

Smoothing a hand across her mouth, Alana takes a deep breath before saying, "Can we talk in private?"

"No," Tristan quips.

"Fine," I reply. I twist around and go up on my toes to kiss Hendrix's lips. "You're taking me on a date tonight."

The harsh frown line marring his forehead disappears. "I am?"

"Make sure the Ducati is gassed up."

"I call dibs on date-night Friday," Tristan chimes in.

"Saturday," Constantine says.

Alana gapes at him. "When did you start talking again?"

He doesn't answer. Not even in sign language.

"Join me outside," I tell her.

I pick up my plate and my coffee and go out onto the back patio.

Through the trees, a faint line glows along the horizon, signaling that the sun is about to rise. Alana takes a seat next to me when I sit down at the deck table and tuck into my breakfast. She settles back and crosses her legs. It almost feels like all the other mornings we shared on the back porch at the farm.

Making small talk, I comment, "The mornings here are pretty."

A cold front must've blown through because the

air carries a nipping bite that penetrates through Constantine's running top I'm wearing. I have it zipped all the way up to cover my neck.

"But nothing compares to the sunrises at home," I add.

I cherish every second of growing up on the farm. Wide open spaces and beauty everywhere I looked. The quiet and serenity. The smells and sounds. Every day was an adventure waiting to be discovered. I'd love to take the guys there for our winter break. Spend Christmas at the farmhouse. Cut down a tree and decorate it. Play in the snow. Bake sugar cookies, drink homemade hot chocolate, and stay up all night waiting for Santa to arrive. The chaos of Christmas morning as we sit around the tree and open presents. All the childishly fun things an adult takes for granted. All the things we missed out on together.

Alana reaches an arm behind me and absentmindedly plays with the ends of my ponytail, just like Tristan does.

"Mike didn't tell me Cocky was here."

As if he heard his name, Cocky Bastard hops up on the roosting bar and lets out a good-morning call.

I grin when Tristan's irritated grumble of how much he hates 'that damn rooster' filters out from the kitchen. Once Cocky B gets used to his new environment, he'll quiet down and not crow as often.

"The guys brought him here as a surprise for me. Bought him a coop and everything."

She makes a short, humming grunt.

"Those boys always adored you. Thought you hung the sun and moon and all the stars in the sky."

"They're not boys anymore."

She turns her head from her view of the rising sun and looks at me. "I know. They're dangerous men."

"We're not having this conversation again." Finished with the pancakes, I sip my coffee.

She tugs on my ponytail. "I'm worried about you."

"You don't need to be. I promise I'm okay." I'm not. I'm nowhere near okay. But I can pretend until I am. "Did Tristan tell you what happened?" I ask.

She looks down at her lap and picks at her cuticles. "I don't know what to feel other than relief. It's messed up. I should have been strong enough to do it. Not you." Her sadness is tangible. "James knew you could, but I don't think he ever anticipated that you'd decide to take over the damn thing."

Ah, yes. The base reason for my existence. Papa raised me to be a weapon he could unleash on the Society and bring about its complete annihilation. I don't know if that's true or what he actually thought, but that's how it feels. Aoife, the would-be queen of death. Not a crown I want to wear on my head.

"At least with me, the guys, and Aleksander on the Council, we can change things for the better."

I have an *oh shit* moment when shock flares her eyes comically wide. Apparently, Tristan didn't tell her everything.

"I hope to god you're referring to someone else named Aleksander because you wouldn't be careless enough, or foolish enough, to trust Aleksander Stepanoff."

When I don't answer, she slaps her hands over her face and shakes her head.

"Dammit, Synthia," a beat, then, "If he knows I'm here, he'll tell Gabriel."

"No, he won't." I say it with a conviction I wholeheartedly believe.

She peers at me through spread fingers. "Christ, he told you what Caroline did."

I guess that answers whether she knew about the marriage contract.

Enough with the damn secrets. I'm sick of all the lies and half-truths and self-serving pronouncements of good intentions.

Getting defensive, I snap, "Anything else you'd like to share or get off your chest? And if you try to tell me it was for my own good, I'm leaving."

She slams her palms on the table, matching my ire. "When was I supposed to tell you? You blocked out who you were, and all those years of therapy didn't work. Sending you here was my last resort."

She threw me to the wolves, to what? Jog my memory? Well, it worked.

"Don't look at me like that," she says when I scowl at her. "Even if you never remembered who you used to be, you wanted to come here. You were so happy when you got the acceptance letter."

"But it wasn't real! I never applied for the scholarship."

She frowns. "Yes, you did."

"I thought you did."

"I didn't."

"Or had the guidance counselor do it."

"No."

"Or Cillian."

"He didn't."

Our gazes clash in dual consternation. Then who the hell did? I want to pull my hair out at the roots because I don't want to deal with yet another mystery.

"I'll get Constantine to look into it."

"What are you going to do about Aleksander?" she asks.

The sun finally pops up into full view. A new day has arrived. There is meaningful symbolism to it. Every sunrise signals a new beginning. A blank canvas that you can paint with whatever you want. If the last ten years of my life were an art gallery, it'd be the same picture mounted in every single frame hanging on the walls. It's time for me to paint something new.

"I don't care what the contract says, I'm not his wife."

"In the eyes of the Society, you are," she unhelpfully points out.

"The contract isn't legal and would never stand up in a court of law," I argue. "Besides, marriages can easily be annulled if they haven't been consummated."

She looks horrified. "On that disturbing note, we need to talk about... *that*." She gestures with a fluttering hand in the direction of the house.

"No, we don't."

I'm not discussing my sex life with her or anyone else. Raquelle is the exception.

"You may not be mine biologically, but in every way that matters you are my daughter. I only want the best for you, so it worries me that you're setting yourself up for heartbreak."

Alana's assessment strikes my heart like an arrow aimed true.

"And you're my mom, which is why we will never be discussing my relationships. All that should matter is that I love them." I finish drinking my coffee that's now cold and change the subject. "I have class this morning, but I'd like for you to meet my friend, Raquelle."

Alana hasn't said how long she plans to stay. With Gabriel still lurking around somewhere, being here might not be the safest place, but it's up to her whether she wants to leave. I made the mistake in Texas of forcing her to go. She would have been safer with Andie.

She thinks about my invitation for a while before replying, "I'd like that."

I unzip the outside thigh pocket of the leggings and remove my phone that I found in Hendrix's room. I snap a quick selfie and send it to Raquelle.

Me: Proof of life.

"What are you doing?" Alana inquires.

"Texting Raquelle a picture. Don't ask. It's a thing with her."

Raquelle: Are you back?
Me: Yep.

"Is she Society?"

"Not that I'm aware," I reply. If she is, I'll find out soon enough.

Raquelle: Have a good trip?

That's a loaded question.

Typing out a response, I flip my phone around and ask Alana, "Is that good with you?"

If she's worried about Gabriel or Aleksander, I don't want to pressure her into going out in public.

She reads what I wrote. "Fine with me."

Me: My mom is here. Want to grab lunch after you get out of art? I'd love for you to meet her.
Raquelle: Absolutely!
Me: See you in calc.

CHAPTER 25

SYN

Walking across campus with my hand held in Constantine's feels different this morning. I soon understand why when strangers come up to greet me as we pass, several with their heads bowed like I'm royalty —*stupid, antiquated Society rules*. These people weren't at the gala, but they seem to know exactly who I am.

"That was fast."

Have you ever felt uncomfortable in your own skin? It's a feeling I've lived with for ten years. But that disembodiment isn't just a physical one. It's also psychological, like struggling with who I am, and who I want to be going forward. Syn won.

However, talking with Alana this morning brought about a new identity crisis. I'm not a child anymore, but I'm also not an adult. Not really. Even though the childhood I was raised in and the shit I've gone through made me mentally older than I really am, I haven't yet lived. I'm twenty years old and have spent half my life hiding, refusing to remember, and now I'm the head of one of the most powerful entities in the world that only a select group of people knows exists. How am I remotely ready for that kind of responsibility?

Constantine lifts our joined hands and brushes his lips across my knuckles. I appreciate that he doesn't try to placate me with false assurances, like trying to convince me that things will settle down soon. The uneasy feeling that hasn't left my stomach taunts that things have only just begun.

"So, date night with Hen," he says.

"I need to talk to him without any distractions. He's hurting because he thinks he hurt me."

We also need to start figuring out our new normal. I'm one woman being split between three men I love equally. Most of our time will be spent together, but we also need time where it's just the two of us without the others.

"Does Hendrix have a place he likes to go to when he wants to be alone?" I ask.

"There is a place, but he's not alone."

That's rather cryptic. "Can you elucidate?"

I love the grin that curves his wonderful mouth. "Do you remember when you memorized the entire Z section of the Webster dictionary?"

I went through a weird phase when I was nine. I wanted to know what every single word meant, so I started at the back of the dictionary. Not many words start with x, y, or z. I was precocious and ambitious, not crazy.

I laugh. "I think I made it through T before…" Before Papa hid me in Ireland.

Constantine grows somber. "When Hen needs to

escape, he goes to the Red Room."

I don't recall seeing a red room at the house.

"Is it in the basement?"

"It's a sex club, baby girl."

Oh. Well. Um...

I'll add it to the things Hendrix and I will need to discuss because there is no way in hell I'll be okay with him fucking other women—and I don't give one damn if it's a double standard.

When we get to the tree outside of Barnaby Hall, Constantine places my bag on the grass and takes out a set of keys from his front pocket.

Curious, I hover over his back while he carves something into the trunk.

"What are you doing?"

"This is our tree," he says.

I guess it is. I fell asleep with my head on his lap under this tree. It was right after what happened in the alley at the Bierkeller. I didn't remember them, and it was disconcerting how much I gravitated toward them anyway. I remember being both terrified and drawn to Constantine for some inexplicable reason.

Constantine also stood under this tree's branches, guitar in hand, waiting for me after class. He had sent me flirtatious texts, asking me to be his girlfriend, then took me on a picnic. It was all so frivolously silly, but so damn endearing. Constantine has a romantic streak a mile wide. He's a man of little words, so he finds these sweet, little ways to show me how he feels, like carving our initials into the tree that is ours.

I slink my arms around him and smile over his shoulder as he cuts a capitalized C-O-N and a plus sign into the bark, then shapes the letters for S-Y-N.

"Add a heart."

"Always so damn bossy."

I nip his earlobe with my teeth.

An electronic shutter click sounds nearby. "Too flipping cute," Raquelle says, snapping pictures with her phone.

"I want copies." I hop away from Constantine and tackle her in an exuberant hug. A first for me, but it feels right, so I do it. "You look amazing," I tell her.

Her long hair has been cut to shoulder-length, making the natural curl more pronounced.

She bounces the ends of the soft spirals in her palms. "It was time for a change."

"I love it. You are a goddess."

Raquelle is beautiful, inside and out. She's the nicest person I've ever met and so open. Nonjudgmental and supportive. It's crazy how instantaneous our friendship has been. Opposites who are also alike. If I were into women, I'd be tripping over myself to steal her away from Drake.

She blows a self-deprecating raspberry. "I wouldn't go that far. Hey, Constantine."

He lifts his hand hello and slips my backpack onto my good shoulder.

See you at home? he signs.

He tends to revert to sign language when he's around other people.

"You could join us for lunch if you want."

He has an hour free between classes around that time.

Enjoy your girl time, he replies but I know my dark angel will be there, somewhere in the shadows, watching over me.

"Damn, that man is fine," she says.

I make sure he's out of earshot before I ask her, "Have you and Drake ever gone to a sex club?"

Her eyes go enormously wide behind her glasses. "Is *that* what you did this weekend?"

"No!" I splutter a little too loudly.

She'd never want anything to do with me if she knew what I really did this weekend.

Raquelle bursts into a fit of mellifluous laughter. "The look on your face is priceless. I don't think I've ever seen that shade of red before. And no, we haven't, but we have gone to an adult store."

Showing my extreme naiveté, I ask, "What do you do there?"

"It's where you buy sex toys. Vibrators. Floggers." She holds her hands wide in front of her to show a length that is anatomically impossible. "Big, vibrating cocks that—"

I push her arms down. "I get it."

Giggling hysterically, she replies, "Girl, if you're going to be with three guys, we need to stomp out that farm-girl pure and dirty you up a bit."

"I can be dirty."

"Uh-huh."

I hook my arm through hers and pull her up the stairs to Barnaby. People part like the Red Sea, and I hope to God she doesn't notice.

"Don't judge this book by its country-girl cover. I've recently discovered I'm into some really weird shit."

"Which you're going to tell me about, right?" She elbows me in the ribcage when I just grin. "Right?"

We walk by a guy wearing black-rimmed glasses, and it reminds me that I haven't spoken to Evan since

Thursday.

"Have you seen Evan?" I ask her.

As soon as we enter the building, the chattering noise in the hallway drops significantly.

"Not since Thursday morning when he works the reception desk at my dorm."

I'll see him tomorrow in bio lab, but I'll try to call him today or drop by his place after calc to see if he's around… if I knew which dorm he resided in. He's never mentioned it. Constantine should be able to find out since he was able to get his digital hands on my student record from the registrar's secure database.

When we get to the seats we usually sit in, someone else is occupying mine next to the aisle. I recognize the raven-haired beauty immediately without seeing her face. I don't need this shit right now.

"Katalina."

She promptly stands up, making sure to keep her head lowered in deference. As much as I hate it, I can't say anything with Raquelle here.

Katalina clasps her hands nervously together. "May I have a second of your time?"

I check my plastic watch I put on this morning. It's cheap and gaudy, but it's so Syn, and I need those little reminders of who I am now.

"Class is about to start, so it'll have to be quick."

Raquelle looks on with interest, and I don't want to be rude, but I'm not going to do the polite thing and make introductions. I want to keep Raquelle as far away as possible from the Society and the people in it. Just being my friend may put a potential target on her back.

I set my bag down in the chair Katalina vacated and cross over to the exit door where the professor enters.

I can tell whose Society by the number of heads that crane their necks with prying curiosity.

I lose count at twenty when Katalina quietly says, "I'm not interested in Tristan."

It wouldn't matter if she was because he's mine.

She fidgets under my resting bitch face. "I mean, I was never interested in him... like that. My father... was insistent."

She distractedly cups the cheek he backhanded before dropping her hand. Unless you know it's there, the bruise barely shows under the makeup she covered it with.

"I just wanted to say thank you. Even though you probably hate me, you were the first person to ever stand up for me."

Not expecting her gratitude for stabbing her father in the eye, I reply, "I don't hate you, Katalina. You may not think so, but you have choices. I will protect you from Mathis if you want something different from what's been dictated to you by him and the Society."

Her big doe-brown eyes blink back tears. "Why would you do that? You don't even know me."

One shoulder lifts in a shrug to hide how much her plight hits home for me. Mathis used her like a bargaining chip. I love my father. I always will, regardless of what he did, but damn him anyway. Papa was my everything, but he failed me in every way a parent can fail a child, and I'm left picking up those mangled pieces he left behind.

The side door clangs open, and the professor walks in. I don't miss the wary glance thrown my way as he scuttles over to the massive wall-length whiteboard. I forgot how many people at Darlington Founders have ties to the Society.

"Let me know what you decide. Stay or leave, I promise you will be safe."

If there is a silver lining to this shitshow, it's that I can back up that promise. I have the power and the resources at my command as the head of the Council, and I plan to use it to protect those who can't protect themselves.

Katalina shakily nods. "Thank you, truly. It means more to me than you'll ever know, but I won't need any protection from my father. He's dead."

I'm about to lie through my teeth by giving her condolences for her loss when she shocks the shit out of me by whispering, "I killed him."

CHAPTER 26

SYN

Entering the bell tower, I take the hidden staircase up to the third floor since the elevator isn't open like it usually is. On my way back to the house after my last class, I decided to stop by and pick up my stuff Aleksander helped me get from my apartment. I should put in my notice to the leasing office that I'll be moving out. Since most of my things were shredded or destroyed, I won't have much to take to the house. I'm still pissed about that. I was sentimentally attached to my cottage-chic garage-sale pieces I found because they represented my first real taste of adulthood and living on my own.

I ascend the stairs at a slower pace when I hear a commotion of raised voices, one of them higher pitched and unmistakably female. I'm going to kill Alana if she sought him out about Gabriel. At lunch, she and Raquelle hit it off immediately. Raquelle makes it effortless to love her because of her funny, bubbly personality, and it made me happy to see Alana laugh. Her laughs were genuine and the conversation at the table easy, but I could tell something was weighing on her mind.

When I get to the door that leads from the stairwell into Aleksander's apartment, I twist the doorknob to open it but meet resistance. It's locked. Aleksander would have been alerted by his security system of my arrival, but with all the yelling going on, I doubt he's even noticed. Thankfully, I watched him enter the code the other night.

When the door unlocks, three rapid beeps announce my arrival but are drowned out by Serena's obnoxiously loud tantrum. My internal groan of displeasure that she's here is as loud as her yelling. I should turn my ass around and leave. Go home and get ready for my date with Hendrix. Instead, I slink down the short hallway and into the kitchen to get the gun duct-taped to the inside of the cabinet beneath the sink.

"She broke my fucking hand!"

Keeping the gun held loosely at my side, neither of them sees me when I stop under the archway. Aleksander's reply is muffled but Serena's outraged response is very loud.

"Get rid of her. Or are you just as pathetic as Hendrix? I never understood how he could ever fuck that ugly cow. The only reason either of you are panting after her is because of who her father is, and Daddy said he's dead! She probably killed him, too."

God, I hate her so much. No one would miss her if I shot her in the head right now.

"Look what she did to me! She's crazy."

Serena bounces her sparkly cast in front of his face.

Did she glue pink rhinestones to it?

Aleksander is in profile, but the anger etched on his face is clear as day. "I'm only going to say this once, Serena. Shut the fuck up about Syn."

She stomps her high heel like a petulant child. "Or what? What are you going to do? My father is a senator. He'll ruin you."

She really loves saying that, but her threats are complete nonsense; nevertheless, I have a sudden urge to jump to Aleksander's defense.

"Senator Worthington will be dead before he even has a chance," I say, making my presence known. "As will you."

At my sudden intrusion, Serena loses her balance and stumbles sideways on her heels. Her facade of confidence and superiority quickly crumbles under my cold glare. Proving she's all bitch and bluster, she lowers her gaze in deference. For once, I don't mind the show of subjugation and take satisfaction in seeing her submit.

"Hey, honey. How was your day?" I slide an arm around Aleksander's waist.

Mischievousness glints in his gray eyes. "Good. How was yours, dearest wife?"

I walked right into that, but I still poke a fingernail into his side in retaliation.

Serena sucks in air so fast, she starts coughing. "You're... *married?*"

"My day was good. Oh, before I forget, Hendrix and I are going out on a date tonight, so don't wait up."

"*What?*"

My gaze cuts to her. "Did I give you permission to speak?" Needing to put her in her place, I rake her with a condescending perusal. "Kneel."

She vacillates, hoping Aleksander will intervene on her behalf. He doesn't. He stays silent, his cold eyes watching with detached amusement.

With difficulty, she awkwardly sinks to her knees in the tight dress and settles to the floor.

"That's better. Now get the fuck out before I bench press your scrawny ass and toss you out the window."

When she struggles to get to her feet, I use the toe of my sneaker to knock her back down.

"Crawl."

Humiliated, Serena hiccups a sniffle as she clambers onto all fours. Black ink blots of mascara leave a trail of teardrops as she shuffles on her hands and knees to the elevator.

"Is it bad that I enjoyed that?" Aleksander says as soon as she's gone.

"Yes."

I'm not proud of myself. A woman should never treat another woman so disrespectfully, but fuck if she didn't have it coming.

Aleksander suddenly shifts and backs me up until my butt hits the wall next to the window. The thick muscles of his outstretched arms contract when he braces them on either side of my shoulders, effectively caging me in. With the afternoon sun shining in through the glass, the light washes the gunmetal color from his irises until they look as translucent as clear quartz.

"I was hoping you'd drop by."

His nearness doesn't make me uncomfortable, but it does make me guarded. Aleksander has a habit of tilting me off my axis because I don't know how to compartmentalize him. At times, he can be as sweet as Constantine or as mercurial as Hendrix. Like his pseudo name's sake, Alexander the Great, Aleksander is extremely intelligent and a master of strategy, which means I can never underestimate him. History is riddled with the demise of people who miscalculated their opponent—and there lies the crux of my confusion because I think of Aleksander as more friend than foe.

"I came by to pick up my stuff."

"Is that the only reason?" he asks.

There's a spark of hopefulness in the cadence of his deep baritone that I squash as soon as I reply, "Do you know where Gabriel is?"

Irritation replaces the hope. "Like I told Tristan last night, I don't know where he is. Pyotr checked out his New York residence this morning. The maid said she hadn't seen him in over a week."

Aleksander trudges out of the living room, and I have no choice but to follow.

"Alana is here. She's staying at the house." I return the pistol to its hiding place under the sink, then wash my hands.

"I honestly don't think she's even a blip on his radar. He's probably in hiding."

"Or planning to retaliate," I argue.

"Gabriel can't do shit. He doesn't have the manpower or resources to come after us that way." Pulling on the freezer drawer, he holds up a frozen meat lover's pizza. "I was going to pop a pizza in the oven for dinner if you're hungry."

I check the time on my phone. "It's four in the afternoon."

I still need to take a quick shower and change before my date with Hendrix. It's been on my mind all day. Our date has an ulterior motive, but I'm also excited about it.

"It's an early dinner," Aleksander replies and sets the oven to preheat.

I squint an eye and side-pucker my mouth. I eventually resign myself to staying since I'm actually starving.

"I could eat," I reply, hopping up onto the counter island and dangling my legs over the side.

"Drink? I've got beer, water, or soda."

"How about we circle back around to what we were talking about and not ignore the elephant in the room?"

Aleksander grabs a beer from the fridge. "I don't see an elephant."

Swiping the bottle from his hand, I take a sip and give it back. "The enormous pink one named Dierdre."

"Alana."

"Your sister."

"She's not my sister."

I jump down from the counter and rush after him when he storms back into the living room.

"She could be if you give her the chance."

He goes over to a secretary desk tucked in the corner and picks up a manilla folder. "Drop it, Syn."

"Have you met me?" One thing I have plenty of is stubbornness.

I take three steps back when he advances before I stop myself and stand my ground. I didn't come here to fight, but I will because it's important. Aleksander needs Tristan and Alana, and I believe with my whole heart that they need him, too.

"Why can't you leave things alone? It's clear as fucking day that we hate each other."

I won't let his anger sway me. Taking a chance, I cup his stubble-roughened cheek and softly say, "No, you don't, and neither does Tristan or Alana."

His eyelids slam shut at my touch, and he exhales a strained breath.

"We've lost so much, Aleksander."

The mood in the room suddenly alters. Like a coiled snake striking, he grabs my wrist and pries my hand from his face.

"And whose fault is that? I had a brother. I don't need another one."

The dark edge to his voice puts me on alert, as does his crushing grip around my wrist. I refuse to feel any more guilt about killing Aleksei. I did what I had to do to protect Constantine. I would gladly sacrifice myself to the devil if it meant he lived.

"Let. Go." It's the only warning I'm going to give.

As if it causes him pain, he swallows as he chokes out, "I *can't*."

This entire conversation is taking a turn down a path that I don't want to travel.

Apprehension rolls out of me when I say, "What do you want from me?"

"I want you to see me."

Not fully understanding because I'm looking right at him, I reply, "I do see you."

He gently releases my forearm, and my fingers curve around the thick paper packet when he places the manilla envelope in my hand.

"No, you don't. Not like you see *them*."

He leaves me standing in front of the large, picturesque window that overlooks the campus, wondering what the hell just happened.

"Aleksander, wait! What about the piz—"

When I hear the three rapid beeps of the exit door being opened, I know he's not coming back.

"That went well," I mumble.

Going back into the kitchen, I turn off the oven, then set the manilla envelope on the counter and stare at it, pondering what's inside. Only one way to find out.

I pinch the two tiny pieces of the metal closure together and open the flap. Shocked at what I find, I dump everything out and rifle through the old photographs. There are so many. Most of them are of Papa and Mama, but there are several with me in them as well.

Aleksander must've found these in the archives.

Inside the compound I had burned to the ground.

The tears come, and I don't stop them.

"Thank you," I whisper to the man who is no longer here.

CHAPTER 27

SYN

"What are you doing?" Constantine asks, coming into my room.

Sitting cross-legged on the bed and surrounded by photographs, I look up from my journal.

"Scrapbooking."

Hendrix wasn't home when I got back, so after getting ready, I decided to add to my journal instead of studying. Unlike the macabre entries on the pages that came before, my new entry is about going on a date with Hendrix. It's silly to feel this childlike giddiness over a date, but it's a rite of passage I never got to experience as a teenager. And with three boyfriends, I have three first dates to look forward to, the romantic picnic with Constantine last week, notwithstanding. I also added a few of the photographs of my parents that Aleksander gave me but want to keep the rest for framing after I make copies.

I clear a place for him, and the mattress dips when Constantine sits down next to me. He picks up one of the photos and studies it.

"Where did you get these?"

"Aleksander."

He makes a nondescript grunt and hands it back to me.

"Here," he says, holding out a gift box wrapped in gold-embossed tissue paper.

I was wondering why he had his hand behind his back.

"You brought me a present?"

I'm not used to seeing him blush, and damn if it isn't sexy.

"It's nothing much."

I place the pen between the pages of my journal to keep my place and set it aside. Before I take the gift from him, I crook my finger for a kiss.

"Important things first." I suck on his bottom lip.

He strokes his tongue inside my mouth, and I get lost in his kiss. I could be ninety years old, and I would still get butterflies every time he kissed me.

"What is it?" I ask, holding the box to my ear and giving it a little shake.

"Open it."

I trace over one of the metallic foil-stamped butterflies that adorn the wrapping.

"It's too pretty to open."

In a rare show of whimsical playfulness, he blows a raspberry on my neck that sends me into a fit of rambunctious giggles.

"Then I'll open it."

He pretends to reach for the box, and I snatch it away.

"Don't you dare!"

With an inordinate amount of care, I cut through the

pieces of tape with my fingernail, so I can preserve the paper and not tear it.

When I begin to remove the lid, he hurriedly explains, "It's nothing special. Just something I saw at the student store and thought of you."

"Whatever it is, I'm going to love it because it came from you."

I peel back more tissue paper to reveal a beautiful pink leather-bound journal. Embossed on the cover is a dandelion puff, its fluffy seeds scattered from spine to edge, carried by an invisible wind.

I remove it from its casing and press it to my nose, breathing in the wonderful smell of new leather and paper.

"Is it too girlie? I wasn't sure if you'd like the pink."

I seem to be a fountain of tears today. "It's perfect. Thank you so much."

He pulls me into his lap, my back to his front, and circles his arms around me.

"I remembered what you once told me about dandelions."

When we were little, we came across a small patch of dandelions during one of our survival training sessions out in the woods that surrounded the Society compound. I explained how your wish would come true if you were able to blow all the fluff off the seed head. I never told him what I wished for, no matter how many times he asked. And as fantastical as it was, my wish became reality. Constantine loves me.

He tucks his chin in the crook of my shoulder and opens the journal to the first page. There's an inscription written in his messy cursive.

Fill the pages with your wishes and know that I will

make every single one come true.

Overwrought with emotion, I flip over and push him back onto the bed. "You already have."

Needing to feel him inside me more than I need air, I eagerly slide my hand to the zipper of his jeans where he's already hard and ready for me.

But before I can undo the top button, I lose all sense of gravity when I'm hefted into the air and thrown over Tristan's shoulder.

"Tristan," I laugh, more than say, when he delivers a stinging slap to my ass.

"Nuh-uh. No fucking. Hen is waiting."

Folded in half over his shoulder, my stomach takes the brunt of the bouncing as he carries me down the stairs.

"Hey, I was just coming up to ask you what you wanted for dinner—where are you going?" Alana says when we pass by the living room.

Using Tristan's back to support me, I manage to execute an awkward pushup and wave at her.

"I'm going out on a date. Love you!" I happily call.

The crisp evening air refreshes my senses as soon as we're outside. There are no clouds to obscure the darkening sky or hide the first pops of stars that appear. A perfect night for a ride on Hendrix's bike.

"Help him get out of his head," Tristan says when we get to the bottom of the porch steps.

"I will."

Or I hope I can. I have something specific planned for my date with Hendrix.

The rumble of a motorcycle engine makes itself known as it starts up. With each torque of the handlebar, the revs crash into me. This will be another first. A new experience that will belong only to Hendrix and me.

"Hold on," is all the warning I get before my butt hits the back of the saddle. "Straddle the seat and move closer to Hen. Put your feet here."

I follow his instructions and widen my legs to slot myself behind Hendrix. He's wearing a dark brown leather jacket that feels buttery soft when I run my hands over it.

"Thank you for this," I say loud enough to be heard over the engine.

Hendrix reaches back and lays his hand on my thigh, his casual touch triggering a flurry of tingles.

The streetlights have turned on, even though it's not yet fully dark, and I get my first top-down view of his bike. It's all matte black and chrome with electric blue trim. Very Hendrix.

"Be careful with her on this thing," Tristan says and kisses me goodbye.

"Fuck off."

Tristan takes the helmet Hendrix hands him and smushes it over my head. It's a tight fit and very uncomfortable.

"Is this really necessary?"

"Yes," they say at the same time.

Tristan secures the clasp under my chin and grins. "You look like a chipmunk."

I feel like one with how squished my cheeks are.

Alana and Constantine come out onto the porch, both aiming the cameras of their phones at us, capturing new memories.

Tristan presses something on the outside of the helmet, and I jump when Hendrix's voice speaks loudly in my ear.

"Where to, firefly?"

The helmet must have a built-in microphone.

"Just drive," I tell him.

I'll let my broken compass lead the way, knowing it will get me exactly where I need to be. It led me back to them, didn't it?

He grabs both my hands and encircles my arms around his torso. "Hold on tight. Never let go. Understand?"

Funny how those words hold such a profound meaning that have nothing to do with being on the back of his motorcycle.

CHAPTER 28

HENDRIX

Speeding down the deserted county highway that connects Darlington to the next town over, I can't stop the grin from forming when Syn lets out a whoop of effervescent joy. We've been riding for almost an hour with no destination in mind. It's been both cathartic and torturous, especially when I feel the heat of her pussy snuggled against my ass. I feel like a bastard with how badly I want to pull over, bend her over my bike, and fuck her. I don't deserve to touch my sweet angel after what I did. I lost control. I let my darkest secret slip. And now she's seen firsthand the animal I turned into.

Without her around to save me, I sunk under the weight of my pernicious shame. It ate at me, morsel by morsel, until there was nothing left but a debased sadist wearing the husk that used to be me.

But then Aoife came back, and what was left of my humanity has been struggling to claw its way to salvation. To her.

So, yeah, I'm a bastard because being with her, loving her, fucking her… hurting her… is the only time I feel anything real. And right now, she's not helping to calm my urges with the way she keeps caressing her hands over my abs. I don't think she realizes she's doing it, but my dick is most definitely aware.

"Up ahead. Take a left."

I snap out of my thoughts and glance around. We're in the middle of no-man's-land, a long stretch of road in the unincorporated outskirts of town. It's not as polished as Darlington or as picturesque. The land out here is cheap, more industrial, and attracts a seedier kind of business. Like bars where the parking lots are filled with more Harleys than cars and—

"Are you sure?" I ask when the only thing I see are the bright pink-and-blue flashing lights promising *Girls, Girls, Girls*. "That's a strip club."

She leans into me and tries to peer over my shoulder. "I know."

"I'm not taking you to a strip club on our first date."

Her breathy chuckle goes straight to my throbbing cock that refuses to settle down.

"It'll be fun."

I've had more than my fair share of fun at strip clubs, but if any woman is going to be naked and grinding on me, it's going to be her. I don't want anyone else, and I'm damn sure not going to disrespect her by looking at other women without their clothes on.

"Please, Hendrix," she says when I don't slow down.

My tiny voice of reason screams curse words at me when I ease off the gas. Gravel crunches and pops under the tires as we pull into the overflowing parking lot. I'd only visited this place once, during our freshman year. My predilections lean more toward the kind of debauchery where I get off on inflicting pain, not nipple tassels and stuffing dollar bills into G-strings, so when I discovered the Red Room, I had no reason to venture out this way anymore.

Syn waits for me to engage the kickstand before sliding off, and I immediately miss the feel of her wrapped around me.

"Can you help me get this thing off?" With her nose scrunched and her mouth puckered in the cutest frown, she fumbles with the clasp for the helmet. Christ, she's adorable.

I nudge her hands out of the way and do it for her.

"Much better," she says.

She does a hair flip thing where she bends over, then arches up like an ethereal mermaid bursting from the water, all scarlet tresses and pale, creamy skin. She gives her long locks a shake and gifts me with a luminous smile that punches a hole in my chest. I'm utterly entranced. The facets of this amazing woman are endless. Badass. Lethal. Sweet. Innocent. Sexy. Funny. Adventurous. And so fucking smart. My childhood best friend has grown into the most amazing woman. I'm obsessed with her. Crave her. Love her with every decrepit, blackened part of my soul.

Which is why we shouldn't be here.

I snag her by the waistband of her blue jeans and roughly haul her to me. Those gorgeous blue-bonnet eyes sparkle under the multicolored lights when they look up at me with trust and love, two things I don't deserve but am selfish enough to keep and not give back.

"You don't have to prove anything to me."

Twin hi-beams from a four-cab pickup shine directly at us when it parks in one of the few open spots remaining. The place is busier than I would expect for a Monday night. From the multitude of more expensive Mercedes and Porsches in the lot, it seems like a lot of students from Darlington Founders frequent here along with the locals.

Syn's small but deceptively strong hands grip either side of my neck at the nape, pulling my gaze back to hers. It's too much of a reminder of what I did to her. I could have killed her, and she would've let me.

"Have you ever considered that maybe I have something to prove to myself?" she asks.

Frustrated, my voice wavers with unwanted vulnerability. "I don't want you to change just to make me happy. You already make me so fucking happy, firefly."

Determination ignites behind her baby blues. Even the tiniest of embers can start the most dangerous blazes, and Syn is nothing if not strong-willed and obstinate as hell.

Taking the tab of my jacket's zipper between her teeth, she stares directly at me as she slides it down. She knows exactly what she's doing, challenging me like this. I sink my hand into her hair, fisting it like a leash. To anyone coming out of the club, it would look like she's about to go down on me, and god help me, I'm tempted to pull out my cock and let her suck me off in full view of everyone.

Sliding up my body, she grasps the two halves of the jacket, moving them out of the way, and places the softest of kisses to the spot where my heart thunders her name.

"I want to be here with you. I want to be your everything, your every desire, even the ones you're afraid to share with me. As Aoife, I loved you as a boy, but as Syn, I fell in love with you because of who you are now. Your demons don't scare me."

I'm torn between my desire for her and the lingering shadows of my past.

"You deserve better," I declare.

"I deserve you, just the way you are."

"I hurt you." And the guilt of that is killing me.

She fits herself to me, chest to thigh, and I can't keep my hands off her.

"You know damn well I could have stopped you at any time if I wanted to. What I have with you is different from what I have with Tristan and Constantine. That darker side of you doesn't make me love you less; it makes me love you more. Constantine is my sweet, safe place. Tristan is my strength. But you, Hendrix, are my freedom. You see the same darkness inside me, the wildness, and instead of caging it, you let me soar when I want to fly."

I drop my forehead to hers, overwhelmed by her, her heart and her love. Nothing I have done in my life warrants such a gift.

"I fucking love you."

"Never doubt, not for one second, that I fucking love you back."

She licks the shape of my mouth, and I open for her, sucking in her tongue. Tasting. Devouring. Taking.

We get a few catcalls from people coming out of the club on their way to their vehicles, but we ignore them.

"We can leave if you don't want to be here," she offers.

"If you want the honest truth, watching other

women who are not you grind on a pole isn't that appealing."

The grin that curves her mouth is as luminous as a ray of sunshine. "And if it was me?"

"Front row center, baby. What?" I ask when she laughs.

"I left that wide open for a dick reference. I'm kind of disappointed. You're off your game tonight, Mister Knight."

She bands her legs around me when I lift her up.

"You want to grind on my pole, dirty girl?"

I groan when she swivels her hips and rubs against my rock-hard dick.

With a seductive, husky rasp, she whispers in my ear, "I want you to fuck me."

The blunt nails of my fingers dig into her ass as lurid fantasies run rampant.

"Here?" I ask, thinking she's kidding.

She proves that she's very serious when she fits her hand between us and flicks open the button of my denims. I almost come in my pants when her clever fingers curve around my shaft and squeeze the tip. She swipes her thumb across the head, through the precum weeping out, and brings it to her mouth, sucking the digit like a fucking lollipop.

"Here," she replies.

Two men stumble their way into an Uber that just pulled in front of the club, and I take a quick glance around when their drunken laughter spills out into the night, a reminder that we're out in public. I may be a deviant, but I'm also a jealous, possessive asshole when it comes to her. If it were Con or Tristan, I'd have no problem, but the thought of another man looking at what's mine, wanting what's mine, makes me rabid.

Finding a more secluded spot, I walk us to the back of the lot and drop her onto the hood of a black Mercedes. The engine is still warm, so whoever just arrived shouldn't be returning anytime soon.

Syn yanks me down and latches onto my neck with a hard suck that makes my cock throb with desperate need.

"Off," she pants, wiggling her hips as she struggles to unfasten her jeans.

I bracket her waist. "Up."

She lifts her hips, and in one hard yank, I have her jeans and panties shucked down her legs and tossed to the ground.

Her throaty laughter echoes around us. "Well done."

"You ain't seen nothing yet."

Bending over her, I bunch the fabric of her shirt and lick a line up the middle of her torso from navel to sternum. Her smooth, soft skin tastes like vanilla. When I get to her luscious, full breasts, her pink-flushed nipples are too much to resist, and my tongue does wicked things to each one that have her moaning my name.

Her fingertips scrape along my scalp. "Hendrix. That feels so good."

I pin her hands above her head on the hood of the car. "I'm going to make you fly."

Her breath hitches when I stretch her out like a sacrifice on an altar. Syn arches her back, beckoning me to take what I want. My gaze travels the curves of her body dappled by moonlight. Her hair creates a crimson halo around her head, and stars reflect in her eyes, bringing out a hint of teal green in the blue of her irises.

Such a beautiful sight.

My mouth goes on a frenzy of exploration across her skin, her breasts, her stomach, and finally to her face where her plush lips welcome me. There's something about the way she kisses me that I've never felt before. No one has ever kissed me the way she does. It's meaningful and soul-shattering, and I'm smart enough to know that it's different with her because I love her. Messy, complicated, terrifying, wonderful love.

"In me now." She hooks her feet around my upper thighs and wiggles down the hood a few inches.

"Not yet."

"*Hendrix*," she whines, and I chuckle.

"Patience."

The heat of my breath cascades over her quivering stomach, inching closer to the heaven of her sweet cunt. I grab her ankles, spread her wide—and feast.

"*Fuck, yes!*" she shouts when I cover her pussy and thrust my tongue deep inside her.

She's so wet and ready, it doesn't take long for me to bring her to the cusp of orgasm. Seconds after I put my mouth on her, Syn explodes, my name falling from her lips in the most erotic way. I don't give her a chance to recover. I attack her clit again like it's my mission in life. I edge her over and over, building her up only to deny her the gratification she's desperate for.

"Dammit, Hendrix!" she says when I won't let her come.

With a devil may care grin, I lick her juices from my lips. "You need something, firefly?"

My naughty girl slips her hand between her legs and tries to get herself off.

"Nice try, sweetheart."

I flip her and push her down on top of the hood of the car. Her entire body shudders when I take out my cock and tease her clit with the metal barbell of my piercing.

"Please fuck me," she begs.

Such filthy words from my sweet angel.

In one punishing, effortless thrust, I'm seated fully inside her. I grit my teeth when her walls clamp down. So tight. Fucking paradise.

In a slow and unhurried tempo, I rock my hips, making sure to hit that sweet spot with my piercing that drives her crazy. I don't pay any heed to the people coming and going from the club. My entire focus is on her. Damn the world and everyone in it.

"Tell me you're mine," I demand.

Her fingernails gouge deep grooves into the black paint as I pound into her pussy. The owner isn't going to be happy.

"I'm yours, Hendrix. Only yours."

"Say you're mine forever."

"Yes. *Yes!*" she shouts.

Another deep thrust has her orgasm slamming into her. Her whole body locks tight, and she climaxes spectacularly.

That euphoria I only feel with her bursts out of me, and I moan as I come. She turns her head and kisses the side of my hand when I collapse on top of her.

This woman is my home and my heart.

I tenderly kiss her shoulder that bears the bites I gave her. "I love you."

CHAPTER 29

CONSTANTINE

The gym is filled with the sounds of punctuated grunts and the smell of testosterone-laden sweat. The musky stench is the first thing that hits you as soon as you walk into the place, but after a while, you get accustomed to it. Dusty beams of sunlight stream in through the glass walls that span the entire front part of the building and cast long, blocky shadows across the felt-covered rubber canvas of the center ring. Every person who walks through the doors either seeks a sanctuary where they can escape their lives for a few short hours, or they come in search of a battlefield where they can test themselves against a worthy adversary.

I come to release stress and hit shit.

Hendrix stands on the other side of the heavy bag and holds it steady for me. "I should bring Syn here again. She seemed to enjoy herself last time. But that was before."

He doesn't have to say what. It was before Aoife

came back. Syn was already a force to be reckoned with when she didn't remember who she was. Aoife is a whole other level of lethality. Beneath her sweet and kind exterior lies the potential for devastation. Syn's formidable strength is like a single atom, seemingly insignificant in its size. But that tiny atom harbors the explosive energy of an atomic bomb which has the power to obliterate everything in its path.

"She'd kick all our asses." And do it with both her hands tied behind her back and blindfolded.

My aggression unleashes a fast rhythm of punches until my arms burn with fatigue. I stop briefly to shake out the soreness and start again. Right hook, front jab, uppercut.

"She's still having nightmares."

I slam my fist into the bag hard enough to make Hen slide backward a good foot.

"I know."

Dumbass. We all sleep in the same bed with her.

I used to keep her nightmares at bay when she slept in my arms, but the last three nights, we've been startled awake by her screams. It fucking guts me that she's still hurting. Nothing we do seems to help, and though Dierdre means well, her hen-peck hovering is driving us batshit.

Breathing heavily, I use the back of my arm to wipe the sweat out of my eyes. "Your turn."

I lean against the bag to catch my breath as Hendrix strikes it at a slower pace. Each of his hits are measured and precise like he has all fucking day. Since their date, he's been acting more like the old Hendrix from our childhood. Calmer. Happier. I've heard him laugh more in the last two days than he's done in ten years.

He moves the bag out of the way. "I don't feel comfortable about going, not with your dad still lurking around somewhere."

That's a sore spot for me. I've chased down every lead, even had Jax look into it. Nothing. Not one fucking clue where my father is. Gabriel Ferreira is a ghost.

"You have to," I remind him.

Suspicions would be raised which might lead to the wrong person asking the right question if he doesn't give Patrick a public wake and play the grieving son who tragically lost his mother and father within weeks of one another. Tristan leaves for Boston on Saturday to keep up the same appearance for Francesco and Helena. Syn wants to go with them, and after a tense hour-long argument last night when she got back from working her shift at the Bierkeller, she finally agreed to stay in Darlington with me and Dierdre. The damn fire at the estate continues to make news, but we control the narrative and have been able to keep the spotlight, and the paparazzi, off us. For now. I have a feeling that will soon change.

Hendrix lets the bag drop and delivers a roundhouse kick. "I don't have to fucking like it."

I wouldn't either. He and Tristan have to deal with the businesses and family estates they inherited, whereas all the money I have is from a trust fund my grandfather gave me that my father could never touch. He tried. Many times.

Hendrix executes a flawless combo of punches. "I'll strangle the first person who tells me what a wonderful man he was and how much he'll be missed."

"Just smile and murder them in your mind. Don't do anything stupid."

He shoves the bag at me. "Thanks for the vote of confidence, fucker."

With his erratic behavior lately, my concern is warranted—and he'll be there by himself with no backup. Maybe Syn should go with him. I could go with Tristan. I dismiss the thoughts as soon as I think them. Syn's safety is our priority and keeping her here is where she'll be most protected.

I jerk my chin in the direction of the sparring ring that has become available. He holds the ropes for me to slip between, then follows me into the square. We're already warmed up and loose, so I start things off with a practice combo of punches that he blocks.

There are three important things about fighting. The first is to build muscle memory so your reflexes act on instinct. The second is to learn how to fall down and get back up. It's counterintuitive, but when your opponent gets you on the ground, it leaves you vulnerable and gives them the upper hand. The third thing is fight dirty.

"Have you noticed anything different about Syn?"

Hendrix gets distracted which allows me to fake a right, then sweep his feet out from under him. Using my leverage, I drop down, hook my forearm under his chin, and use my left leg to pin his right arm to the mat.

He taps out and sits up when I roll off him.

"Other than the nightmares, she seems fine. This morning in the shower, she asked me if I wanted to go to therapy with her."

I'd suggested it to her, so am fucking happy that she's thinking about doing it. Hen, too.

"Are you?"

He stares off into the distance, his chest rising and

falling. "I don't know how much good it'll do, but I'll go if it helps her."

I slap his back, so damn proud of him for taking that first step. First steps always lead to a second and third, and then before you know it, you've walked a mile.

"But that's not what you were referring to, is it?" he asks.

I fold my arms over my bent knees. "She's been crying a lot."

"Yeah."

"And throwing up."

"A few times, but yeah. No fever, so I don't think she's sick."

"She ate two steaks last night."

"I make a fucking awesome steak..." His mouth drops open. Closes. Opens. I think he's figured out what I'm getting at. "Oh shit. *Oh shit*. Oh shit!" He surprises me when the biggest smile spreads across his face. "She's pregnant?"

"I may be wrong," I quickly rush in. But I hope not.

I want a house full of our kids. I want a forever with her. But if kids are not what she wants right now, I'll support her a hundred fucking percent with whatever she decides.

"Syn's pregnant?"

Hen and I look over to see Evan standing at the side of the ring. And he doesn't look happy.

"You can fuck right off with the eavesdropping," Hen says, pushing off the floor to stand.

"It's not eavesdropping when you shout something to the entire room."

"It is when I'm not talking to you, jackass."

Hen climbs out of the ring and shoulder checks Evan

on his way to grab a towel from the stack. Evan sends Hendrix a fuck-you glare at his back.

"Syn's been looking for you. You ghosting her for a reason?" Hen says.

She said he didn't show up to lab Tuesday or work the reception desk this morning at Raquelle's dorm. She asked me to find out where he lived. Turns out, he lives off-campus in a small one-bedroom Craftsman leased under his father's name. Not what I expected the son of the head of the Irish mafia to live in. Or the financial aid. Maybe Cillian thought it was the best way for Evan to blend in. Just another regular college student. Not wealthy like the Society kids who attend Darlington. Protection through anonymity.

Evan shoves his hands into his front trouser pockets. "Had to do something for Dad. Is she really pregnant?"

I hop out and catch the towel Hen throws at me. My knee-jerk reaction is to tell him to mind his own business.

I don't know, I sign.

"I don't know ASL and don't insult me by pretending you can't talk because I heard you just now and when we were in Texas."

With his glasses and boy-next door charm, Evan may appear non-threatening, but I know better. He and Aleksander are very much alike in many ways, and it would be stupid to underestimate either one of them.

"She's not pregnant." It's not a lie because we don't know for sure.

"But you think she might be."

"That's not what he said." Hendrix signs the word for *dick*, and I peer down at my feet to hide my grin.

"Can you drop the attitude?"

"Nope."

He cants his head at the ceiling, like he's asking the higher power for divine intervention before mumbling, "What the hell she sees in you—"

"She works tonight if you want to drop by the Bierkeller and let her see you're alive and well," I interpose.

Without looking at his watch, he replies, "She gets out of class in a half hour. I'll catch her then. FYI, Dad is putting some of his men in place to watch her and Alana."

I hold my hand up to stop Hendrix from talking because I know whatever comes out of his mouth will include *no* and *fuck you*, neither of them helpful.

"Why?"

"Someone recognized Andie and Liam this weekend. Word is out about Syn's connection to the McCarthys and the Irish mafia. What in the hell were you thinking getting them involved? Our family has a lot of enemies."

That familiar rage bangs against the steel bars I continuously have to erect to contain it.

"We'll handle it."

"Yes, *we* will. Syn is family. McCarthy family, and we take care of our own."

CHAPTER 30

SYN

Me: Class done. Heading home.

Hendrix is the first to respond in the group chat.

Hendrix: Made spaghetti bolognaise, garlic bread, and a triple chocolate cake for dessert. Picked up some cookies and cream ice cream and a jar of dill pickles at the store.

He had my mouth watering until he mentioned pickles.

Me: Just the cake and ice cream. No pickles.

Hendrix: Be prepared. T and Dierdre are in the backyard. Yelling. Staying out of it. Con is babysitting to make sure things don't come to blows.

Oh, crap.

Me: Be there in 10.

As soon as I exit the auditorium, I see Evan waiting for me out in the hall. He doesn't smile when our gazes meet.

Strolling over to where he's leaning on the opposite wall, I lightly pinch his cheeks, then lift his arm and let it fall back down.

"What are you doing?"

"Making sure you're real and not a figment of my imagination."

Hazel eyes circle skyward. "Ha. Funny."

I punch him in the chest. "Where have you been?"

At least he looks contrite when he replies, "Had to do something for Dad."

"There are things called smartphones that send text messages."

He pulls out his phone. "Did you text? I didn't get anything."

"I also stopped by your house. I thought you lived in the dorms."

"Heck, no. Too noisy."

There's so much I don't know about Evan, but I'd like to. Distantly related or not, he's basically one of the only blood relatives I have left. Him and Andie and Cillian. I guess Declan as well. And Liam. And those guys, Lochlan and Seamus, who work for Andie. All of them are cousins to some degree.

Huh. I guess I have more family than I realized.

The strap of my bag slides off my shoulder. Evan catches it and pushes it back into place, his frowning gaze locked on the zipped-up collar around my neck. I'm suddenly pulled by the arm around the corner and dragged into the men's restroom.

"Evan—"

He tugs the zipper a fraction, and I slap his hand away, but not before he gets an eyeful of the bruise on my neck.

"Jesus, Syn. What in God's name happened?"

I pull the zipper back up. I've been so careful to hide it.

Alana hasn't even noticed.

"I'm fine. Things were a little crazy at the gala."

"I should have been there for you. I'm sorry I wasn't."

He cradles my face, his thumb brushing over the apple of my cheek. It feels too intimate, so I sidestep out of his way and go over to the sinks to wash my hands.

"Things happened. It's done. We're in control of the Council now."

He comes up behind me. He's not as tall as the guys, but he tops me by a couple of inches. I search our reflection in the mirror, trying to find any genetic resemblance—a mole or freckle or the shape of the eye or ear—but find none. Evan and I don't share any obvious phenotypes, but I doubt we would, given we're distant cousins, not first or second.

"I heard. And so did a lot of other people. That's what I wanted to talk with you about."

That doesn't sound good.

I turn around and prop my butt against the sink's edge. "Oh?"

When my bookbag slips down my arm again, this time he takes it and hooks it over his shoulder.

"One of our rivals, the Petrovs, a syndicate that controls half the Eastern block, knows you're one of us. Word travels fast in our world. With your new position of power in the Society, you're now a target for our enemies."

I'll talk to the guys and Aleksander. Put extra eyes and ears on things to find out more about the Petrovs. They would be stupid to come after the Society. It would start a war they would lose because we're not only global but are now aligned with the Rossis, Agostis, McCarthys, and Levines.

"Thanks for the head's up."

Evan slowly shakes his head. "Syn, you need to be careful. Aleksander has ties to the Petrovs. You can't trust him."

But I do. And trust isn't something I give freely. It has to be earned, and Aleksander has earned mine.

"I'll take that under advisement."

The restroom door pushes open. "Shit. Sorry. Didn't know it was occupied," a guy says.

"We're finished." I try to take my bag back from Evan, but he won't give it up.

"I'll walk you home," he insists.

The guy holds the door for us to pass. He must be Society because he keeps his head lowered and won't look me in the eye.

The humidity jacked up during the time I was in class. I'm sweating by the time we reach the bottom of the steps of the lecture hall. Fall doesn't officially begin until September twenty-third, so most of the month is this peculiar yo-yo of weather where summer and autumn duke it out. One day is nice and cool, the next, it's sweltering and hot. The only good thing about it is the changing of the leaves which has already begun.

"Hendrix will have supper ready when I get home since I work tonight. Stay and eat, and we can catch up. Alana would love to see you."

Evan stops in his tracks. "She's here?"

Suddenly feeling like I'm missing something, I reply, "You didn't know?"

He rakes his hands through his hair and makes the ends stand up in messy, odd angles. "No. Dad forgot to mention that tidbit of information." He starts walking again. "I hate how he expects me to do his bidding but refuses to tell me anything. Typical."

I'm not going to pry into his personal business. It's interesting that Andie and Alana sing Cillian's praises, but his own son feels alienated. Why can't parents just love their children? Full stop. Love them without any expectations or strings attached or make grandiose plans about their future instead of letting them find their own path.

"I'm having a big cookout at the house next weekend. Raquelle's boyfriend, Drake, is coming for homecoming. Open invitation if you like backyard barbecues."

He kicks a pinecone off the sidewalk that catches the interest of a busy squirrel. Immediately pouncing, it snags its prize and scampers off with it up a tree.

"I'd like that. There's a post-game party on fraternity row that Friday night after the game. I went last year. It was a lot of fun."

I've never been to a party before. Another rite of passage I'd like to check off my to-do list.

"We'll be at the football game. I'll talk to the guys about the party."

We step off the sidewalk onto the cushioned grass. It's just a short three-minute walk across an open community park to get to the house.

"You don't need their permission to go to a party, Syn."

"I'm not asking their permission."

I kind of am, but that's part of being in a relationship. It's not just myself to consider anymore, and I can't go off and do whatever the hell I feel like.

"You get to have your own friends and do stuff you want to do without them tagging along everywhere you go."

"I do. And they don't," I answer in order.

Grabbing his wrist, I pull him out of the line of sight of the door camera just as we reach the front walkway of the house. Constantine was finally able to repair the wiring massacre I created when I disabled the security system.

"Why are you ranting at me?"

"I'm not." He exhales an exasperated breath. "Sorry. Knight and Constantine said something that pissed me off and put me in a bad mood. I didn't mean to take it out on you."

I notice how he calls Hendrix by his last name and Constantine by his first.

"When?"

"At the gym earlier."

Raised voices carry from the backyard, including Cocky B's trumpeting crow.

Evan looks around, perplexed. "Is that a chicken?"

I smile with pride. "My pet rooster. He's better than any guard dog."

Cocky has excellent hearing and will make a racket if he senses anything that shouldn't be there.

Fisting one of the straps, I give Evan no choice but to return my backpack. "Maybe you should skip sticking around for supper. World War Three might erupt at any second. Rain check?"

With a crestfallen moue, he steps in front of me and kisses my cheek before I can evade it. My aversion to people in my personal space hasn't completely gone away. I'm getting better with the spontaneous hugs with Raquelle.

"We could catch a movie this weekend if you're up for

it."

I breathe easier when he takes two steps back.

"I can't. I already have plans tomorrow night and Saturday, and Tristan and Hendrix will be out of town."

"When are they coming back?"

"Sunday night."

He bumps my foot with his shoe. "I'll be around. Call me. Anytime for any reason, even just to talk."

Evan is such a nice guy, seemingly untainted by the mobster world he grew up in. I hope he never loses that part of himself.

"I will. And thank you. For everything."

He rushes back into my space and embraces me in a tight hug. "I will always protect you, Syn. Always."

Mired in contemplation, I wait until he crosses the yard and heads into the park before I go inside the house.

Standing at the end of the counter island, Hendrix raptly stares out the open back door. I cuddle up to him, nuzzling my nose into his shirt because he smells delectable.

"Are they still alive?" I ask.

He curves his hand around my waist to rest across my stomach.

"See for yourself."

I follow his gaze, and happiness explodes like a glitter cannon as I watch Tristan and Alana hug. I think it's the first time I've seen them touch one another. There's been a lot of distance and enmity between them lately, and I hope that whatever is transpiring in the backyard is the catalyst that will lead to them repairing their relationship.

Sniffling, I lift my arm and wipe the tears off on my

jacket sleeve.

"You emotional, baby girl?"

"A little."

A dill pickle spear appears in front of my face, and I bite into it before realizing what it is. It's really good, and I'm really hungry, so I eat the entire thing.

"I'm starving. Where's the ice cream?"

Hendrix bursts out laughing, then proceeds to kiss the ever-living hell out of me.

CHAPTER 31

SYN

Collapsing onto the bar stool like a woman rung dry, Shelby groans in relief. "My feet are killing me."

We have an hour to go before our shift ends, but things have thankfully quieted down after a very busy night.

"You need this more than I do."

I pass her the glass of sweet iced tea I just made, and she guzzles it like water.

"I think it's the first night you haven't gotten beer spilled on you."

I reply to that with an amused chuckle. There are some perks that come with people being terrified of you. No more unwanted grabby hands trying to feel up my ass, no more spilled beer, and an added bonus —very generous tips. I made over five thousand dollars tonight. Something I cannot report to Keith without rousing questions. I turned in a hundred of it and will put the rest in an interest-bearing account I'll open in Shelby's son's name. Never too early to start planning for college or whatever he wants to do when he grows up. Once I find out what happened to my inheritance, I hope to add significantly to the account, so that Christian is set for life.

"Miracles do happen," I reply. "What trouble has Christian been getting into?"

Every time anyone mentions her son's name, she lights up with such joy, it's infectious.

"I think I may need to call an exorcist."

Playing along, I reply, "Why?"

She takes out her phone from the front pocket of her server's waist apron and flips through a slideshow of pictures she took of Christian with a rainbow of colors all over him—and the walls and the floor and the sofa.

I giggle. "Oh, no."

"Oh, yes. My son has been possessed by Picasso. It took me and Mom most of a day to clean it up. Thank god for non-toxic, water-based fingerpaints."

Cheers erupt from the back corner table of guys as they celebrate a touchdown from the game being replayed on the large screen.

"What happened to your boyfriends?" she asks.

It's pretty clear to everyone that I'm dating all three guys, and not once has anyone acted weird about it.

"Hendrix had to go to New York."

She pitches in and helps me refill sweetener packets. I have a specific way I like the colors to show in the dishes. White, pink, blue, yellow.

"No, the other ones."

Tristan is with Alana. She decided to stay at my studio apartment. She didn't come right out and say it, but she wasn't comfortable being in the house and hearing me... well, us, and... sex, so yeah.

Constantine was here but left. I noticed two men hanging around and recognized one immediately as the guy who Cillian had watching over Raquelle. Evan really needs to talk to him about being less conspicuous, and I really need to talk to Evan to find out why Cillian has men shadowing me. Not after tonight if Constantine has anything to say about it.

"Tristan is hanging with a friend, and Constantine will be back to pick me up."

She reaches past me to grab the white sugar packets. "I like your friend, Raquelle."

Raquelle stopped by earlier, but we were so swamped, she didn't stick around for long.

"Me, too."

Finished with the sweetener dishes, we start on rolling utensils in large paper napkins.

"Let's plan to do a girls' night sometime. It'll be nice to get out and have a conversation with an adult. I love my kid, but I need some grown-up time that doesn't involve fingerpaints or potty training."

"Thanks for reminding me."

"About potty training? Do I even want to ask which one?"

She says it so deadpan, it takes me a second to get the joke, and when I do, I can't stop laughing. It wasn't even that funny.

"Cookout next Saturday at the house. Bring Christian."

She makes an *eek* face. "You sure? He can be a handful, and that's on his good days."

"Absolutely."

I'm actually looking forward to having a house filled with noise and people and kids... well, one kid...

running around.

She acknowledges the table that waves her down. A guy holds up three fingers to indicate another round of beer for him and his two friends.

"Three more pints for table six," she calls to Keith, who's working the bar.

"Don't go anywhere," he tells me as he pours the drafts and hands them to her.

I busy myself by wiping down the bar, so he doesn't have to. There's not much to do since my section is empty and the only people left are watching the game.

"See if this is okay." He produces a printout and slides it across the bar top.

I stare at the rows and columns of a work schedule. Every Monday and Wednesday for the month is blocked out between six p.m. and nine p.m.

"Who's this for?"

"You."

I frown at the piece of paper, then at him.

"I work Wednesdays, Fridays, and Saturdays."

The only reason I'm here tonight is because Keith was short-staffed and needed a fill-in.

He throws his hand towel over one shoulder and leans his elbows on the bar. The bar lights play a muted kaleidoscope over his shaved head. I finally remembered the name of the actor I thought he looked like. Keith is a burlier, lumber-jack version of Bruce Willis.

"You don't like it?"

Having my weekends completely free? Who wouldn't like that?

"Well, yeah, but—"

Pleased, he taps the wood with his knuckles and gets

back to work. "Then it's settled."

I follow him down the bar where he stops at the register.

"I don't understand. Weekends are your busiest times. Don't you need me here?"

He looks around and motions for Dirk, a new hire who started two weeks ago. I've barely spoken three words to him because our schedules hardly ever align.

"Announce last call in ten minutes," Keith tells him.

"You got it." Dirk flashes me a flirtatious grin, but I noticed that he did that with every female he encountered tonight.

He's already scored four phone numbers, and if the moony-eyed redhead at the end of the bar has anything to say about it, she'll be leaving with him when he gets off work.

"My office," Keith says, and by his brusque tone, I'm left wondering if I did something wrong.

Keith has been acting weird all night, and now, he gave me a new schedule with fewer working hours. To me that sounds like he's upset with me or about to fire me. It shouldn't come as a surprise since I've been unexpectedly gone a lot the last two weeks.

"Okay," I hedge.

I follow him to the back office. Every time I walk down this hallway, I remember the first night I literally ran into Tristan. He was so arrogant and cocky and handsome. That one small encounter changed my life. I like to think of it as a promise fulfilled. My heart found theirs again.

He unlocks the door and waits for me to enter before closing it. The lock clicks into place. Going over to where I store my bag while I work, I untie my waist apron and hang it on the hook. Keith ambles behind his messy desk stacked with bills, receipts, and purchase orders he hasn't yet filed, and sits down in his oversized leather armchair. With steepled fingers and a serious expression, he waits for me to take a seat.

Suddenly feeling like a kid under her father's reproachful gaze, I wipe my hands down my jeans and lower myself into the chair across from him.

"Do I need to apologize for anything or plead my case? I really like my job here, and I love working with Shelby and having you as a boss. You've been so kind to me, and I'm so sorry I've been absent a lot lately. I promise to do better. Please don't fire me."

I can stand in front of a room full of the wealthiest, most intimidating members of the Society and not feel one ounce of nervousness, but one staid look from Keith has me rambling like an idiot.

Picking up the framed photograph of his wife and two daughters, his chair creaks when he sits back. He reverently touches their happy faces through the glass before putting the frame back in its place.

"Thirty years ago, I was not the man I am now."

Unsure of what he's getting at, I ask, "What kind of man were you?"

He slides a silver letter opener from the desktop and manipulates it between his fingers, much like a magic coin trick. It floats over his knuckles. Under, over, under, over.

He stares at me long and hard to the point I get very uncomfortable.

"A dangerous one."

I tense at his implied threat.

Please don't.

Please don't be another false face. He's a good man. He adores his daughters. He works long hours to provide for his family. But I know better than anyone how appearances can be deceiving, and the persona you show to the public is not who you really are.

"Keith—"

"I built an empire from death. Made a fortune as an assassin for hire. I didn't care who I killed as long as the money was good. And the money was always good," he emphasizes.

Keith may be twice my size, but I've killed much bigger men than him when I was a little girl. I took out a dozen guards at the compound without hesitation or mercy.

"And how much are you being paid to kill me?"

His brow furrows. "You think I want to kill you?"

If he wants to confuse me, he's doing an excellent job.

"Then what's the point of the monologue?"

His face breaks out in the biggest smile. Keith never smiles.

"I was trying to give you a little backstory so you would understand."

Feeling like I'm on a merry-go-round going nowhere, I ask, "Understand what exactly?"

He shifts his big body and reaches for something under the desk. Not giving him a chance to go for a hidden weapon, I hurtle over the desk. My momentum tips him backward in his chair, the crash resonating with a loud crack against the wall when I land on his chest. I snatch the letter opener from his hand and press the rounded, dulled point into his neck at the carotid artery. He doesn't even flinch.

"I never took you for a stupid man, so do not fuck

with me."

"You'd be wrong about my ignorance, otherwise, I would have known exactly who you were the moment you walked through the door—Aoife Fitzpatrick."

Blood begins to ooze when I break through the skin. "How do you know my name?"

"If you stop trying to decapitate me, I'll tell you."

I increase the pressure. "Tell me now."

"You were never this hostile as a child."

He knew me as a child? *Shit.* Is he Society?

Keith uses my momentary distraction to disarm me. He tosses the letter opener across the room.

"James was a good friend. I am not going to harm you, Aoife. Can we please talk now?"

He doesn't move when I set my feet on the floor and create several feet of distance between us. Once I'm far enough away, he carefully rights his chair and uses the square napkin his coffee cup is sitting on to wipe the blood from his neck.

"I'm listening."

He holds up one burly hand. "I'm going to get something from the drawer. I promise it's not a gun."

I give him a nod to proceed. "Slowly. No sudden movements."

"I know."

He takes a worn, frayed-edge photograph from the drawer and places it on the edge of the desk. I'm in disbelief when I see him standing next to Papa in the photo. Keith has hair.

"I used to be Society. James helped me get out. A clean break. New life. Even though I'm no longer part of that world anymore, I still have connections. I hear things. I heard about what happened at the gala. How in the hell are you alive? Are your parents—"

"No. They're dead. I'm only here because someone pulled me from the fire." I pick up the photo. It looks real. Not AI or photoshopped. "You used to be Society?"

He said he was, but I ask again anyway.

"Yes. A long time ago. I left when you were..." He looks up as he does the math. "Three, I think. You look so different."

"So I've been told. Why did you leave?"

Keith glances at the picture frame. "I met a wonderful woman and fell in love. I wanted my life to be with her. I wanted a family. I couldn't have that if I stayed, so James made sure it happened. Your father was a good man, Aoife. I'm so sorry for your loss."

I walk to the other side of the office, still wary and unsure. Keith just dropped a revelation bomb on me. Another crater added to the multitude that already potmarks my psyche.

"Thank you. Why live in Darlington?" I ask because if he fully wanted out of the Society, he picked the wrong town to live in.

"My wife, Evelyn, was from here. It was her home. She loved it here, and I loved her. It was an easy choice."

That's really very sweet. You can tell the merit of a man by the way he loves his woman. It isn't just about saying the words to her every day, you also have to show her.

"So, the Bierkeller?"

This time, his grin comes swiftly. "I'd always wanted to own my own bar. It's not much, but it's mine. It's allowed me to live a normal life, be a good husband and a good dad. You would have loved Evelyn. She used to teach kindergarten. The sweetest woman you'd ever meet. She saved me."

We don't talk about it, but everyone who works here knows that his wife died from breast cancer three years ago.

It's amazing how someone can come into your life and change it in the most unexpected ways. How love can be transformative and make you a better person. Keith found that kind of love with Evelyn. I found it with Constantine, Tristan, and Hendrix. I'd like to think that Papa and Mama found it with each other.

Keith lifts his massive body from the chair. "You can walk away, Aoife. If it's not what you want, just walk away. James would want you to. He'd want you to be happy."

Thoughts of my father flood my subconscious. His features are more prominent, not as blurred anymore. Having pictures of him and Mama have helped keep what they used to look like fresh in my memories.

"Please call me Syn. Aoife's dead."

"If that's what you want."

"It is."

Like Morse code, he *tap-taps* the photograph on the desk with his finger. "I owe James a debt. If you ever need me to repay it, I will."

His meaning is obvious. He'll become the man he used to be. I just have to say the word.

"About that new schedule."

His belly laugh is deep but brief. "You don't have to work here, but if you decide to stay, you make your own hours. God knows, you have enough on your plate."

I want to work here. Like he wanted a normal life, I want the same kind of normalcy. I can't let the Society take over and become my entire existence.

"Mondays and Wednesdays are perfect."

CHAPTER 32

SYN

"Do you think she'll be okay by herself?"

Tristan enters the code to disable the alarm as soon as we walk into the house. He came with Constantine to pick me up from work when my shift ended.

"She'll be fine. Cillian's men will be lurking around to make sure."

With my arm halfway out of the sleeve of the sports jacket, I turn around. "I'm calling him tomorrow. I don't care if we're related, he can't keep doing stuff without talking to me first."

Peeling out of my clothes until I'm in nothing but my T-shirt and undies, I pad into the kitchen. Ice cream is calling my name. I need the sugar infusion to sustain me through a couple hours of studying.

"I actually don't mind. It's free security we don't have to pay for."

I place my palm on his forehead.

His eyes rove upward. "What are you doing?"

"Seeing if you have a fever because there is no way

you'd be so amicable about this, therefore, you must be delusional with fever."

He removes my hand and sucks my index finger into his mouth. The tug and pull of his tongue have my belly swooping violently with desire.

"I can promise you, Red, I feel just fine. You, however, look a little peaked."

A demure blush tints my cheeks pink, and he laughs. I catalog it into memory with the other smiles and laughs they've given me, each one special and wonderful.

Tristan smacks a playful kiss to my lips. "You are so damn cute."

"Ice cream," I reply.

"Already on it. How many scoops?"

Constantine puts out three bowls on the counter island, along with what's left in the half-gallon container of cookies and cream.

"Two really big ones. And whipped cream. Do we still have that bag of chocolate chips?" I ask, going inside the pantry to find it.

"Shelf on the left."

"Where?" I ask when I don't see it.

"Top."

I go up on tiptoe.

"Higher," Constantine says.

I don't see it.

"Are you messing with me so you can stare at my ass?"

Finding the chocolate chips on the middle shelf, I grab it and the bag of mini marshmallows.

"You've got a very fine ass," he replies and lightly swats it as I walk out of the pantry.

"Babe, you want a beer?" Tristan asks.

"No beer." Constantine deftly grabs the bottle Tristan offers me and puts it back into the fridge.

"I was going to say no," I tell him.

Beer and ice cream are two things that do not go together. Beer with pizza. Yes. Root beer and ice cream. Also yes.

Going back to the conversation we were having on our way home, I ask, "When did you find out about Keith?"

It makes sense now why the guys and Keith were on such friendly terms that went beyond them being merely regular patrons at the Bierkeller.

Constantine doubles the size of the scoop of ice cream before plopping the large ball into my bowl. "The first night we walked into the bar."

Tristan sprays out a generous mountain of whipped topping in each bowl, while I sprinkle on chocolate chips.

"He said if we brought any trouble to his bar, he didn't care who our daddies were, he'd kick our asses."

"And to stay the fuck away from his daughters or he'd castrate us," Tristan adds.

"He said that to Hendrix," Constantine reminds him.

Tristan licks his spoon clean, and my damn pussy clenches.

"They're teenagers," I state, which would've made them preteens when the guys started Darlington Founders.

"Teenagers now, but women when they grow up. And the *royal we* was very apparent. He may have said it to Hen, but he meant it for all mankind." Tristan's phone vibrates. "Speaking of Hen."

Ice cream forgotten, I swipe his phone. My ecstatic heart soars as soon as the screen lights up with Hendrix's face.

"Hey!"

The top buttons of his dress shirt are undone, allowing me a tantalizing glimpse of his inked chest. The ends of his dark-blue tie hang loose on either side. He tamed his hair with a clean side part and shaved. Reclined against the headboard, Hendrix Knight is the epitome of sexy, billionaire bad boy.

"There's my gorgeous girl. Miss you like crazy."

"I miss you, too. Are you sure you don't want me there? I could take one of the private jets."

The flight from here to New York is short. I could stay a day, then fly to Boston to be with Tristan.

Hendrix shakes his head. "As much as I want you with me, it's safer there. You'd hate it anyway. Nothing but sycophants and lawyers."

He looks worn out. Dark half-moons line his undereye, making the blue of his irises stand out more.

"You ready for the wolves to descend, brother? You get to experience this hell all weekend," he says to Tristan.

I prop the phone against my bowl, so Hendrix can see us both.

Absentmindedly coiling a lock of my hair around his finger, Tristan lets it unwind. "No, but it has to be done."

"Work go okay?" Hendrix asks.

I bite on my bottom lip. "I may have physically assaulted my boss."

He sits up. "Keith?"

"Uh-huh."

Seeing the anger about to geyser out, Tristan rushes

to explain. "It's all good. He told her who he was."

The tension gouging lines into Hendrix's face disappears. "You beat Keith up? The man is a brickhouse. I'm even afraid of going toe-to-toe with him."

I hold my finger and thumb an inch apart. "Maybe a tiny bit. In my defense, I thought he was going for a gun."

He emits a throaty laugh. "Botched it up that bad, huh?"

I shrug. "Like Tristan said, it's all good now. When are you coming back?"

"Late Sunday. Tomorrow is the wake, then on Saturday, I've got to check on the repairs at the estate. I'll come back to New York that afternoon and deal with the staff here, so I can close up the penthouse. I'm talking to a realtor tomorrow evening. I want to put it on the market as soon as all the legal shit is taken care of. Bryce went over the will with me this afternoon. I get everything."

"Did you doubt that you would?" Tristan inquires as he eats.

I grab my bowl and dig in. It's basically a milkshake now.

"Yeah, I did. It would've been just like Patrick to stick it to me in death. Then again, he had no idea it was coming, so no impetus to change the will."

The ice cream I'd been thoroughly enjoying settles like lead in my stomach. "Can we talk about that stuff later?"

"Hey, man," Constantine says, getting in the huddle in front of the phone's camera lens.

"You assholes are making me hungry. Is everybody

eating ice cream?"

I hold my spoon up for him to see. "With all the toppings except hot fudge."

Hendrix gets a ribald twinkle in his eyes. "Are you enjoying that ice cream, sweetness?"

It's not the term of endearment but the way he says it that knocks a hole of lust straight through me.

I suggestively slide my tongue around the spoon and lick it clean. "It's *really* good."

Hendrix lies back on the pillows, and I get a top-down view of him in bed. "How good?"

Holding the spoon up, I dribble drops of ice cream over my tongue, intentionally spilling some. Frosty wetness soaks through my T-shirt.

"Oops. I'm a little messy. Let me take care of this."

Standing back far enough that he gets a full frontal view, I wiggle out of my shirt, which draws Constantine's and Tristan's rapt attention.

With a seductive twist of my wrist, I release the clasps to my black lace bra, sliding it down to reveal a scintillating peek of cleavage.

Hunger flares in Hendrix's cobalt gaze. "Fuck, firefly. You make me so hard."

"Show me."

The camera pans down his body and lingers on the very obvious bulge of his trousers. My own desire ignites, and my pussy clamps down with unfulfilled need when he strokes himself. I watch with bated breath as he brings the camera back to his face. I know I'm in trouble when a cocky smirk curves his lips.

"T, you hungry for more dessert?"

My heart races when Tristan's whiskey eyes pin me in place. "Starving."

"Don't you dare," I warn him, laughing, when he grabs the canister of whipped topping and gives it a shake.

He takes a predatory step forward, and I try to retreat but am stopped by a solid wall of tattooed muscle. Constantine shreds my bra from my grasp, his calloused hands molding to my breasts and tweaking my nipples until they bead into stiff peaks.

Tristan sprays out a dollop of whipped cream on his fingertip. "Open."

His pupils dilate when I suck his finger into my mouth.

"Good girl," he praises.

He covers my nipples in creamy, white foam, and I gasp at the unexpected shock of cold against my sensitive flesh. The jolting sensation is compounded by the hot sear of his mouth as he torments me with slow, sensual flicks of his tongue.

My moan echoes around the kitchen when Constantine slips his hand under my panties, his fingers delving deep between my slick folds. They manipulate my pleasure with ease, and I freefall into the journey they take me on.

Stepping closer, Tristan gently strokes my cheek, his touch feather-light and his gaze intense. His breath fans across my lips as he gently presses his thumb against them, tempting a response. My mouth opens, and Tristan's lips crash down onto mine, his tongue thrusting deep. I arch against him, succumbing to his possession, while also seeking the orgasm Constantine's fingers are promising.

"Con, let's see how sweet our girl tastes," Hendrix says.

I whimper in protest when I'm suddenly pulled away and lifted by the hips. Once the counter island is cleared, Constantine lays me out like a sinful feast.

Tristan aims the phone at me, giving Hendrix a clear view.

"This seems familiar," he says, referring to what happened in Texas.

His arm moves in and out of camera view with measured strokes. Just the thought of his hand around his inked cock, touching himself, has liquid desire soaking my panties.

"I wish I was there with you, baby girl."

I run my hands over my breasts and down my stomach to the belly chain. "What would you do if you were here right now?"

Hendrix lets his fantasy play out as he describes in vivid detail every filthy thing he would do to me.

"I'd want to mark you."

I tilt my head to expose my neck. "Here?"

Constantine crawls up onto the countertop, fitting himself between my thighs as he hovers over me. The corded muscles of his arms bulge when he lowers, his lips poised at my pulse point.

"I would kiss you there, then move lower."

Constantine follows Hendrix's instructions, kissing a path down my neck to my breast.

"I'd French kiss your gorgeous tits, making sure to graze your nipples with my teeth."

My fingers play through Constantine's hair, holding on as he does wonderful things to me with his mouth.

"T, let me see her tits."

Constantine pulls back to give Tristan an unobstructed view for the phone.

"Fucking perfect. Your nipples look like the sweetest red berries. I'd feast on your tits, biting each one. Can you feel my mouth on you, firefly?"

"God, yes," I moan, the image playing like a movie behind my closed eyelids.

I feel Hendrix's remote presence as if he's physically there, whispering his desires in my ear.

My back slides across the granite when Constantine dismounts and pulls me to him. He props one foot on his shoulder and kisses up the other leg, his mouth branding my skin with every press of his lips.

"Bite her inner thigh, right there," Hendrix says.

I cry out when Constantine nips his teeth into my quivering flesh, flying high on the pinch of pain that melds perfectly with the pleasure.

"How wet is she?"

Cold air washes over my pussy when Constantine removes my underwear.

"Soaking," he relays, nuzzling his nose through my pubic hair. "She smells like vanilla."

"I need to see."

Tristan angles the phone directly above my pussy, his gaze feral. The sexual tension in the room is barely contained and about to break. It vibrates through me with the power of an earthquake.

"Use your fingers. T, bring the camera closer."

Constantine does as he's told. The throbbing between my legs intensifies. *So good. So fucking good.* He pushes a finger into me, then two, then three. Dear god, the stretch is unimaginable, like I'm a helium balloon about to pop under the pressure.

"Suck her clit. Eat her. Fuck her cunt with your tongue. Make her come."

As soon as Constantine puts his mouth on me, the dam bursts, and I'm thrown into a state of rapture as I explode.

"You're so beautiful, Syn. Again, love. I need one more."

"Oh, god!" I scream when Constantine opens me wide and buries his cock deep inside me.

My hips buck and convulse with the electric thrill of constant stimulation. My spine bows off the cold granite surface with his punishing thrusts. He keeps up his relentless attack, never wavering, never stopping until I can no longer hold back.

When I climax a second time, it hits suddenly, made endless when Constantine follows right behind me.

"Syn," Hendrix moans, giving in to his own orgasm.

The phone clatters to the countertop near my ear, and I welcome Tristan when he takes Constantine's place between my legs.

In one smooth push, he enters me.

"Ready for me, Red?"

"Always, Boston."

This is my paradise, and I'm drowning in it.

The way these men love me is like the most magnificent watercolor painted upon the canvas of my soul. Love isn't merely the flutter of butterfly wings or the pounding of excited heartbeats; it's a transformative force that sculpts us into better versions of ourselves. Through their unwavering belief in my worth, I discovered a courage I never knew existed. With each shared moment, with every kiss and touch and word spoken, they're the mirror through which I no longer see my flaws, only my strengths. They inspire me to strive for greatness. To be more than I ever dreamed possible. Love has the ability to turn the ordinary into the extraordinary, and the broken into the beautiful.

CHAPTER 33

SYN

"Wake up, sleepyhead."

I burrow deeper into Tristan. "Five more minutes."

Hendrix's morning-husked chuckle is distant and barely audible. "That's what you said five minutes ago. You have class, baby doll, and I have an impatient lawyer waiting for me downstairs. Wakey, wakey."

Rousing enough to grab the phone wedged between Tristan and me, I hold it to my ear, not caring that it's on speaker and will probably deafen me.

"I'm up," I yawn out.

I fell asleep last night to Hendrix reading *Romeo and Juliet*. I love that he found a way to be with us, even if he couldn't physically be here with us.

"Morning, sunshine. Miss you," he says.

"Miss you more," Tristan mockingly replies, rolling on top of me. "Now bugger off so I can wake her up properly."

"Bugger off? Is my snooty British rubbing off on you?"

I fly into a fit of giggles when Tristan snuffles my neck.

"Seems so."

My giggles turn into moans when he slithers down my body.

"No time for that. She's going to be late to calc," Constantine says, walking into the bedroom, carrying a tray of coffee and pastries.

I wiggle out from under Tristan and make grabby hands for the coffee.

"Seriously?" Tristan bemoans.

I pat his naked chest as I take my first sip of gloriously scalding caffeine. "Morning orgasms will have to wait. Coffee comes first. What time is it?"

"Quarter after seven," Hendrix says.

I have a half hour to eat, shower, and dash to class.

Constantine sets the tray down on the bed, and I immediately shove a raspberry-filled cronut into my mouth.

"Did you get everything set up?" Hendrix asks.

"I did," Tristan replies.

He wipes a smear of raspberry filling from the corner of my mouth with his pinky, and I bring it to my lips, licking it off.

"What did you set up?" I ask and go for the apple strudel. "These are good. Where did you get them?"

Constantine tears off a piece of my puff pastry and pops it into his mouth. "Bakery off Chestnut."

"That place sucks," Hendrix chimes in, but he would say that about anything he doesn't make himself.

"What did you set up?" I prod.

Tristan kisses the apple-cinnamon filling off my mouth. "You'll find out tonight."

My grin is a mile wide. Date night with Tristan is tonight, something I'm absurdly excited about. I've known the three of them since I was a child, yet everything with them now seems new and unexpected—kind of like the excitement a kid feels on Christmas morning when they get to see what Santa brought them.

"Hint?" I ask anyway, knowing he's not going to give one.

"Nope."

I press quick kisses to his and Constantine's lips, then hop off the bed and dash into the bathroom to get ready. The area on my shoulder has scabbed over nicely. I don't need to gauze it anymore, but I do need to keep the bruise around my neck covered. It's changed from purple to greenish-yellow. A few more days, and I should be able to conceal it completely with makeup.

After a fast, four-minute shower, I throw my hair up in a wet bun and swipe a little mascara on my lashes.

"I put a clean running shirt on the bed for you. High, zip-up collar," Constantine says.

"Thanks."

He saunters in and stands directly behind me. Every part of me is aware of him. His body heat, his natural musk, his touch as he skates a hand over the curvature of my hipbone to my abdomen.

"Any nightmares last night?"

Our eyes meet in the mirror. They've been worried about me. Hell, *I've* been worried about me. But since I finally reconciled Aoife with Syn, I've been better. Not perfect, but I'm getting there. It's all about the baby steps.

"If I did, I don't remember, so yay."

His fingers flex over my naval and goose bumps scatter like falling stars. "Nausea?"

"Nope." I smear on a little matte lipstick and twist around to look up at him. He's in those fucking hot black boxer briefs, so my hands naturally gravitate to that delicious vee that demarcates his six-pack abs.

"Can I ask you about something?"

He drags his thumbs across the ridge of my clavicle. "You know you can ask me anything."

"About the Red Room."

Tristan booms from the bedroom, "You told her about the Red Room? Does Hendrix know that she knows?"

Constantine quirks a questioning brow in askance.

"I was going to ask him about it the other night. That was the whole point of going to the strip club."

Tristan appears on the other side of the open doorway. "When did you go to a strip club?"

"I told you…" I blink, and blink again. "I didn't tell you?" I say when he frowns. "I meant to. And in my defense, Hendrix and I didn't go into one. Just the parking lot."

"Now I'm confused as fuck."

I slide past him and hurry into the clothes Constantine left out for me.

"My date night with Hendrix. I thought going to a strip club would be fun. I had planned to broach the subject of the Red Room with him, but we got sidetracked."

"By what?" Constantine asks.

My face goes up in tattletale flames when I recall what Hendrix and I did in the parking lot. There will be things I do with each guy that are private and belong between the two of us, not the four of us.

"Syn, you need to tell him you know," Tristan says.

"I will."

"Don't be surprised if he flips the fuck out."

Sitting on the edge of the bed, I take great pains to tie an intricate double knot in the laces of my tennis shoes.

Keeping my eyes downcast at what I'm doing, I ask, "Has he, uh… has he gone there recently?"

I get a very emphatic hard no in stereo, and relief thunders down over me like a rainstorm.

"I want to go. All of us."

I'm met with dual stunned expressions and gaping mouths. *Okay, then.*

Heading into my room, I grab my backpack. I've got ten minutes to hoof it across campus.

Tristan and Constantine trail after me down the stairs. "Red, you can't say something like that and let it just hang there."

"We can talk about it tonight."

"Babe," Constantine says as I open the front door—

And run right into Alana.

"Oh, hey! I've got to get to cla—"

Her enraged glare locks onto Tristan. "Aleksander Stepanoff is our fucking *brother*?" she shouts.

CHAPTER 34

S Y N

Sitting on the grass in the quad, I tip my face up to the cloudless sky to soak in the golden rays of the afternoon sun. It's a good day. A great day in fact. I found out this morning that Serena left DF. The good senator sent her ass to Arles, France to live with her mother.

"He won't even give a little hint about where he's taking you tonight?" Raquelle asks, shuffling through her bag's contents.

Her art lecture let out early, and we ran into each other as I was on my way back to the house after my last class.

I swat away a bee that keeps buzzing around my face. "Only to dress casually and wear sneakers."

"Found it!" She holds up sheets of notebook paper in victory and passes them to me.

"Thank you so much. You are the most wonderful friend in the world."

I glance through her calculus notes. Alana's surprise visit this morning derailed me, and I didn't make it to class because I was too busy refereeing the fight she and Tristan got into. However, my question about whether Alana knew about Aleksander is finally answered. She didn't. I'm going to murder Evan. I don't know how he found out about that well-guarded secret, but he spilled it all over Alana this morning when they spoke. *I'd* like to speak with him as well—if he'd answer his damn phone or return my texts. He told Alana that Cillian needed him in New York today. Something to do with a guy named Dante, who works for Keane.

"How weird is it that your mom is your boyfriend's sister?" She cracks up laughing.

My face screws up with disgust. "When you put it that way, it sounds incestuous."

I told her about Alana and Tristan and their recent tempestuous relationship that I thought they were reconciling. If there's anyone I trust as a confidant other than the guys, it's Raquelle. You never know how much you need something until you have it. I can tell the guys anything, but it's nice to have another woman to talk to—someone else who isn't my adoptive mother. Unfortunately, I can't tell Raquelle *everything*. Maybe someday. Maybe never. But I hope it's the former.

"Switching subjects, are you excited about next weekend?"

Raquelle enthusiastically bounces in place. "I can't freaking wait. We talk all the time and video, but it's not the same as being with him, you know?"

I pluck a four-leaf clover from the small patch growing beside me and tuck it behind her ear. "Hendrix has only been gone a day, and my heart already aches. You haven't seen Drake in weeks."

She removes the clover and twirls it by the stem.

"It's been hard, but we knew it would be. Long distance relationships suck."

And here comes the guilt. I've been so preoccupied with all my drama, I haven't been there for her like she has for me.

"I'm a shit friend for being absent so much."

She bumps my shoulder. "No, you aren't. Your life is busier than mine. You have three guys to juggle, work, and school. All I do is paint all day. Not a hardship by any means."

Not liking her self-deprecating putdown, I reply, "Your talent and your art are amazing. You inspire me to pursue my dreams."

She clicks her tongue. "Aww. Getting all the feels."

"I'm serious. That oil painting you did with all the different reds, I want it if you ever decide to sell it."

She said she painted it with me in mind. My hair was her muse.

She gawks at me, and her brown eyes appear huge behind her glasses. "Are you serious?"

"Of course I'm serious. Don't you dare cry," I say when her eyes fill to overflowing.

Whipping off her glasses, she wipes the moisture from her lashes. "It's just... no one has ever said that to me."

Surprised, I ask, "Not even Drake?" Surely, he and her family support her art.

She makes a *pfft* sound. "I love that man, but an art connoisseur he is not. He's proud of me, supports me one hundred percent, but he doesn't get it, if that makes sense. When he looks at the stuff I do, all he sees is a bunch of colors, not the message or the emotion it evokes. Art is alive. It's supposed to make you feel."

As she talks, she waves her hands around animatedly. She's so passionate about what she does. She *loves* what she does. When I become a doctor, will I have that same passion and love for my job? I hope so. I want to be someone's inspiration.

Raquelle presses the four-leaf clover between the pages of her art history textbook. "Hate to run but I have to get to the art store before they close, and you have a date to get ready for."

We both stand up at the same time and brush errant broken blades of grass from our legs.

"Shelby wants to do a girls' night soon. You in?"

"I met her last night, right? The dark-haired single mom."

I sling the strap of my pack over my shoulder. "That's her."

My phone vibrates against my leg where I have it stored in the side zipper pocket of my sports leggings.

Raquelle gives me a hug. "That sounds like fun. Tell her yes. And text me tomorrow."

"I will," I reply, taking out my phone.

Thinking it's one of the guys, probably Tristan, I open the text message without checking who the sender is.

Unknown: *Omnis Magna Potestas Ex Sanguine Et Morte Nascitur.*

All great power is born of blood and death. The dictum of the Society.

Unknown: You can't protect her.

Attached is a picture of Raquelle and me. I'm tucking the clover into her hair.

My head jerks up in alarm, and I scan the quad. Whoever sent the message is here.

Another text comes in.

Unknown: You can't protect any of them.

The attached photograph is dark and grainy, but realization of what I'm looking at batters me with sickening thuds. It's me. And Hendrix. In the parking lot of the strip club. Having sex.

Someone else was there. Watching.

What the fuck?

Fury rolls through me, but more than that, I feel violated. Some sick asshole has been watching me. Invading my private, intimate moments.

I type, **Who is this?**

It bounces back as undeliverable almost immediately after I hit send.

Sunlight and shadows play tricks of illusions as I search the quad for the source of the texts. Students and faculty members mill about. A group of guys toss a frisbee back and forth. A few people laze in the sun with their laptops. And then, I catch a glimpse of a dark figure slipping behind an oak tree near the fountain.

My surroundings blur in my periphery, and my vision tunnels in on the man wearing a black hoodie that conceals him from head to waist, blue jeans, and white sneakers. I can't see his face or what he looks like because of the damn hoodie.

With determined, purposeful strides, I follow him. The quad seems to stretch endlessly before me. The distance I traverse that should take a smattering of seconds, feels like an eternity to cross. Just as I'm closing in, he must sense me because he suddenly bolts, disappearing out of my line of sight. *Dammit.* Without a second thought, I break into a sprint and go after him.

My backpack makes running cumbersome as I knock into several people in my haste to catch up to the man. Just as I'm able to gain some ground, the sneaky fucker takes a sharp turn around a corner between two buildings. I give chase, but he's nowhere to be seen. Breathless, I skid to a stop in front of the bell tower. Frantically searching my surroundings, I try to even out my jagged respirations. How could I have lost him?

Feeling a surge of anger-fueled frustration, I let it out with a very loud, "*God dammit!*"

"Someone is having a bad day."

I turn toward the voice and the cocky smirk it belongs to.

"And someone is about to get his ass kicked," I reply, advancing on Pyotr.

He's made sure to stay invisible since he ambushed me and knocked me out in the catacombs. He should have remained that way.

"You shouldn't hold grudges," he says, backing up.

"Fuck you."

"If you're looking for your husband—"

I slam him up against the glass door of the building. "Aleksander is not my husband. Give me your phone."

Pyotr isn't the man I was just chasing because he isn't sweating or wearing a hoodie. I'm still going to check his phone.

"Front pocket. Fish it out yourself." His moss-green eyes shimmer with mirth, and a grin plays across his lips. He's enjoying this.

"For fuck's sake, stop flirting with her," Aleksander says, firmly pulling me away from his friend.

Aleksander's hair is slicked back, and he's wearing a Henley that sticks to his damp chest.

"Why are you wet?"

My suspicious tone doesn't go unnoticed.

"Went for a jog. Was getting out of the shower when I saw you out here. You look upset," he says with concern.

I temper my skepticism when I detect the fresh, woodsy cedar soap from his shower.

"I am upset." I hold out my hand. "Unlock your phones and give them to me. Now."

"Not until you say please," Pyotr replies and gets a nasty look from Aleksander.

"Just give her your phone," he says as he puts his in my outstretched palm.

I open the text chain and scroll through them. Nothing of importance. A few to Pyotr, some about business. One with Tristan? I skip over that one and don't read it. I may be snooping in their personal stuff, but I do possess a modicum of moral restraint.

With a rankled roll of the eyes, Pyotr slides his phone out but holds it up in the air. "What if I have dick pics on here? Do you want your wife to leave you once she sees what I'm packing?"

I punch the side of his arm, hitting the pressure point that paralyzes the muscle, and catch his phone when it drops from his limp fingers.

"Fuck! What the fuck was that?" he exclaims, shaking out his arm.

It'll be another ten minutes before he gets full function back.

"That was for being a jackass," Aleksander replies.

He holds up Pyotr's phone for him to unlock it with his fingerprint.

"Thank you."

I check through Pyotr's most recent text messages… and immediately turn off his phone and shove it back at him. He wasn't lying about the dick pics.

"Told you," he quips.

Aleksander motions with a tilt of his dark-blond head for Pyotr to get lost. "Go put a heating pad on your arm. It'll help with the circulation."

Pyotr walks backward, pushing the entrance door open with his butt. With a smile as big as the Montana sky, he says, "See you around, Mrs. S."

"I'm really sorry about him," Aleksander says as soon as the door clicks shut.

Pyotr's annoying, but I give him credit where credit is due. He's loyal to Aleksander. They have a deep bond that can only be formed through a lifetime of trust and devotion. Ride or die, I think it's called. Good friends like that are a rare breed.

"He's harmless."

Aleksander emits a snort of laughter. "You'd emasculate him if he heard you say that. Trust me, he may act like a twelve-year-old, but he's far from harmless. You want to tell me what's going on?" he asks, waggling his phone.

I give him my biggest, sweetest smile. "Not particularly."

Hendrix and Tristan have too much to deal with already, and I'm not about to dump this on them. It can wait until Sunday when they're both back. Hopefully, Constantine can do his techie magic and find the person who sent the texts.

Aleksander suddenly sidesteps in front of me, his attention on something at my back. "Do you have someone shadowing you?"

I was wondering when he'd pop up after I took off from the quad.

"Guy with wavy strawberry-blond hair. Tall and

lanky?"

He nods an affirmative.

"That's Patrick. Cillian put one of his men on me. Another guy is watching over Alana."

Andie said they were solid, and I trust her. I need to ask Patrick if he saw the man in the hoodie.

"I would have been happy to do that."

I don't need or want Pyotr or anyone else following me around. One is enough.

"Thanks, but Cillian has it covered."

"Why doesn't Tristan have someone on you?"

Why do men assume women are helpless?

"Because he knows I can take care of myself."

Dropping back on my heels, I'm forced to tilt my head to look at him. Under the sun's ochre rays, his hair looks like it's made from spun copper threads.

"I'm sorry about the other day," he says at the same time I blurt, "Evan told Alana about you."

He blows out a saw-edged breath. "So that's why Tristan called me this morning and wants to meet when he gets back from Boston."

His shoulders hunch when he pushes the sleeves of his Henley up to his elbows. Aleksander's arms are covered in tattoos all the way down to his fingertips, and like the first time we met in the library's elevator, my gaze is drawn to the letters written across the upper knuckles of each finger that spell out ANGEL and DEVIL.

What I didn't notice before are the smaller letters inside the bigger ones. He stiffens when I take his left hand and run my fingertips along the black script. A-O-I-F-E are in tiny cursive inside of ANGEL. I lift his right hand. A-L-E-K-S is hidden inside of DEVIL.

He has my name inked on his skin much like Hendrix

and Constantine have symbols of me tattooed on theirs. The timepiece and words. The weeping angels on their backs. Angel. Aleksander has my name inside ANGEL.

"Syn," he quietly says when I keep staring at his hands.

"I need to go."

CHAPTER 35

TRISTAN

Syn sits back in the seat with a pout pursing her gorgeous mouth. "Are we there yet?"

With one hand on the steering wheel and the other holding hers on my thigh, I take my eyes off the road for a second to glance over at her. I could look at her every second for eternity and still lose my goddamn breath.

"Almost there," I promise.

"That's what you said five minutes ago."

For the first half of our eighty-minute helicopter ride to Nantucket Island, she peppered me with question after question about our destination. I wouldn't tell her. Once we got over water, she finally figured out where I was taking her and has been a ball of energy ever since.

I've never planned a date before. I fuck women. I don't romance them. But I want our first date to be special because Syn is special. I hope I don't screw this up.

She leans across the console as much as the seat belt allows and huffs when she sees the car's speedometer.

"Can't you go any faster?"

I bring our joined hands up to my lips and kiss the backs of her fingers. "We'll be there soon."

I chuckle at her long, drawn-out groan.

The darkness along the road is cut by the car's headlights and a few pole lights spaced at various points. Silhouettes of gnarled, stunted trees whose craggy branches twist and turn in chaotic patterns dot the roadside.

With the push of a button, she rolls her window down. Wind whips through the car's interior, thrashing her hair around her face in a whirlwind.

Breathing deeply, she sighs. "I can smell the ocean," she says of the light odor of salt and seaweed that perfumes the air. Draping her arm out the window, she furls her fingers through the rushing wind. "I remembered this. I thought it was a dream, but it was a memory of two children dancing in the rain on a white sand beach."

Our families had been vacationing at the Knight's summer home on Martha's Vineyard for the Fourth of July. It wasn't really a vacation. It was a gathering of the Council members. All business, no fun. So we made our own fun. Snuck out and took one of the boats and sailed across Nantucket Sound to the island. It was one of a handful of times we could escape the shackles of our responsibilities and just be kids. Play and laugh and be free. We stayed out all day and returned that evening. Francesco beat me unconscious for leaving without his permission. That day was worth every lash mark from his whip.

Slowing down, I turn right onto a narrow, shell-lined road; they crack and pop under the tires as I navigate the thoroughfare that leads to a private beach.

She sits forward and peers out the front windshield. Faint flickers of light up ahead greet us when I pull to a stop and park the car.

"Tiki torches?" she asks.

"Paper lanterns," I reply.

Cylindrical lanterns hang like stars from suspended ropes that extend out from a central pole. Underneath the canopy of makeshift starlight is a large, quilted blanket piled with pillows. A picnic basket sits at the corner.

Syn turns her head and renders me stupid with the most refulgent smile I've ever seen.

"Tristan, it's beautiful. How did you do all this?"

I brush my thumb over her cheek, so absolutely fucking in love with this woman. "I have my ways."

And hired help, but I'm going to take all the credit.

Her hand settles on the door handle. "Race you there," she says and leaps out of the vehicle.

I'm a grown-ass man. The king of a shipping empire and heir to the Amato fortune. I shouldn't feel this childlike exuberance at her challenge, but fuck if I don't.

Barreling out of my side of the car, I catch up to her when she stops to remove her canvas-top sneakers. Her laughter spills out into the night when I snatch her around the waist and swing her around in a pinwheel until we're both dizzy.

When I set her on her feet, she butterflies kisses all over my face. "Best first date ever."

Kicking off my loafers I wore with no socks, I point out with amusement, "It hasn't even started yet."

Syn pulls me along, eager to get to the breakers and dip her feet in. The beach is empty, not a soul around.

Only the sound of the lapping waves and the starlit sky above are our company.

"Our date started the second you smiled at me when I walked through the door," she replies.

My girl. The hopeless romantic.

Hand in hand, we stroll down the gentle slope where the dunes meet the high tide line. The sand is coarse and cool under our bare feet and pebbled with bits of shell. The frothy wash runs between our toes as we stand at the shoreline and gaze out over the sound that separates Nantucket from Martha's Vineyard. The beacon from a lighthouse shimmers in the distance, guiding lost souls at sea back to the safe harbor of home.

We enjoy the serenity of the darkness while listening to the rhythmic pounding of the waves against the shore. The night seems to hold its breath, as if time itself has paused to enjoy this moment with us.

"The guys bought Andie an island."

Unfiltered laughter rumbles up my throat. "Is that a hint, baby girl?"

She wraps her arms around me and presses flush to my side. "Maybe," she teases. "It would be nice to have someplace that's our own. A secret place no one else knows about where we can just... be. No Society. No outside world."

Her wish fills my head with so many thoughts of what I want for our future. Things I hadn't thought were possible until she reappeared into our lives.

"The greenish waters of the Atlantic are so different from the majestic, deeper sapphires of the Pacific," I comment, even though it's night and the water resembles a giant ink blot. "I like the blue of the Pacific, but I prefer the sand beaches of the East Coast over the rocky coastline of the Pacific Northwest."

She wiggles her pink-painted toes and digs them into the saturated quartz grains. "I'd like to see the Pacific one day."

I keep forgetting how much she missed out on. Half her life was stolen from her.

"Anytime you want to go, Red."

I wonder if she likes snow globes. I could buy her one from every place we visit. Give her wonderful adventures and new experiences she can bring home with her. Something she can hold in her hand and remember all the good times we had together while there.

Kissing the top of her head, her apple blossom scent entices me. "You hungry?"

Her cheek nuzzles the cotton of my shirt when she nods yes.

Giving my back to her, I squat down, and she climbs on for a piggyback ride.

"This makes me feel ten years old all over again."

I like that she says that. I like that she's kept that innocent, untainted part of herself, the part she never allowed the Society and its brutality to ever destroy.

When we get to the blanket that's laid out, she hops down and turns in a slow circle, hand to heart, as she gazes up at the paper lanterns.

"This really is incredible, Tristan. Thank you so much. I wish we could stay and sleep out under the stars."

We will. I'll make sure of it. It fucking kills me to leave her while I go to Boston tomorrow, but I have no choice. Neither does Hendrix. Papers have to be signed and legal matters tended to. Since Hen and I dropped out of Darlington, we'll have more responsibility heaped on our shoulders when we transition into the businesses our fathers left behind. There's so much that needs to be done, and not one iota of me gives a damn right now. Tonight, I want to focus on my woman and the future we're building as a family. Syn, me, Con, and Hen. Nothing else matters. Not Amato Shipping or the fucking Society or finding Gabriel. Syn and I deserve to carve out a few hours of time and just exist with each other.

Folding my legs, I lower to the ground and open up the picnic basket. I unpack the containers, one at a time, and lay out the spread of food, so she can choose what she wants. I didn't know what to order from the local café, but whatever it is smells good.

Syn wipes off the sand that dusts her calves before sitting cross-legged next to me. She pulls off an aluminum lid from a tray to reveal roasted chicken and rosemary. In another container, fresh strawberries glisten under the soft glow of the lanterns, a hint of whipped foam on the side for dipping. She uncovers dill potatoes, garlic green beans with almonds, and toasted baguette slices smeared with olive tapenade.

"Dessert first," she says with elation when she sees the cheesecake.

I pass her a fork.

"Oh, my god," she breathes with the first bite. "Try this. So good. Not Hendrix good, but pretty damn good."

I take the bite she offers and hum my approval. I doubt I'll get any more with the way she's inhaling it.

"How did you manage all of this anyway? Because I have to tell you, you knocked this first date thing out of the park."

Warmth spreads through my chest at her compliment. "I had a little help from the locals."

I hold up a bottle of champagne and another of sparkling water. She points to the one that's not alcoholic. We throw class right out the damn window and drink straight from the bottle.

As we eat, we talk about nothing and everything. Syn shares stories of growing up on the farm, painting vivid pictures with her words that transport me to a world I will never know but would like to learn more about. Her eyes sparkle with mirth when she tells me about how she found Cocky Bastard, and I find myself captivated by the way her face lights up over that damn rooster.

I listen intently, hanging on to everything she says, feeling myself falling deeper and deeper for this incredible woman in front of me. She endured a nightmare of pain every single day, yet she woke up every morning with gratitude. When she tells me about her high school experience, the bullying and the loneliness, I reach for her hand, and my fingers intertwine with hers in a silent promise that every day from now on, she will know nothing but happiness.

"I'm stuffed," she says and collapses onto her back on the blanket. She points up and traces a pattern in the sky. "Found your constellation."

I lie back, our shoulders touching, and follow the outline she draws. We used to stargaze from the roof of the Society compound. She made her own constellations for us and declared herself Sirius, the brightest star in the night sky. She said if we ever lost our way, we were to look up and find her. That our souls were bound together by an invisible thread of fate born from stardust and the universe.

Rolling on top of me, Syn straddles my waist. Her scarlet hair waterfalls down around her, the ends brushing my chest.

"Want to go for a swim?"

I grab her hip and slide my hand up the curvature of her waist to her breast. Her torso elongates, preening under my touch.

"The water will be cold." I pinch her nipple, and it beads beautifully. "We don't have our swimsuits."

Her smile transforms into a sexy smirk. "We won't need them."

Every molecule of air gets pulled right out of my lungs at her implication. With a deliberateness that has my heart pounding, she slowly unties her wrap blouse. The panels fall open to reveal a see-through gossamer pale pink bra that leaves little to the imagination.

Her seduction begins with just a promise of what's to come when she slips the sleeves of her blouse down her arms and cups her gorgeous tits. Tweaking her nipples, she rolls her hips, sliding her pussy over my rapidly hardening cock.

Bracing her waist, I guide her undulations, thrusting up into her as she uses me to seek her pleasure. Hands in her hair, head thrown back, her torso bowed in a sinuous arch, she moans as she shatters, the fine tremors of her shudders vibrating through my fingertips. I can't take my eyes off her. She's a voyeur's feast of beauty and sex.

"Magnificent."

Her cornflower-blue gaze sweeps over me with so much heat and want. No woman has ever looked at me the way she does. Syn sees *me*, not my money or what my last name entails. She knows every decrepit inch of my soul and loves me with her whole heart. I love her back just the same. What we have should be impossible—me, her, Hen, and Con. But it's the most perfect, the most real thing I've ever known.

She glides a fingernail up the hollow of my neck. "Take off your clothes."

She's in command, and I'm her slave.

Pushing the button of my jeans through the buttonhole, I hook my thumbs under the waistband. One inch. Two. Three. The denim slides over my glutes. Kneeling between my thighs, she helps me shed my jeans the rest of the way off and licks her plush lips when my cock springs free. I moan when she takes me at the base, pumping me with hard tugs just how I like it.

"I love how thick you are. How incredible it feels when you stretch me."

My cock wants to die in the heaven of her pussy. Feel her slick warmth and the flutters of her orgasm squeeze my shaft as she comes.

Needing to feel her soft skin, I run my hands up her thighs. "My beautiful Syn."

Her breath hitches in response. Praise is her addiction, just like pain. She craves them.

Rising to her feet like a Titian goddess, I watch with half-lidded eyes as she shimmies out of her pants. Dark blonde hair frames her perfect pink cunt, glistening with her essence. She's dripping. For me. My tongue hungers to taste her. My body aches with the need to fill her.

Our hands reach for one another at the same time, and I bring her down on top of me. The long, fluid lines of her body under my hands are nirvana. Being kissed by her, a rapture.

With her lips on mine, she whispers, "*Gheobhaidh mo chroí do chroí.*"

She takes my mouth and makes love to me with her tongue, sweeping deeply and tasting me thoroughly.

She places my hand to her breast. "Feel how my heart beats only for you."

I do. I feel its strong beat declare its love to mine.

"Feel how much I love you," she says.

The heat of her cunt envelops me as she lowers onto my cock. Jackknifing upright, I cradle her in my arms. Everywhere my tongue strokes her silky flesh ignites sybaritic flames. She rises and falls in a hedonistic rhythm, riding me hard, her tits bouncing with every downstroke.

Resplendent sensations spark along my nerve endings. My muscles tremble as a direct line of electric current mainlines into my bloodstream. Higher and higher we climb, hurling ourselves toward the release we want so badly.

I fist her hair and expose her neck for the taking, giving her the sting of pain she wants with strong sucks on her skin. Her eyes roll back in ecstasy, only to fly wide on a gasp when I broach a finger into her forbidden hole. The sounds she makes are wonderfully pornographic, her sultry *Tristan* music to my ears.

I add a second finger and fuck her ass as I fuck her pussy. Her walls clamp down, and I try to hold back the orgasm barreling my way, but she's too tight. My balls draw up, and I shout her name as I pump her full of cum just as her climax sends her soaring.

She rocks her hips, riding the aftershocks, before slumping forward into my arms, a sweaty, gorgeous mess of sated woman.

"That was intense. Amazing."

I lick the seam of her kiss-swollen lips, and our tongues meet in a lazy, soft kiss.

"Better than amazing."

I brush her hair away from her face. Her blue eyes are luminous; her cheeks flushed a rosy hue. So damn gorgeous.

She giggles. "I think some sand found its way into… some interesting places."

CHAPTER 36

SYN

Full lips kiss a decadent line across my shoulder. I stir from my deep slumber when Tristan's teeth nip my earlobe.

"Red, I've got to go."

"Come back to bed," I mumble.

His husky chuckle fans over my neck. "Baby, I seriously have to go."

Coming fully awake, I find that I'm lying on top of Constantine, using him as a body pillow. Pushing my hair out of my face, I slide off Constantine and sit up.

My eyes sleepily open, and I get my first glimpse at a devastatingly handsome Tristan dressed in a dark suit and jacquard tie.

Yawning widely, I grouse, "Why didn't you wake me?"

I wanted to cook breakfast and spend time with him before he left.

"I just did." He kisses me—my lips, my cheek, my nose, my eyes.

"I'm too tired for you to be obtuse."

His smile does the trick of perking me right up.

"And that's exactly why I didn't wake you. You need your sleep. Go back to bed."

"I'm up. Have you eaten?"

He kisses me. "Bowl of cereal." Another kiss. "I've got to get going, or I'll be late to the meeting with the lawyers."

"I'll walk you out."

Constantine rolls to his side and throws his arm over me when I try to get up.

"Stay in bed. That's an order." Tristan leans over and sucks a nipple into his mouth. I'm fully awake now. And horny. "Now give me some tongue, so I can go."

Our goodbye kiss gets a bit out of hand. Constantine intervenes by pushing Tristan off me with his foot.

"I'll be home before you know it. Have fun on your date tonight." He bumps fists with Constantine and gives me one last kiss before leaving.

"I love you!"

Tristan stops in the doorway and pretends to catch the kiss I blow him. "Love you back."

There's a pull in my chest when I hear his footsteps descend the stairs, as if a string tethers my heart to his. I guess that's why they call them heartstrings.

I get distracted by the gentle glide of Constantine's hand across my pebble-roughened skin. "They'll be home tomorrow."

"I know. Still miss them."

I fly into a fit of laughter when he attacks my ribcage and tickles me.

"Con!" I snort-giggle, unable to squirm away from his fingers.

He pulls me under him and settles his weight on top of me. The head of his cock pushes at my entrance, and my heart rate speeds up at the delicious contact.

"I love hearing you laugh."

His lips softly touch mine, a wispy brush of mouths that have me floating. Pulling back just a fraction, I touch fingertips to his mouth, tracing the contours of the top, before doing the same to the bottom.

"You have such a beautiful mouth."

He smiles as he kisses the tip of my finger. Every part of this man is beautiful. Sometimes, it literally hurts to look at him. It's a good hurt where my heart feels about to burst with how much I love him.

"What do you want to do today?" he asks.

A long, masculine finger brushes up my ribcage to stroke the underside of my breast. Back and forth, back and forth.

"Honestly? I just want to spend the day with you."

We're all so busy with school and the other stuff I refuse to think about right now, and the times we get to be just *us* are rare.

His thumb swipes over the puckered bud of my areola. "That sounds perfect. But first…" he says, and I moan when he pushes inside me.

Tucking the pen between the pages, I look up from the pink journal Constantine gave me when Alana steps out onto the back patio, two coffee cups in hand. She passes me one, and I hold it between my hands to warm them up.

Repositioning the deck chair next to me, she sits down. "I should have gone with him."

"No one can know Dierdre is alive," I remind her.

Tristan was firm on that. He didn't want to take the chance of anyone recognizing her. She has no desire to return to the Society in any capacity. Dierdre is dead and will remain that way.

She sips her coffee and gazes out over at the chicken coop where Cocky B happily pecks feed off the ground. He seems to have settled down and gotten used to his new enclosure and the guys. Last night was the first time he didn't crow all night long and keep us up.

"Aleksander knows," she replies.

She just opened the door, so may as well walk on through.

"You need to give him a chance. He shouldn't be held responsible for the sins Francesco committed."

She shields her eyes from the severe mid-morning sun and turns her head to look at me. "You care about him."

I meet her disbelief with firm resolve. "Not in the way it sounds like you're insinuating, but yes. We're the only family he has left. He needs you and Tristan."

"And you need to stop being so trusting of men with ulterior motives who only want to use you to get what they want."

I don't see how he's using me. He went through all the trouble of staging an internal coup, then stepped aside and let me and the guys take over, even with all the animosity between him and Tristan still rife.

Coffee spills over the lip of the cup when I put it down harder than intended. "Your cynicism is duly noted."

Sitting back in the chair, she shakes her head. "Always

so damn stubborn."

"I got it from my mom."

The tension between us dissipates when she comically snorts out a short laugh. "Like mother, like daughter, huh?"

"Absolutely."

We grin at each other before she turns serious.

"I love you, Synthia. I just want you to be happy. And safe."

I lean an elbow on the table and rest my chin in my upturned hand. "I am happy. It might sound weird, given everything that has gone down recently, but I'm happier than I've ever been because I have them."

"People don't understand poly relationships. Are you prepared for that? The ridicule and judgmental attitudes that you'll get?"

Been there, done that. Have the T-shirt to prove it. Wait. That doesn't sound right. How does that saying go?

"I've lived most of my life subjected to ridicule and judgmental attitudes because of the way I look. Nothing anyone can say or do can hurt me anymore. I know my worth, and I trust what I have with Tristan, Hendrix, and Constantine. I won't stop them if they feel like they need to walk away, but I will *never*, not ever, walk away from them. I mean it when I say they are my forever."

There's a long pause where we do nothing but stare at one another.

"Okay," she eventually replies.

Our hands meet in the middle of the table, fingers accordioning and holding tight. Alana isn't my birthmother, but she's been the best mother a daughter could ever wish for.

"I read something once that really stuck with me," she says. "I find that its words are particularly apt at this moment. The passage was, *'The mother, once cradling her daughter in tender arms, now watches with a bittersweet ache as her little girl blossoms into a woman before her eyes. There's a poignant realization that she must loosen her grasp, allowing her daughter to spread her wings and soar into the vast unknown of adulthood. Yet, intertwined with the pangs of letting go, is an unwavering commitment to support her daughter's growth, to be her guiding light through life's labyrinthine paths. The mother finds solace in the understanding that love will always bind their souls together, no matter where their individual journeys may lead.'"*

And here come the tears. "You memorized all that?"

"I liked how it sounded."

"Am I interrupting?" Constantine's rough, raspy voice politely intrudes, and I smile up at him when he bends to kiss me on the lips.

"Not at all."

He spent the morning chasing down cyber leads with no luck. He won't give up until he finds who sent those texts to me yesterday. Alana was understandably upset when I told her about the texts—not the images.

Alana sips her coffee and quietly studies him. She hasn't warmed up to him or Hendrix yet, and her relationship with Tristan is in the early, foundling stages of repair. It's going to take time.

"Isn't tonight your date night?" she asks.

"It is. We're keeping it simple. Dinner and a movie."

I'm just as excited about that as I was for my date nights with Hendrix and Tristan. I don't need fancy dinners or grand romantic gestures all the time.

Spending time with them doing nothing at all is just as important and just as special.

A monarch butterfly tilts this way and that as it rides the air currents. We should be seeing a lot more of them soon as they make their long migration south to their wintering grounds in Mexico.

"I think I'm going to head back to Dilliwyll this week."

I'm a little surprised, but I knew it was coming. "You can stay as long as you like. No rush to go back."

"I miss the farm."

I do, too.

My quick infusion of melancholy goes away when Constantine produces a guitar from behind his back. Getting up from my chair, I motion for him to sit down, then take a seat in his lap and get the guitar positioned comfortably over my legs.

"Do you mind if we skip the Blue Ridge at Christmas?"

"But it's your birthday trip," Alana replies.

I turn twenty-one on Christmas.

"I'd like to celebrate both at home, if that's okay."

Her eyes move to Constantine, and whatever exchange they have with that one look seems to work.

"I'd like that. I have a lot of Christmases to make up for with Tristan… and Aleksander."

She didn't just say what I think she said.

My smile is blinding. I'm so fucking proud of her in that moment.

"You sure that's a good idea?" Constantine says in my ear.

I twist my neck and kiss the side of his stubbled jaw. "It's a great idea. You'll see."

Brokering no further argument about the subject, his arms come around me, and his fingers rest on top of mine. My foot taps out the four-beat he counts out loud. When he gets to four, we strum the beginning notes to a song we started working on together. A love ballad. We haven't come up with the lyrics for it yet, just the main melody. It flows effortlessly as we play, a beautiful dance of notes that fills the air and melds with the birdsong being sung on the high branches of nearby trees. The music connects us in a way that words never could, similar to how Constantine and I could have a deep conversation without uttering a single sentence. The language of soulmates, I guess you could call it, where you're able to say so much to the other person with a simple glance or a smile.

When the last chord fades away into silence, Alana releases the breath she'd been holding. "That was absolutely beautiful. How in the world can you both play the guitar at the same time? I've never seen anyone do that."

"Lots of practice," I reply, but am drowned out when Cocky lets loose a screeching crow just as the doorbell rings. It's followed by a loud knock on the front door.

"Aleksander?" Alana queries, getting up.

"I don't think so."

Maybe Raquelle, but she would have texted first before coming over.

Constantine carefully lifts me off his lap. "I'll get it."

Holding the acoustic by the neck, I stand up, trying to overhear who he's talking to.

"It's Evan," I say when I hear his voice.

The front door slams shut with a *bang*. Sometimes I forget that Constantine can be just as possessive as Hendrix and Tristan. And rude.

"Let me go catch him."

I don't have to because the man in question appears in the back doorway. He's not wearing his glasses. Without them, he looks completely different. No more Clark Kent.

"Hey! I was—"

"I'm sorry."

A violent explosion of pain slams into my chest, and every muscle in my body locks tight in fiery convulsions when fifty-thousand volts of electricity surge through me.

CHAPTER 37

Hendrix to Syn: Miss you. Call me before you and Con go out. I'll be around.

Tristan to group chat: Dinner with the estate lawyers. Don't know when I'll be free, but I'll text when I can. Love you.

Hendrix to group chat: Love you too, baby.

Tristan to group chat: I was talking to Syn, jackass.

Hendrix to group chat: Suck it, ass-twat <middle finger emoji>

Tristan to group chat: Mature. Seriously have to go now. Putting phone on vibrate.

Hendrix to group chat: FYI. The paps have descended like wolves. Mayor has half the police force here to keep things under control.

Hendrix to group chat: WhereTF is everyone?

…

…

Hendrix to Syn: Baby, you there?

Hendrix to Constantine: I'm bored, and Syn isn't

answering her phone. Are you guys fucking? Can I watch?

...

...

Hendrix to group chat: What the fuck is with the ghosting? Pick up your fucking phones.

Tristan to Hendrix: Stop being so damn needy and leave them alone. They're out on a date. Con didn't bug the shit out of you when you and Syn went out.

Hendrix to Tristan: No one will answer. Syn hasn't texted back. Not once. Have you heard from them?

Tristan to Hendrix: They'll call when they get back. What are u doing?

Hendrix to Tristan: Do U really want to know? <eggplant emoji> <sweat droplets emoji>

Tristan to Hendrix: Didn't need that visual.

Tristan to Syn: Red, text the group chat as soon as you see this. Don't care what time you and Con get in, call me. Love you.

...

...

Hendrix to Tristan: Where the fuck are they? It's three in the morning.

Hendrix to Tristan: I can't access the server to check the security feed.

Tristan to Hendrix: I haven't gotten any notifications. Hold on. Let me check.

Hendrix to Syn: Baby, I'm getting worried. Please call me.

Tristan to Constantine: Is the server down? Hen and I can't access anything.

Tristan to Constantine: Con, pick up, dammit. Text. Anything. Send a signal that you and Syn are okay.

Tristan to Dierdre: Hey. Can you go by the house and check on Syn. Text me back. Better yet, call me. Forget that. I'm calling you.

Hendrix to Tristan: This is fucked up. I'm coming back. Plane is already fueled and ready.

Tristan to Hendrix: Dierdre won't answer either. I'm in the car and will be in Darlington in two hours.

…
…

A phone rings.
"What?"
"Aleksander, I need you to go to the house. Something's wrong."

CHAPTER 38

SYN

With me sitting snuggled on his lap, Papa twirls his thick finger around a curl of my blonde hair and loops it behind my ear. The wood fire warms my bare toes and draws a sleepy yawn from my lips. Drowsy and content, I rest my head in the crook of his shoulder, breathing in the comforting notes of the vanilla in his aftershave as he tells me the story of Boudicca, a Celtic queen. Upon her husband's death, she rebelled against the Romans who had seized her kingdom, raped her daughters, and publicly whipped her as a message not to defy them.

"And when the Romans took everything Boudicca loved, the queen vowed, 'Win the battle or perish, that is what I, a woman, will do.'" Taking my chin, he tips my face up and pecks a soft kiss to the button of my nose. "You are my fierce little queen, Aoife. Even when all seems lost, never stop fighting."

Never stop fighting.
Never stop fighting.
I am the phoenix.

AOIFE, WAKE THE FUCK UP.

I come to with a choking gasp as vomit singes a path up my throat. It spills out of me and drips down my chin and neck, setting fire to my lungs when I aspirate it. Jagged coughs wreck me as my body instinctively tries to expel the acrid liquid that invaded my airways.

My head falls listlessly to the side as my stomach revolts again, but there's nothing left to come out.

Why can't I move?

My throat is scraped raw, making it painful to draw a breath, but once I'm able to, my senses click back on, one by one. First is the smell. The godawful stench of bile that covers me and makes my stomach roll violently once again. Then sound. A monotonous *drip, drip, drip* sneaks past the white static buzzing in my ears. When my eyelids finally blink open, all I see is... nothing. Complete blackness swims in front of me.

Forcing my arm to move, I raise a trembling hand to my forehead where the pounding headache is trying to burst right out of my skull.

"Ow, fuck." I hurt everywhere, like one giant muscle cramp.

My legs are bent at the knee and at an angle. Something hard and cold digs into my back and shoulders. Not a bed. Not Constantine's bed where I'm safe and warm with his arms around me.

"Constantine?" His name comes out as barely a croak.

I need my dark angel. My safe place. He'll hold me and make the pain go away.

"Constantine," I say louder.

He doesn't answer back, only the echo of my own voice.

I wince when light suddenly pours into the room and

blinds me.

A door.

The light is coming through a door.

A way out.

But a way out from where?

Footsteps approach, but I can't see who they belong to. As my senses return, I become painfully aware of my surroundings. Thick silver bars enclose me on all sides.

I'm in a cage. *I'm in a fucking cage.* And I'm naked.

I refuse to succumb to the panic that wants to overtake me. No matter how scared I am, I can't let it win. Think, god dammit. Think.

We were at the house on the patio. Me, Constantine, and Alana. Someone came. Evan. Evan was there.

"I'm sorry."

He tased me. Evan fucking tased me.

Black sneakers partially hidden below the ankle by the frayed hem of denim come into view on the other side of the bars.

Evan's blurred visage materializes when he lowers down on his haunches. His finger taps out an ominous tune on the metal grating, similar to how a xylophonist hits the tone bars of a xylophone.

"Maximillian Rossi used to lock Andie in a dog cage. You like being a good girl. You're my good girl," he croons, his hand making petting motions. "Such a good girl."

The fuck?

I try to sit up but can't, the confines I'm trapped inside are too small.

"Where's Constantine? Where's my mother?"

Evan doesn't answer me.

What the hell is going on? My mind can't reconcile

the Evan I've come to know—the kind, sweet guy I first met in my biology lab—to the stranger staring at me now.

My skin crawls when his hazel eyes take their time tracking over my naked body. He took off my clothes when I was unconscious. He touched me without my consent. What else has he done to me without me knowing?

Noticing the vomit, he makes a *tsk* with his tongue. "You're a mess."

Evan rises to his feet and walks over to the far wall. He picks up something from the floor that resembles a thick green rope. With his back turned, I frantically examine the room. It's barren. Empty. There's nothing distinguishable or identifiable for me to tell where I am. Am I at his house? I dismiss that notion. He wouldn't be stupid enough to take me somewhere the guys could easily find me.

But they're not here. Hendrix is in New York, and Tristan is in Boston. Evan knew they'd be out of town —*because I told him*. Oh my god. What did he do to Constantine?

"Evan, where's Constantine?"

Silence.

I grow more desperate when the unknown assaults me. Constantine would have stopped him. He wouldn't have let Evan take me.

The crash at the house. I thought it was the front door slamming shut.

Snapshots of images from the garden bombard me. Aleksei with a gun at Constantine's head while his men kicked him. The torment and sorrow in his eyes when he looked at me. He was ready to die to save me.

"Evan! Where's Constantine? Where's Alana?" I scream their names to the heavens, terrified that they're already there. "Evan! Answer me!"

He turns around, the end of a water hose in his hand. He's seriously not going to—

Motherfucker!

A frigid blast of water pummels my chest with bruising force. I'm trapped like an animal, unable to escape. All I can do is curl into a ball and wait for it to end. The strong jet of water scours the tender skin of my scarred arm and hip, then moves up to my face. It feels like I'm drowning on dry land when water penetrates my mouth and nose.

As suddenly as it began, it stops, and Evan drops the hose to the floor.

"There. All clean."

A cold I've never experienced seeps deep into my bones. It's like having every drop of blood in your body replaced with a slurry of glacial ice.

Through chattering teeth, I splutter, "Why... are you... doing... this?"

His head tilts, his bewildered expression like that of a child's. "You don't belong to them." A glint of silver catches the light when he dangles my belly chain from his middle finger and twirls it around. "They took you from me. They put chains on you. They don't love you. You're a possession. Something to play with. I kept trying to tell you, Aoife, but you wouldn't listen. They were corrupting you. I saved you. You belong to me. You're mine now. I'll take care of you."

He's not making any sense.

Evan pockets the diamond chain. Like a chameleon that can change its appearance on a whim, he smiles.

It's not a nice or genuine smile. It's full of malevolence, just like his eyes. They're no longer masked behind the guise of black-rimmed glasses. I can see it now—the demented soul that hides underneath his false boy-next-door veneer.

"Don't feel sad about the baby. I'll give you more. A whole family. I'll give you everything, Aoife. You'll be happy."

He's out of his fucking mind.

Then it hits me. He said baby.

For a second, I thought I might be pregnant, especially after the mornings spent draped over the toilet. I wanted it to be true. Wished for it with my entire heart. Tristan and I talked about starting a family. Kids, a house, a beautiful future with the men I love more than anything. I don't know how Constantine or Hendrix feel about children because we haven't broached the subject yet, but I know without a doubt, they would love any child I brought into this world.

But I'm not pregnant. Four at-home pregnancy tests say that I'm not. I didn't tell the guys. There wasn't any point since every result came back negative.

But how did Evan know I bought the tests unless—

Has he been following me? Spying on me?

My mind jumps to the man in the hoodie and the threatening messages, and my shock turns to outrage.

Bending my legs as much as I can, I kick at the cage, striking it with my bare feet until the soles crack open. Blood drips down my heels, but I don't care. I don't stop.

I trusted Evan. I let him in. And he betrayed me. He targeted my family and my men. He hurt them.

"Stop it!" Evan shouts, but my screams are louder.

"Where's my mother?" *Kick.* The metal bars clang like

a gong being struck with a mallet. "What have you done to Constantine?" *Kick.*

The door to the cage suddenly swings open, and I'm dragged out by the hair. Metal cuts into my back and legs as I thrash about, trying to fight the hands that have me. My feet slip on the slick blood coating them, unable to gain traction.

Clumps of my hair are ripped out when I'm harshly shoved face-first to the floor. I muster every ounce of strength I can and push up from the cold concrete, but all the air gets knocked out of me from the kick delivered to my side. There's an audible *crack* of bone. An eruption of pain.

I can't breathe.

I can't breathe.

"Don't hurt her!" Evan's pleas fall on deaf ears.

Another brutal kick flips me onto my back, and a shadow falls over me, made fuzzy by the tears weeping from my eyes.

"Hello, Aoife," Gabriel says.

The sound of his voice fills me with terror. Not for me, but for Constantine. Gabriel wouldn't just kill his son. No. He would torture him first. Make him suffer in horrific ways. Bring Constantine to the brink of death, just to deny him, because he gets off on it. He'll do the same to Alana. He'll punish her viciously for what she did.

I scrabble a hand across the floor, searching for a weapon, anything I can use. He crushes my fingers under the hard heel of his shoe, and I choke back the whimper that tries to escape. I will not show weakness in front of this man. He will not break me.

Hatred blazes in my eyes when I meet his dark gaze.

Gabriel Ferreira looks exactly the same as I remember. Constantine shares his dark features. Same hair and eyes. But Constantine is *nothing* like his cold, heartless, sadistic father.

"I'm going to kill you," I promise him.

Gabriel's mouth twists in a merciless smirk. "I'd like to see you try."

"No!" Evan yells just as starlight splinters behind my eyes when Gabriel brings his foot down on my head.

I wonder if I'll become a phoenix, like the one in the story Papa reads to me at bedtime. I'd like that. I'd like to be able to spread my wings and fly.

I feel like I'm flying now. Higher and higher toward a bright light. It's beautiful. Peaceful.

I am the phoenix.

CHAPTER 39

TRISTAN

"God dammit, move, asshole!"

Gravel spits up and peppers the truck behind me when I swerve the Porsche onto the shoulder of the road to get around the slow-as-hell car that decided to drive the speed limit. I ignore the horns honking at me and increase my speed.

I'm coming, baby. Please be okay.

When the screen of my phone lights up with a video call from Aleksander, I clip it into the dash mount and jab at the green icon to accept.

Eyes half on the road and half on my phone, I bark, "Aleksander—"

"Pyotr and I are at the house."

"And?" I practically shout.

I'm about to go out of my fucking mind. Hen and I haven't heard from Syn or Con since yesterday after I arrived in Boston. It's now after four in the morning and still no word. The location shared on their phones says they're at the house. Something is very, very wrong.

"*And* hold on," Aleksander snaps.

He switches his phone's camera view from front-facing to back-facing, so I can see what he's seeing.

The walkway to the house fills my screen, then pans up to the front porch.

In a hushed tone, Aleksander tells Pyotr, "Go around back." Aleksander's footsteps are silent as he moves up the steps. "The front door is ajar."

My heart, which has been racing since I left the house in Boston, pounds a triple beat of trepidation.

"I see it."

Con would never leave the door unlocked or left open. *Fuckfuckfuck.* I pound the steering wheel at the helplessness I feel. My woman and my best friend are missing. Two of the most important people in my life have vanished.

The tip of Aleksander's gun comes on screen as he pushes the front door open with it.

"Clear," he says.

Pyotr appears from the kitchen. "Back door was unlocked. One of the patio chairs was on its side. Other than that, nothing."

A weighted stone drops in my stomach. I shouldn't have left. I should have taken her with me. Too many *should haves* circle my conscience like a vulture patiently circling a dying animal.

"The bedrooms," I tell him.

Aleksander takes the stairs at a snail's pace to the second floor. My knuckles go white when my grip tightens on the steering wheel, every passing second an eternity of uncertainty. With a surge of dread, I watch as he navigates the dimly lit hallway, his movements cautious yet purposeful. He thoroughly checks each room, but there's no sign of Syn or Constantine.

"Nothing appears to be touched. Nothing of value taken," Pyotr says, not talking to me but to Aleksander.

The camera view flips to Aleksander's grim face. "How long before you get here?"

Panic morphs into blind rage, and I lash out, hurling accusations like serrated daggers.

"What the fuck did you do? Where is she? I'm going to fucking gut you if you laid a hand on her!"

Aleksander's expression contorts with fury, but beneath the anger, I see something else—genuine hurt, raw and unfiltered.

"You think I would harm her? Fuck you!" he seethes.

A moment of silence hangs between us, heavy with unspoken accusations and bitter resentments.

As angry as I am, and as much as I'd like to lay the blame at his feet, I don't think he would intentionally hurt Syn. But the shit he set into motion and the games he's been playing carry the threat of repercussions, with Syn right in the middle of the bullseye.

"This her phone?" Pyotr asks in the background.

Aleksander's camera view switches once again. Pyotr is holding up the new phone Con gave her with a rooster soft case.

"That's hers," I say.

Going around the truck in front of me, I jerk the car hard to the right to avoid being plowed into by a tractor trailer coming in the opposite direction. I'm doing over a hundred and will be lucky if I'm able to get to the town limits of Darlington without attracting the attention of a passerby sheriff.

"What's her password?"

My gaze darts to the green road sign saying I'm fifty

miles from Darlington. At the speed I'm traveling, I'll be there in a half hour.

"I'm not giving you her fucking password."

"Try Cocky Bastard, no caps, no space," Aleksander replies, and I want to reach through the phone and choke him. How the hell does he know that?

"You may want to see this," Pyotr says, and acid curls my insides.

"What? Show me," I demand.

"Fucking hell. Any way to find the sender?" Aleksander asks.

Sender?

"If it's a burner, no. We can get an approximate location of where the texts were sent using the cell towers it pinged. I don't know how useful that would be."

"Do that."

Fed up with them talking to each other, I shout, "Aleksander, show me!"

"Pull off the road," he says.

"Not stopping."

"Syn doesn't need you lying in a hospital bed and eating from a tube because you wreck the car. I won't show you until you pull off the fucking road."

Smoke billows up from the tires when I slam on the brakes and skid off the road onto the shoulder. Luckily, no one was behind me.

"I'm parked."

There's a swish of bedcovers when he places Syn's phone on top of her duvet and hovers his phone over it to show me the texts.

"When did she get them?" I ask, incensed at what I'm reading.

"Friday."

She didn't say anything. Why didn't she tell us?

"That's not all. Whoever sent her the texts was watching her. This was attached." Aleksander pulls up an image of her and Raquelle. "And this one."

Murderous rage fills me when I see the image of her and Hen.

Putting the car in first, I stomp on the gas. "No one else sees that."

"They won't." Aleksander deletes the image before handing Syn's phone to Pyotr. "Get anything you can off this." His phone flips back around to his face. "We'll find her."

His firm declaration is incongruent with the worry marring his face. A worry I feel a thousand-fold.

"Hen and I haven't been able to log into the server that stores the videos from the cameras. Someone knew to disable it."

"Fuck. *Fuck!*" he shouts, the sound of something crashing to the floor blasting through the audio.

"Aleksander, whoever took her and Con also has Dierdre."

We made a lot of enemies this past weekend, but one in particular flashes his malevolent face in my mind's eye.

Aleksander comes to the same conclusion. "Gabriel."

CHAPTER 40

CONSTANTINE

Syn screams my name. It pierces the empty void I'm trapped inside and sends a jolt of desperation through me.

"Don't hurt her!"

Evan's shout invades my subconscious, his voice mingling with the haunting shadows that seem to taunt me, preventing me from finding her.

"*Syn!*" I yell, frantic for her, but she doesn't answer.

"Constantine."

A woman's voice cuts through the darkness, but it's not the one I want to hear.

"Constantine," the woman says more urgently. A sob tears through the air, sharp and agonizing like the cry of a wounded animal. "He's hurting her."

The woman's words crash into me with brute force, dragging me back to reality. I fight against the restraints, a metallic clang ringing in my ears as I struggle against the chains binding my wrists, straining to break free. My efforts prove futile, my arms stretched above my head and bound so tightly it feels like they could snap at any moment. My fingers are completely numb, and my shoulders are strained to the point of dislocating. How long was I out?

"Constantine, wake up."

Crust grits my eyelashes when I open them. Blinking furiously, my vision gradually adjusts, and I try to make sense of my surroundings. Everything blurs in and out before bare cinder block walls come into focus, their bleak, gray color adding to the oppressive atmosphere.

"Dierdre," I rasp when our eyes meet. She's also bound and dangling from her wrists, her toes barely scraping the floor.

She's been beaten badly. Her face is a horror show of blood and bruises. I can barely see the slits of her eyes through the swelling around the sockets.

"Synthia," she says through puffy lips.

My mind races with fragmented memories as everything rushes back all at once in a deluge of snapshots.

Evan was at the house. The son of a bitch tased me as soon as I opened the door. He must have drugged me too. It would explain the viscous stupor weighing down my limbs, making it hard to think straight.

"He's hurting her. He's going to kill her," Dierdre slurs. Her head lolls forward, then jerks upright. She's seconds away from blacking out.

Panic claws at me. The scream I heard through the delirium was real.

I promised Syn I wouldn't let anyone hurt her ever again. I should have trusted my gut. I knew something was off about Evan. I felt it from the moment I saw him when I picked Syn up from her biology lab. And now he has her, and it's my fault.

"Do you know where Evan took us? Do you know where we are? Dierdre!" I bark when her body goes limp, and she dangles from her wrists like a broken marionette. "Alana," I say this time.

She's unresponsive.

Shit.

I need to find a way to get free from the shackles, then find Syn.

She needs you. Do not fail her again.

I sway from side to side as I test if there is any give in the chains, my movements sloppy and lethargic from whatever I was given. I gaze up at the fifteen-foot-high ceiling. Pipes run in parallel lines across the length of the small room. I think we're in the subbasement of a building.

I follow the path the plumbing takes. The chains aren't anchored to the ceiling but thrown over the thickest pipe. The joint where two pipes meet could be a potential weak spot that I can take advantage of.

Engaging my core, I hop my body and thrust upward. There's a loud *clack* of metal on metal that vibrates from the pipe to my feet when gravity pulls me back down. My shoulders scream in agony from the hard jolt. I don't pay attention to the pain and do it again, but the damn thing doesn't budge.

My lungs haul in dusty air, hoping the infusion of oxygen will help dispel the brain fog. Pearls of sweat drip down my face and into my eyes, the salt stinging my irises like lemon juice on a paper cut.

The door to the room suddenly smacks open and crashes against the wall. Debilitating anguish slashes my heart when I watch my father drag Syn's nude, lifeless body into the room. Her head is bent at an odd angle from the grip he has on her hair.

Not like this. She can't be taken away from me like this. We just found each other again. We were going to spend the rest of our lives together. Syn, me, Hen, Tristan, our child—

Ohgodohgod. No! *No!*

A strangled, mournful wail erupts from what's left of my shattered soul.

"Good. You're awake. Brought you something."

As if she's nothing more than garbage to be thrown out with the rest of the trash, my father tosses Syn in the corner, then goes over to Dierdre.

"Deceiving cunt," he growls.

He slaps her across the face hard enough to make her head whip back. Like a ragdoll, it droops forward, blood-tinted drool pouring from her mouth.

"What have you done? You promised that if I helped you…" Evan runs into the room and falls to the floor at Syn's side, his hands all over her body. "I'm sorry. I'm here now. I'll make it all better." He softly kisses her, and I lose it.

Like a rabid animal caught in a snare, I thrash about, wishing he was closer and my feet weren't zip-tied together, so I could snap his neck with a twist of my legs.

"Get away from her. Don't you fucking touch her!"

My father turns sharply and looks at me. He hasn't heard me utter a word since the night he choked me. A cruel curve graces his lips when he takes out a gun and points it at me.

"Thank you for your service to the Society, but it is no longer required."

His arm swings toward Evan, and he fires a bullet directly into the back of his head. The boom of gunfire deafens me for several seconds, a chaotic ringing in my ears that's loud as fuck.

"You just started a war with the Irish mafia."

Thin tendrils of smoke rise and disappear quickly from the barrel of his pistol as my father holsters it.

"I hate hearing your fucking voice. It was better when you were mute. And Cillian McCarthy will believe the narrative given to him."

He approaches an unmoving Evan, his coal eyes void and empty. Syn had once commented that she hated the cold expression I would get when I shuttered my emotions and detached from the world, and I despise that I see the same look in my father's eyes now.

He rolls Evan off Syn with a push of his shoe. "I have to say, finding out she was alive was surprising. James was always two steps ahead of everyone else."

A stark epiphany flashes its bright warning light as the truth comes tumbling down around me. It was never Aleksander pulling the strings. It was my father. He orchestrated everything, using Aleksander's revenge to pave the way for *him* to take control. But he never counted on Syn returning.

My gaze darts to her. I can barely breathe past the pain, every inhalation a struggle against the suffocating despair I'm drowning in. My soul cries out for her, begging her to answer back. Syn was the beacon of light in the darkness of my existence, and he took her from me.

I love you. I love you. I'll be with you soon, sweet girl. Wait for me.

Taunting him, I say, "I bet it pisses you off that she

messed up everything."

He tears his gaze from her crumpled form, victory shining in his eyes. "I think I've rectified that little problem, don't you?"

I fucking hate him. I hate that I look like him. I hate that my last moments on this earth will be with him.

"I'm going to kill you."

I've never heard my father laugh before. It sounds off. Demented. "That's exactly what she said."

Blood ejects sideways from my mouth when his fist slams against my face. His next punch breaks my nose. My father unleashes hell upon me with unrestrained brutality, hit after hit that are as cruel as his heart.

When his arm tires, he stumbles out of the reach of my legs. He's not stupid. He knows not to let his guard down.

"That's all you've got? Pathetic." I smile through blood-soaked teeth. "You know you can't break me. You never could. Might as well kill me."

I'm coming, baby. Just a little while longer.

His contemptuous glare turns smug. "Your suffering has only begun. I'm going to carve her up into pieces in front of you, then let you watch her body rot with the maggots as I slowly and painfully drain your life. And right when you're on the edge of death, I'll burn what's left of her and finish the job Francesco failed to do."

I can't block out the gruesome things he describes. Those unbearable images play like a grotesque movie in my mind. My father has never been able to break me, not with his fists or his punishments, but hearing what he plans to do to Syn destroys me completely.

I spit at him. "See you in hell."

"Worthless piece of shit."

I don't feel the next crushing blow his fist delivers. Or the next. I dissociate and go somewhere else. I go to her. My beautiful girl with the flame-red hair and sky-blue eyes. *Meu coração.*

Constantine, open your eyes.

I don't want to. I want to stay here where it's peaceful. But I never could deny her anything.

Through the cerise haze that obscures my sight, Syn rises from the floor like a specter, a gorgeous visage of blood and carnage. My angel is here to take me with her. I'm ready.

Except she's not an apparition.

"*Is i mbás amháin a éireoidh mé.*"

My father's eyes widen in surprise, but it's too late. His chest suddenly bows out in a severe arc, his body pulled taut with invisible strings.

Syn wrenches his head back and presses her mouth to his ear. "I am the phoenix, motherfucker."

When his legs give out and he falls to the ground, that's when I see the knife. Where the fuck did she get a knife? Did Evan have one on him?

Syn drops to sit on top of Gabriel's chest. "Did you know that fifty percent of patients with spinal cord injuries suffer from neuropathic pain?" She drags the tip of the knife down the left side of his face. "I severed your spinal cord in a very unique place. It's why you can't move. But you can feel. *Everything.*"

His pain-filled moan reverberates between the cinder block walls when she slices the creases of his mouth and carves a Joker smile on his face.

This magnificent, amazing woman.

"Syn."

She struggles to stand up, clearly hurting from her

injuries. "Titanium," she says.

Seeing her smile at me is the most beautiful fucking thing I have ever seen.

I want to go to her, hold her, carry her out of here. I can't do any of those things while still restrained.

She pokes Gabriel in the neck with her bare toe. "Be right back. Don't go anywhere."

Chuckling at her own joke, she limps over to me and cuts through the zip tie around my feet, while I work on freeing my hands from the chains.

"Help Dierdre."

Syn's momentary frown turns to one of distress when she sees Dierdre.

"Mom?" Syn cries and rushes over to her. "Mom, wake up. Please wake up. Constantine, she's not moving. I can't get her down."

I'm able to manipulate my left hand and pop my thumb and first two fingers out of joint, making it possible to finally slip free from the chains. Once my feet touch the floor, I snap things back into place. Fuck, that hurt. Not the most pleasant sensation.

"Can you support her legs?" Syn asks.

Even with the two of us, Dierdre is difficult to get down. She's nothing but dead weight.

"Careful," Syn says as we lay her gently on the floor. Dierdre still hasn't come around.

Syn checks her pulse. "It's weak but I feel it. We need to get her to a hospital."

The look of pure hatred Syn delivers to my father would burn him to cinder and ash if it could manifest itself into physical form.

She crawls across the dirty concrete floor to where he lies paralyzed. "You will never hurt anyone else I love," she vows.

Her fists pulverize his face with unyielding blows. I hope she smashes in his fucking skull.

Pop. Pop. Pop.

We look over at the door when we hear gunfire. It's muffled but unmistakable.

"Gabriel's men?" she asks, coming to stand beside me.

"I don't know."

I take her hand. We'll fight to the death if we have to.

A shout echoes from somewhere far away. "Syn! Con!"

Seems the guys have arrived. I had no doubt they'd find us at some point.

"Tristan!" Syn yells, answering him.

Her reply has a chaos of shouts exploding in unison. I promptly whip off my shirt and pull it over her head. No way is Aleksander seeing her naked.

Syn grabs my wrist, her hand small but so fucking strong—just like she is.

"Are you okay?"

I know my face must look like a slab of raw meat. "Never better."

"Liar." She brings my hand to her cheek and nuzzles it.

Gathering her as tenderly as I'm capable of with the desperation I'm feeling, I hold her as close as possible.

"Are *you* okay?"

Her cheek caresses my chest. "My head hurts, and my ribs," she replies.

"I thought I'd lost you again." I don't stop the tears from coming. I welcome them.

"I thought the same thing. Let's not get kidnapped again."

"Deal." I bury my face in her neck, too terrified to ask

her about the baby.

"What do you want to do about him?"

Not wanting to let her go, I gently pull away and stand over my father. He blinks up at me as he chokes on the blood that pools in his throat. I bring my foot down on his neck and crush his windpipe.

"Karma, asshole."

CHAPTER 41

ONE WEEK LATER

SYN

"Nope. Don't you move."

Raquelle races to pick up Alana's bottle of water before I can.

Wincing when she sits up, Alana grouses, "I'm not an invalid."

"While I'm here, you are," Raquelle replies.

To explain the beat-up state we were in, Tristan told her that Constantine, me, and Alana were in a car accident. She's been in mothering mode all week. Constantine and I only had to stay in the hospital for two days, but Alana was there longer because of her severe facial subperiosteal hematomas. She was discharged yesterday and is recouping here at the house.

The swelling on her face has gone down considerably, and the bruising has turned from bluish purple to an ugly shade of pea-soup green. But she's alive, and that's all that matters. I'm faring a little better, even if my cracked rib is killing me. Every time I breathe in, or god forbid, cough, it feels like a knife is being shoved into my chest. I've survived worse trauma, so I'm not complaining.

"What the fuck was that? Foul!" Hendrix shouts, hands on his hips.

Cocky Bastard trumpets a loud crow from his roosting perch, and his tiny, three-hen girl group cluck in response. Tristan had Henny, Penny, and Jenny brought up from the farm, and Cocky has been in rooster-rutting heaven. We'll be overflowing with eggs by tomorrow.

"See, even the demon bird agrees with me."

Tristan spirals the football to Constantine. "There are no fouls in football, dumbass, only penalties."

Hendrix flips him off. "Same difference. And this shit isn't real football. Real football involves actually kicking the ball down a field with your foot. Hence, *foot*ball."

A very intense game of touch football—the American version, not the European one as Hendrix likes to point out—is taking place in our backyard. Hendrix, Pyotr, and Drake against Constantine, Tristan, and Aleksander.

"What's the score?" Alana asks.

"I have no idea," I reply.

My rapt attention has been on watching six bare-chested men run around. I couldn't care less about the game.

"I'm horny," Raquelle suddenly blurts. "Are you horny? God, I can't take much more of this. Too much man candy."

I burst out laughing when she fans her flushed face, squirms on the lounger, then takes a long drink of iced tea.

But she does have a point.

The guys are shirtless and sweaty. All those tattoos and muscles and... *Jesus*.

"Yep," I reply, sipping my water.

Alana makes a disgusted face. "Not a visual I want about my brothers—what?" she asks when I give her a blinding smile.

"Nothing."

Like I knew she would, and despite all the shit that came before, Alana opened her great, big heart and accepted Aleksander as her brother. And as much as he'll deny it, Aleksander has enjoyed having a big sister to boss him around, which she's been doing all day. His and Tristan's brotherly bond is slower to take root. They're trying, but there's a lot of baggage to unpack. Over a decade of animosity and rivalry can't be erased overnight. Constantine has taken Aleksander's newfound presence in our life with a metaphorical shrug of the shoulder. Hendrix is a whole other story. He still hates him. Baby steps, as I always say.

"I'll get it."

I make Raquelle sit back down when the doorbell rings. "I've got it. Anyone want me to bring back anything?"

"Can you grab me the bag of Red Vines?" Alana asks.

"Red Vines. On it. Raquelle?"

"The bag of sour cream and onion potato chips sitting on the counter would be good."

Hendrix won't start up the grill for another hour. We plan to eat, then head to the college stadium to watch DF play the Carolina University Wildcats. We'll hit fraternity row afterward for the parties. I can't wait.

The front door cracks open just when I round the corner from the kitchen.

"Hello?" Shelby calls, then says, "Christian, don't—"

The front door swings wide, and a tiny raven-haired blur flies past me, shouting, "Football!"

He skids across the floor and bumps into the wall, then hits me with a blue-eyed petulant scowl when he doesn't see anyone in the living room.

"Football." His l's come out as w's, and it reminds me so much of Sarah.

"Christian Thomas Pender. Manners, young man. Say hello first. And take off your shoes."

He hurriedly kicks them off, and those big blue eyes turn puppy-dog when he peers up at me. "Hi. Football, please."

Trying not to smile, I point in the direction of the kitchen. "Backyard is that way."

Like a bundle of chaos, he slips and slides his way into the kitchen.

"He's been bouncing off the freaking walls all morning, wanting to come and play with the big boys," Shelby says exasperatedly, giving me a gentle hug.

She looks like a mom today. Jeans and a graphic tee, with her hair pulled back in a low ponytail.

"Wait until you meet Sarah. She'll give him a run for his money."

"You look so much better today," she comments.

"I feel better."

Like Raquelle, Shelby has been coming over every day to check on me.

"From Keith. Hot wings and potato skins." She slips

off her sandals and hands me a large paper bag.

I peek inside, and my mouth waters at the scrumptious, greasy smells wafting out. "Not sharing."

"Didn't think you would."

Two blacked-out sedans pull up, and I wave, already knowing who's in them. Keane is the first to get out, followed by an exuberant Sarah, then Jax, Rafael, and Liam.

Shelby's eyes grow saucer-big as she gawks. "*Holy shit*," she whispers.

I close her mouth with my finger under her chin. "Those are my cousin's husbands. Want me to introduce you?"

"Hell, yes. And if you'd like to adopt me, I would appreciate it."

Amused at how serious she sounds, I ask, "Why?"

"Because hot men harems run in your family, and I'd like one very much."

"Auntie Aoife!" Wearing the cutest pink dress and matching pink cowgirl boots, Sarah runs up the porch steps and ferociously hugs my legs. "I missed you." Her little arms rubber band around me tighter.

Every time with this girl, I lose my heart.

"Missed you, too, squirt," I reply, running my hand through her soft, brown curls.

"I drew this for you," she exclaims, holding up a crumpled piece of paper in her little fist. "It's our family."

I gingerly squat to be at her level. While I take an inordinate amount of care to smooth out the wrinkles, she plays with the flower on my necklace. Tristan had the pressed flower he gave me made into a charm that now hangs from a delicate platinum chain around my neck.

"I love it," I enthuse about her drawing, not able to hide my emotions.

The picture is a stick family with me and Andie in the middle holding the hands of a smaller stick girl. The guys fill up the rest of the page, and I think the extra two stick men are Declan and Pearson, based on the one with the scribbles on his face for a beard and the other with huge, loopy bumps for muscles.

MY FAMILY, she wrote in blocky print.

My family.

It's surreal how you can lose so much but gain so much more.

Sarah pokes one of her cherubic fingers at the small cut on my eyebrow. "Auntie Andie said to be careful of your boo-boos. Want me to kiss them better?"

I point to my cheek. "Here."

She smacks a kiss on the bruise then gives me three more in various places.

"Four angel kisses," she says, and I smile when she holds up six fingers.

I absolutely adore this girl.

Not caring when my ribs protest, I embrace her tiny body in a hug. "My boo-boos feel so much better."

"Hey, Red," Liam says, bending down to pick up Sarah.

She wraps her arms around his neck and begins smacking enthusiastic kisses on his cheek.

"Shelby, this is my cousin, Liam."

"Nice to meet you," he says.

Her mouth falls open again. "Uhhhh…"

"S'up, queen," Rafe cheekily greets me, and I roll my eyes at the moniker.

Keane and Jax join us on the porch, and I make the

rest of the introductions to a starry-eyed Shelby.

"Play," Sarah insists, trying to climb down from Liam.

Shelby finally comes out of whatever hot guy fantasy she was having. "I can take her. My son's here. Christian. He... and... play... and... yeah." She blushes a million different shades of fuchsia when the guys grin at her.

Sarah perks up at the mention of a potential play buddy. "Can I? Pretty please."

"No rough housing," Keane says.

She pouts. "I promise."

Jax leans in to my side. "Andie's been teaching her Krav Maga."

"Where is Andie?" I ask when she hasn't materialized from one of the cars.

"And that's our cue," Keane says, taking the food bag from me and herding everyone inside the house until only Liam and I are left on the front porch.

"Cue for what?" I ask suspiciously.

"He wasn't sure if you'd want him here."

"Why would Keane think he's not welcome?"

"Not him."

Liam glances toward the driveway, and my stomach drops when I see Cillian standing next to Andie. I haven't spoken to him since the first time I met him at his house. I'm not entirely sure I want to speak with him now. I'm trying to put what happened with Evan behind me and move forward with my life. There's also a part of me that blames Cillian for his son's actions. I don't care how ridiculous it sounds, it's how I feel. Evan complained all the time about how his father ignored him and treated him like an employee instead of a son. If Cillian had been more involved in Evan's life... paid more attention... I don't know.

"If you want him to leave, he'll leave. He just wants to talk, and Andie thought here would be good. Safety in numbers."

I balk at that. If Cillian is here to seek any form of retribution for Evan's death, he's come to the wrong house. Gabriel killed his son, not me. But I would have, given the chance. I would've killed Evan without a second thought.

My skin electrifies at his presence, and I know without looking that Constantine is standing in the doorway. I twist around, and our eyes meet. Everything we want to say to one another is conveyed in that one look.

With my curt nod of assent, Liam cuffs my shoulder in support, or maybe approval, and heads indoors without saying anything else.

Constantine brushes up to my back, and I reach behind me, threading our fingers together as we watch Andie and Cillian ascend the walkway to the house. Their footsteps up the porch steps are as trepidatious as the thump of my heartbeat.

Andie cups my face and sweeps an apprising perusal over the damage Gabriel's boot inflicted. My hair can only hide so much of where he kicked me.

"Things are healing nicely. You look good."

I snort at that lie. I look like someone kicked the crap out of me.

She and I have videoed a lot this week. Andie went through something similar—the kidnapping and the cage—and it helped being able to talk to someone who got it.

"Any more headaches?" she asks.

"No."

By some miracle, I only sustained a minor concussion, but the migraine that took up residence for days wasn't fun.

She gives me a tender kiss to my good cheek, and without another word, goes inside. The quiet *click* of the door closing sounds more like a *boom*.

A brisk gust of wind swirls leaves around our feet as silence suffocates the air. So damn awkward.

"I'm sorry, lass."

He doesn't try to make excuses for Evan like a parent tends to do when their child does something wrong.

I don't know what else to say, other than, "I appreciate that. Did you love him?"

Evan went through life thinking his father didn't care about him.

Cillian looks out at the sun-dappled horizon, melancholy hidden behind his green eyes. With a weighted sigh, he says, "I loved my son as much as a man like me could."

Evan fixated on me to fill that void. I've come to understand that fixation began when he first saw me in the hospital after the attack. When he would sit by my bedside and read me stories. Aleksander and Pyotr found a box of journals when they searched Evan's house, similar to the journals I have. I've spent the past couple of days reading them. Evan lied. He knew exactly where I was the entire time. He kept tabs on me. Watched and waited. He never knew about Constantine, Tristan, or Hendrix, or my connection with them. Everything that happened after I first met Tristan at the Bierkeller fucked up Evan's plans for me to fall in love with him.

I miss him. Not the Evan he was in the basement, but

the kind, caring Evan who was my friend.

I can feel Cillian's gaze on me. "I'm so fecking sorry. I just wanted ye to know that. I'll get out of yer hair, so ye can enjoy the rest of yer day."

He holds out a thick yellow envelope, and I hesitate before accepting it. I don't know what I expected exactly, but he said everything that really needs to be said. *I'm sorry.* It's good enough for me.

"No matter what, the McCarthys will always be your family. You need us, and we'll be there. No questions asked." He walks down two steps before stopping. "James would be so fecking proud of the woman you've become, Aoife."

"It's Syn."

He pauses. Nods. "Take care, lass."

It's so easy to lay blame. Even easier to hate. But that's not who I want to be. My life has always been about fate versus destiny. Fuck them. I'm carving my own path from now on.

Cillian is almost to the second sedan when I raise my voice and call out, "We're having hamburgers and hot dogs on the grill if you'd like to join us."

His small smile gets lost in his red beard. "I'd like that."

Constantine opens the door for us, and I walk Cillian through the house and to the back patio. As soon as Alana sees him, she lights up. The smile she gifts him is that of a woman in love. We are most definitely going to talk about that look later.

"Seems that Dierdre has a crush," Constantine says.

"You saw that, too?"

Of course, he saw it. He sees everything.

Constantine and I hang back for a while and just

take in the beautiful scene of our family. Our beautiful, crazy, complicated family.

Sarah and Christian are in the chicken coop with Shelby, feeding the hens. The three-on-three touch football game has now turned into four-on-four with the addition of Keane, Rafe, and Liam. Andie is sitting in Jax's lap and talking to Raquelle. So many smiles. So much laughter.

Constantine wraps his arms around me and rests his chin on the top of my head.

"I think we just witnessed a miracle," I say when Tristan laughs at something Aleksander says.

"*You're* our miracle."

This man and his words.

His hands move down and settle over my stomach. "One day, I hope we can make a second miracle."

At the hospital, he and Hendrix were devastated when they found out I wasn't pregnant. Tristan was understandably upset because it was the first he'd heard about it.

Angling my head, I look up at my beautiful dark angel. "A home full of miracles."

He kisses my lips, then the button of my nose. "What did Cillian give you?"

My fingers clench around the envelope I forgot I was holding.

"Let's find out."

I untwist the cord from the string and button closure, pull out the stack of papers—and suck in a sharp breath when I see THE LAST WILL AND TESTAMENT OF JAMES FITZPATRICK. But that's not all. Flipping through the papers, there are financial records, deeds of ownership, a trust. All of them are in my name. My inheritance.

Billions of dollars of assets and money.

"*Holy fucking shit.*"

Constantine chuckles. "James really was always two steps ahead of everyone else."

CHAPTER 42

THREE MONTHS LATER

THE RED ROOM

SYN

The heavy oak door to the Red Room swings open, and a rush of cooled air kisses my cheeks. With my hand gripped tightly in Tristan's, we cross over the intimidating threshold into the unknown. Music pulsates around us like a living thing, a throbbing drumbeat of writhing bodies, sex, and good times. The Red Room is a foreign world of debauchery, but one I'm excited to explore with my guys.

Hendrix brushes his fingers down my lower back, his touch a silent vow of possession.

"Ready, firefly?" His husky whisper is laced with the promise of what's to come, and I shiver from its effects.

I nod, giving him a daring tip of my lips. "More than ready."

They asked me what I wanted for my birthday. I told them this.

Constantine hovers close to my side when we stop in the entryway, his coal eyes reflecting the flickering candlelight of the antique chandelier hanging above our heads. The low light gives an otherworldly ambience to the sanguine silk wall coverings and black velvet drapes that adorn the entry hall. The décor is all red, black, and gold but tastefully done and not tacky like I thought it would be. I envisioned sticky floors and matte black walls that would be a cornucopia of stains under a black light. It's not that. The entryway of the Red Room is elegant and refined, the bold colors giving it a sensual allure.

Uncertainty falters my confidence when I see the mass of people already here, some dressed in elegant attire, some not wearing any clothes at all. Hendrix chuckles when I quickly avert my gaze from the two men openly fucking a woman on a red upholstered chaise lounge. Her face is a display of carnality as one man thrusts into her from underneath, and the other man takes her from behind.

"That's tame compared to what you'll see in the back rooms," Hendrix whispers in my ear.

At his insinuation, heat infuses my cheeks.

Heads turn our way in interest as I'm pulled deeper into the Dionysian chaos. I don't know where to look or if it's rude to stare, so I keep my eyes pointed directly in front of me.

A woman steps out from behind a standing glass reception desk. She's already tall, made even taller by her thigh-high stiletto boots. Her midnight-black hair is sleeked back in a ponytail, and she gives it a flirtatious swish over her shoulder when she approaches. Her skirt leaves little to the imagination, but the lack of a top definitely does. Her large, round breasts barely move as she walks.

"Mister Knight," she greets in a purr, and my eyebrows hit my hairline when I look at Hendrix.

Tristan cracks up beside me, and I dig my nails into his palm. I didn't think about how I would handle meeting any of Hendrix's past playthings. Gouging her eyes out with a nail file for looking at him would be a good start.

"Belinda, this is Syn."

I give him props when his eyes never stray past her face.

Her mauve-glossed lips spread in a sincere smile, and she holds out her hand for me to shake.

"It's so nice to finally meet you, Miss Carmichael. I'm the manager of the establishment. Anything you need, please let me know. Your comfort is our priority." She greets Tristan and Constantine in turn, then turns her attention back to Hendrix. "Everything is prepared as you specified."

"Thank you."

"Enjoy," Belinda says.

I watch her sashay her curvy ass back to her station behind the reception desk where a couple waits to speak with her.

"She seems… nice."

"She's my employee, baby girl," Hendrix says. "And the answer to the question I see bouncing around your gorgeous brain is no. Belinda is an employee, nothing more."

"You own this place?"

"Silent partner as of three years ago."

I'm guided farther into the den of decadence as they take me down a long, darkened hallway to a central underground rotunda made of Romanesque archways with more hallways branching from it in different directions.

The pungent musk of sex and leather permeates the air. I can almost taste it on my tongue. Moans of various pitch and volume drift down the hallways, their song causing a visceral pull between my legs. I'm shocked by how turned on I'm getting listening to it.

Hendrix brushes my hair off my shoulder and runs his lips up the curve of my neck. "Hear that? That's the sound of fantasies coming to life."

A woman's sharp cry as she orgasms melts my legs right from under me. Constantine steadies me when I sway backward.

"Look at you, all wild-eyed and breathless," Hendrix says with a cocky British cadence.

He chuckles when I can only nod in reply, unable to articulate the storm of arousal brewing within me.

"Want to watch?" Tristan asks.

"We can watch?" The idea intrigues me. "Will people be able to see us when we're... *you know*?"

I'm more comfortable in my scarred skin, and we don't confine sex to just the bedroom, but I want tonight to be just us, no one else.

Hendrix shakes his head. "The room we'll be in has no windows or cameras and is completely soundproof."

Tension I didn't know I was holding eases from my shoulders. "I'd like to see, if that's okay."

"More than okay."

Hendrix leads us down the hallway to the right of

where we're standing. Glass walls showcase Epicurean scenes on either side of me. A *tableau vivant* of unrestrained pleasure plays out in every room I stop at. The acts taking place are a kaleidoscope of passion. In one room, a man guides a crop along the inner curve of a woman's thigh. She quivers in anticipation, then cries out in ecstasy when he slaps her pussy. Her eyes go dreamy, and she sighs when the man strokes her with tenderness before delivering another punishing snap of leather tassels.

"There's such beauty in surrender," I whisper out loud, my thoughts escaping before I can catch them.

Tristan's whiskey-browns glint with seduction. "Are you ready to surrender?" His dark tone is like a velvet caress that sends tingles down my spine.

My mouth goes dry. The thought of what tonight entails fills me with a mix of trepidation and exhilaration.

"Yes," I reply.

No other words are spoken as I'm taken to a red door at the end of the long hallway. This must be the Red Room.

Hendrix produces a keycard from his pocket. One swipe, and the door unlocks.

"Will we still be us in there?" I ask Hendrix.

Going to therapy together has helped us battle the demons from our past. However, those demons will never truly disappear. They are a part of who we are. But I would hate myself if coming here triggers him in some way, and he gets lost in the darkness again like he did at the gala.

He takes my face between roughened hands, his cobalt gaze boring into me. "I don't need this. I don't need any of it. What I can't live without—*is you*."

Tristan grabs the back of my neck, his touch reassuring instead of possessive. "We don't need any of this shit, Syn. We need *you*."

Constantine twists my face around and softly kisses me. "You control what happens here. Anytime you want to leave, say the word."

The way they love me is a very powerful thing. But it's not only love. It's trusting the person holding your heart to protect it and nurture it.

"I want this."

I want to explore this unknown world with them and test my boundaries.

Hendrix pushes the door open, and every nerve ending stands at attention as I'm whisked over the threshold and into the Red Room.

A ripple of shockwaves undulates through me at the sight that unfurls before my eyes. Silk curtains cascade from ceiling to floor in a waterfall of black. The air is thick with the sharp tang of leather furniture placed strategically around the room. The centerpiece is a large circular bed covered with pillows in various sizes that sits on top of a raised platform. Towering racks filled with sex toys and sensory tools stand like sentinels along the walls; however, it's the odd-looking equipment that holds my complete attention. *Holy hell.*

My gaze darts from one thing to the next—a stripper pole, a St. Andrew's cross, what I think is called a spanking bench, a complicated contraption that looks like a suspension rig. Each one whispers promises of sweet torment and beckons me with an allure that I can't deny. The room is a temple to all things taboo, and it calls out to something primal inside me.

"Ready to be worshipped?" Tristan's touch on my hip anchors me in the sea of sensuality that threatens to sweep me away.

"Yes." I breathe out, barely recognizing my voice.

"On the bed, firefly."

My knees slide over satin sheets as I climb onto the pillowtop mattress.

"Where do you want me?" I ask, pushing pillows out of my way.

"Right there. Don't move," Hendrix replies.

Those stormy ocean eyes hit me with a punch of lust when he takes off his shirt, then my throat constricts when Tristan and Constantine follow suit. I'm overwhelmed by their masculine beauty, each man so different and so goddamn gorgeous.

Hendrix saunters over to the bed. His fingers trace the line of my jaw as he leans in, his breath warm on my cheek.

"I want to blindfold you, to enhance every sensation as we worship your body with our touch and our mouths… and our cocks."

Before I can say yes, Constantine's presence is in front of me, his dark eyes pulling me into their inky depths. He runs a length of silken rope through his fingers, the sound it makes a whoosh of a whisper that sends my heart rate soaring.

He's usually content to let Tristan or Hendrix take the lead, but not tonight. Tonight, my broody man is going to play, and I fucking love it.

Tristan crooks a finger, and I crawl to the end of the bed.

"Ready to be ruined, pretty girl?"

I smile at the memory of when he first said that to

me. "Do your worst, Boston."

"We will." His lips graze my earlobe, sending a jolt straight to my core.

Hendrix circles the bed, a predatory alpha staking his territory. This is his domain, and we wait expectantly for him to begin.

"Kinbaku."

The word rolls off his tongue like an invocation as he takes the rope from Constantine.

"What's that?" My voice goes tight as he stalks closer.

"A type of bondage. You'll be suspended and at our mercy to do whatever filthy thing we want to do to you."

My pulse hammers in my ears, a frenetic staccato that matches the drumbeat of my escalating desires. The idea of being held captive by silken threads, of surrendering to them, is intoxicating.

"It can be painful, but the pleasure will be incredible," he promises. The hunger in his tone is palpable as he waits for me to give my consent.

Bringing my wrists together, I hold my hands out to them. "I'm yours."

The air suddenly electrifies against my skin, every synapse coming to life. I'm standing on the precipice of uncharted territory, and my entire body palpitates with the sweet, heavy weight of anticipation.

Tristan's touch is gentle yet firm as he secures the blindfold over my eyes. The loss of one sense heightens the others, and I become acutely aware of every sound and movement.

"Green for good. Stop to stop," he says, brushing his lips over mine.

I process his words. There's power here, in this surrender, a potent kind of trust created by the bonds of love.

"Not red?"

"That may confuse things," he replies.

Oh, because of his nickname for me.

He tightens the knot in the sash and kisses me again. "Good?"

"Green."

"Good girl."

A rush of arousal pools between my legs at his spoken plaudit.

"I don't want to be a good girl tonight," I say, echoing the pronouncement I gave them in Texas.

Like the flick of a switch, the room crackles with a deafening silence, an all-consuming expectancy that ignites my heart into a wild frenzy. It sears through me like a blazing fire, so intense and overwhelming, my soul vibrates with its raw power.

Hands grip my legs and pull me down the bed. *Tristan.* I know each man's touch well.

He lifts my right foot and smooths his hand down the long length of my leg and back up to my calf. The straps of my high-heeled sandal fall away, and the shoe slips from my foot and falls to the floor. He does the same to the other sandal, then crawls up my body and tenderly pushes me back onto the mattress.

I sigh when he kisses me. Just a feather-light caress of my lips. "I love you, Red."

When I try to reach for him, fingers shackle my wrists. *Hendrix.*

"Let yourself feel."

My stomach pebbles with goosebumps when Tristan tugs down the zipper of my skinny jeans. His weight lifts off me, and soft lips touch my navel. *Constantine.*

My abdominals quiver as he kisses along the concave of my stomach. Hendrix pins my arms above my head, pushing my breasts up for Tristan's mouth. He sucks my nipple until it hardens into a tight bud under my halter top. My pussy responds to the stimulation. They know they can make me come from breast play, and he's using that knowledge to make me squirm.

"Tristan."

"This shirt needs to come off."

He edges the stretchy fabric up my chest. Hendrix takes over and pulls the halter up my arms and the rest of the way off. Constantine drags my pants down my legs, taking his sweet-ass time as he stops to kiss and touch me everywhere. It's the most beautiful torture. Their hands and mouths are all over me, short circuiting my senses. Tears gather behind my lashes when they take turns pressing kisses to every scar and burn that mars my left side. Each touch and tender stroke of flesh tears at the fabric of my restraint, leaving me bare and aching for more.

Hendrix lets go of my wrists and bundles my hair to the side and out of the way. Bending over me, he runs his tongue down my face from cheek to neck. I gasp when Tristan pinches my nipples between his fingers. The electric sensation travels directly to my clit.

"You're dripping, baby."

Constantine's warm breath fans over my mound, and a delirious moan escapes when he slips a finger through my folds.

"Taste her," Hendrix says.

I cry out when Constantine French kisses me in the most erotic way. His tongue thrusts deep, fucking me with his mouth at the same time Tristan makes love to my breasts. Every pull of his hot mouth burns a current of desire low in my belly.

Hendrix's dirty promise whispers in my ear. "You're going to take all of us tonight, baby girl. We're going to ruin you *so good*."

Lurid images play in my mind of me taking the three of them at the same time, and I climax in an explosion of rapture.

"Fucking magnificent," Hendrix says, releasing my wrists.

Tristan sucks a nipple. "I love your tits."

I know he does. He can't ever keep his hands off them.

"Color?"

Is he serious?

"So fucking green," I moan, still riding the high of my orgasm because Constantine hasn't stopped eating me.

I curl my fingers in his dark, wavy locks and tug. "Fuck me," I entreat.

His chest expands with a deep groan. Through the bottom gap of the blindfold, I'm able to see him strip out of his trousers, exposing the rest of his wonderfully tanned skin, dark hair, and gorgeous ink. My gaze falls to his hard cock. Precum glistens at the tip. Not able to stop myself, I slide my hand between my legs and play with my clit.

"Fuck, firefly. I love watching you touch yourself."

Hendrix seals our mouths together, our tongues tangling in a sloppy, perfect, upside-down kiss. Constantine pushes my hand away with his cock, and he rubs me with his piercing. He slides the head through my wetness, then sinks into me with a hiss of pleasure.

"Every time. So tight. So good."

He groans the sexiest sound when he pulls out, ever so slowly, savoring the way my pussy envelops him, not wanting to let him go.

With one hand curved around my ass, he presses the other to my heart, and I remember what he said to me when he made love to me the first time. *You are my heartbeat.*

He pulls a guttural moan from my lips when he thrusts deep. His hands grab my thighs and stretch them wide, opening me fully to him. My moans turn desperate when he fucks me with a wild intensity that rocks the bed and sets my breasts bouncing with each snap of his hips.

Hendrix reaches over me and slaps my clit, and *holy shit*. I tumble over the edge, coming hard. Constantine groans my name as he fucks me through my orgasm, then follows me into sweet oblivion. Pulling out, he shoves his cum back inside me with his fingers.

After finding out I wasn't pregnant, we had a very long talk about starting a family. It was a really good talk. We want a house full of kids. We want that beautiful future. Marriage. Family. A lifetime together. Little do they know, we're going to start that family very soon. I'm eight weeks pregnant. Something that's been easy to keep secret because I haven't had any morning sickness yet.

"T, grab that," Hendrix says, and I push the blindfold up to see what he's referring to.

There's a pulley system directly above the bed I hadn't noticed.

Hendrix pushes the silky fabric down over my eyes. "No cheating, or you'll punished."

That's not exactly a threat.

He cradles my hands and ghosts his lips over the knuckles. "I'm going to bind your wrists first."

My pulse quickens. "Okay… I mean, green."

I'm flipped over onto my stomach.

With precision and care, he positions my hands at my lower back and weaves one of the ropes around my wrists and down to mid-forearm. Constantine wraps my left leg with the same tenderness Hendrix uses. He does the right leg next. More ropes weave around my torso like a spider's web. Lying face down, I can't see what else they are doing. There's a tug on my arms, then each leg raises separately, bowing my body in a gentle U-shape.

Hendrix glides a fingertip under my chin, tipping my face up. "Ready?"

I'm curious to know what happens next.

"Green."

A gasp of breath gusts out when I'm lifted off the bed. The ropes cradle me in an intimate lattice of confinement as I hover in the air, arms straining against the pull, and legs bent at the knees and spread wide. The feeling of being so intricately bound is both a comfort and a thrill. There's a certain seduction in relinquishing control to them. I know that I'm safe with them. That soul-deep and unwavering trust is what sets me free to explore this new realm of sex and intimacy.

"Absolutely stunning." Tristan shimmies a reverent hand down my hair, stroking the soft tresses and letting them sift through his fingers.

His words are a tender caress, wrapping around me just as securely as the ropes.

With a light push on my leg, Hendrix spins me around in a lazy circle. My belly swoops at the absence of gravity. It feels like I'm flying.

"I want to watch. Please."

I love being blindfolded, but for this new experience, I want to see everything.

Constantine stops my revolution and deftly removes the blindfold. His ebony-brown gaze skims appreciatively over my contours and curves, and the hot look he gives me makes my damn toes curl.

"You look fucking perfect, baby girl."

His lips seize mine hostage, his tongue delving inside, taking and claiming until I'm breathless with want.

"Seeing you like this—fuck, baby. You're my every fantasy come to life," Hendrix says, the edge in his voice sharp enough to cut through the haze of my arousal.

I'm literally vibrating with need—need for them and a need to be claimed by them.

"Green."

The room falls away as they descend upon me; the press of bodies around me is disorienting. Tristan's skilled hands chart a path over my body, mapping each response, each hitch of breath. Constantine's lips trace a trail of kisses along my spine, his tongue painting strokes of ecstasy that leave me gasping for air. Hendrix's fingers dance along my skin, teasing and tormenting in equal measure. I'm submerged in a trifecta of hands and mouths and dirty whispers.

I arch into their touch, moan at the sweet sting of a playful slap, revel in the rush of heat as they explore and claim. Each sensation is amplified, each kiss a brand upon my skin. I'm floating, lost in the sea of sensation, when suddenly, the energy in the room shifts again to something darker. A shadow looms over me, and I know without looking that it's Hendrix.

"Ready for more?"

"More."

I'm punished with a stinging slap to my pussy.

"Green," I correct.

There's a rustle of bedsheets, and then Hendrix is beneath me.

"A few inches," he says.

I jump when the ropes slowly lower me until my nipples brush the hard plains of his chest and his hard cock presses into my stomach. My arms strain against the ropes, and my thighs burn from holding the bent position for so long. Beads of sweat pop along my hairline as tension fills my body.

"Look at me," he commands firmly.

I obey, seeking comfort in the stark blue of his irises.

"Tristan is going to lube you. Don't tense up."

I try not to. Breathing in deeply, I exhale out in a five-count.

"That's it, love." With a warm smile, Hendrix caresses my face.

His uncharacteristic tenderness helps relax me until my muscles go slack.

There's a *snap* right before cold liquid drizzles between my ass cheeks.

Tristan circles a finger around the puckered ring of skin at my back entrance. "I want you so fucking badly."

A full-body shudder overtakes me when he spreads the lube to my pussy and fingers me.

Hendrix uses the give in the ropes to swing me forward. His lips latch on to my sensitive nipple, and he sucks with gentle pressure. Constantine crawls onto the bed and settles on his knees in front of me. I'm about to take all three of them at once, and all I can think is...

finally.

Hendrix lets go, and Tristan catches me by the hips on the backswing.

Pushing past my barrier, he sinks one knuckle deep into my ass. "I can't wait to feel you choking my cock with this tight ass."

The perception of fullness is excruciating. He goes deeper, pumping lightly, just as Hendrix prods my pussy with his cock.

My eyes flicker to Constantine stroking his length with long pulls.

This is really happening. Happiness like I've never experienced crashes into me at the expectation of being truly, thoroughly, unequivocally dominated by these three men.

"You're doing so well, Syn," Constantine murmurs, and his approval is a bolt of warmth straight to my core.

Tristan sinks a second finger inside me and scissors them. *Holy shit. Holy shit.*

"She's ready."

The ropes lower me a fraction of an inch, and Hendrix surges upward, impaling me on his cock.

I emit a long, drawn-out whimper when Tristan takes my ass, his thick girth rending me in two in the most amazing way.

"*Fuuuuck.* Fucking hell, baby. You feel so good."

My eyes roll into the back of my head as I straddle that wonderful line between agony and ecstasy.

Tristan uses the ropes to rock me back and forth to meet his shallow thrusts. The motion slides me over Hendrix at the same time, effectively fucking me on his cock. I've never felt anything like it.

"Let go, baby. We've got you," Hendrix says, his

voice a seductive melody that weaves through the air, a hypnotic rhythm that coaxes my body into surrendering further.

Constantine fists my hair and forces my head back. I immediately welcome him into my mouth, deep throating him until I gag.

"Syn," he moans as I hollow my cheeks and suck him like a fucking Hoover.

I exist in that moment with them, raw and open, nothing held back. This is intimacy in its purest form—challenging, freeing, and utterly transformative.

Every searing thrust of their cocks—in my pussy, my mouth, my ass—drives me toward nirvana. The rush of pleasure and pain coursing through me is like lightning under my skin. Everything feels bigger, more powerful, and I know the orgasm that's about to slam into me is going to tear me apart.

I'm tied up, unable to move, and being fucked by three men. It's twisted, filthy sex of the best kind.

Tristan's thrusts grow more and more frenetic, and I'm given no time to catch my breath when Constantine's cock thickens in my mouth, telling me he's close. Hendrix wedges his hand between us and taps my clitoris with two hard beats. Everything coalesces into a dense ball of intense pressure. It coils tauter and tauter. It's too much. Too big. And then...

...I fucking explode.

Like a bomb detonating inside me, my orgasm smashes through me, an uncontrollable force that splinters every cell apart.

My scream gets lost around Constantine's cock as thick pulses of his cum release down my throat. Strangled noises sound around me when Hendrix and

Tristan find their own release. They fill me completely, possess me thoroughly, and love me absolutely.

My lungs heave in much-needed oxygen when Constantine slips free from my mouth. He collapses beside Hendrix on the bed, his chest rising and falling with effort. I swing back and forth in a lazy pendulum, my thoughts incoherent and fuzzy.

I wince when Tristan pulls out next, then sigh when he rains kisses over my lower back.

"Thank you for such a precious gift," he says, and I want to laugh at the fact that he's thanking me for anal sex, but I don't have the strength to do anything more than make a small hum.

"Aftercare," Hendrix says.

He kisses me so sweetly, those tears come back with a vengeance. Damn pregnancy hormones.

I zone out as they lower me fully to the bed. Their hands are gentle as they unknot the ropes and remove them.

"Ow," I mumble into the mattress when my spine straightens out, and my legs fall listlessly to the bed covers.

I moan like the biggest whore when they massage me, *everywhere*. It's almost as good as the sex, but I won't tell them that.

It takes effort to roll over. Constantine sweeps my sweat-damp hair off my face, his dark eyes conveying so much.

"Love you, pretty girl," Hendrix says, kissing each of my fingers.

"Love you more."

Tristan's smile turns quizzical when I take each of their hands and place them over my stomach. Can you feel your daddies, little bean?

The goofiest, biggest smile creases my cheeks when I tell the men who are my everything…

"I'm pregnant."

EPILOGUE

FIVE YEARS LATER

The bed sheets rustle and are pulled off my legs when Hendrix stirs.

"Baby girl," he sleepily mumbles.

"I'm stopping," I whisper and shut my laptop, not wanting him to see what I'm getting him for Christmas.

Ryder Cutton, a former street racer who now operates Randy's Custom Auto in Fallen Brook, is designing a custom Ducati for me to give to Hendrix. From the images he sent, it's going to look amazing.

Tristan grunts and rolls over onto his back, slapping Hendrix in the head when he throws his arm over his face.

"Fucker," Hendrix grumbles into his pillow.

Bending over, I kiss his shoulder. "I'm going to peek in on the twins."

He turns his face but doesn't open his eyes. "Want me to?"

The baby monitor has been quiet, but I'm still in the habit of checking on them every few hours, not used to them sleeping through the night. That only started happening about two weeks ago.

Classes dismiss for the holidays soon, and I plan to catch up on some much-needed sleep. Three glorious weeks of being able to take naps with the kids. Raquelle, Drake, and their son, Troy, will be spending Christmas with us this year. Alana and Cillian will be here, too. It's a little weird he's my stepfather now. I wish Andie and the rest of the fam could come, but we'll see them after the New Year. One week of beach and sun on their private island before I have to be back for the start of the spring semester.

I have three more semesters of laboratory and coursework in medical school before I begin my clinical period. Two years of that, and I'll start my residency. I don't regret a single sleepless night, no matter how drag-ass tired I was during the day in class. I'm living my dream, and it's the most magnificent dream. I wake up every morning so damn grateful to have my husbands and my children and the life *we* choose.

I kiss Hendrix's sleep-softened lips. "I've got it. Go back to sleep."

"Gonna fuck you when you come back to bed."

He'll be dead to the world by the time I turn in, but I'll make sure to wake him with a blow job.

Putting my laptop on the nightstand, I slip out from under his arm and quietly pad barefoot down the dark hallway, stopping at Fénix's doorway first. He's snuggled in his father's arms, the most content expression on his slumbering face. There is nothing more beautiful than seeing Constantine with our son.

And Fénix is most definitely biologically Constantine's. I knew the moment they put him in my arms and those big, dark eyes looked right at me.

But it doesn't matter who our children resemble. Their daddies love them to the depths of their souls. Our home is filled with so much laughter and even more love. We've kept Fénix away from the Society as much as we can, wanting him to have the normal, happy, carefree childhood we never did. I know the day will come when the three of them start noticing things and have questions. Questions about my scars or why they have so many daddies or about the Society.

Coal-black eyes blink open. I still lose my damn breath and get those wonderful belly flutters every time Constantine looks at me. He peers down at Fénix, a smile ghosting his mouth, and shuts his eyes once again. I just stand there for a few minutes, memorizing the way they look together, wishing I had my phone so I could take a picture.

Heading back down the hallway, I stop to close our bedroom door just in case the babies wake up. Going into the twins' room, the nightlight Tristan bought before they were born casts butterflies on the ceiling. Quiet classical music plays softly from the wireless speaker on the dresser. The room smells like lavender and baby powder. Baby smell is the best smell.

I check on Niamh first. She's been a little congested. Nothing bad, just a bit of a cold. Her perfect pink lips are puckered, and she's making the cutest sucking noise. I stroke her satin-soft cheek and brush her silky blonde fuzz. She's Hendrix's mini me and has him wrapped around her teeny finger. I peek over into the other crib at Caoimhe. She's all Tristan. She was born with a full head of thick brown hair. Her eyes are a mix of mine and his—light brown with a pale-blue halo around the irises.

I had a heteropaternal superfecundation pregnancy with the twins. It's rare, but it happens. Two separate eggs fertilized by two different fathers.

I retuck their blankets around them until they look like miniature burritos. Snug as a bug in a rug. It's something Mama used to say to me.

"Love you, sweet angels."

Hopefully, I can eke in a couple of hours of sleep before they wake up hungry and need to be fed.

Covering my giant yawn, I tiptoe out of the room and go downstairs for a glass of milk.

The house we built northeast of Hillsborough, North Carolina is big. Not ostentatious—because I can't stand that bullshit—just big, like Cillian's place in Boston. It's also less than a thirty-minute drive to Duke where I go to medical school, and why we chose this area. It can be a pain for the guys, but they try to work remotely as much as possible and only travel for business when absolutely necessary, mostly for Society stuff, which is a whole other story. It took a couple of years to root out the people who were still loyal to Francesco, Patrick, and Gabriel. Those were difficult, bloody years of infighting and civil war, but we survived, and the Society is better because of the changes we've enacted.

"Shit," I whisper-hiss when I get to the bottom of the stairs and almost trip over the small toy cars that Fénix forgot to put away.

He created a racetrack across the foyer floor using blue painter's tape and wood blocks. The boy is obsessed with cars. He gets it from Hendrix. Fénix is going to go nuts when Santa brings him a go-cart that looks like an F1 race car for Christmas this year. The guys built a dirt track in the back of the property that Fénix doesn't know about yet. The big reveal will be on Christmas morning.

The house sits on a ton of land we purchased, plenty of open country for the animals to free range and the kids to explore. Along with Cocky B and the hens, we have three horses, two labradors, and a bunch of feral cats and raccoons that keep coming around because Fénix keeps sneaking food scraps to them. Mostly stuff he doesn't want to eat, like broccoli and fish. I can't wait to see what kind of personalities the twins will have. They're both quiet babies, always content to watch the world around them. Then again, they're only six months old. Once they start crawling and getting into things they shouldn't, we're going to have our hands full.

The kitchen is dark when I enter, illuminated only by a spear of moonlight coming in from the French doors that lead out onto the back deck. Humming the song from the radio I heard today, I shimmy my ass to the refrigerator and reach for the gallon of milk, only to stop short when I sense I'm not alone.

Happiness detonates inside my chest when arms band around me. Pirouetting around, I climb his massive body like a freaking jungle gym and hook my legs around his waist.

"When did you get ba—"

The rest of my question morphs into a moan when I'm pushed against the industrial-size fridge and passionately kissed.

"Miss me, *pevchaya ptitsa*?"

Aleksander had been in Dubai on business and wasn't supposed to get back until Monday.

I pepper enthusiastic kisses all over his face, so happy that he's here. "You know damn well I did. Why didn't you tell me you were coming back early?"

He cups my face between his large, inked hands, and I get lost in his gunmetal gray eyes.

"Wanted to surprise you."

My smile is effulgent. "Best surprise."

He brushes a soft kiss over my lips. "You know what time it is?"

The brilliance of my smile increases. "After midnight, which means…"

"The two-year anniversary of the first time I kissed you," he finishes for me.

"As I recall, kissing wasn't the only thing we did," I remind him.

The long and winding road of our relationship is an interesting one. Enemy turned friend turned something more. Aleksander *earned* his fucking place in this family and in my heart. With Tristan as the ringleader, it was actually the guys who played *Emma* and encouraged Aleksander and me to explore the feelings that had been building between us for years. He's a good man, a great brother to Tristan and Alana, a fantastic father to my kids, and he loves me with his whole heart. I love him back just the same. It's different from the love I have for the guys but just as powerful. I may not have the history with Aleksander that I do with Tristan, Constantine, and Hendrix, but that's what's special about sharing a lifetime together. We have the rest of our lives to make new memories that belong to only us.

Aleksander sets me down on the counter island, but I keep my arms and legs locked around him. I kiss up his neck, inhaling his spicy aftershave, and nip a love bite to his chin.

"Kids are asleep. House is quiet. Want to fuck your wife hello?"

Technically, we're not married, but I never ripped up the contract. In my heart, I'm as much his wife as I am the guys'.

He curves a hand around the back of my neck, and my legs turn to jelly when his grin turns wicked.

"I'd very much like to fuck my wife."

"Hey, man," Hendrix says, shuffling into the kitchen. "Thought I heard voices. Welcome back."

He and Aleksander tap fists.

Their friendship took a while to solidify, but once it did, they've been thick as thieves. Aleksander's calm demeanor helps ground Hendrix, much in the same way as I do.

Grabbing a chilled bottle of water from the fridge, Hendrix rests a hip to the counter. "By all means, please carry on with what you were doing."

Tristan enters the kitchen with Constantine. Guess all the adults are up. Our sleep schedules are screwier than the kids.

"Welcome home," Tristan says, slapping Aleksander on the back in the way men hug each other without actually hugging each other.

"What were they doing?" Constantine asks. He leans around Aleksander to kiss me.

Hendrix puts his water down, the glint in his baby blues as wicked as Aleksander's smile was moments ago. "About to fuck. I was going to watch, but since we're all here. Grab the whipped cream."

I dissolve into a fit of giggles when I'm laid out on the countertop.

Best thing about my husbands? All the fucking-fantastic orgasms.

Want to read an exclusive sneak peek chapter of my upcoming dark romance stand-alone starring Sarah? Well, she's grown up now and very much the badass, like her auntie Syn and adoptive mother, Andie. To download the exclusive bonus sneak peek, copy and paste https://storyoriginapp.com/giveaways/07f442f6-eaae-11ee-a5bb-dfd262781b9f into your browser.

Curious about Andie and her savage men? The Savage Kingdom series is available on Amazon, Kindle Unlimited, and audiobooks.

#1 Savage Princess
* *HOLT Medallion Finalist*
#2 Savage Kings
#3 Savage Kingdom
The Savage Kingdom Series is now available as audiobooks (Narrated by Keira Grace)

ALSO BY THE AUTHOR

Under Jennilynn Wyer (New Adult & College, Contemporary romance)

The Fallen Brook Series

#1 All Our Next Times

#2 Paper Stars Rewritten

#3 Broken Butterfly

The Fallen Brook Boxed Set

4 Reflections of You (Coming Soon)

The Montgomerys: Fallen Brook Stand-alone Novels

That Girl [Aurora + JD]
* *Winner of the Rudy Award for Romantic Suspense*
* *A Contemporary Romance Writers Stiletto Finalist*

Wanderlost [Harper + Bennett]
* *Contemporary Romance Writers Reader's Choice Award Winner*
* *Contemporary Romance Writers Stiletto Finalist*
* *HOLT Medallion Finalist*
* *Carolyn Reader's Choice Award Finalist*

About That Night [Jordan + Douglass]

The Fallen Brook Romance Series: The Montgomerys

Love Everlasting [Mason + Aria]

Savage Kingdom Series: A dark, enemies to lovers, mafia, why choose romance

#1 Savage Princess
* *HOLT Medallion Finalist*

#2 Savage Kings

#3 Savage Kingdom

The Savage Kingdom Series is now available as audiobooks (Narrated by Keira Grace)

Forever M/M Romance Series (A Fallen Brook Spin-off)

#1 Forever His (Julien's POV)
* *A Contemporary Romance Writers Stiletto Finalist*

#2 Forever Yours (Elijah's POV)

#3 Forever Mine (Dual POV)

Beautiful Sin Series: A dark, enemies to lovers, reverse harem/why choose

#1 Beautiful Sin

#2 Beautiful Sinners

#3 Beautiful Chaos

The Beautiful Sin Series is now available as audiobooks (Narrated by Devon Wilder)

◆◆◆

Under J.L. Wyer (High School & Young Adult)

The Fallen Brook High School Young Adult Romance Series: a reimagining of the adult Fallen Brook Series for a YA audience

#1 Jayson

#2 Ryder

#3 Fallon

#4 Elizabeth

The Fallen Brook High School YA Romance Series Boxed Set (Books 1-4) with bonus alternate endings

YA Standalones

The Boyfriend List
* HOLT Medallion Award Winner*
* A Contemporary Romance Writers 2022 Stiletto Finalist*

LETTER TO READERS

Dear Reader,

Noooo! This can't be the end. I absolutely adore these characters. Syn was such a fun FMC to write, and the guys… I love them all and wouldn't be able to pick a favorite. Hopefully, somewhere down the line, Syn, Tristan, Hendrix, Constantine, and Aleksander will pop up in another story, just like Andie and her men (from my Savage Kingdom series) did in this series.

Don't forget to **sign up for my newsletter to get the exclusive first chapter of Sarah's story** (https://storyoriginapp.com/giveaways/07f442f6-eaae-11ee-a5bb-dfd262781b9f). I'm hoping to release it sometime in 2025. You can also **join my private reader group, The J-Crew** (https://www.facebook.com/groups/jennilynnsjcrewreadergroup), to stay up to date on book releases, cover reveals, and enjoy special member-only giveaways.

Now for my thank yous.

Thank you to Ellie, my awesome copy editor at My Brother's Editor, for your support and love for my stories, and for the hard work you put in.

Thank you to my readers who have given me daily doses of excitement about getting this series done and published. Whether it's fighting over the men or begging me for hints on how things would end, I loved hearing from you.

Thank you to all the book bloggers who support me, and the supportive author community on Instagram.

Thank you, Nala, for our weekly author meetings where I can hash out ideas, get inspiration, and meet my goals. Your organizing skills are truly inspirational!

A huge shout out to my awesome ARC and Hype teams! You ladies are the absolute best!

Thank you to my husband and family who support me one hundred percent every day. Love you so much!

And thank you, reader, for coming along this crazy journey with me and supporting independent authors like myself.

If you haven't read my other books, check them out. I have a reputation for drinking the tears of my readers and have been crowned the queen of WTF cliffhangers and twists. My Fallen Brook Series (*All Our Next Times, Paper Stars Rewritten, and Broken Butterfly*) is an angsty, twisty-turny emotional roller coaster that involves a love quadrangle between childhood friends. You'll definitely want some tissues for *Broken Butterfly*. The Montgomerys series of stand-alones takes place right after *Broken Butterfly* and each book focuses on one of the half siblings of Fallon Montgomery. *That Girl* is Aurora + JD's story; *Wanderlost* is Harper + Bennett's; *About That Night* is Jordan + Douglass's; and *Love Everlasting* is Mason + Aria. If you want something darker, check out my Savage Kingdom reverse harem/why choose series (*Savage Princess, Savage Kings, Savage Kingdom*). My books are packed with my signature WTF moments, strong women, and swoon-worthy men. You can find them on Amazon and Kindle Unlimited. You can also visit https://www.jennilynnwyer.com for a complete list.

    Until next time,
    Love and happy reading,
    Jennilynn

ABOUT THE AUTHOR

Jennilynn Wyer is multi-award-winning romance author (Rudy Award winner for Romantic Suspense, HOLT Medallion Award winner, Contemporary Romance Writers Reader's Choice Award winner, four-time Contemporary Romance Writers Stiletto Finalist, three-time HOLT Medallion Award Finalist, Carolyn Reader's Choice Award Finalist) and an international Amazon best-selling author of romantic fiction. She writes steamy, New Adult romances as well as dark reverse harem romances. She also pens YA romance under the pen name JL Wyer.

Jennilynn is a sassy Southern belle who lives a real-life friends-to-lovers trope with her blue-eyed British husband. When not writing, she's nestled in her favorite reading spot, e-reader in one hand and a cup of coffee in the other, enjoying the latest romance novel.

Connect with the Author

Website: https://www.jennilynnwyer.com
Linktree: https://linktr.ee/jennilynnwyer
Email: jennilynnwyerauthor@gmail.com

Facebook: https://www.facebook.com/JennilynnWyerAuthor

Twitter: https://www.twitter.com/JennilynnWyer

Instagram: https://www.instagram.com/jennilynnwyer

TikTok: https://www.tiktok.com/@jennilynnwyer

Goodreads: https://www.goodreads.com/author/show/20502667.Jennilynn_Wyer

Bookbub: https://www.bookbub.com/authors/jennilynn-wyer

Books2Read: https://books2read.com/ap/nAAgBb/Jennilynn-Wyer

Amazon Author Page: https://www.amazon.com/author/jennilynnwyer

Newsletter: https://forms.gle/vYX64JHJVBX7iQvy8

SUBSCRIBE TO MY NEWSLETTER at https://forms.gle/vYX64JHJVBX7iQvy8 for news on upcoming releases, cover reveals, sneak peeks, author giveaways, and other fun stuff!

JOIN THE J-CREW: A JENNILYNN WYER ROMANCE READER GROUP

Join link https://www.facebook.com/groups/jennilynnsjcrewreadergroup

Printed in Great Britain
by Amazon